T0086786

All Things Tending towards the Eternal

All Things Tending towards the Eternal

Kathleen Lee

TRIQUARTERLY BOOKS
NORTHWESTERN UNIVERSITY PRESS
EVANSTON, ILLINOIS

TriQuarterly Books
Northwestern University Press
www.nupress.northwestern.edu

Copyright © 2015 by Kathleen Lee. Published 2015 by TriQuarterly Books/
Northwestern University Press. All rights reserved.

Printed in the United States of America

10   9   8   7   6   5   4   3   2   1

This is a work of fiction. Characters, places, and events are the product of the author's imagination or are used fictitiously and do not represent actual people, places,
or events.

Library of Congress Cataloging-in-Publication Data

Lee, Kathleen, author.
    All things tending towards the eternal / Kathleen Lee.
        pages cm
    Includes bibliographical references.
    ISBN 978-0-8101-3061-6 (pbk. : alk. paper) — ISBN 978-0-8101-3062-3
        (ebook)
    I. Title.
    PS3612.E344A79 2014
    813.6—dc23
 2014033233

♾ The paper used in this publication meets the minimum requirements of the
American National Standard for Information Sciences—Permanence of Paper for
Printed Library Materials, ANSI Z39.48–1992.

For Tony, my traveling companion

Traveling is a brutality. It forces you to trust strangers and to lose sight of all that familiar comfort of home and friends. You are constantly off balance. Nothing is yours except the essential things—air, sleep, dreams, the sea, the sky—all things tending towards the eternal or what we imagine of it.

—CESARE PAVESE

To awaken quite alone in a strange town is one of the pleasantest sensations in the world.

—FREYA STARK

CONTENTS

ACKNOWLEDGMENTS

I am grateful to the Rona Jaffe Foundation, the Ellen Levine Fund for Writers, and the Ucross Foundation. Thanks to the *Colorado Review* and *Puerto del Sol*, in which excerpts from this book appeared previously, in different versions.

Thanks to Mike Levine at Northwestern University Press.

Thank you to those who gave me (possibly unwittingly) their anecdotes and stories: Nick Evangelos, the Lee family, and Robert Winson. I'm deeply grateful for the insights of Laura Hendrie, Eddie Lewis, Toni Nelson, Alex Parsons, Miriam Sagan, Eve Schaenen, and Rob Wilder. Thank you to the editing crew of Floating House. I'm also grateful to Robert Boswell, who, more than once, rescued my drafts and my attitude. And especially, I'm thankful for Tony Hoagland.

All Things Tending towards the Eternal

Chapter 1

In the East China Sea somewhere between Osaka and Shanghai on the second of a three-day journey, Fanny Molinari witnessed a murder. An accidental murder. Death inadvertent.

This was in the middle of August, 1989. The *Red Star*, flying the flag of the People's Republic of China, slipped free of Osaka harbor. Passengers crowded against the deck rails, snapping photos, laughing and talking, squinting into the high glare. Why did sailing away make people jubilant, Fanny wondered. Alongside her fellow passengers she stood at the rail: tall, pale, separate, in her traveler's skirt of soft gray, with her long braid; her face alert, amused, shining with sweat like a diver surfacing from the dark into a bright, unexpected world. No one touched her, not even accidentally. Japan receded. The bay water twitched and glinted and a warm, salty breeze blew across the deck. Ahead lay a plate of gray ocean rimmed in the distance by a smudged line dividing water from sky.

By the next afternoon the same deck would be deserted, everyone below in air-conditioned shadow; crew and ship officials attending to their duties, the surrounding ocean a sheet of steel.

Fanny paced the decks, scouting for distraction in the form of someone to talk with. Up and down stairs, around the front and back of the ship, along the sides; nothing, nobody. She peered into the no-smoking lounge where a young girl played the piano while her mother coached in shrill Cantonese; the smoking lounge, filled with chairs dressed in pleated skirts; and a couple of gift shops. One shop offered brightly colored swim trunks (to swim *where?*), liquor, biscuits. The shop across the hall sold buttons, washers, screwdrivers, plastic cigarette lighters, cheap flashlights. The salesclerk stood stiffly in a red polyester skirt and jacket. Fanny approached. "Do you sell batteries?" she asked.

"Yes," the clerk said, unsmiling.

"What sizes?" She needed batteries for her headlamp.

"Yes," the clerk said.

The clerk stood with her hands clasped in front of her, unmoving. Fanny waited a beat. "Is there another shop that sells batteries?" The clerk nodded and said yes.

"Is this the only shop that sells batteries?" The clerk nodded and said yes.

"Thank you." Fanny bowed—a remnant gesture from traveling in Japan. So much for batteries.

She circled back to her cabin, flung herself onto her bunk, and listened to her berthmates. Mandarin. Fanny didn't understand a word, but how much could be surmised from tone and inflection. One minute the language sounded like nails hammered into a coffin, the next like a broom sweeping the floor. Her berthmates were two women, seated facing each other on a lower bunk. Fanny occupied an upper bunk; the fourth bunk was empty. The older of the two women, dressed in a gray silk Mao jacket, did most of the talking, her finger jabbing the air in front of the other's nose, her eyes narrowed. The other, in a shiny flowered blouse and fashionable sunglasses, grunted now and then. The old woman's voice sank, conspiratorial, and rose, emphatic. She imitated someone ironically, then segued into indignation. Her hair was parted on the side and clipped neatly behind each ear with a hairpin. Then, as if they'd arrived at an impasse, they pulled out cigarettes and lighters and fled the cabin to smoke.

Wistfully, Fanny watched them depart, then sank into a minor internal skirmish over her tolerance—or lack of it—for the stillness and boredom imposed by travel. This was the great myth of travel: there you were, off to China (from Japan!), how exotic. Except the exotic didn't diminish the quotidian. You're *traveling*, a word implying movement, but it meant you had to be still for hours and days on end. It wasn't as if she were walking or swimming to China. Travel involved waiting for one thing to be over so that you could wait for another thing to start, and so on and on. Three days trapped on this boat, to be followed by days trapped on a train or a bus or another boat. Separated by a scattering of nights in bad hotels. At times the waiting was featureless, like the first moment after you awaken in the morning and you don't know who or where you are. Or the waiting was dense with misunderstandings and blunders; a topography of minor disasters. What envy this trip had generated—a one-way ticket to Asia. Not working. People imagined a *vacation*; they didn't imagine tedium, or weeks of *talking to yourself*. Or, thinking. She had a few topics she rotated through, one of which was: what next? At home she kept a folder labeled *Should I Do Something Else*, stuffed with graduate and certificate program information and job descriptions: X-ray tech, social worker, ESL teacher, hospice nurse, woodworker, nutritionist, permaculturist. She longed to find a means of being more useful in the world, and wouldn't it be nice to unearth as-yet-undiscovered talents and skills? But from the vantage point of her forties, nothing had the irresistible sheen of possibility. The trip so far had yielded no progress on this topic. She opened the first, then the second of her two knapsacks and gazed at her possessions, calmed by the items which comprised her companionship: her worn gray sweatshirt, a blue soapbox, a rock from Atalaya, Bruno's journal.

The young man seated beside Fanny at dinner wore a gold turtleneck with a heavy gold zipper. He told her that he lived in East Africa, worked in textiles, and was on his way home to Shanghai for a vacation. His teeth were yellow-brown from smoking. He kept an unlit cigarette beside his chopsticks, touching it now and then. At each of the round tables, waiters slapped down great bowls of white rice and platters of steamed buns. The food was bad, evidence that they had left Japan. Her dining partner asked the questions Fanny had grown accustomed to, and her answers were rote. "I live in New Mexico, in the western part of the United States." By the way he nodded, she knew this meant nothing to him. Probably he imagined she was from Mexico. His hair was clean and he smelled powerfully of cologne; he was attractive in a sad, garish way, like someone on their way to

Las Vegas for a funeral. In answer to the next questions, she reported flatly that she was forty-three years old, unmarried, without children. Fanny had always believed that the best way to live an interesting life was to remain solitary. She secretly held that the single-minded pursuit of romantic love was for the unimaginative. This streak of austerity in her character—like a nun's—did not extend to sex. She was like a nun who had sex. A bad nun. A very bad nun.

But instead of the usual undisguised expression of shock, sorrow, and sympathy, the man with the gold zipper laughed cheerfully.

Fanny laughed too, as if her answers *were* amusing.

When she'd turned forty, she'd hardly noticed. Now, three years later, her back bothered her, a formless anxiety often woke her in the night, and she felt her life sliding away under its own volition. Not only unmarried, without children or property, she had never been divorced or fired from a job, never filed for bankruptcy, never taken antidepressants or gone to a therapist, *and* she still wasn't sure what to do with herself. Soon she'd be invisible, an aging woman, her access to the currency of romance gone, and she couldn't decide if she ought to lean forward like a runner trying to be the first to break the tape, or if she should jog at the back of the pack, reluctant for it all to be over before anything had come of it. Traveling in Asia, where she was repeatedly asked about her age and marital and motherhood status, had made her acutely aware of what her life was not. Was this funny? In any case, it felt good to laugh.

His next question should be about work. Questions came in order: place of origin, age, marital status, children, work, income. Sometimes she said she made fine wooden furniture because she'd taken Introduction to Woodworking at the community college and had made exactly one piece of furniture: a small table. Sometimes she said, "I work in a hospital." Which was true. Most people assumed she was a nurse, or maybe even a doctor, which was not true, and when she was asked for medical advice, things grew awkward. He held up his index finger, eyebrows raised in question. "One people?" he said.

She considered the wall mural over his shoulder, one of those cliché oriental scenes of green spiky peaks and tiny monk figures meditating in miniature lonely shacks. She offered a smile and nodded. Hell, yes. She was alone.

Their conversation was interrupted by a man across the table raising his voice, rubbing his bony chest, and grunting in a kind of percussive accompaniment to his declarations. He held up his mug—painted with bamboo and a panda—filled with duty-free cognac (the bottle on the floor beside his chair). "I'm a happy man," he shouted, and everyone in the dining room turned. A manifesto. He'd worked as a chauffeur at the Mandarin Hotel in Hong Kong. Now he was retired, on a tour of Asia. The skin on his face was so thin it appeared glued to his bones. His Adam's apple pumped up and down. "Shanghainese are," he declaimed, "the cleverest people in China." He took a swig of his drink. "Look at me." He jabbed his own chest with a forefinger. "I worked my way up to chief chauffeur." Fanny and Gold Zipper exchanged a look. The way Happy Man went on to speak about pachinko and mahjongg, it was apparent that he'd lost a great deal to gambling.

Fanny felt light after her exchange with Gold Zipper; even if they didn't run into each other again, it had been enough contact to make her feel human. Under the darkening sky, she went up on deck and stared out to sea, the expanse of dark water shiny with moonlight, surging softly. Here was the reason people rejoiced at setting sail: a ship's deck to survey from, the curve of the earth to roll over, a spit of land to round. The seen to the unseen, the known to the unknown; the unfamiliar turning by mysterious alchemy into her own experience before sliding into the past. Far from home, riding the watery flanks of the world. She knew this, had discovered it with Bruno long ago, but each time she encountered it, it felt fresh, a source of pleasure that she stumbled upon again and again. After an inconclusive month in Japan, she was restless. To be on the move was like scratching an itch, voluptuous scratching.

She pulled Bruno's journal from her pocket. It was a worn address book, narrow, maroon-colored. She'd taken it from his house thinking she'd need it to contact his friends, but when she'd opened it a week later, she found that it was a journal of the trip he'd made to Asia the previous year. An odd journal, employing an abbreviated accounting of experience. It was cryptic in a way that suggested something hidden, a message embedded among the entries. This, anyway, was what she wished for: that Bruno had left her a message. One that would occupy her time and require her intelligence and attention in order to decipher. She felt sure that he would have left her something. Not an object, more like a directive—advice, a piece of wisdom. With Bruno's journal and Wen Li's letters to him, Fanny was composing her own pursuit. Maybe she would discover that he'd left her something, or nothing, or maybe she'd discover that he'd meant to leave her something if only he'd had time and foresight. She flipped through the journal and halted at *H*, reading in the dim light:

> *HongKong. turnip cake shrimp dumplings roast duck congee*
> *lamb chops & mint jelly. tea, buckets of. Dense clouds, no rain.*
> *roasted pig on a board down a bus aisle.*
> *Friday ferry to Lantau, sweaty hike, bee-chased through rice*
>   *fields,*
> *cows on a beach in the morning glories & large snail shells.*
> *Scottish Julia F! met at a bar cum hair salon by day.*
> *her blue room, 15th floor of Chungking*
> *I took the stairs (quads strong)*
> *landings full of garbage & turbaned men smoking*
> *salty neck, opinionated, kind, light & hefty.*
> *julia julia*
> *shall we shall we meet meet again again*

Fanny shut the book, feeling guilty for eavesdropping even though, well, even though. Julia F, whoever she was, appeared under the letter *J*, too, as Wen Li appeared under *W* and under *E* in the entry for Emei Shan, Fanny's designated destination. The entries for Wen Li were not at all revealing. Still, this was where Fanny was going: the People's Republic of China, Sichuan Province, a town called Emei Shan to meet a woman named Wen Li. Who was this person who had written so many letters to Bruno?

Fanny observed an older couple at the ship's rail. The man stepped behind the woman and massaged her shoulders and neck. She leaned into him and the two stood facing the ocean. The air was sweet and briny. *The world is made of couples*, Fanny thought. Not exactly a brilliant deduction. How had this couple met? What chance encounter in their past had led to this moment, studying the South China Sea from the deck of the *Red Star*? There was enough white in their hair to catch the moonlight and make their heads gleam.

The couple moved away and Fanny picked at the coil of rope on which she was sitting. She had no companion and this had begun to feel barbed; she would not entertain desperation. Her habit was to deflect any but light attachments (wasn't detachment Buddhist? she asked Bruno) so that she would not suffer when the attachment was severed. Bruno the Buddhist often reminded her that when she attempted to avoid suffering she was separating herself from experience and the mystery of being, thereby increasing her suffering.

Bruno used to have a lot of girlfriends; later, it seemed there were fewer. A memory of Bruno at a party, bent and rummaging in a refrigerator, extracting a large onion which he peeled and bit into. He ate it, whole and raw, glass of red wine in one hand, onion-as-apple in the other. It made Fanny laugh and Bruno liked to make his sister laugh. After their parents died, making Fanny laugh had become his avocation. At the party, he said he'd eat the onion, then a few garlic cloves, and see how many women he could get to kiss him. What did Fanny wanna bet? They had years of bets going, a long complex accounting that only occasionally resulted in money changing hands. He chewed through two fat cloves of garlic, shedding their thin skin with his fingers. He started in the back patio, talking first to a woman in a flowing skirt with curly blonde hair. Fanny caught bits of their conversation. You've got a wonderful mouth, he said to the woman. Then something about how best to juice an orange and how to draw a perfectly straight line with your eyes closed. Could he kiss her, he asked. Then he did. After which he'd glanced at Fanny, the light of success in his face, the index finger of his left hand rising discreetly: there was one.

So long ago, just after Bruno had moved to Berkeley, when he was beginning to take Buddhism seriously, before everything that was to come. Her chest tightened. She was resilient, often unflappable, used to things not going her way, practiced at gathering herself in trouble or after failure. If he were to appear beside her on this deck, she'd slug him. The *asshole*. Who would make her laugh now? *How could he have left her alone?* She considered the dark water churned into a white froth by the ship's passage.

On the afternoon of the second day, Fanny sat on deck on the same rope coil, wiping sweat from her face with a bandanna. Failure was another of her topics: she had no career (only an ordinary job, one that let her take a three-month leave, no less, but shouldn't she have a career by now?), no relationship (never longer than nine months, her love life on a school calendar), and now, she was no longer a sister (she was unsure how she'd failed Bruno). She glanced around the worn plank deck at the various rails, pipes, and vents, the purposes of which she was entirely ignorant. A woman came around the corner and leaned against the railing. Was it starboard or port? It was the older woman from the couple Fanny had seen the night before. Her khakis were crisp, the sleeves of her yellow blouse rolled neatly to her elbows. Fanny considered going to talk to her, but then a young man approached the woman. Did they know each other? He strolled past, the woman didn't turn. No, they didn't know each other.

But the young man retraced his steps and stopped behind the woman, grasped her hips, and smoothly lifted her. The woman's legs paddled in a pantomime of someone trying to run away. He raised her higher, above the railing, held her briefly over the water, and released, letting her go. She fell, her yellow sleeves and khaki pants filled with air, her arms and legs moving in a slow-motion dance of hesitation. She was gone from sight; vanished. *What?* Sweat poured down Fanny's temples; what had she just seen? It happened so quickly, it was so shocking, that she didn't trust her senses. A woman thrown overboard. More dropped than thrown. There was the man's back, receding. Fanny ran after him, calling out, "Hey, hey!" He turned a corner and disappeared.

Within an hour, crammed into a tiny cabin deep in the ship with the captain and two other uniformed ship's officers, Fanny was describing what she'd witnessed. She glanced around for a place to sit. The cabin was too warm, there was no air flow, there were no chairs. Metal walls painted white, no porthole; it was practically a closet. The walls thrummed with vibrations from the engines. She paused in her account, wanting to remember something, like a sound just out of range. A soft panic took hold of her.

One of the uniforms gestured impatiently for her to proceed, and the captain, his hat tucked under one arm, gave a restraining look.

"The man lifted her easily." It had been surprising because he wasn't a big man. Had it been the fluke strength of someone under the spell of a terrible compulsion?

The captain's expression was stern, the sternness softened by bad skin, which made him appear kind. Fanny regarded him. "He dropped her over the deck rail. She fell without a sound. I mean, no splash." Fanny clasped her own hands. "No cry." She stopped again.

"Please, continue." The impatient official again.

The captain tilted his head slightly, indicating, Fanny thought, that she could take her time. The scene playing in her head gleamed like an offering: here was a kind of death, quick, magnetic, drawing you down into that eternal immensity of water. Fanny was too antihysterical to have ever considered suicide; when her life was hard, she increased her capacity for suffering. The woman's body falling over and over again in her mind made her lean forward and hold her breath. "The man put his hands in his pockets and looked out to sea. He rocked back on his heels and walked quickly away. I thought, *A man has just thrown someone overboard*. I ran to the rail and looked down but there was nothing. I shouted at him. He was very fast, gone."

"What did you say to the man?"

"Hey! Stop!" Absurd. "I ran after him but . . ." A faint stink of warm diesel filtered into the cabin. The white paint was bubbled on the wall behind the three uniforms. She felt nauseated and trembly. She'd had no idea what she would have done if she had caught up to him.

"And then?"

"I ran for help." The store clerk from whom Fanny had tried to buy batteries stared speechless. Then, down one more flight to the reception desk, calling for help, repeating the word "Overboard," trying to slow her breathing and sound reasonable, though she wanted to scream. Someone—not just anyone, someone particular—was drowning! Could the woman swim? Were there sharks?

The second clerk, in his rumpled black suit, had regarded Fanny as if she might be fanciful, as if she'd watched too many movies. Was she quite sure?

Quite, Fanny had said, and she had begged him to stop the ship.

"What did the man look like?" the uniforms asked. One of them held a pen poised over the page of a notepad.

"He was wearing sandals with dark socks," Fanny said. A nerdy look. "He had thin light hair in an old-fashioned haircut, parted on the side, hair across one eye." She paused. "He was young." It had seemed like he knew what he was doing and also like he had no idea of what he was doing.

The ship's engines shuddered into reverse and then shut off, a ripping sound. They closed off the doors; no one could go on deck. Fanny was taken to the officers' lounge, where she was left alone. She was thirsty and sweating in the overly air-conditioned room. The memory she'd been trying to retrieve came to her: she and Bruno at a swimming pool. It was a private swim club in Albuquerque, up against the Sandias, their parents at an afternoon barbeque with friends. Bruno was four or five, which meant Fanny was three or four. He'd been holding on to the edge, going around the pool hand over hand. Fanny was playing in the warm shallow water near the steps, where her father and the husband (which family friends were they?) were talking, drinks in hand. Her father scanned the pool, shading his eyes, and asked Fanny, "Where's your brother?" She didn't know. He rose, started briskly around the pool, and stopped when he saw a shape at the bottom of the deep end. For years Fanny had pictured her father diving into the pool in a suit and tie, slipping out of his hard, shiny leather shoes at the pool's edge. But of course he'd been wearing a swimsuit. He pulled up Bruno's small body dripping water, laid him on the pool deck, and breathed into his mouth. The adults crowded around. Fanny stood alone in the shallow end, the warm chlorinated water soaking the ruffled skirt of her favorite red flowered swimsuit. An ambulance came, her family was whisked off to a hospital, and she was left in the care of the friends. She couldn't remember who they were. She had not cried. She couldn't cry among strangers, and besides, she felt it was her fault, and you didn't cry unless something had happened to you, not over something you'd done yourself. She'd let her father down, not keeping watch over Bruno. She already knew that she and her brother were responsible for each other.

Friends brought presents for Bruno to the house; a green dump truck that Fanny coveted. Afterward, Bruno had no memory of the experience and, when enrolled in swim classes later that summer, learned to swim easily. Fanny was less successful. She screamed if the instructor tried to pry her hands off his arm. Everyone in her class learned to swim, and Fanny? At the end of the class she would hold on to the edge of the pool by herself, anxiously. She never wanted to go swimming, no matter how hot it was. She never had another favorite swimsuit. Some summers she didn't buy a swimsuit. When had she stopped keeping watch over Bruno?

Stewards combed the ship for the suspect—that's how they referred to him—and dropped dinghies with search parties. The ship languished through the evening. Fanny was joined in the officers' lounge by the disappeared woman's husband. His name was Bertrand and his wife was Emily; they were from a small town outside Montreal. Bertrand wore silver-rimmed glasses that sat on his face crookedly, and he dyed his hair brown, his white roots beginning to show. He blew his nose into a cream handkerchief and wiped his eyes behind his glasses. Emily didn't know how to swim, he said, as if he were rehearsing his explanation to their family back home, how it happened that he was returning without Emily. Not even Emily's body. He would return with something missing, an absence. He was certain, with a lack of hope or doubt that Fanny found admirable (what did it take not to cling to life?), that she had drowned quickly. Bertrand thanked Fanny, in the tone of an apology. Fanny saw in the blue shadows of his face that grief was always a solitary experience. She knew this. She forgot it again and again because she wished otherwise. He touched his ear carefully, as if it were a delicate pastry. Fanny squeezed his hand once but didn't want to overstep and didn't touch him again. They spent long moments staring at a dish of flat dry biscuits and sipping bitter, tepid tea. Worms of gray cigarette ash sat in an ashtray.

Not long after, the thrower was found: a young man from Switzerland traveling with his parents. He had returned to his cabin as if nothing had happened. He was twenty-three, and his mother, with a tight, emotionless face, declared that he was fine as long as he took his medication. It came out that he'd stopped taking the medication when they left Switzerland. He wanted to feel the world, he said. He didn't know the woman, had never seen her before.

Fanny was brought into the same white closet she'd been questioned in earlier, to identify him. The captain, his cap gripped under his arm, nodded reassuringly at her. The young man appeared unaware that he'd sent someone to her death. He seemed pathetic rather than evil, a lost boy. She could be wrong; maybe he was pathetic *and* evil. Fanny studied the young man's mother, her blonde hair attractive and short. Shiny, healthy hair, without any gray, her face strained but unlined. He might have dropped his mother overboard, he might have thrown Fanny. She made the possibility vivid in her mind; an encounter with chaos. You wouldn't survive it, then what? Nothing. Who was there to notice if Fanny went missing? She felt the danger close to her; solitary people were more apt to die of simple illnesses and in ordinary circumstances. She nodded at the captain. Yes, this was the man she had seen throw overboard Emily, wife of Bertrand.

Eighteen hours behind schedule the ship steamed into Shanghai. A Sousa march blared over the loudspeakers. Fanny fidgeted in the line to disembark. Next, to Guangzhou, where Bruno had begun his China travels, then from Guangzhou to Emei Shan to meet Wen Li. She wanted to follow in Bruno's tracks, as much as she could surmise those tracks. Luck was generous with her in small matters, withholding in large. Often she could not tell if she was in or out of luck; they could seem, to her bafflement, the same. Below and beyond stretched the indifferent gray water. What kind of luck was it to have witnessed a person thrown overboard?

Between Fanny and Bruno, so much had been unspoken; they had no pacts. That didn't mean that Fanny was without assumptions. She assumed they were watching out for each other; she assumed full disclosure, so that the other might anticipate risks and dangers. Yet it turned out that she had been the only one of the two of them following rules; rules, it also turned out, she had imagined. Why be surprised at this? Bruno liked to set rules—establishing an uncrossable border in the backseat of the car—which Fanny would obediently adhere to, and which he would break, flapping his hand onto Fanny's assigned side, touching her arm, toeing her shoe. Bruno breaking his own rules. He'd been so close to her he was out of focus.

The gangplank dropped into place and the shoving and jostling commenced.

Chapter 2

Bliss Beer & Guest House served bitter, watery coffee in the morning, and if you could tolerate the smell of fermented fish sauce, spilled Tiger beer, and cigarettes, you could happily sit beside the spotted window, warm, damp air wafting down from the turgid fans clicking overhead, listening to opera. Opera was the feature that distinguished Bliss Beer from other establishments on Khao San Road in Bangkok.

You could have at least an hour of very loud Puccini or Verdi before anyone offered you an elephant trek around Chiang Mai or a fake Rolex or a girl, before anyone tried to sell you hash or opium, before a distraught Belgian girl told you about the boyfriend who'd abandoned her in Kunming, before the exhaust from a million *tuk-tuks*, motorcycles, and automobiles rose into the air and wrapped your lungs and mind in the suffocating shroud of its embrace.

Early on a Saturday morning in August, 1989, Yevgeny Velasquez sat at the window table, heaping sugar into his coffee. This was his final day in Bangkok. He was on the evening flight to Guangzhou. An aria from *Rigoletto* blared. Yevgo stared out the window, thinking of skin, of stroking the arm of a woman he'd met at a bar last night. There was nothing in the world like human skin; what else gave equally of pleasure and horror? There were thousands of people he hoped never to touch. He flapped a fly buzzing around his head, flicking its light body once with the back of his hand. Street vendors were setting up for another day selling tribal fabrics, drawstring pants, crocheted bikinis. Last night's girl—her name was Ingrid—was big with long legs that had put him in a state. The fly landed in the bristly hair of his forearm. He slapped himself, missing the fly. The chain of events that had brought Yevgo to this morning, sobering up alone in a cheap café in a large Asian city, seemed opaque to him. He didn't recognize his own hand flipping his fate like an egg in a pan.

Ingrid probably didn't consider him a possibility for the exercise of a little lust. It was age. You got over a certain age (Yevgo remembered the first time, a few years back in a San Francisco bar, when a woman's eyes had slid over him as if he was a featureless prairie and she in search of a mountain), and everyone younger thought that you were another species. They thought you didn't need or didn't want sex; they thought that money, stability, pinochle were your chief interests. Everyone your own age, on the other hand, thought that you couldn't quit your job and wander around the world without a tour group or destination; they thought that beer and spectator sports and visiting your grandchildren was enough of a life. The fly circled his head, settled on the back of his neck. He slapped and missed.

Yevgeny Velasquez, called Yevgo, was sixty-three, short, dark, formerly handsome, badly dressed, with an accent somewhere between Moscow and Havana, spiked with California. He had a round, soft belly, thick hair changing from black to gray, and a missing tip of his right index finger. His face was falling, with soft flaps of skin along what had once been a strong jaw. Heavy eyebrows lay flat above a pair of sad eyes that made women want to take care of him. He was alternately fatalistic, stoic, joyful. He gave his money away when his heart was touched; he was quick to anger and quick to fall into troughs of despair. He loved to eat, drink, laugh, and weep. Though he showed physical signs of aging, his expression was almost unchanged from his youth, and it was an irresistible combination of mournfulness and joie de vivre. He was someone who could, without cause, be happy. Because outright joy was so rare in a person, it affected others like a blow to the solar plexus.

He didn't know how old Ingrid was. She had unwrinkled, unblemished skin. She was in those golden years between adolescence and middle age. What was an acceptable age? He rolled the *Bangkok Post* and tracked the fly as it lifted off and landed: the back of a chair, out of reach; edge of the table, too awkward. His daughters were thirty and thirty-two. So nobody under thirty. The fly landed on the window, turning in a tight circle. It paused and rubbed its front legs together in a mime of anticipation. He lifted the *Bangkok Post*, aimed, and slammed the paper against the window. The fly stuck to the glass. He regarded the rolled newspaper as if it had done the damage.

At his elbow, the owner stood holding aloft a pot of coffee with a questioning expression on her broad face.

Yevgo covered the cup with his hand. "Good morning, beautiful. How's business?" Too much of her coffee and he'd get the runs. She was a serious, solidly built, middle-aged woman whose name Yevgo could not remember or pronounce. They had to shout to hear each other over the music.

She pressed her lips together, glanced around the empty room. "Last night, okay." She liked and respected Yevgo, whose name she could not remember or pronounce, because he was older than the rest of her patrons and because he was older than she was. He stayed in a room behind the café and came down early; he'd been here two or three times already, in and out of Bangkok.

"You like this big, sad music, eh?" Pavarotti was singing about pain and betrayal. Yevgo wanted to pinch the thick part of the owner's arm, the bare flesh like a limb of polished wood. The music swelled, the tenor piercing through the violins.

"So suffering. This life," she shouted, setting the coffeepot on the table with a bang. "You want eggs?" Her voice was naturally strong, but early in the morning, with opera in the background, it was the screech and caw of an untuned instrument.

The food here was terrible, even the eggs were inedible. "Forget suffering. What about pleasure?" Yevgeny shouted back. It was deflating to have to face Buddhism when he was still half-asleep and hungover.

"What?" she yelled, her eyes settling on the dead fly.

"No eggs," he shouted. Flirting with her was hopeless; it would be better to teach her to make good coffee.

She shrugged. "No coffee?" Her gaze still on the dead fly.

"Take the day off, we'll have fun." What would he do if she said yes? Her English was okay, but it revolved around food, drink, and Buddhist precepts; he spoke no Thai. She wasn't beautiful but he liked her face with its expression of vigorous composure.

Wagging a finger, she said something in Thai. "No kill," she shouted. "Short life, bad health." She picked up the pot of coffee and trotted into the back, her dark blue sarong tight across her hips. Asian women had flat butts, a little wide sometimes, but always flat.

Yevgo had started his trip in Bali, traveling from beach to jungle, through Indonesia and Malaysia into Thailand. After years of working steadily as a San Francisco taxi driver, after paying for a mortgage, for insurance, for college, after obligation and duty, there was this: the secret indulgence of aimlessness. By tonight, he'd be in China. Enchanted by the momentum and inertia of travel, he was relieved to have, for the time being, the driving taken out of his hands.

Yevgo imagined he was happy, even if he hadn't gotten laid in a couple of months, even if he was sweating away any sense of purpose in the bottomlands of Asia, even if nobody knew where he was or what he was doing, even though nobody cared if he encountered death or a fate worse than death.

A man approached and slapped a piece of paper against the café window at Yevgo's eye level. Color photographs of vaginas, close-up views of eight or ten, some blown up larger than life, some miniaturized. The man's face was sternly inviting, as if he were presenting Yevgo with a display of pets requiring adoption. Take one of these vaginas home, feed it, save it. As detached parts they were more like landscapes than pets. He felt a moment of despair over what men could do: fuck a piece of land. Not that Yevgo wouldn't be capable.

He waved the man away. Marketing was the strange aspect of capitalism; any small-minded idea could be tried out, any offensive attempt to sell your product was okay as long as it resulted in sales. The man seemed to press the photos closer against the glass, as if they might permeate the surface; vaginas breaking through to make a personal appeal. Then he peered around the deserted café, folded the paper, and walked off. Yevgo shot back the syrupy dregs of coffee, wincing. It was not yet eight in the morning and already over ninety degrees on Khao San Road. He'd showered and donned a semi-clean shirt but he could smell himself, last night's vodka and beer, and other things, things that might not wash out.

He picked up his pack and left the owner a hefty tip, glancing at the dead fly. Buddhists weren't supposed to kill living creatures. They weren't supposed to serve alcohol either.

Just after noon, Yevgo took a pedicab to the General Post Office, an imposing gray colonial building occupying an entire block. He entered the cool interior which, with its high, arched ceilings, felt like a church, and headed for the poste restante boxes on a counter against the back wall. Standing beside a young woman with dreadlocked blonde hair who smelled of cigarettes and patchouli, he trolled the box of letters and cards filed under *V*. There were letters with stamps from Sweden, Chile, South Africa, the United States, England, Malaysia. He read a folded note for someone named Victor from Willow: *We waited until the 4th. Where are you??? What happened? god, I hope you're okay. We're in Kathmandu if you get this soon—then on the Annapurna circuit, then back in Kath by next month. Leave a note, we're worried . . .* What had happened to this Victor, he wondered. Then he moved to the *Y*s, even though there was no chance he'd have mail. His ex-wife wouldn't write to him, his daughters refused to encourage this trip. His friends weren't the writing types. He liked the way his heart lifted at the prospect of mail. He loved equally the gradual sink into disappointment and despair. Yevgo wasn't above enjoying his own sorrow, the sad state of his life.

His final Bangkok mail check. Next: China. This was open-ended travel; after awhile in one place you moved onward, not back home, but to the next country. He paused on the wide, shallow steps outside the GPO, fingering the matryoshka doll in his pocket. It was the smallest doll, solid rather than hollow, with painted-on arms and a painted-on babushka. She had pink dots for cheeks, narrow eyes, thin brows, and bangs that lay flat and dark like a Tartar. Yevgo's mother was not Tartar—she was a Russian Jew, his father a Cuban Catholic—but there was something in the implacable calm of the doll's face that reminded him of his mother.

He strolled away from the GPO, feeling his solitude; land and oceans stretching away from this piece of earth, hundreds of square kilometers of space filled with people who didn't give a shit about him. If his mother were alive, she would write to him. The suffering of solitude was so clean, like having your insides sanded down.

Nobody who had a choice walked along Rama IV Road—six lanes of vehicles spewing gaseous particulates that seized your lungs into a cramped fist and singed the lining of your nostrils. Traffic streamed past, then piled to a halt behind a distant signal and sat for ten minutes, then fifteen minutes, then twenty, engines throbbing, veils of exhaust hanging low. Bangkok was not a great walking city but Yevgo had learned that a traveler walked. You never drove yourself anywhere. Sometimes you were driven and often you walked. You walked because there was time to fill. You walked because you wanted to go nowhere while going somewhere. You walked because your obligation was to encounter, to discover, to meet surprise. His feet hurt. Even in his expensive, custom-made sandals—a necessary extravagance—his arches and toes ached. He rubbed the matryoshka doll in his pocket. His mother had not been saintly, but he preferred to remember her as nearly perfect.

Walking helped his back, ruined from years of driving a cab. He turned off Rama IV into a snake farm where antivenom for most of the world's deadly snakebites was produced. He read this on a plaque. Traffic sounds rose from beyond the walls, filtered through a screen of trees. The grounds were quiet. Snakes were silent creatures. Yevgo yawned. Another sign listed the times for venom milking; he'd missed one by twenty minutes. He stood before a snake cage, staring at a heap of enormous thick snakes, piled on top of each other like skeins of rope, vaguely shiny as if they'd been rubbed with oil. Why weren't the snakes on the bottom crushed to death? Snakes didn't actually resemble rope, they were more tensile, giving an impression of vigor. They seemed simultaneously unconscious and alert.

Yevgo stretched out on a bench and checked his watch for no reason; he had nowhere to be for hours. He gazed up into the shade. Fiera used to massage his shoulders, lower back, and butt when he finished a driving shift. Her fingers like picks jabbing painfully and deliciously into flesh and muscle. Fiera, his wife, his conflagration. She had been a woman who could get herself to the head of any line. He remembered how, when they were first married, she'd gotten chickens in Tashkent when there were no chickens to be had, and always the thickest, creamiest grade of sour cream. She was one of those Jewesses with pale skin, dark reddish hair, *chinita* eyes, and eyebrows that slashed her forehead like a couple of sword strokes. He took out the matryoshka doll. Fiera: his wife no longer.

A vision of Tashkent appeared behind his closed eyes: piercing light, poplar leaves like a thousand tiny fans stirring crisp, dry air. He stared up. How did trees thrive in Bangkok, breathing air dense with exhaust fumes? Cicadas screeched and horns honked in the distance. *Tashkent,* he whispered, the word rich in his mouth. What if he stuck a hand into one of the snake cages? He'd get bit, someone would give him a dose of antivenom, and he would live. Or he'd get bit and die. He considered his hands, the foreshortened right index finger familiar and stubby, wishing he hadn't quit smoking.

Chapter 3

The opening entry under *G* in Bruno's address book–journal:

> *room 212 Shamian Binguan, Shamian island, Guangzhou,*
> *Guangdong Province, People's Republic of China.*
> *fka Canton.*
> *I feel as if I'm breathing air leftover from the opium days*
> *rank, thick, oof.*

When she'd checked into the Shamian Binguan, Fanny couldn't bring herself to request Room 212. What reason would she give, what reason did she have? She wasn't the type to imagine an encounter with Bruno's spirit. Fate, in the form of an indifferent front desk clerk, assigned her Room 227, a spare, windowless space the size of a closet. A room with no view. She dropped her bags on the chair, flicked on the fan, and let the tepid air blow against her damp neck, lifting her arms, turning her sweat-soaked back into the airflow. Her throat was sore. She was just off two trains from Shanghai (a great deal of smoking, spitting, and coughing) and a bus from the train station. It was not quite eight o'clock in the morning. She washed up and went out for a walk.

There was something about Guangzhou, with its frantic traffic, heat, pollution, that made you immediately consider by what means and how soon you were going to leave. Shamian Island seemed one of the nicer spots in the city with its grand trees stirring a breeze and a dusty park flanked by elegantly decrepit colonial buildings. A sandbank, it had been won in the Opium War by the French and British and turned into an enclave for Europeans. Colonization, war, greed; here was distant history, impersonal, and here, too, was recent history, personal. Bruno had been here, had gotten a coffee (abysmal) and a pastry (abysmal) every morning at the White Swan, just as she intended to do. They had arrived by different routes, in different years, but they were each here: Fanny and Bruno, Fanny following Bruno, as it ever had been.

At first, she'd written to Wen Li because she was notifying people, going through Bruno's actual address book—which she'd eventually found—sending out sad news notes. The notes were unpadded: Bruno had died, unexpectedly and suddenly. Wen Li didn't respond. Later, Fanny found the stack of letters from Wen Li to Bruno. When she'd decided to make this trip to Asia, Fanny wrote again to ask if Wen Li might want to meet. This time, a response came: Wen Li "extremely desired" meeting with Fanny. "So very sorrow" to hear about Bruno, her "English too poor say my heart." Fanny was to leave a note at a café in a town called Emei Shan, and somehow Wen Li would get this note. In any case, that place was Fanny's goal, which meant that Guangzhou was, technically, out of her way. So? There was no point in pretending she knew what she was doing, no point in imagining that she wasn't carrying a clumsy load of grief into the world, hauling it on and off trains and buses and boats, into hostels and cafés, museums and parks.

A couple walking toward her were laughing loudly. "You don't have to view every relationship through the lens of Marxist labor," the woman was saying.

"If not the lens of Marxist labor ontology, then it's Freudian sexual psychology–which would you prefer?" the man said.

The woman exploded with a sigh.

Dressed in shorts, sandals, and oversized T-shirts, the couple and especially their bare legs—pale and stout like logs peeled of bark—embarrassed Fanny.

"Hey, fellow alien," the man addressed Fanny. "You look like you need a drink. Follow us."

"At this hour?" Fanny laughed.

"Why not?" They introduced themselves, Canadians arriving from Hong Kong. They'd been teaching in Indonesia and were getting in a bit of traveling before returning to Canada.

"Did you get a whiff of the canal?" the man asked. "It bubbles as if it's alive, and the stink . . . Holy crap!" He raised his eyebrows. "Communists don't believe in the holy but they sure believe in crap."

The woman gave him a look and turned to Fanny. "How easy do you think it'll be to get supplies for my period?"

"In China?" Fanny said.

"Why didn't you think of that before?" the man said. "You never think ahead. It's like traveling with a kid."

"Give it a rest, okay?"

Fanny let her gaze roam. These people were tedious. *Always looking to be amused*—she could hear Bruno teasing. There: a good-looking westerner. A tall, dark-haired man was eavesdropping on their little group, his mouth curved in a smile. *American*, she thought. He appeared unlikely to discuss bodily functions.

The Canadians invited her to meet them for a beer later.

"Sure," she said and excused herself, flipping her braid over her shoulder as she set out after the eavesdropper. Chase down that handsome man.

On the bridge off Shamian (the smell, as advertised, overpowering), Fanny trailed the man. He was easy to spot because of his height but he wasn't easy to follow. The sidewalk was thick with people. Shopping bundles kept banging against her legs, and people turned to stare at her after she bumped them. She lost sight of him and stood still, perspiration slipping down her neck.

A man approached, one of those young men whose lives revolve around finding foreigners with whom to practice their English. "May I help?" he said. What could she say, *Please help me follow a man I don't know*? Then she spied a head of dark, curly hair in line for a bus. She hurried to the bus, paid the fare, and pushed on board. An *escapade*, that's what she was on.

Fanny followed the handsome man into a cemetery shaped like an amphitheater—curved terracing set into a steep hillside. Stadium seating for the dead. A cemetery fitted *her* agenda; what was *he* doing here? He walked on the far side of the curved rows of gray headstones, most of which had porcelain photos of the dead. Shrunken, small-faced women, sage men with droopy mustaches, an occasional bright-eyed younger person, collar buttoned to the neck. Fanny climbed the stairs along one side, hitching her skirt and turning at the sound of leaves rustling. A dove fluttered from some bushes. The sun was high, but there was an aura of dusk about the place. A woman watered plants at a headstone, a straw-brimmed hat with a curtained fringe of black lace hiding her face. The stairs were steep and irregular. Her legs grew heavy, her body like a sponge weighted with water. Three bony dogs stopped eating at her approach, hunched over a flowered enamel platter of rice, hindquarters tensed. Fanny's face and neck streamed with sweat as if sprayed with a hose. The cemetery was quiet, a large space nearly devoid of living people, a bowl of graves.

Bruno wasn't buried anywhere. He'd been cremated in Berkeley, his funeral held at San Francisco Zen Center's Green Gulch farm. Several hundred people attended, most of whom Fanny had never met and had never heard about from Bruno. Bikers in leather jackets and bandannas, Zen students with prayer beads around their wrists, priests and monks in robes, and customers from both his jobs. He'd moved to the Bay Area to become a Buddhist monk and found work in the produce section of a natural grocery and as a motorcycle re-pairman. *Greens and machines*, he used to say. Some of his friends in-troduced themselves to her and talked about her brother—revealing things about him that she had not known. The piece of information that shocked her the most was that roughly six months before he died, he'd left his teacher, at the end of a four-month practice period at a monastery in the Rockies. Why hadn't he told her? Why hadn't she sensed that something significant was happening to him? In Zen, a monk who leaves his teacher is called "nine-fingered" for having cut off an essential digit. Experimenting with other Buddhist lineages, Bruno had continued to study and practice. She was told, in a whis-per, that nothing was more insulting to Zen practitioners than reject-ing Zen for other Buddhist traditions.

There were moments when it had seemed possible she'd stumbled into the funeral of a stranger. Not only had she lost the Bruno she knew, she'd lost a Bruno she hadn't known. A cool fog drifted up from an ocean she couldn't see. Once or twice she thought she heard the boom of surf but maybe it was the roar in her head. When the service was over, Bruno's former teacher corralled her to ask why Bruno had stopped being his student—what did she know? He regarded her with moist eyes. Her face had grown warm. He was handsome, charismatic, brilliant, at least about Buddhism. How could a spiritual teacher understand so little about the dynamics between human beings?

A week later she'd accompanied a few of her brother's friends to Muir Beach where they'd tossed most of Bruno's ashes into the waves. It was a bitter, windy, gray October day; nobody had wanted to linger. She was too disoriented and confused to cry but a couple of guys had sobbed behind their sunglasses. Turned out they'd ridden with Bruno that day and felt responsible without having any idea how the accident had happened. She kept the rest of the ashes, packed into two ziplock sandwich baggies. In his will, he'd handwritten at the bottom, in his odd, lumpy printing: *Fanny, take a trip.* She was surprised at the existence of a will. What single person with few assets and no dependents had a will? Apparently Bruno. He'd left his Norton Commando (mangled beyond use) to the shop where he'd worked, his Buddhist accoutrements to a couple of his meditation pals, and the rest to Fanny, along with that handwritten note. She was afraid that it would prove to be all that he'd left her. Over forty years as siblings and that was it? *Fanny, take a trip* was like saying *Fanny, you're a girl.* Together, they'd become masters of the long, unstructured wander fueled by trouble. Take your sorrow, anxiety, heartbreak on the road.

She was sitting on one of the stone steps, skirt tucked between her legs, arms crossed around her bent knees. Here's what she knew: her brother had had a secret life; he died in an ambiguous manner. These small facts might mean nothing. Who didn't have a secret life? What did the ambiguous circumstances of his death mean, since the essential fact was that he was dead?

Below lay the Pearl River and beyond that ranks of Soviet-style block apartments. Fanny wished she could cry, give her grief some exercise, walk it like a dog on a leash. Oh, for the relief of weeping. She should have spent the afternoon reading *Light Years* in the air-conditioned lobby of the White Swan. Reading was one of the most reliable of pleasures and that novel could make ugly surroundings extraordinary, even beautiful, its sentences reshaping reality. Without the influence of literature, without the benefits of distraction, the present could feel so hard, so far from joy. Into her view came the eavesdropper.

"I saw you in that park earlier, right? Shamian?" He stood beside her, his left hand fingering change in his pocket, a big warm smile lighting his features. "I thought that was you on the bus." He gestured as if the bus lurked behind him. "Know why it's called a Permanent Cemetery?"

Fanny shook her head. She had no idea where she was or what it was called. She'd let herself be carried away.

"The bodies get to stay permanently. Other cemeteries, you're buried for six months, then exhumed and cremated so someone else can use the spot for six months. Ingenious, yeah? Give people six months of graveside mourning, then *get over it*."

His accent was English, which caused her to reconsider her first impression. Why had she assumed he was American? Something about him signaled American.

"Nice out here, isn't it?" He sat on the step and she scooted over to make room.

Not exactly nice, she thought, following his gaze through tree branches to the gray flannel sky, but she said yes and nodded. She wanted to agree with him, and here at least the noise of traffic was at a distance. Clink clink clink—the change being moved around in his pocket. Surreptitiously, she checked him out: a belt—a rich reddish leather—worn with olive-green pants, a cream shirt with the sleeves rolled, dark hair curled over the collar. Her mouth started to water, which rattled her. Who was she turning into?

They introduced themselves, Fanny, Daniel. Daniel removed his hand from the change in his pocket and began bouncing one knee, up and down, up and down. They stared out at the oily gray river. Fanny wasn't uncomfortable with the silence; it felt unexpectedly companionable. She considered the city from this remove: stuffed with factories, exhaling a foul breath, Guangzhou was crammed into a tight bend in the river. There was a uniformity of color and tone; the same murky gray-brown washed over the land, the river, and the air, as if the entire city had been dipped in muddy water. Fanny said, "The river got its name from pearl shells found on its bottom."

"Wasn't it a monk who lost a pearl in the river and it glowed at night but nobody could ever find it, try as they might."

"An irretrievable pearl is better than actual pearls." She paused. "Hard to believe this used to be a fast, clear river. Now it's like molten mud."

They fell silent.

"There used to be islands offshore." Fanny had read an odd little leaflet about the history of Guangzhou in which the word *primordial* appeared multiple times.

Daniel recited in a deep announcer's voice, "A couple of thousand years past, the Pearl River flowed from primordial forests." Then in his normal voice, "I read that pamphlet, too." Making air-quotes with his fingers, he said, "The Pearl River, like an obedient domesticated animal, hoisted its load of silt to the sea. Something like that."

"No mention of obedience."

"I'm embellishing." He began humming "We Built This City" and then broke into song, "*They built this river, they built this river on silt 'n' silk . . .*" He drummed his hands on his knees.

"Hey, I've traveled a long way to get away from bad pop music."

"Eighties rock is not my preferred oeuvre." He began singing again doing a creditable imitation of Neil Young's mournful pitch. "*Four foul winds that push lonely, dirty rivers past our eyes . . .*"

The song was crap—she wasn't a fan of Neil Young—but his voice was deep and warm. "You a rock star?" she teased.

He continued singing.

"In a band?"

"I like to sing."

"You're good."

"And you? A historian?"

She shook her head. "Enough time to read anything I find." She paused. "If not a lead singer, what, then?"

"Before quitting to wander the world? A sommelier."

"Surely you jest."

He laughed. "Pretentious, you reckon? It means I've had training in the science and art of wine."

"Oh." A wine guy? He didn't seem like a wine guy. She gestured across the spread of river and city. "I wonder how many square feet of silt the river has been carrying daily for the last three hundred years." Fanny paused. "There's a formula—always a formula—which I'd guess requires width and depth. What do you think, thirty-five meters wide, nine meters deep?"

"So, you're not interested in wine," he said.

"I like wine."

"I'll go with forty meters wide, ten deep, to make it easy," he said.

"Make it easy, that's no fun."

"Have it your way. Thirty-five times nine is . . ."

"Three hundred fifteen square feet," Fanny said.

"Velocity requires a time factor."

"Right, I'd have to time a float, which I haven't a chance of doing, so . . . never mind." Here was her handsome attraction-distraction, which she'd pursued to a cemetery, and of course she couldn't summon an ounce of flirtation or charm. He was charming *and* a good singer and all she could do was talk about mud.

"Guangzhou is not what I expected," he said. "I'm curious how much money is made here. I reckon there's a flow rate for that, don't you think?" His smile was crooked and winning. "This town has a pedigree of trade, anteceding even opium. Back when it was called Canton and this was the Canton River. I studied Chinese history— I'm sounding like a wonk, aren't I?"

"No worse than cubic feet of silt."

He laughed, and they both relaxed. They exchanged the requisite information of travelers. He had come to China via Hong Kong from the Philippines where he'd been traveling with a friend, playing golf and visiting World War II sites. He'd arrived in Guangzhou the previous day.

"You hungry?" he asked.

Fanny counted out bus fare, her native reticence wrestling with the urge to fling herself at him. She hadn't had company since . . . she didn't know how long, days of solitary eating.

"Famished," she said.

"Splendid." He smiled as if she'd saved him from some dreadful obligation. "Dim sum at the White Swan?" He took her elbow.

Standing side by side—they were the same height—she was sur-prised to find herself staring into his eyes: straight black brows, long eyelashes, blue eyes.

"You're quite tall, aren't you?" Daniel said.

She swallowed a sarcastic quip.

"I like that. I like a tall woman."

Fanny's heart fluttered. What might happen or what might not happen appeared simultaneously in her mind, making her feel a little manic. *Down*, she thought. Here was the perfect aspect of travel: she would never see him again.

The White Swan, Guangzhou's swankiest hotel, with a soaring lobby and several floors of restaurants, offered respite from the grit of the city and a taste of Chinese absurdity—the waterfall in the lobby, for example. Evidence in Bruno's journal suggested that he'd lounged around the White Swan a fair amount. The dim sum restaurant took up one noisy floor. Children chased each other through the tables, waiters wheeled carts up and down, slapping bamboo steamers of barbequed pork buns, shrimp dumplings, pork dumplings, onto ta-bles. Small plates of fried octopus, sweet and sour prawns, bean curd with Chinese mushrooms, jellyfish, black sesame roll, sweet bean in fried dough, coconut milk pudding. The food rolled across the room. Daniel ate with enthusiasm, trying one of each, then seconds. Fanny, not a delicate eater, found that her hunger had vanished. She poked at a dumpling and some seaweed salad with her chopsticks. They drank a couple of beers quickly and their talk eased: food, travel. Light con-versation, not quite personal, topics coming and going like the stacks of little plates. He touched her forearm once, to emphasize a point, and leaned across the table. His face had no wrinkles. His chopstick skills were abysmal. She resisted the urge to show him how to use them properly.

"Tell me how you became good with numbers," Daniel said.

"I'm not that good."

"You work with numbers?"

"I work with people."

"Okay." He laughed. "You work at . . . ?"

"A hospital." She paused. "I'm not a nurse, or a doctor. I just . . ."

"—don't want to tell me what exactly you do. Where is this hospital at which you work?"

"Santa Fe, New Mexico. Why the cemetery?"

"I read about it in the guidebook. You?"

Say she'd followed him there? "The dead are some of my favorite people." She heard herself laugh and thought, *You're drunk, Fanny, please don't be an idiot.* She finished her third beer. "I'm taking my brother's ashes to Tibet." Plausible. She and Bruno had talked about traveling to Tibet together, and Bruno had been near Tibet when he'd been in Asia the year before he died. Could she meet Wen Li in Emei Shan in September and make it into Tibet by the anniversary of Bruno's death—October 8?

Daniel murmured sympathetically. "You were close?"

Fanny talked about her brother. How witty and talented he'd been—always the most charismatic person in the room—how everyone loved him. "He was careful and attentive. You should've seen his arrangements of fruit and vegetables at the market where he worked; they were works of art. Red, yellow, and green peppers in alternating waves of color. Pears and apples in sculptural piles. You've never seen produce like that. When he worked on a motorcycle, it was like surgery, tools and parts practically sterilized and catalogued. He wasn't sloppy or forgetful. The minute he walked into a party, it became more fun, more interesting."

"I'm terribly sorry." Daniel spooned a cube of spicy braised tofu onto her plate. "Try some of this. It's nice."

"Our parents died when we were in high school." Her voice softened. "After that, it was only us two." She wasn't being entirely honest about Bruno. He was capable of teasing someone to tears, capable of great kindness and generosity, capable of furious outbursts. He could make someone laugh right up to the point where they would crumple beneath his wit. Bruno, the cardboard box he'd been cremated in, the drift of smoke disappearing into a foggy morning. He was her sidekick in dreams. He was the person with whom she'd laughed more than with anyone else.

Fanny rummaged through her bag, trying to get her eyes to focus, and finally resorted to feeling for what she wanted. She dropped a ziplock sandwich baggie onto the table. Gray powder puffed from it in a gust of breath. "Oh," she said, fingering the baggie, searching for holes.

Daniel blanched.

"My brother."

"The tofu really is very nice." He leaned back, his eyes averted from the baggie.

"He wore a helmet when he rode. Except for the once." Fanny picked up the tofu with her chopsticks, set it down. That warm Saturday in early October Bruno had on blue jeans and a long-sleeved black T-shirt. Like a diver going without a tank, wetsuit, or fins, entering the ocean anyway. No padded leather jacket, leather pants, helmet. No belt, no watch. His driver's license and a twenty-dollar bill were found in his back pocket. He appeared to have freshly shaven his head. Most likely, he'd meditated for an hour, then gone out for a newspaper and tea at a local café. By nine, he was riding south with friends, a pack of guys on motorcycles. When his friends turned off to Bonnie Doon, Bruno had waved and continued down the highway, alone. The guys who'd cried at the beach when they'd scattered Bruno's ashes felt guilty that they hadn't stopped him from going off on his own.

She forgot where she was, sinking down through beer into a review of the details of that day, less than a year ago. She'd imagined it so many times it seemed as if she'd been there, getting up at dawn, the gray unwashed light turning into a yellow glare that made her squint as she watched, in her mind, Bruno return from the neighborhood café, cut through the alley, unlock the back gate to the yard where he lived in a garden shed he'd renovated. She watched him not put on his helmet or his jacket, watched him wheel the bike out to the street, swing a leg over, and kick it on, and while she watched, her heart swelled. Now she knew what was going to happen. Had *he* known? Then she skipped forward to the moment when his friends turned off and Bruno waved, continuing down Highway 1. It didn't seem unusual, really, that Bruno would want to ride solo, so why did that moment strike her as meaningful? Who could know whether he'd crashed his motorcycle on a California highway intentionally, or if it had been an accident?

"You don't like tofu?" Daniel said.

She gazed at the square of tofu on her plate. "A motorcycle helmet weighs three maybe four pounds. They fit pretty snug, meant to cradle and pad the cranium."

"Try this oniony pancake."

He seemed about to feed her himself, put the food into her mouth. She tasted the pancake. Bruno's biker buddies had not questioned the absence of his helmet. Some of them rode helmetless and Bruno had an unassailable manner—you trusted he had his reasons. His helmet sat on a splintery bench in the entry of his studio while he flew out of control on Highway 1, the bike finally lying down, spinning around and around, the road scraping away Bruno's left side—his unprotected leg and torso and arm, his shorn white scalp hard against the black asphalt.

"Nice, isn't it?" Daniel was watching her face.

Fanny stared in confusion, then realized Daniel was referring to the pancake. Brits talked about food being nice, like a person. "It's good."

"I haven't got any siblings," Daniel said.

Grief was supposed to ease with time, and it had, slowly and painfully, after her parents' deaths but she found the opposite to be true with Bruno. The memorial services, the going out to California and emptying out his studio, had given her the impression of his presence. People asked after him and she could talk about him. Sometimes it had seemed that he was on a long trip, merely out of reach for awhile. Once the flurry of activity ended, once it was apparent he wasn't on a trip, she began to feel what lay ahead of her: the rest of her life without a close family member. Nobody to remember things that she forgot, nobody to tolerate her even when she was cranky and ill-behaved. At first, the fineness of the ash in its ziplock baggies had surprised her. Also that a person was not reduced to an even consistency. Chunky bits of bone were mixed in with the ash. Bruno's bones. The ashes felt not like company, but like a focus, an imperative.

As if she had no idea how it'd gotten there, she snatched up the baggie of Bruno's ashes and returned it to her bag. "Oh god." She flagged a waiter and asked for plain rice. "I've had too much to drink." The waiter slid a bowl from his cart onto their table. She was a social danger, taking out Bruno's ashes at lunch with a stranger in a restaurant with linen tablecloths.

"I'm honored that you, you know, would talk about it."

"You're being kind. Can we please change the subject?"

"Right. China! Where next?"

Fanny scooped rice with her chopsticks. "Emei Shan, I mean, eventually, somehow. You?" She felt shaky, as if she'd run too far.

"Playing it by ear." He explained that he and Simon, his best friend with whom he'd just been in the Philippines, had read history together at Oxford; Simon's area, World War II and the Pacific. Simon had returned to London because his wife was pregnant so he, Daniel, was on his own to tour the locus of his study: China. He began a comparison of the French Revolution and China's communist Revolution.

She tried to track the communist takeover of China, nodding and saying the occasional "Really?" while she worked on an image of herself with this British Daniel in the tiny, airless room she occupied at the Shamian. How long had it been since she'd had sex? A couple of Bruno's friends had made passes at her at his funeral, and one night when she'd been emptying out Bruno's studio, his friend Leonard stopped by and they'd ended up making out, Fanny's back against the bare wall that Bruno faced when he meditated. She'd balked when Leonard tried to move her up the ladder to the loft bed. "Want some tea?" It made her smile to remember the look on Leonard's face when she'd posed that question. As if she'd turned into a prim 1940s girl, offering tea instead of sex. Now here I am in China, eating dim sum with a handsome Englishman who can sing! Lifting her own spirits with a hoist. His nose was too long, it didn't fit his face, and he was certainly younger than she was, but so what? The tablecloth was cool beneath her palm, its dense weave the signature of a high-quality life. Out the large windows the afternoon was a warm embrace of gray. Think of the air as soft rather than polluted.

"I'm digging on being here, ready for a nice spot of unscripted travel, right?" Putting on a broad Cockney accent.

"The best kind," Fanny said.

"Do you want to hear a communist joke?" Daniel said.

Oh please, not a joke-teller.

"Russian communism, not Chinese, but they're cousins, right?" He cleared his throat, began to speak in Russian-accented English. "In a prison cell in the Soviet Union, full of people convicted of, nobody knows vhat. A new man is thrown in by the police and everybody rushes over and asks, How many? How many years of prison have you received? The man says, ten," Daniel's voice imitating dejection. "What for, they ask. For nothing, he answers. Ach, you are a liar, they say. For nothing, they give five years."

Not a stupid joke. It felt good to laugh.

Daniel smiled. He gestured at a waiter for the bill and then excused himself.

He was gone a long time. Fanny waited. Finally, she paid—it was expensive only by Chinese standards—gathered her things, wondering what had happened to him, and there he was by the stairs, holding his stomach. "Terribly sorry, my stomach hasn't been right lately." He patted his trim belly and looked rueful. "I can't count on it. I was feeling fine. Shall we go, then?" He offered his elbow.

She made sympathetic noises while thinking he shouldn't have eaten quite so heartily if he was having stomach trouble. The offered elbow made her feel foolish. She was suspicious of the ways in which men tried to manipulate a woman simply by being polite. He wasn't going to pay his share, and this little dance he was doing to evade the subject struck her as idiotic, if amusing.

"You really are a lovely height, you know that, don't you?" Daniel said.

She swallowed a laugh. Her height! She was tipsy enough still to be on the verge of the inappropriate.

Downstairs they paused in the lobby near the entrance to another of the hotel's restaurants. Fish tanks along one wall burbled behind them, and an ornate red and gold design framed the doorway.

"It was nice meeting you, Daniel." She said this formally, trying to forget her semidrunken ravings about her brother, trying to avoid images of Daniel naked. His eyes were the blue of a cold ocean, grayish and dark. "I hope your stomach is better." She glanced at the fish tanks. She had an uneasy sensation of regression, as if she had no experience with men or human relations. The fish, focus on the fish. One obligingly swam up to the front of the tank and pursed its large lips into a comical fish kiss, like in a cartoon. Again, she nearly burst into laughter. Fish kiss.

"Right-o. Maybe we'll run into each other out there in the wild blue yonder." He cocked his head, his gaze moving from her face to her hips, from her hips to her feet, from her feet to her hair.

"Mmm." Could she get him past the floor attendant into her room? Maybe there was a chance she'd get pregnant. Accidentally, of course. She pictured a beautiful toddler with an English accent. A boy. Boys were easier than girls. A boy who could sing. She couldn't believe what she was thinking. What was happening to her? A few beers and she was off her head. The fish sucked its lips. The word *giggle*, a silly word, came to mind and she blurted, "See you later." Then stared helplessly at his mouth, his white teeth and curved lips.

He leaned forward and kissed her. A kiss like buttered toast, simple and irresistible. Fanny opened her eyes and saw a clean-shaven, un-lined cheek.

The room appeared worse under the glare of the bare bulb, its green and white walls a sickly cast. Fanny switched the light off and flicked on the fan which rotated its face at an angle to the end of the bed, sweeping air across the narrow mattress. Lying in bed, you could put a hand on two walls. Sex in a closet. They shed their clothes, pulled back the sheet, and, with a certain amount of fumbling, lay close. Fanny's legs were unshaven and she hoped Daniel wouldn't notice. Quick, quick, under the sheet. Not much preamble: their lips soften-ing as they kissed, the startling first touch of tongues, a few whispered questions and checks. They shared the taste of garlic and beer and soon were sweating, the unavoidable fact of it washing away self-consciousness. Fanny never could account for her mind during sex. One reason to like sex was to have the necessity of coherent thought taken from her. She could think, or not, or not pay attention to what she thought. She saw a lake she often hiked to in the Pecos, the water frigidly cold though she always made herself jump in. She recalled her most recent former not-a-real-relationship boyfriend, the dense bulk of Ian's chest, his boring monologues. For some reason this loosened her mind and she forgot herself, where she was and who she was with.

The bed was meant for one person. Daniel's leg lay over Fanny, pin-ning her in place. When he reached for her hand, she felt unaccountably moved and pressed down on her heart with her other hand, as if she might turn off the tears that started in her eyes. Sex after a long hiatus was such a relief; she felt she was allowed back into the world of humanity and she was grateful.

He jerked awake, turned to check his watch. "Sorry, just have to . . ."

Fanny rolled on top of him, put her hands on his shoulders, and closed her eyes the better to feel. Bare skin.

"We shouldn't . . ." After a minute he said, "Hang on."

She watched him reach for the condom packet, trying to think of a way to put a stop to it, but she hardly knew the guy and he'd think she was crazy and he'd be right.

Their bodies worked together, far ahead of the rest of them.

She pulled up the sheet and watched him dress. He wore boxers, navy with white stripes. Nice legs, muscled and lean. Buckling his fine belt with his fine hands. Images of sliding came to mind—down a smooth chute into water, skimming across ice.

"Want to go exploring?" he said.

"Thanks, I've got stuff to do."

"In Guangzhou? You're joking."

"Let's just say I've had enough activity for one day," she said.

"Right." He gave her a measuring look. "The mistress of moderation."

He sat on the bed, shoving his feet into his shoes. "Tell me again where you're going next." When she didn't say anything, he continued, "We could conspire to accidentally run into each other."

"I don't travel with a plan."

"No encore?" There was a pause. "Fanny?"

Her name in his voice, inflected with his accent, pleased her. "Daniel who?"

"My surname for your itinerary."

"Not an itinerary."

He tugged her braid gently.

"Yangshuo, maybe Chongqing. There are ancient Buddhist cave carvings somewhere between here and Chengdu. Anyway, by one way or another, to the Buddhist mountain called Emei Shan, in Sichuan Province. Then Tibet." She was having trouble thinking. He stroked her arm.

He stood and sang into an imaginary microphone, "*Never would she tell a man her plan . . .*"

Fanny laughed. The tune was "Ruby Tuesday." She loved the Stones.

He raised his eyebrows. "Sichuan Province. Say the place again?"

"Emei Shan."

"There." He pointed at her.

"I don't do that kind of travel—being in a certain place at a certain time," she said. "I don't have a return ticket."

"*Try to meet her someplace if you dare, she won't care*," he sang. Shoving his shirt in, rolling his sleeves higher, he continued singing. "Let's rendezvous at the mountain." He buckled his belt. "I am Daniel Lowe." He smiled down at her. "You are Fanny Molinari."

"Pleased to make your acquaintance, Daniel Lowe. You going to pay your share of lunch?"

He looked embarrassed. "Look, it's not what you think."

She waited.

"I *am* sorry. I . . ."

"Thought you'd get away with a little dine and dash?"

"No. No, I, it was . . ." He ran his hands through his hair and gazed down at her with an expression of charming chagrin. "A mistake."

"A mistake."

"Let me give you what I have." He began to pull yuan out of a pocket.

"It's okay." She sat up, found her T-shirt, began to dress. It wasn't the right moment to be handed money.

"I'll treat when I see you at the Buddhist mountain. Truly."

Fanny was quiet, feeling herself alone again.

"So, travel queen, how much time do you need for your walkabout?"

"Three weeks. I guess. I don't know."

He was bent over, lacing his shoes. "What was your brother's name?" His tone turned gentle.

She hesitated. "Bruno." She hadn't given him her last name, had she? How many beers had she drunk?

He leaned over her. "I'm really, really sorry about Bruno." He kissed her on the cheek. A soft brush of lips, slightly damp. "Two and a half weeks?"

She shrugged. "Sure." Now she wanted him gone, resenting that she'd told this stranger about Bruno.

"But wait." He straightened. "We could have dinner tonight. What do you reckon?"

She considered teasing him about who would pay for dinner, decided against it. "Thanks, I've got stuff . . ." She trailed off.

"Right." He reached for the door.

"Hold on." She motioned for him to stand back while she opened the door and checked up and down the hallway for the floor clerk. "Clear." She let him leave, preventing herself from thanking him profusely. Thanking him for what? Fucking her. Ending her self-imposed, accidental period of celibacy. Releasing some pent-up toxic sadness. Putting an end to the feeling she'd had since Bruno died that she wanted no one and no one wanted her.

He brushed past her, singing under his breath.

Chapter 4

Zhou Chi figured he probably was not the worst driver in Guangzhou but he was certainly very bad. He had trouble getting into first gear. He didn't know his way around the city. He was supposed to be a *taxi* driver. He was behind the wheel of a dented Toyota Corolla, creeping forward like a gassy cat along an abandoned stretch of the Pearl River. Newer docks had been built downriver so this place—a crumbling brick warehouse, some bent metal sheds, and several rusted boats—was deserted. A perfect place for a cabbie to learn to drive.

The brick-colored car he drove was shabby and hard-used, its engine cranky, the vinyl seats split. Zhou's passenger, his friend Liu Po, hacked and spat out the open window then pursed his lips toward a lit cigarette.

Payment's due, Liu Po said. Five hundred kuai, in a week.

The payment was an unofficial gratuity to local party officials, required of every Guangzhou taxi driver. Five hundred kuai was a lot of money. So far Zhou had earned almost nothing. The car belonged to Zhou's twin brother, Yuyi, who had been dragged from his taxi on these abandoned docks, robbed, beaten, and left to die. It was one of a series of unsolved attacks on taxi drivers; probably the assailants bribed police into bumbling incompetence. Now Yuyi lay in a hospital bed, unconscious, and Zhou drove the taxi—stalling in intersections, bouncing onto curbs, lost in the confusing maze of

Guangzhou's streets that no map could untangle. He had been coming to the dock, to practice, yes, but also thinking maybe he'd have the chance for revenge. An absurd idea. His brother had probably just been dumped here.

Hunched over the steering wheel as if he were hiding it, Zhou failed to give the car enough gas and it lurched, sputtered, died. Liu Po flicked ash out the window. They had been friends for nearly twenty-five years. They liked to say that they'd been friends before they could talk. Zhou turned the key without depressing the clutch. Nothing happened. He pumped the accelerator. Nothing. Liu jabbed his cigarette at Zhou.

Think, he said.

Zhou remembered the clutch.

Get aggressive, Liu said. Don't be a model worker. Yank their pants down.

Like Pan? Zhou asked.

Pan was an older man who'd wrestled a younger driver to the ground over a passenger and lost a tooth in the scuffle. Neither driver got the fare.

Liu cut a shrewd glance at Zhou: did he *want* to do this? He had to make the monthly rental on the car, as well as the gratuity to party officials, and there was the expense of gasoline. This was no game. It was serious business. Glorious business! One could make money, and if Zhou did not keep earning, he would lose Yuyi's lease on the car.

Zhou depressed the clutch, started the car, shifted into first, and let up the clutch. The car leapt forward and died.

This is crazy, Liu said. He sounded offended. You don't even *like* to drive.

More like, I don't know how to drive, Zhou said.

Liu chewed and spat out a bit of thumbnail. If you are doing this only because of your brother . . . he began, but he did not finish.

Of course Zhou was doing this because of Yuyi. If not for Yuyi, Zhou would still be in Hangzhou, working at the guesthouse, reading Dickens in bed at night.

What does your soul crave? Liu asked.

Zhou knew precisely what his friend wanted: Liu Po wanted to shove success in the form of money, joy in life, and freedom down the throat of the Chinese Communist Party. Birds swooped above the turbid water. Zhou peered into the shadows alongside a building, as if he were expecting someone.

Liu lit a fresh cigarette with the burning butt of the one he was finishing. Stocky, with wild, unkempt hair, dressed in cheap gray slacks, thin socks, and black shoes with a slight high heel, he sported a few wisps of beard, a retro effect that he imagined a fashion groundbreaker. Working his teeth into another fingernail, he asked Zhou how often he drove down to the docks.

Zhou was still contemplating Liu's first question. An apparently straightforward question: *what do you want?* But what he wanted was misty and out of focus. He was so practiced at hiding his hopes and dreams from others that he was not sure of them himself. It was hard to be Chinese. At least he had Liu for a friend, someone to irritate him into action, someone he could trust.

They had an unusual friendship; they had never betrayed each other. Liu's family, labeled class enemies during the Cultural Revolution, had been off-limits. The boys—Liu, Zhou, and his brother, Yuyi— had turned the secrecy of their surroundings to their advantage; secretly, they stayed friends. They used a rock and stick in a wall near their apartments as a signal, and they met away from their neighborhood to play. Their secret friendship had given them strength; the vitality of survival.

You shouldn't come here, Liu said of the dockyard. It's bad to haunt such a place.

Zhou smiled. Liu would talk on and on, answering his own questions, filling every fragment of silence. Zhou waited for his friend to continue.

The problem is . . . Liu paused, staring out the window. The problem is that you don't properly value money. Cash, sweet, sweet cash. Liu lifted his chin and crooned the words. Like many fat men, he could appear either thuggish or jolly. He punched Zhou on the shoulder. What you need? You need a chick. What about that drop of honey at the corner shop? She's a ripe melon. Liu belched then patted his stomach. If you had a girl, you'd get interested in money. She's a shy one but you could crack her rind.

Why did women turn soft over Liu? Zhou wondered. They were

always trying to cook for him, mend his clothes. Anyway, what shop girl? Zhou didn't know any shop girls. Ailin's face came to mind, her typical expression of furious disdain. She addressed her co-clerks at the hotel identically, as Comrade. Ailin would never be his girlfriend, with or without cash in his pockets.

Come on, tell Uncle Liu how often you've been coming here, Liu said. Once a week? What will you do if the hoodlums show up?

Zhou said nothing. Here's something he wanted: he wanted to read Thomas Hardy and the rest of Dickens. Sure, he wanted a girlfriend, a wife, a son. He glanced at himself in the rearview mirror. A man without heft. A face that could seem clever: narrow jaw, pretty mouth, small ears. Look again, and you noticed that the face was without a shadow of guile. He sighed. He wanted to be unassailable.

More often? Liu prodded.

It was dusk, night coming like a secret everyone knows about. The light faded from a thick, dirty white into a flannel gray, soggy with pollution and humidity. Zhou had been driving to the docks once a day.

There is nothing you can do, Liu said. Give it up.

Despite being twins, Zhou and Yuyi weren't alike and they weren't close. Yuyi held a flinty, practical view of life. He had taught himself to drive and worked long hours, determined to live a modern life. Yuyi was garrulous, energetic. Zhou was reserved and moody. He was the only one among their friends to go to university. The small hotel where he clerked accepted only Chinese guests, which meant he didn't even have the chance to use his English language skills. Yuyi had been angry with Zhou—he felt that Zhou didn't do enough for their parents, only thinking of himself. The brothers hadn't spoken in months and Zhou hadn't been home in a year. When he heard about Yuyi—his parents had used the telephone at the corner shop to call the hotel which had sent a clerk on a bicycle to Zhou's rooming house—Zhou had immediately returned. Now he was pretending that he knew how to drive a taxi, trying to bring in the money Yuyi had provided.

Did you hear about Chen? Zhou asked, changing the subject, whispering, glancing over his shoulder out the rear window.

Sure, Liu said. Chen built a raft, rowed it to a yacht, and was at this moment en route to Australia. Or Chen had gone to Shanghai to be a movie star. Or Deng Xiaoping sprinted across Tiananmen Square and tackled Chen at Mao's feet. Liu laughed. Personally arrested by Old Uncle Deng. Liu turned around, too, as if someone might appear to listen to their conversation.

Chen'll end up a party deputy, Zhou said.

Party deputy was their personal euphemism for *political prisoner*. Chen was a former schoolmate who'd gotten fired up and somehow scraped together enough money to go to Beijing during the May 1 holiday after hearing rumors of demonstrations. Chen was loud, bitter, not that smart.

Zhou leaned against his door, took a cigarette from Liu's pack, and twirled it between his fingers, an activity that never failed to soothe. The cigarette flashed across his knuckles. The rumors of demonstrations were evidently true: Chen *had* been arrested. Zhou had picked up Chen's brother-in-law near the bus station the day before. The brother-in-law had gone to Beijing to see if he could discover what had happened to Chen, who had not been heard from. Zhou explained this, whispering. The two friends regarded each other. They'd heard about the democracy demonstrations but trusting what they heard was another matter.

Chen: disappeared for democracy, Zhou said, his tone sarcastic.

Only an ordinary worker, Chen had no connections. In China no connections meant no hope. Chen would never be seen again by either of them.

It's a trade: a donkey for a horse, Liu said. China won't be the same, everything will change.

Everything will stay the same, Zhou said.

He was always surprised by Liu's optimism. Where did it come from? Their life of balancings and evasions, of habitual maneuvering around officials and restrictions, would never change.

Why so glum? Liu said. For example, our parents aren't in private business but we are, right?

Zhou grunted. Not exactly true. Liu was paying off the boss of his work unit in order not to work at the factory to which he'd been assigned. As for himself? What he was doing was such a tangled illegal mess, he couldn't think about it. First, things would go backwards. That's the way crackdowns worked.

Liu grabbed Zhou's arm. Do what *you* want, he said. Live coura-geously! He let go, slumped in his seat and said, With a car you're as good as a cadre. Get a woman and the next thing you know you'll be cramming fistfuls of kuai down your belly like plates of dumplings. This is your chance. He tapped a beat on the dash. Let's eat, he said. I'm hungry.

This is your chance, Zhou repeated silently, though he saw no logi-cal connection between a girlfriend and making money. He cast his eyes around the inside of the taxi, the place his brother had spent most of his time. A red plastic rose stuck out of the ashtray, and a strand of plastic lilacs stretched across the shelf behind the rear seat. A small wooden Buddha figure was tucked in the glove box, unob-trusive protection that had failed. These details surprised Zhou. He didn't know his own twin. Maybe he didn't know himself.

Zhou started the engine and began to turn the car around, con-centrating on shifting into first gear. There was a man walking toward them. Here it was. Zhou flicked a glance at Liu, who straightened and hooked his right elbow into the open window.

Zhou shifted roughly, the car stalled. The dead-fish smell of the river stuck in his throat. Liu drummed his fingers against the roof of the car, Zhou worked the key, the clutch, the gear shift. A man was walking toward them. He'd imagined this countless times. Now he could think of nothing, his brain gone oily, slithering down by his feet. He felt pounded by his own heart. The tips of his fingers tingled.

The car shot forward and the glove box crashed open onto Liu's knees. As he drew closer, Zhou saw with surprise that the man was a foreigner. Tall, with curly dark hair, a sharp foreigner's nose, large eyes. What was he doing *here*?

"*Ni hao*," the man said.

Zhou guessed the man meant hello but it sounded like nothing.

"Do you speak English?" the man asked. Zhou glanced at Liu, who was gawking at the man as if the sounds issuing from his mouth were miraculous.

"Indeed. So my capacity permit. Permits," Zhou corrected. He gathered his brain from down by his feet, his stomach from his throat, his heart from his solar plexus.

"Can you get me out of here?"

What was the foreign devil saying, Liu wanted to know.

The man was lost.

Zhou had studied foreign languages at university: Russian and English. He hadn't been good at Russian, but he'd done very well in English. Since graduating, he'd worked on his English by attending Hangzhou's English corner—locals gathering at a park weekly to practice their English conversational skills—and by reading Charles Dickens. Several years earlier, he'd found *Bleak House* at the back of a junk shop and he'd read it at least a dozen times. His parents were confused and frightened by his interest in English; they worried it would get him into trouble. Hadn't they been taught that America was a source of evil, and didn't that include, by association, its language? Liu found Zhou's ability to speak English mildly amusing. Nobody imagined the thrill.

"Sir, to where are the destination desired?" Zhou said, flustered.

"The White Swan." The man laughed a high-pitched laugh. "I'm not staying there, but nearby." He flopped into the backseat.

Zhou shifted into gear, flipped on the meter, and threw a quick, pleased smile at Liu. He let the clutch up too fast and the car jerked to a standstill.

Liu told him not to use the meter; he could charge more because foreigners didn't know anything. They were so full of money it made their blood fat.

Why are you whispering? Zhou wanted to know. The man doesn't speak Chinese.

Going where? Liu asked. The White Swan. Ha! Exactly as he suspected. The foreigner *is* rich.

Zhou didn't tell Liu that he wasn't interested in getting rich off a foreigner. "Where are you from?" Zhou glanced in the rearview mirror at the man, who seemed as handsome as a movie star with a square jaw and dark curls drifting across the flat rock of his forehead. Absurd, those curls, but Zhou felt envious nonetheless. There was a short silence. Had he made a mistake?

"England."

"Tower of London, Thames, Chancery," Zhou said. An Englishman!

"You've been?"

"No. Alas. I read books." A trip to England? Impossible.

The man nodded, meeting Zhou's eyes in the mirror. "I see."

"One day I wish for visiting there." A useless wish. Zhou was producing poor, plain sentences. He wanted to speak beautiful English, to deliver whole paragraphs like his hero Dickens. He was speaking English with an Englishman! A sheen of pleasure spread over him. This was his first happy moment in months. "Where to your home?"

The man laughed his nervous laugh. "London." But he'd been traveling for awhile.

Liu turned round in his seat to stare. Easy meat, he said to Zhou. Get him drunk, play checkers, win cash. Look at him: hair like a bird's nest, and that nose. I don't see how he got out of his poor mother.

We aren't going to make five hundred kuai betting on checkers, said Zhou.

Come on, Liu groaned. The foreigner is a pig on a platter. Now is not the time for your porcelain scruples. For once, be courageous! Liu's voice rose.

Zhou concentrated. "I implore you, sir, appease your appetite to drink. I pray you accept my invitation." Zhou had favorite phrases from *Bleak House* which he savored like a sweet. How accomplished he would feel if he could use a few of them: *upon the whole, quite so, very much obliged.* He loved particular words for their sound and the feel of the syllables in his mouth: *distinguished, graciously, lamentable.* Some passages he'd reread so often he could recite them from memory. He imagined that the characters in *Bleak House* were his closest English-speaking friends.

The foreigner said, "Lovely. I could use a beer."

Liu demanded translation. A beer. Perfection. Guoren's place.

Zhou pondered *use a beer*, a phrase he'd not encountered. He turned left through a yellow light, dodging bicyclists and cars running the yellow light in the other direction. The screech of honking horns trailed after him.

Daniel Lowe, sitting in the back, gripped the cracked armrest. He'd been lost and now he was found and he was about to die or be maimed in a sweltering taxi on the foul, seething streets of Guangzhou. Sour fumes wafted up his nose and down his throat: China's rancid flavor of the day. He was lucky the driver spoke English (odd English), lucky that he wasn't getting robbed and beaten, but the bugger was a maniac at the wheel, throwing them heedlessly into oncoming traffic and driving—stabbing the brake and shifting in crashing hatchet strokes—as if he were waging class warfare against the internal combustion engine.

Guoren's, four low tables and sixteen stools, occupied a section of crumpled sidewalk in a busy neighborhood. Liu ordered a bottle of bai jiu, three beers, peanuts. Guoren kept beers on blocks of ice in bins beside his small kiosk. Only talk, Zhou said sternly. No games, no bets. Liu pursed his lips and poured three shot glasses to the trembling brim.

Zhou and Liu lifted their glasses and tossed the liquid down. Daniel followed suit. Liu slammed his glass on the table and wiped his mouth with the back of his hand.

Daniel coughed. "What is it?" The stool was so short, his knees nearly touched his chin.

"This is bai jiu. The significance of which means white ghost. It is composed of rice." Zhou couldn't stop staring at the foreigner's face, the way the nose and cheekbones were mountainous, creating shadowy valleys, and a ravine for each eye. A steep face, dangerous, nothing like the flat plains of Chinese faces. "Pardon, please may you confer the favor of your distinguished name?"

"Daniel. Daniel Lowe," Daniel said.

"I trust I ought refer you Mr. Lowe."

"Please call me Daniel."

"Dan yell," Zhou said. "I am honored to favor your acquaintance. Extremely amiable." Zhou bowed his head. Charles Dickens was in his pocket, nay, in his very throat. "My name is Zhou Chi. That is, Mr. Zhou, but I beg you, please confer the simple name Joe." Chi was his given name, and he proudly knew that English speakers called each other by their given names. In English he should properly be called Chi but he wanted to use his surname because it sounded like an English name.

"Joe?"

"Exactly precisely." Zhou smiled, thinking of sweet, poor Jo, "the outlaw with the broom," in *Bleak House*.

"I introduce to you my particular friend, Liu." Zhou waved a hand at Liu. "Lee-you." They downed another round of bai jiu. "I beg you, Mr. Daniel, partake the peanut, a particular China specialty. Do you meet it?" Zhou held a peanut aloft.

"Sure." Daniel smashed the shell between thumb and forefinger.

Liu wanted to know what they were talking about.

Just talking, Zhou said.

Guoren pulled up a stool. He was thin with a girlish waist so narrow his belt wrapped around to the middle of his back. He leaned forward like a long-stemmed flower. Where'd you find Big Nose? he asked Liu.

He's a famous American actor, going to make a movie in Guangzhou. In search of Chinese people to act in the movie, Liu said.

Guoren raised his eyebrows. From Holy Worm? He examined Daniel, starting at his shoes and working up to his hair.

Holy *Word*, Liu corrected. The foreigner had told Liu that he was the perfect tough guy, plus Holy Word handsome. Liu turned his profile, round and soft as bread dough.

Gongster. That's what they called criminals. Guoren rotated a forefinger into one nostril. So, this was how movie stars dressed. Guoren leaned across and ran a finger over Daniel's fine leather belt. Daniel jerked away. Guoren smiled and nodded. That belt must be worth a lot of money, he said to Liu. He didn't like me touching it.

Liu's eyes followed a young woman in a tight skirt weighted with fringe and lace wobble past on a pair of pumps. See that.

They both watched the woman's backside as she picked her way across the buckled sidewalk. She's nothing, Guoren said. He saw women all day and she was not the most beautiful. He sighed.

The foreign man was thirty-three years old, not married, Zhou translated.

What is wrong with him? Liu said. Thirty-three was old to be unmarried. Even Zhou, at twenty-five, was old to be unmarried.

Speaking of marriage. Guoren winked at Liu. Was Liu going to marry Yang Mei?

Don't be stupid, Liu said. He was still married, and once the nightclub opened, he'd be surrounded by beauties.

Guoren looked confused. He thought Liu had gotten divorced.

What about Guoren's marriage prospects, Liu prompted.

Guoren blushed.

The foreigner had been to the Philippines and Hong Kong, Zhou reported. Zhou had requested that Daniel bestow upon him slow speech. He'd never before spoken with an actual flesh-and-blood Englishman and understanding was harder than he imagined.

What kind of person takes such a long vacation? Liu said. He inhaled on a cigarette, his puffy cheeks sucked in, eyes squinting.

"What's he saying?" Daniel asked Zhou of Liu.

"Travel is a particular favorite to my friend," Zhou said. *To*, or *of?* English small words were confounding.

I've no time for getting married, Guoren said, sweeping an arm over his modest operation. Also his parents weren't healthy and that was taking a lot of time.

What's wrong now? Liu yawned.

Hemorrhoids, Guoren announced without embarrassment. His father had hemorrhoids and his mother had loose bowels. What they do for hemorrhoids . . . Guoren spoke in a megaphone voice. They stick a finger up there and massage them flat. Guoren illustrated with his index finger.

Please. Liu grimaced.

The foreigner had studied Chinese history at a famous university in England, Zhou reported to Liu. Right now, he didn't have a job. His name was Dan-yell. Confidence was flooding through Zhou. Maybe he wasn't a good driver, but he could understand English.

What kind of idiot doesn't work? Liu said. His father must be rich.

Guoren continued: his mother spent all morning in the latrine— very mysterious, nobody knew the cause—and then she had to lie down the rest of the day.

I'm pleading with you, have some decency, Liu said, putting his head in his hands.

Mr. Daniel is not rich, Zhou said.

Liu scowled. Useless foreigner. Liu stabbed his cigarette into the sidewalk. Let's go.

Liu should listen, Guoren advised. Everybody was going to have aging parents.

No. Liu shoved money at Guoren and stood. Guoren went to make change, a little dejected.

Mr. Daniel has an idea for making money, Zhou said.

Let him find his own way to the White Swan.

No. Zhou patted Liu's stool. They were going to listen to the foreigner's idea.

Liu knew a turtle egg when he saw one. He kicked his stool in disgust.

Sit down, Zhou ordered. He'd had enough of Liu's puffed up torch and gutter style. It's time to do what *I* want, he said. Zhou turned back to Daniel. How could anybody trust a face like that? He indicated for Daniel to continue, thinking, This is my chance.

"My idea requires two actors, you because you speak English—very good English, I might add—and your friend." Daniel nodded at Liu. "Or, another friend if he isn't interested." He paused, wiped perspiration from his temples. "You translate while your friend acts as an escaped demonstrator from the democracy demonstrations in Beijing. Together—one in Chinese, one in English—you tell a story. The story of a chap who was at the demonstrations, got arrested, and escaped. I'll find tourists to be our audience, and we'll charge them. Presto, income! We'll tell them we're raising money for the cause of democracy in China and they'll get to hear something unique , right?"

Zhou glanced around when Daniel stopped talking. The other people at Guoren's were absorbed in their own conversations. A couple of young men talking about bicycles, a young woman and man mooning into each other's eyes. He thought about Chen.

"We split the money three ways." Daniel fingered a peanut. "Each person plays an important role. I find tourists who will pay, you and Liu tell a good story—maybe you know things, maybe you make it up. It doesn't have to be true." Daniel waited.

"Where shall this plan discharge?"

"Your apartment? Here?" Daniel said.

Zhou nodded. There was, of course, no possibility of doing it here, in public, or at his parents' apartment. The thought frightened him. "Very well. I beg you, wait." He turned to Liu, speaking so softly Liu had to put his ear near Zhou's mouth.

You still, Liu said, don't understand the art of whispering.

Zhou waved impatiently.

How much will we make? Liu asked.

Zhou turned to Daniel then reported his answer to Liu: ten or twenty dollars a person.

Liu snorted. Foreigners were surpassingly foolish. Why would they pay *so much* money for lies?

Zhou asked Daniel and reported back to Liu. Westerners believed democracy was the best kind of government, and that the people in Tiananmen Square had been very brave. It would be an adventure for them to meet someone who had been there, someone who was fighting for democracy in China.

Daniel squashed one peanut shell after another while he watched the two men confer. The day was waning. The sidewalks filled with people hurrying home from work.

Democracy in China! Liu laughed. He paused, staring at the cracked sidewalk. Okay, he said at last.

Zhou, woozy with drink, giddy from speaking the King's English and hatching a scheme, turned the wheel too sharply while crossing an intersection and tapped the side of a bicycle. He nudged the bicycle like he might have grazed someone's shoulder walking through a crowd. The rider toppled. Another bicyclist plowed into both the car and the first rider, then another, and soon there was an unsightly heap of bicycles against the right front bumper of Zhou's car. In the back seat, Daniel, after bai jiu and beers, wondered dreamily if the Queen of England had ever been in a car accident in a foreign country, or if that was one more experience royalty missed out on.

Zhou couldn't move and even Liu's hissing exhortations had no effect. An older man in a worn Mao jacket and cap and a sturdy, middle-aged woman with a voice like a fire alarm crowded at Zhou's window, waggling fingers in his face. The evil proliferation of cars and the horrors of private ownership were responsible for everything that was wrong about China today. There was no respect for the virtuous bicycle! The two stepped aside only when a policeman appeared; he leaned in the window and asked to see Zhou's papers. Zhou was flooded with a familiar feeling: dread of being caught in the midst of trying to get away with something. Zhou looked exactly like Yuyi but he still broke into a sweat; driving a car on someone else's papers was illegal.

The policeman, at the end of an oppressively hot, dull day, had half-seen the accident. He worked one of Guangzhou's vast intersections that, despite traffic lights, lane lines, and two policemen, was loose anarchy. Another bribed license, the policeman thought. Nobody learned how to drive; too many people wanted licenses and the necessary paperwork was overwhelming. It made no difference to him; hit one bicyclist, hit a thousand. Anybody could ride a bicycle: the unco-ordinated, the careless, the distracted, the aged, the grief-stricken, the love-struck, the enraged, the drunk. He checked the driver's papers, staring at them for a long time. He couldn't focus what with the old man honking in his ear and the woman shaped like a block of apartments holding forth on how disappointed Mao would be, were he alive, by the ongoing corruption of socialist values. *In Chairman Mao's name . . . oh, please,* he thought. Nobody gave a solid shit for Mao these days. He handed the papers to the driver with his palm open and turned his attention to mollifying the stale Maoists. Comrades, he began. It flowed from there, a stream of rhetoric that he could deliver in his sleep. It was meaningless, and it shut up the pious pair. They shot glances of hatred at the car as they rode away.

The episode took an hour—making sure nobody was hurt, checking everyone's papers, checking everyone's bicycles. He didn't release the taxi until last, and before he did, he inspected the backseat. Sight of the white foreign face shocked the policeman. The foreigner, asleep with his mouth agape, head draped over the back of the seat like a flaccid pillow, snored. A gentle, flatulent sound. The policeman, backing away in alarm, waved the car off.

When he left London, Daniel had vowed to give up lying, cold turkey. Telling the truth was a cornerstone in his plan to revise his life, which was, he understood, his plan to revise himself. Here he was, at loose in the world where no one knew anything about him or his past. This was his chance to be himself, that is, his true self. The real Daniel Lowe. He was sitting on a bench in a park near the White Swan, still a little drunk, feeling fragile, the sun dipping into a chemical bath of orange rimming the skyline. If he didn't say anything, didn't offer the truth, was that lying? He hadn't told Fanny the complete unadorned, fully reported truth because he knew that a New Mexican would not be charmed by a Texan. Not easily. *Half*-Texan. His life was made of remorse, shaped and layered and frosted with remorse. This was how he'd gotten lost in the afternoon: walking and thinking. Regretting that he hadn't told Fanny that his father was from Texas and that he'd spent summers and school breaks in Houston and that he'd been to New Mexico many times, including Santa Fe. He'd skied in Taos and summered in Angel Fire. Thinking about Fanny, about how fantastic it was to fall into bed with someone interesting. He'd not *compared* to Vivian so much as noticed that his hands were encountering not-Vivian. He thought about Vivian, he thought about becoming a better person, about making money on the road, and he'd come up with a good idea—potentially a *great* idea—and suddenly he'd come to, like surfacing after a long swim underwater, sputtering and breathless; where the hell was he? Lost out on some decaying docks, a stinking river sliding past, the heaving chaos of Guangzhou eerily absent. He'd panicked. He hadn't been eating much (austerity measures) and was vulnerable to overreaction. When he'd seen the taxi he was elated and then so nervous he thought he might puke. He couldn't say more than hello in Chinese. As he walked toward the taxi, he flashed on a bullet going through his heart, thinking of Hong Kong triads, the Chinese mafia. He was in the sort of place where he might end up dead or beaten so violently no one would know who he was. *Pay attention, for god's sake.*

A breeze rustled through the shabby trees overhead. Daniel wiped sweat from his forehead, seeing again the taxi as it turned clumsily. How it lined him up like a target, nosing toward him with belches of black exhaust. He'd held his breath, touched the stiffness of his passport stashed against the small of his back, and stood still, as if he would escape harm if he didn't move.

He drank down the rest of the water in his water bottle. Nasty business, that rice alcohol. Since he'd left Simon in the Philippines, Daniel had the impression that everything that happened to him was either a lesson or a test. First test passed: he'd come up with a money-making scheme. The idea had occurred to him because westerners were talking about what had happened in Tiananmen Square, and one traveler claimed to have met someone who had been there. Today's lesson? *Pay attention.* A lesson he regularly failed. Daniel sensed that he was trying to learn the same things over and over. It took everything he had to keep his head above the fray of solo travel. So much to do: find places to eat and sleep, figure out where to go, and how to get there, all in a language he didn't speak. But hey, he was in China! The country whose history he'd studied (for a time, at least). It was *amazing* to be here. Everything was going great. He'd met Fanny Molinari: unflappable, good company, not exactly beautiful but sexy. He had made her laugh! Thank god he could sing. He'd gotten laid, then he'd gotten lost, and then he'd met Joe. He wondered if those abandoned docks were from the opium days. It seemed thrillingly possible. No lying, he promised himself. Fresh start, clean slate, new man. He stood and stretched, bounced up and down a few times. Next: find Fanny.

Gone was the cavernous quiet of night. By nine o'clock in the old days, the streets of Guangzhou would have been nearly empty: a few bicyclists riding home, their desultory conversation and the creak of wheels and pedals the only sounds in an echoing silence. There were still bicyclists, but now there were also taxis and buses and street-side stalls open late. The general buzz and hum like a distracting fly. Zhou used to like to go on night walks, imagining China the only country on earth, and he, Zhou Chi, the only person awake, brooding through the dark secret streets.

He stopped some distance from where the cabs gathered at the train station. He could watch the taxis and not interfere with the people spilling onto the pavement, spreading in a flood of baggage and confusion; the late train had arrived from the Hong Kong border. The first time he'd accepted a fare at the station, a driver had removed the passenger to his own taxi while two other drivers berated Zhou. Humiliated, he hadn't heard a thing. Now he watched as two drivers elbowed each other and another stuck his foot out to trip up a comrade bearing down on a customer. The tripper clapped his hands and laughed. The train station was where the money was, and Zhou was working up the nerve to re-enter the fray. Dirty tactics were acceptable, but when and which kinds? He fretted that he would never become a good taxi driver. To calm himself, he recited a favorite passage from *Bleak House*. "It is night in Lincoln's Inn—perplexed and troublous valley of the shadow of the law, where suitors generally find but little day—and fat candles are snuffed out in offices, and clerks have rattled down the crazy wooden stairs, and dispersed." *Troublous valley of the shadow of the law.* "The bell that rings at nine o'clock, has ceased its doleful clangour about nothing; the gates are shut . . ." Zhou started the engine and headed toward the airport, a less intimidating work area.

At an intersection several miles from the airport, he saw a man fling himself from a taxi, slam the door, and flag Zhou. Zhou slowed and the man, a foreigner, threw his bag in the back, then himself. "Go." The foreigner waved frantically. "Get me out of here." Zhou drove away, seeing in his rearview mirror the angry gestures of the rejected taxi driver. Now whose ire had he earned?

"Goddamn taxi drivers, they'll take advantage of anybody, their own brother. Son of a bitch." The man leaned forward and said, "If you're thinking of cheating me, I'm warning you."

Zhou smiled, shook his head. "Not at all, sir."

"You speak English?" The man raised his arms. "Thank you, thank you Jesus."

Zhou had heard that foreigners were religious and often prayed in public, or spoke aloud to God or Jesus. "Quite so. If you please, sir, to which may I deliver you?"

The man leaned over the front seat and stuck out his hand. "Yevgeny Velasquez. Call me Yevgo."

"I am honored, to be sure. My name is Zhou Chi. Please call me Joe." It struck him as strange and wonderful that he'd taken over his brother's life and he was speaking English more than he ever did in his own life. His English was already improving. Zhou turned into a street that stank of crushed ginkgo.

Yevgo flopped back, swabbing his temples. "Greedy motherfuckers. I know what I'm talking about. I *am* a taxi driver." He touched the plastic lilacs on the shelf beneath the rear window. "Nice touch."

"Pray, what is your destination?" *Nice touch?*

"Let me buy you something to eat."

They drank beer and ate dumplings from a cart underneath an overpass near the river. Yevgo talked while plowing through three orders of dumplings. Yevgo had known immediately that asshole driver was taking a detour because he'd fixed in his mind where the airport was in relation to his destination. He always knew where he was and where he was going; he'd never been lost in his life. He was good with directions and maps because he used to be an engineer; he'd become a cab driver twenty-five years ago when he'd emigrated to the United States. Taxi-driving Lesson Number One: never assume your fares are foolish.

Zhou listened, working hard to follow the words in the thicket of Yevgo's accent.

A dumpling wobbled between Yevgo's chopsticks; it had taken him three tries to lift it. "Even when life is bad, life is good." He chewed the dumpling. "You're a good man, Joe."

It was late, the hour of confessions and confidences. "What is necessary," Zhou asked, "of a top-notch taxi driver?"

The street lamp cast a circular yolk-colored glow of light, shapes and figures beyond blurred in shadow. A few bicycles swished by, the silent dark river slipped toward the ocean. "Good people instincts—who is likely to be sick on your backseat, run like a rabbit without paying, or hold a knife to your throat." Yevgo speared the last slippery dumpling with his chopsticks. "And you have to like people. Talk to them, get involved in their problems. People get in a car with a stranger at the wheel and their mouths turn into well-oiled machines. Taxi drivers are therapists. I give out a lot of advice, free of charge. Sometimes people even take my advice. Maybe my own life is a mess, but I give good advice."

The two men Zhou had met on this single wondrous day—the only foreigners Zhou had ever met—talked freely of their lives as if the information was not delicate, as if anybody might know it. They were so frank!

"An instinct for not getting killed helps. The thing about danger? Smell it before it hits." Yevgo paused. "You've got to enjoy the scene, the gang of drivers. It's a small world; once you're in, it's better than family." Yevgo chewed. "Naturally, you need navigational skills. One other thing. Driving a taxi messes up your back and you get hemorrhoids—do you know hemorrhoids? Look it up in a dictionary. The traffic! It's stressful. It's hard on your eyes—looking at maps or street signs, driving at night." He was working himself into an emotional state. He'd ruined his health, his family life, his peace of mind, and for what? If he'd obeyed Fiera, he would have had a desk job as an engineer. He wiped the back of his neck with a bandanna and took yuan out of his pocket.

Zhou dropped Yevgo at a hostel near the White Swan, on impulse inviting him to come on the expedition in the morning. Afterward, he drove to his parents' apartment, headlights off, the taxi gliding through the darkness, pretending he felt relaxed.

Chapter 5

Fanny was squashed into the middle of the backseat between an older guy in a batik shirt who smelled powerfully of garlic and the woman from Canada. The leaves from a strand of plastic lilacs laid out across the back shelf of the car poked Fanny's neck. In the front were Daniel, the Canadian guy, and the driver. Daniel seemed to be friends with the driver, called Joe, and some friend of Joe's. The friend had been arrested in the democracy demonstrations in Beijing. They were going to hear his story.

When Fanny had run into Daniel in the park earlier that morning, she'd felt awkward, conscious of the sweat on her chest and her clothes that were not freshly washed. Daniel was relaxed and casually flirtatious without a trace of unease. How could someone be so smooth and clean while traveling in China? It filled her with admiration and anxiety. She tried to hold up her end of their flirtation but she wasn't good at flirting. That had been Bruno's forte; he was the flirt, the charmer, the one everyone fell for instantly. Fanny was self-contained, honest to the point of making others uneasy, an acquired taste.

The taxi traveled in jerks and abrupt brakings, turns that were either too wide or too tight. Fanny gripped the upholstery of the front seat in an effort to keep her balance, fruitlessly trying not to touch either of her seatmates. What was the old guy's accent? Maybe eastern European. He was missing part of a finger, had a soft belly and a hooked nose, dark eyes, thick hair, an expression that suggested familiarity with tragedy. His name was Yevgo.

They walked up to the fourth floor of an apartment block painted an unsightly shade of pea-soup green, then down an unlit corridor that smelled of rusting pipes and cooking oil, halting in front of a door with peeling bits of pasted-up red paper around the doorframe. Fanny wished she hadn't accepted Daniel's invitation to come along; it was going to be a trial—boring, tedious. She envisioned cups of tea, stilted conversation, the strain of stifling yawns. She'd said yes in a moment of weakness, feeling she ought to be polite and agreeable. Why did having sex with someone obligate you to them? Joe knocked, a fleshy man opened the door, and they were whisked into a room filled with cigarette smoke. Behind them, the door clicked shut.

It was a one-bedroom apartment and the sofa was also Liu's bed. He'd strewn some wall posters and pamphlets around, advocating the one-child policy, or with slogans such as, "Prepare to Fight Imperialists!" On the table, he'd arranged a bottle and shot glass of bai jiu. Mao's communists had been stolid and serious, sternly rejecting life's pleasures. Supposedly. Hardly anybody believed that party officials denied themselves luxuries now. Liu imagined that democracy revolutionaries (he knew none) would be drinkers and carousers. Behind the calculated mess was evidence of a genteel room; a small jungle of well-tended plants on the tiny balcony, lace antimacassars on the chair and sofa arms. They had an hour before Liu's father returned from sitting with his birds in a park, or his mother from shopping. Impossible to account for the presence of five foreigners in their home.

Zhou squatted on a low stool. Liu launched into an account of the demonstrations in Tiananmen Square. How it had felt like the wilds of Africa (not that Liu had any idea what the wilds of Africa were like—on the other hand, he hadn't been at the demonstrations either) with soldiers filling the vast savannah of the square.

Savannah? Zhou said, glancing up at Liu. Why are you talking about Africa?

"It sounds poetic."

Don't make it hard. Zhou didn't like to admit weakness in the realm of English, but *savannah*?

Translate, Liu commanded.

Zhou took a deep breath.

Liu smiled at the sound of his words in English. He went on to describe how at first the demonstrators had resembled crickets, tender, delicate beings before the callous elephants advancing upon them. But the cause of freedom, the power of united action (here Liu exchanged cautious glances with Zhou—he was sliding toward communist rhetoric), turned the crickets into lions, and they, too, began to advance.

Crickets, elephants, and lions? What is this, the zoo? Zhou said.

Translate, Liu commanded.

Be serious, this is . . . think of Chen, Zhou said. Still, he found himself imagining the scene as he listened, then retold the story. He thought his translations very good. He described the crickets as "delicate honorable creatures" that were "transformed" under the heat of circumstance, as in the ancient art of alchemy. He used the word *indomitable* to describe the advancing lions of democracy and *menacing* for the elephants of the army. For *savannah*, he settled on *grassland*.

It was similar to, Liu said, the first days when the Communist Party was formed (something else of which he had no experience—he gave Zhou a guilty apologetic look), a righteous cause for the good of the Chinese people. Though the experiences they were describing were unknown to them, both Liu and Zhou knew what it was like to be caught in large unruly crowds. As boys, they'd been on the fringes of Red Guard marches through Guangzhou, and it had been wild and chaotic, thrilling and frightening. Much more violent and disturbing than what Liu was now describing.

Liu paced two steps back and forth. Down with corruption, Liu shouted. Long live democracy! Freedom and liberty! He raised his arm in a fist.

Zhou imagined the famous square he'd never visited filled with thousands of people shouting for democracy, raising their arms. Was this what had happened?

Liu thumped down onto a stool and socked Zhou in the arm. Translate, he said roughly.

Zhou could see that Liu's eyes were damp—were those tears?—and he was sweating. Zhou made himself turn to the foreigners. Yevgo opened his eyes. Zhou cleared his throat and the four leaned forward. He wasn't sure what would come out of his mouth, suddenly afraid it would be the old chants, the fanatical ideology that had permeated his life and the lives of Yuyi, Liu, their parents, everyone they knew. He felt a thickness in his throat. He coughed. But his voice was unperturbed as he spoke the words in English: freedom and liberty, democracy, permit the people to choose. He thought of Chen. Stupid, loud Chen, surrounded by soldiers or tanks. Or, Chen in a dank cell. Or, maybe he was sitting right now in a restaurant, drinking beer and eating peanuts. No. Zhou felt it his duty to imagine the worst. When he finished, his audience was silent.

You should get a foreign girlfriend, Liu said cheerfully. These women aren't bad.

What had Chen been thinking? Zhou thought.

Maybe *I'll* get a foreign girlfriend, Liu said.

Would Liu have gone to Beijing to support the students? Zhou wanted to know.

Don't be stupid.

But, Zhou said, you're in favor of an open economy. Do you believe democracy is important, better than socialism?

Maybe, Liu said, his tone indifferent. But it's no big deal: certainly not worth arrest.

Liu had told a good story, even if it wasn't true, Zhou said. He felt relieved that this was almost over, that they seemed to have convinced the foreigners of the lie. He wanted to bolt up, hustle them out. He didn't care about the money, he only wanted not to be caught.

Liu nodded, pleased. Maybe I should become an actor, he said.

Zhou was always surprised by the absence of humility in Liu. Anybody else would have said, no, not worthy storytelling. Liu made money easily, he could have his pick of women. There was something not very Chinese about him.

Liu said he never expected to hear his words in English—it sounded wonderfully strange. Look at them. He thrust his chin at the foreigners sitting on his parents' sofa. They would eat live frogs if we dished them up.

"Did he," Fanny asked of Zhou, pointing at Liu, "know the man who stood in front of the tank?"

"I shall inquire," Zhou said, hiding his confusion.

Tank? Liu said. Man?

Lie! Zhou said. A ribbon of sunlight shot through the window behind the plants, turning particles of dust yellow.

I'm not an idiot. Liu paused. Say this: I did not have the honor of meeting this great man.

Fanny nodded when she heard the answer. Something about this performance made her uneasy; perhaps the problem was that word—*performance*—which popped into her head unbidden. Daniel didn't seem sufficiently wary; he trusted too easily, leaving himself open to being taken advantage of. She felt worried that he was being duped.

The return drive to Shamian Island was silent, but when they unloaded at the dusty park, the Canadians gushed over how *wonderful* it was to meet *real* Chinese people. It had been the most fascinating thing they'd done on their travels. They pushed kuai at Joe, adding extra for "the cause." Which, to Fanny, seemed ridiculous. Who, apart from the inattentive and moronic, would imagine that democracy was now, or would be anytime soon, a genuine cause in China? Observing the glow on their faces (two people who seemed not unfamiliar with irony) made her feel ungenerous; she kept quiet and contributed ten kuai. She hadn't believed the performance, not really. There'd been a few moments in that stuffy room when she'd been swept along, but she thought she could tell the difference between wanting to believe and truly believing, between a seductive lie and a difficult truth. She gave money because the driver had a kind face and because Daniel had invited her, and because she wanted to protect him from what she feared: that those two Chinese men were fooling him.

The Canadians left, Zhou drove off with Yevgo, and Fanny and Daniel stood side by side on the cracked sidewalk gazing into the forlorn park. Already checked out of the hostel, she had a couple of hours before she needed to collect her bag, buy fruit for the trip, and head to Dashatou Wharf to catch the boat. She'd planned to while away the afternoon reading in the air-conditioned lobby of the White Swan with the sound of the waterfall in the background. Fly across a continent and an ocean, endure hours of discomfort on public transportation, to read in a hotel lobby. Who could admit to this kind of travel? A tepid breeze rustled through the plane trees. The plump matrons practicing tai chi on the chewed grass dipped their knees in unison. Fanny considered the possibility of sex, and the possibility—coming to mind again, like that extra drink you shouldn't order when you have to drive home—of pregnancy. An accidental pregnancy. An accidental pregnancy resulting in an accidental life. But she didn't have a hotel room anymore. Maybe then a cup of bad instant coffee in one of the White Swan's restaurants and break it to Daniel that he was being duped by a couple of local slicks. It was hard for her to resist the truth. Wave it like a flag, wear it like a banner, the truth, undeniable, unwanted.

"Your destination is Emei Shan because . . . ?" Daniel glanced at her.

"I liked Joe and Liu," she said. "Where'd you meet them?" *Flirt, Fanny, for god's sake.*

"Great blokes. I was at one of those roadside bars. You've seen them. Tiny stools?"

Fanny nodded. "Are you sure . . ."

"For a person who travels without an itinerary, you seem awfully definite about that mountain."

"I know, I know."

"So?"

She hesitated. "I'm meeting someone. A friend of my brother's."

"I didn't realize your brother had been in China."

"Year before he died."

"He's got a friend in Emei Shan?"

"Apparently. I don't know anything about her." Though Fanny had drawn a hundred conclusions about Wen Li from her many letters to Bruno. She pictured a plump, plain person with a face smooth and square as a butter pat. Someone with burdensome family responsibilities and an impatient nature.

Daniel nodded. "I looked up the mountain in a guidebook. There are two towns near the mountain. The larger, closer one has a café called the Teddy Bear. Easy to remember."

Jesus, the Teddy Bear Café must be the only café in Emei Shan. "Want to get a cup of crap coffee at the White Swan?" Still not flirtation.

He took hold of her hand and lifted it to his mouth. "Fact is, I've got a *blistering* hangover. I drank too much with those chaps and I'm knackered. Desperately need a shower, shave, and a kip." He squeezed her hand, gazed into her eyes. "Nothing more do I want than to see you in a couple of weeks at the Teddy Bear Café. We'll scale the flanks of a sacred Buddhist mountain and earn our place in the book of eternity, sleep in a monastery, and . . ." He raised his eyebrows.

Once again she found herself uneasy with his chivalrous act—kissing the back of her hand! Absurd. "Do you think that really happened? To Liu," she blurted.

"What?" He was puzzled. "Sure, yeah."

"Never mind," she said. "I'm a skeptic." A cynic. Tactless. Sarcastic. A judge, a critic. A fortune-teller had once told Fanny that she lacked tact and to her irritation she knew this to be true. She didn't believe in fortune-tellers.

"The Teddy Bear? Two and a half weeks?" He leaned over, kissed both her cheeks, then her lips. "I'll wait for you," he said.

Fanny shoved her hands into her pockets and nodded without speaking. *Wait* for her? She suppressed an impulse to snort a laugh at an image of Daniel sitting in a place called the Teddy Bear Café day after day, week upon week, waiting for someone he hardly knew . . . that someone being herself. Then it seemed sad and hopeless and she didn't know what to do with her face.

Chapter 6

Zhou had agreed to take Yevgo on a tour of Guangzhou. He held the steering wheel lightly—as if it were a new friend. Something about speaking English and the money in his pocket, or having Yevgo calmly seated beside him, made Zhou feel that he was driving better. Yevgo wasn't *perfectly* American, the way Daniel was perfectly English, but Zhou liked and admired him nonetheless.

They strolled around a congenial, ratty park. The day stretched ahead like an empty familiar road. Trees with faded leaves spread a weak shade. Instead of grass there were swept ovals of dirt. Elderly men chatted while their birds perched in teak cages hooked onto tree branches, and a cluster of women rotated their hips, slapped their arms, swung their legs. A man practiced tai chi, lifting and pressing his arms through the air as if it were a weighty object.

At the top of a hill stood a pavilion once brightly painted. From one of its benches they surveyed the patch of gasping urban nature below. Gray apartment blocks shouldered up against the park, every balcony obscured by hanging laundry. Beyond lay buildings under construction wrapped in brown burlap as if they were packages to be mailed.

Yevgo said, "Will you drive me to China's western border? I'll pay expenses—including your return expenses—plus a fee." Yevgo knew that scene back in the apartment had been a charade, and not because the details didn't add up. The anxiety hadn't been fearful anxiety, the self-satisfaction a wrong note. If Liu had been arrested, he would not act so pleased when talking about it. Yevgo figured if Joe could participate in something like that, he was available for hire.

Zhou bent to fold his pants over his knees, arranging the hem so that his shins were exposed to the air.

Yevgo let the silence lengthen. The sounds of Guangzhou boiled below: bicycle bells, car engines, staccato tones of Cantonese. "I want to go home," Yevgo said. "My real home: Tashkent. I'd like to see some of China on the way, and I'm an old man." Not that old, he thought, but never mind. "It will be comfortable in your car; it will be more interesting with you as translator." Had he heard any birds in Guangzhou? Uncaged birds? He spoke slowly, to be sure that Joe understood. Yevgo had grown accustomed to the American style of travel, everyone in his own vehicle. He didn't want to be stuffed onto one more bus or train, people hacking and coughing. He could spend his money the way he liked. He had to remind himself of this, still aware of Fiera's notions of which expenses were essential—makeup and shoes—and inessential—vodka and pool.

"Here is Grudge Dissolving Pavilion," Zhou said. He gestured to the decrepit structure they were sitting beneath. Zhou was registered to live and work in Hangzhou; the taxi was registered in Guangzhou. Drive Yuyi's taxi across China? Hire himself out to a foreigner? It was dangerously illegal. Not to mention he could barely drive across Guangzhou. "In behind to us is the Poem Reciting Tower where in olden days . . ."

"I'll pay you a hundred yuan a day." Less than twenty dollars. The men stared ahead as if there was a television before them. "Plus expenses."

"Traditional Chinese scholars learned very many ancient poem to memory. By heart, I believe you say in English." Zhou was dumbfounded. Such a sum!

"It'll be an adventure," Yevgo was saying.

"Here men said poem for calm and intelligent sensation," Zhou said.

"Think about it."

Zhou was thinking. *This is your chance.*

On their way out of the park they were intercepted by a stooped man with pocked skin and a wispy gray beard who asked, in formal, heavily accented English, if Yevgo were American. Yevgo, his mind on home, said no, he was Russian. The man's obvious disappointment irritated Yevgo. Why were people interested only in Americans who, in his opinion, were not always worthy of such interest? Americans are shallow, he wanted to shout. Americans don't care about anybody outside of America; they don't care about anybody in China. Why not ask if I'm Italian or Greek or Cuban? The man was talking about how he'd worked for the Americans during the war. Later Yevgo pondered if the man's story could be true. Could a Chinese man in Guangzhou have worked for the Americans in wartime? Or, was the old man one more person telling a story to give himself a heroic life. Everyone wanted to appear better than they were.

"That friend of yours, Lou?" Yevgo said.

Zhou was driving them to a restaurant to discuss details of Yevgo's proposed trip.

"Liu. Lee-you."

"He ever been to Beijing?"

Zhou grunted. Of course Liu had never been to Beijing. Who had the money to go all the way to Beijing? Each layer of deceit Zhou was enmeshed in stacked up in his mind: lying to these foreigners, taking their money, missing the date of his expected return to his work unit, using a taxi illegally, driving on someone else's license, using a hospitalized person's identification.

"It didn't seem like he'd been at those demonstrations," Yevgo said in a musing tone.

The engine died. A knife sharpener walked past, banging his tools together, like a shrill clock ticking, shouting, Sharpen knives, sharpen knives!

"First the clutch, then the key, then shift," Yevgo said. "Take your time."

Zhou did as he was told.

"Now, check your mirrors before you pull into traffic. Side mirror, rearview mirror. You want to get into the habit of doing this every time you pull into traffic."

This kind man, Zhou thought. His hand cramped as he gripped the key.

"As far west as you can take me," Yevgo said. He spread open a map of China. It was the same map that had hung in Zhou's grammar school, before the school was shut down by rioting students in answer to Mao's call for perpetual revolution. They were eating—chili garlic shrimp, rice, beer—on the deck of a docked riverboat restaurant. Small, colored lights were strung around the deck rail.

With his foreshortened finger, Yevgo sketched his plan, pointing out two western border towns. "Yining, or Kashi," he said. "Near the border. Or are they Ghulja and Kashgar?" Even minor details of life were complicated in China. Two names for some towns—one Chinese, the other in the local language. Two currencies (one for foreigners and one for locals), two prices (one for foreigners, one for locals), two times (local time and Beijing time; the government set Beijing's time for the entire country). All the more reason he needed Joe. From Ghulja, he could get to Tashkent via Alma-Ata, from Kashgar via Bishkek. Once in Russian-speaking territory, he could take care of himself.

Zhou ate another shrimp. Delicious. Shrimp were expensive and he never ate them. Now he couldn't stop. Both towns Yevgo mentioned were in the Xinjiang Autonomous Region, a large slab of pale yellow on the map. The edge of nowhere. There was only a sparse scattering of dots for towns and a few thin, black lines for roads. The far west! A place of banishment, populated with political prisoners, home of strange peoples and ancient, buried cities. Nobody went west. Everybody wanted to go to Hong Kong right next door.

"The small roads will be interesting. We're going to see some of China, boy." Yevgo loved the intricacies of navigation. He was an admirer of the extensive and efficient highway system in America but there were few roads on this map. China was a country of train tracks, not highways.

Mouth full of shrimp, Zhou nodded.

Yevgo smoothed the map and calculated. Guangzhou to the border was maybe around three thousand miles. On small roads, with stops . . . still, he might be home in October, the month of anniversaries: his mother's death, his marriage to Fiera, his departure from

Tashkent. The section between Lanzhou and Ürümqi was impressively blank. An area larger—he measured—than the span of his hand, with few dots for towns. For a minute he pictured himself beside a broken-down car under a pitiless sun with a single canteen of water. There would be little traffic on that solitary road.

Zhou swallowed and glanced at the dry patch of yellow yawning between Yevgo's fingers. Was he going to drive into this place of exile? He averted his eyes, imagining the narrow road with its population of prisoners turned road workers in their bright pink T-shirts. Hadn't he heard rumors of recent prison uprisings in Xinjiang? Perhaps along that very road. Prisoners would have nothing to lose, sent far away to do hard labor. What if prisoners attacked the taxi? He pictured himself in a heroic pose, sickle in hand, red kerchief around his neck. He shook his head. A confusion of images from political posters. Perhaps he was meant to be thrown into the world with strangers.

"What do you think?" Yevgo said.

Zhou popped a shrimp into his mouth whole, chewing noisily. *Enjoy this rare moment*, he told himself, *in which you are eating rich food in a rich restaurant*. "Very well, very well." He scanned the other diners, all couples.

"A trip across China," Yevgo murmured. "A chance to see your country."

Zhou thought of how complicated it was for a Chinese person to see his own country; Yevgo knew nothing of life in China.

In fact, Yevgo had forgotten what he knew of restrictions. Twenty-five years of living in America had spoiled him. Years of owning his own house, a washer and dryer, stereo, and car. Years of exposure to marketing and advertising and buying newer models. Now he was for the open road.

Zhou pinched the last shrimp between his chopsticks. It was rude, but he couldn't help himself.

Yevgo said, "You like shrimp? Order more, and more beer." Everything was cheap in China and Yevgo didn't care about money, had never cared about money. It was one reason Fiera had left him. It didn't matter how much this trip cost: he was going home, with a comfortable ride, a guide and translator, and if it meant buying Joe shrimp and anything else he wanted, Yevgo was willing.

"No more," Zhou said. Stomach full of beer and shrimp, he was feeling a little sick.

Yevgo was quiet for a moment. "I have never seen my mother's grave. She died before détente and I couldn't go back." The Guangzhou skyline, velvety with pollution, was crowded with blocky buildings as unattractive as any Soviet creation. Was this what was making him think of home? These ugly buildings? Yevgo liked the way Joe leaned across the table and listened. "She had a heart attack one afternoon and was found the next day when my aunt came by. Lucky they had a date, otherwise, how long would it have been before someone found her?" He ran a hand across his eyes. "She died alone." They were silent for awhile. "You're a good man, Joe." Yevgo lifted his beer bottle. "To China," he said. They touched bottles.

Zhou saw Yevgo's face soften when he talked about his mother and the watery glisten in his dark eyes. Belching, Zhou signaled the waiter.

Yevgo wandered Guangzhou's back streets without aim, dodging greasy puddles and gobs of spit. For the locals all of this was normal: the army of bicycles, cacophony of honking horns, canals of putrid, bubbling water. To Yevgo, it seemed picturesque and distinctive. With its body odor and strong breath, China was a country that was not spruced. Guangzhou could never be mistaken for Bangkok or San Francisco or Tashkent.

He stopped at a low table where four elderly ladies were drinking tea. Tiny toylike furniture. The bitter smell of coal from cooking fires scorched the air. He smiled and bowed, hoping to see their faces change, or maybe catch a glimpse of their teeth. How much you could judge by teeth. He had a sudden urge to embrace a woman. Everyone needed to be touched but you couldn't give a friendly squeeze to a strange woman. The vagina peddler in Bangkok flashed in Yevgo's mind. Life was a sorrowful thing. How about a little dance? He danced a few steps in demonstration and offered his hand. The smallest woman, with round cheeks that hung at her jawline like gauzy curtains, allowed him her tiny hand and stood, lifting her chin like a bird's. He led her in a waltz, counting in Spanish, holding her safely distant from his body. Her feet were very small, he noted, but not bound. The others were excited, shielding their mouths. He could not see their teeth. He twirled her gently, for she seemed fragile and old though her hair was dyed the black of a moonless night. A woman in his arms. When he released her, she was bright-eyed. The ladies wanted him to take one of the tiny stools and drink tea, but he bowed and continued on.

His mind floated and roamed: his former life driving taxis in San Francisco, drinking with Edwin and Moritz, being married to Fiera, Fiera's classically shaped bottom, the fog of San Francisco compared to the heat of Guangzhou, compared to the dryness of Tashkent. He thought about learning Spanish from his father while they walked the streets or waited in Tashkent's grand subway stations surrounded by the heavy cadences of Russian. His father had been in the merchant marine, had fallen in love with Yevgo's mother in Leningrad (where she had gone to visit an aunt), and had let that love change his life. He'd jumped ship, married her, and died in Tashkent instead of Havana.

Yevgo understood what a great effort his father had made to teach his son Spanish so that he would always have someone to speak with in his native tongue. Formal lessons, yes, but mainly long rambling conversations as they moved around Tashkent or picked cherries in the countryside. In winter, with his earflaps pulled down, his coat buttoned, and his scarf thick about his neck, his father described Cuba's warm, moist climate, the feel of salt water, the fruits ending in vowels—papaya, mango, guava, banana. Spanish was their secret language, affording them the opportunity to discuss politics and family problems in public with impunity.

Yevgo stopped walking. Now he spoke English better than he did Russian and his Spanish was about the same as it had always been. He was in a residential area of apartment blocks, a small vegetable market set out along the edge of the street. He didn't notice the mounds of cabbages, green beans, onions. Nor did he notice the clutch of live chickens or the people staring at him, wondering what this foreigner was doing in their neighborhood. His father had died before his mother, but Yevgo was living in San Francisco by then, fighting with Fiera over having left Tashkent and raising two daughters more American than Russian or Cuban.

Since his mother's death, he'd rarely heard from anyone in Tashkent. You stopped making the effort for a few indistinct words, for a letter that said, *There is nothing to buy. You left during Brezhnev, those were the good years, when there were sausages.* During phone calls to his mother before she died, he'd open his large white American refrigerator and gape at its contents: jars of pickles and bottles of beer, eggs, a roast chicken and potatoes, butter, sour cream, jam. It brought tears to his eyes; he had so much and he could not share it with his mother. He thought about that friend of Joe's, telling lies about democracy. What did he know of its compromises and sacrifices? Its joys and disappointments?

The sun was setting in a fizzy orange haze. He turned west and then north; from Guangzhou, he could walk to Tashkent if necessary. After he left Tashkent in 1969, he did not dream of its wide tree-lined boulevards, or the countryside, rippled like a brown ocean beneath vivid skies. He touched the matryoshka doll in his pocket. No Fiera to say they were never going back, no obligation to save money for his daughters, no vast ocean to cross. He rubbed a thumb over the doll. He could do what he wanted. Bicycle bells dinged behind him and he stepped out of the way, into a puddle. Bikes streamed past. Workers on their way home. Yevgo didn't have to be anywhere; no one was longing for him to return or to arrive. *I'm going home, too.*

Chapter 7

A fat-faced party cadre moved into the cabin across from Fanny's. He followed her up on deck, casting suspicious, lecherous glances at her between swigs from a beer bottle. When it was empty, he tossed the bottle into the river. Fanny glared at him—polluting cretin. The Xi River was the largest tributary of the Pearl, second in volume only to the great Yangtze; it provided water to countless towns and villages in the Pearl River Delta. She made herself look away. What was she doing, staring down a drunk party cadre? As an often-solitary woman traveler, she'd perfected the art of presenting as nonsexual. It seemed a useful, if not vital, skill for a woman alone in the world. Out of habit she tucked any desirability, any hints of her own longings or hunger for sex, out of sight. Sometimes she didn't do such a thorough job of it, and before long one man or another came nosing around in sometimes amusing, sometimes welcome, sometimes unpleasant ways.

Retreating to her cabin was not an escape; there slouched her roommate, a young woman wearing a tight shirt and plenty of makeup, belching and sucking her teeth. Fanny wandered the boat, past the packed-in crowds in third class, the slop of rice and cabbage on the floor of the cafeteria, the sewage smell from the toilets. A river boat was smaller than an oceangoing ship, the body of water more intimate. Stories of overcrowded, poorly maintained, capsized boats shot up in her imagination; she hoped the captain wasn't a drunk or irresponsible and that this boat, whatever its name, was in good repair. She could not keep from thinking about the Canadian woman, lifted and tossed into the South China Sea. No doubt she'd thought herself safe from harm. In Fanny's mind, the woman's toes were pointed, her neat figure stiff with shock and cold, drifting back and forth, beyond the golden reach of sunlight into the dark. Maybe to the young man who'd thrown her overboard death was no different than being hungry or tired, a temporary state. Wasn't that somewhat Buddhist? Except a Buddhist would not cause loss of life. Even when you think you have no expectations, you have expectations: you expect to arrive in Shanghai when you buy a ticket from Osaka to Shanghai. No matter what people felt in their souls, nobody said, My fate is to die. Everybody knows death is coming, few expect it.

Mist licked the river, a brown scarf spread over flat land. Bruno had not taken this route; he'd gotten to Emei Shan by train and then bus. Fanny completed one circuit of the boat and began another. Restlessness and loneliness. One precipitated the other; restlessness breeding loneliness, loneliness breeding restlessness. She had an appetite for restlessness; she took her doses of loneliness like medicine, dutifully, with the belief that it would cure her of what ailed her. What ailed her? The fact that she was forty-three and didn't know what to do with herself. Her chronic failure to prosper and settle. Her semi-hysterical, melodramatic core that she permitted no one—except her now-dead brother—to see. Her grief.

The other passengers snacked, tossing into the river chewed sugar-cane stalks, orange and banana peels, beer bottles, biscuit wrappers. Apart from eating, their chief entertainment was keeping an eye on Fanny. Nobody, it seemed, wanted to talk to her, but everybody wanted to get a look at the foreigner on board. Fanny settled on a bench on the aft deck with a notebook, pencil, and *Light Years*. A crowd gathered as if they were pigeons and she a scattering of seeds. What did they see? A creature of mystery and romance come from a far-off land? Alone. Fanny believed in solitude even if it was hard: her parents were dead, her brother was dead. She was alone in the world and it felt right to be, in fact, alone in the world. But to be alone in the world! Suddenly, a voice spoke from the crowd: "You writer?" The speaker was a confident, well-dressed, middle-aged woman. Fanny, surprised to be addressed in English, said yes, she was a writer, the lie giving her a flush of pleasure. Lying presented you with a fantasy different from your actual life; it turned life into a bit of a game. Once the answer was given, the woman disappeared.

What would her friends say about Daniel? He'd get enthusiastic reviews, with perhaps one or two notes of caution. Fanny had a couple of women friends who assumed that every good-looking guy was trouble—narcissistic or needy or both. She wasn't sure that her guy friends would like him. At the least he was someone to have sex with, good sex. Her agreement to meet him tethered her to a specific future. With two people expecting her arrival at the Teddy Bear Café, she could not accidentally float away. She hummed quietly.

Back in her cabin, Fanny's roommate was lounging with her pants unbuttoned, popping salted plums into her mouth. Fanny pulled a chocolate bar—Dutch chocolate she'd purchased in Japan and had been reserving with care—from her bag and offered a couple of squares. The roommate ate the chocolate with relish. Soon Fanny had a handful of salted plums with which to chase her chocolate, and the roommate was making herself comfortable on Fanny's bed, loosening Fanny's braid, running her hands through her hair, prompting Fanny for a brush. The roommate talked and talked, undeterred by the lack of response. She brushed Fanny's hair, twisted it into a roll, undid that, and began to braid. Fanny closed her eyes. Nobody had brushed her hair for years. Even after she was old enough to braid her own hair, if her mother was home, she would brush and braid Fanny's hair. When her mother was home. Fanny and Bruno's parents had run an import business and traveled a great deal, leaving Bruno and Fanny behind. When they were small, a retired Swedish couple stayed with them. Mrs. Karlsson used to braid Fanny's hair into painfully tight French braids which were pretty but not as comfortable, or as perfect, as her mother's braids. By the time Fanny and Bruno were teenagers, they begged to take care of themselves, which meant that when their parents died in the crash of a small aircraft—Fanny fifteen and Bruno sixteen—they were a tight unit. Bruno had borne the bulk of the responsibility. Over the years, Fanny had wondered if it had worn on him, that responsibility, though she'd never asked. Neither one of them ever married, or had children.

She could hardly recall her parents' funeral. Two images only, not related to the funeral itself: a hot-air balloon afloat in a blue sky above the valley, and coyote droppings in the Sandia foothills, where they'd dispersed the ashes. Nothing else. Her cabinmate, a little scary with her excess makeup and shiny, tight clothing, had done an expert braid job. Fanny thanked her; the young woman beamed. Fanny almost hugged her: here was the pleasure of making an unexpected connection, without language.

Night descended. Fanny went out into the warm dark to watch the creamy river churn and listen to the thrum of the engines. The past felt painfully close without the density of ordinary life as a counterweight. Here was the promise in solo travel: time to think about every event, every important period of your life. You could lay your life out one way, then another, extract messages and meaning, give those up for others. You could do this over and over again until you felt desperate and unhinged, or until your past flattened and the present, the messy, circumscribed, insubstantial present, trumped everything that had ever happened to you. A thin rain began to fall, glittering in the boat's lights. At least she could think about her career problem without feeling too hopeless. She could slip into it, then back to the present relatively un-scathed. Maybe she'd *like* a career, maybe she was grown-up enough for one. She'd only ever held jobs: frame shop assistant, paint shop assistant, administrative assistant at a small private school (an assistant by nature perhaps), most recently per diem unit clerk at the hospital. It was a decent job with variety in tasks and personalities, and she was good at it. She liked to work—her aim was not to get out of work. Her general studies degree—years ago now—prepared her for anything and nothing. She prized flexibility, by which she meant the time to take classes, travel, hike on a whim. She resisted a set schedule; she was adept at living on just enough money. All of these things were hindrances to taking up a more meaningful work life. But, what good was she to anyone? She rubbed her eyes and blinked back a sudden blurriness. That was a question to take seriously: of what good was she to anyone.

In the warm foggy dawn, Fanny's roommate buttoned her jeans, took out a mirror, applied thick sweeps of eye shadow. She offered the makeup to Fanny, who declined. A skinny boy—staring dreamily at Fanny—sat on her roommate's bed for a heart-to-heart. He sounded upset, she sympathetic. When the departure marching music began, Fanny pressed herself into the line to file off the boat, relieved at the prospect of geographical change. In the crowd waiting to disembark, she spotted the party cadre. He was wearing a V-necked sweater-vest, like a golfer. She recognized him because of the stare—the same suspicious, lustful stare he'd given her when she'd boarded. She turned away.

Chapter 8

Zhou and Liu performed Escaped Democracy Demonstrator two more times, though only once more at Liu's parents' apartment. The day after the second performance, for a trio from France, Liu's mother was waiting for them. She wanted to know, was it true they'd been dancing cheek to cheek with foreign girls in the apartment?

Not true, Liu said. He lit a cigarette while Zhou dusted the taxi. They were parked in an alley behind Liu's building where Liu's mother had intercepted them. It came out that Wang Taitai, who lived down the hall and had been sent home by her work unit for bed rest because her blood pressure was 210 over 80, had watched Zhou and Liu leave the building. People called her Old Shoe Tofu because what came out of her mouth was as pungent as the fermented tofu dish by that name.

Liu's mother wanted him to know she didn't approve of his disco idea.

Zhou knew everything that Liu's mother did not approve of in Liu's life: she disapproved of Liu's estrangement from his wife and the absence of children, she disapproved of every single one of his numerous work schemes and ideas, she did not like most of his friends, nor did she like the way he dressed. Zhou also knew that Liu's father spent his days alone in the park with his birds, smoking. Nobody ever talked about the past, what was the point? That didn't mean it was forgotten.

Are you trying to ruin yourself? His mother jabbed Liu's chest then turned to Zhou and smiled, saying, Please excuse. She stroked her hair; dyed black and twisted into a roll, her hair was her vanity. Don't bring foreigners here, she ordered, looking back and forth between the two men and giving them her do-what-I-say-or-else face.

There was no music, Liu said, no dancing. He turned to Zhou, who nodded vigorously. Only talk, he said. Liu extracted a second cigarette but didn't light it. He explained that the foreigners were people Zhou had met in order to practice speaking English. They wanted to see a "nice" Chinese apartment. He thought his mother would be proud.

She shot him a look.

Zhou speaks good English, Liu blathered on, turning to Zhou who nodded less enthusiastically. Zhou will get a job as a translator. Or, he'll become one of the taxi drivers at the White Swan, Liu said. Zhou hid his skepticism. Liu and his lies and fantasies.

You know what that Old Shoe Tofu will do, Liu's mother said.

Zhou understood every nuance of this conversation. Wang Taitai would report them to the neighborhood Public Security Bureau thug. *Improper contact with foreigners.* Not to worry, Zhou heard Liu saying, *it's nothing.* This is 1989 not 1969; things are different. Zhou admired Liu's lying abilities, his confident tone, his lack of anxiety. He thought of Liu's father, who couldn't work, couldn't shop or cook, couldn't do anything except smoke and sit with his birds. That was the kind of trouble they could get themselves into.

They took the third group—two large, thick men, one from New Zealand and the other from Australia—to the deserted docks. They pulled folding stools from the trunk of the car and set them on the weedy asphalt, the car doors open as if for a quick escape. That worked surprisingly well; the big men liked going away from the city. They kept peering around and making jokes about being *sitting targets, on the waterfront.*

The location and its implications were distracting to Zhou; he thought of his brother who was still in the hospital. He and Liu honed the story, changing fine points, keeping it fresh. They'd queried friends about the demonstrations in Tiananmen Square. For awhile the events had been a topic of conversation, conjecture about what had happened ranging from a party plot to a fabrication of the foreign media, though there were those who hadn't heard even rumors. Recently people claimed to accept the government's story: students had been permitted to demonstrate and the demonstrations had gotten out of hand and the army had been called in and put an end to the gathering. No casualties. Out of habit, people believed the government without believing the government. Wild rumors lingered: the government had panicked, the army was called in, thousands were dead. Or: nothing, there had been no demonstrations. In China, the truth was like wet clay, changing shape depending on who was handling it.

Some said the demonstrations had not been about democracy— communism was good—but rather they'd been protests against corruption. People supported the students and they also thought the central government was doing a good job. People said one thing, then its opposite, the contradictions presented with equal firmness. Only an unemployed, bohemian friend of Liu's said that the communist system was a dead fish and that the demonstrations had sought to overthrow the government. Revolution, he shouted, continuous revolution! Then he collapsed in laughter and coughing and asked for a cigarette. You can't kill a fish that's already dead and stinking, he said.

Zhou found out about the tank man from Daniel. They worked it into their routine. Liu enjoyed the performances: he soaked up the attention, the praise, the money. Liu wanted more drama, and he suggested they recruit a third friend to play the part of a People's Liberation Army soldier. The soldier would appear and he and Liu would scuffle, Liu would escape while Zhou stayed to spin a tale. Zhou said no; too complicated, not believable. Daniel wanted to bring groups of five or six, maybe get another driver in on it, but both Zhou and Liu were opposed. Small groups were less conspicuous and they didn't want to draw attention. The audiences gave generously, imagining that they were supporting democracy in China.

The performances made Zhou uneasy. The business of knowing or not-knowing was complicated. He'd pretended not to know that similar demonstrations had occurred in Hangzhou, bringing the city nearly to the edge of collapse, though he'd recognized the tension, excitement, and fear in the air. The demonstrators were young and didn't have memories of shouting in the streets, windows being smashed, smoke billowing, piles of half-burnt books, ash and broken glass on the ground. Zhou and his friends were of a generation that had mixed feelings about large group gatherings. In the late sixties Zhou had been eight years old, and he could easily recall the sensation of pressurized quiet in their courtyard while his parents whispered in their darkened kitchen. It was a time of heavy silences split by violent noise. All the adults had seemed to be waiting. Waiting for spring, waiting for change, waiting for trouble to break out. He used to stare up at the portrait of Mao that hung in their apartment, trying to catch the eyes moving. Not surprisingly, he'd believed that those portraits, which were in every room of every building, could see. The Escaped Democracy Demonstrator performances took him back to the past in a way that made him anxious. What about Chen? It was the unknown aspect of Chen's fate that troubled Zhou.

Daniel and Yevgo ran into each other every morning at the White Swan, getting the same breakfast: weak, overpriced instant coffee— the last coffee they would encounter in China—and rubbery imitation croissants. They'd sit together and regale each other with their Guangzhou misadventures: getting lost, the sight of eels being skinned and of pink-fleshed rabbits hung on hooks; the smells—bitter, sour, ancient; worms of cigarette ash on a dish of pork and cabbage; the limitless exasperating enchanting energy of the city. Daniel gave impromptu mini-lectures on the Opium War of 1840–1842. He confessed to having persuaded Zhou and Liu into the escaped democracy demonstrator episodes. Yevgo was amused. Daniel liked Yevgo's generosity and sense of humor. They laughed a lot. Yevgo was a good listener. When Daniel asked if he could come along on Yevgo's trip, offering to share expenses, Yevgo said sure. Daniel put Emei Shan on the itinerary, not hiding the reason and promising to entertain them with songs on the drive. The success of the democracy demonstrator episodes made Daniel buoyant. His connection with Zhou and Liu gave him cachet in the world of travelers; people bought him drinks. Though there was no guarantee that Liu would come along, Daniel was eager to take the show on the road.

Liu had agreed to help Zhou sort out strategies for his illegal journey. They were sitting in the taxi on the deserted docks, Liu eating peanuts, Zhou holding the steering wheel, the engine off. An oppressively humid, warm afternoon. Both men were sweating. They folded their shirts up, their bare bellies appearing oiled.

Liu sucked a peanut out of its shell, smacking the air.

Don't drop peanut shells in here, Zhou said.

Liu tossed a shell out the window. What a fussy grandmother you are, he said.

Zhou didn't want any peanut *skins* in the car either.

Liu pointed out that he was here to help and Zhou could show some appreciation, be a little less particular. Liu was splitting peanuts between his teeth at a ferocious rate, sloughing the skins with his arm hung out the window, tossing the shattered shells away without a glance. He was constructing the lies; the front lies, the supporting lies, the whole delicate structure. Liu would procure a letter of introduction for Zhou from Sun, his friend in the provincial agricultural department. Sun, a party member, owed him. Sun would put a shiny gold seal on the letter. Very impressive. Liu fondled a peanut between his thick fingers, papery peanut skin fluttering to the ground.

A letter saying what?

Hold on. Liu chewed with his mouth open, working a wad of peanut meat into pulp. Okay, the story is this: Zhou is the escort for a foreign agriculture expert come to China to see the miracle of communal farms. Write this down. Liu jabbed a peanut at Zhou.

Zhou opened the glove box and there was the Buddha, sitting amidst a pad of rice paper receipts, a folded rag, a pen, a length of twine. Its small, fat, smiling face eased the tension in his chest. He took the pad of rice paper and a pen. A nearly dry pen which skipped ink. Actually, he said, there would be two foreigners. The Englishman is coming, too.

Liu stopped chewing. Big mistake. Zhou should *not* let the Englishman come.

I like him. Anyway, he's coming.

You'll see, Liu said ominously. Write this: "The miracle" of communal farms. The experts want to see the way agriculture in China is a bridge between socialism and free markets. That's *good*. Liu pursed his lips.

Zhou placed the rice paper on the middle of the steering wheel and wrote. He couldn't press too hard because the paper would tear, but if he didn't press hard enough the characters were too faint.

The foreign experts are here to learn from the greatness of China, a country which feeds all its people. Liu tossed a peanut shell out the window and held his arm high, fingers in a fist. Long Live China! Every Chinese person had enough rice, enough meat! Liu coughed and bits of chewed peanut sprayed from his mouth. Except, he said, for the mass starvation caused by economically induced famines. Liu glanced at Zhou and smiled.

Zhou's pen stopped, poised. You don't know that. He stabbed the pen toward the white specks on the dash. Don't cough with your mouth full.

Liu flapped his hand. Skip that last part. He swiped up peanut pulp from the dash and relocated the chewed peanut bits against the outside of his door.

Zhou watched with a pained expression.

Okay. Our visiting foreign agriculture experts want to see irrigation techniques; they want to see how Chinese farmers brilliantly combine traditional farming methods with new technology. Liu picked peanut out of his teeth with a forefinger. The story was sounding good, *very* eloquent. *I* should be a party cadre. Maybe I can still become one. Liu smiled at Zhou.

Zhou said nothing.

Are those foreigners going to kill your sense of humor? Liu shook his head in disgust. The letter would say that Zhou was the driver, translator, and handler. Liu snorted. Some driver, huh? Anyway, they'd let Sun choose the final words. Sun knew how to set the right wrinkles.

Zhou wanted to know what he was supposed to tell his parents.

That was easy: he should tell them he changed the taxi registration to Hangzhou so he could work his old job—work two jobs—and also because he had a girlfriend there. He wanted to work hard in order to get married. They couldn't say anything against that.

Would they believe him? It was impossible to change a registration.

Liu mangled a peanut between thumb and forefinger. Don't worry about every small detail. When you tell people something, they believe you if you have the right tone.

Exactly what was worrying Zhou. He tapped the pen against the steering wheel. He was passing himself off as his brother, Zhou Yuyi, a taxi driver. He was himself, Zhou Chi, pretending to be a translator and a caretaker of two foreigners. He was going to drive around China without permits, with only a flimsy letter, two different ID cards, and Guangzhou license plates between himself and trouble of the prison variety. He *had* to worry about every detail. One unforeseen gap and he could slip into a hole that he wouldn't be able to extricate himself from. The more he contemplated going off alone with a couple of foreigners—meeting zealous police officers, nosy clerks, and officials (whom Liu called ratholers, every single one of them suspicious and practiced at spying and reporting)—the more he felt he couldn't go through with it, no matter how much money he'd make, no matter that he'd acquire driving experience and have the chance to speak English with a genuine, true Englishman. He was terrified of being discovered in his lies. Zhou loved his country. Love of the People's Republic of China was obligatory, not optional. But faith in China's capacity for fairness and justice was another matter. He spoke English; he might be mistaken for an imperialist, a capitalist roader. Though it was the prospect of speaking English that was drawing him forward. Forward into what?

Will you come? Zhou asked. He needed Liu. For one thing, you're a better liar. Spontaneous, creative.

Liu rubbed a peanut and smiled, pleased to be complimented. Zhou was going to be fine. Once he got going, he'd get cozy.

I can't lie, Zhou said.

What kind of a poor excuse for a Chinese are you?

I don't like to lie.

You don't like to lie. Ridiculous! How can you call yourself a communist? Liu manipulated three peanuts in his palm, working them over as if they were Baoding balls.

Lying in the China of the late eighties was not overtly condoned; every Chinese person would say it was bad practice. But it was an acknowledged necessity. You could not hope to prosper if you weren't willing and able to lie.

Remember what you said to me, Zhou said, *here's your chance*. This can be *your* chance, too.

Liu crushed the three peanuts simultaneously between his palms and then began to pick through the mess, dropping slivers of shell and flakes of peanut skin over the seat and floor.

Zhou sighed. Liu didn't need anybody's help, he took all of his chances.

Leave the Englishman.

Don't worry about Dan-yell. Plus, they could keep making money while they traveled. Liu should admit that Daniel's idea had worked. He'd find tourists and they'd perform. Liu would save a lot of money for his disco. Liu had started a business acting as middleman for a group of farmers who wanted to sell their produce on the free market, and he was working on opening a nightclub, though drinking and dancing had recently been labeled antisocial behavior. Peanut skins and shells littered the floor at Liu's feet. Money was usually a persuasive argument with Liu. Zhou suddenly felt desperate for Liu to come along.

Liu grunted and chewed. I'll put my affairs in order.

Zhou exhaled. He was starting to like this place, the pair of rusted boats that leaned against the rotting, half-sunk dock. It was hard to imagine that bad things had happened here. Places, unlike people, did not appear to retain the aura left by traumatic events. Or, perhaps they did.

Chapter 9

To get into a hotel room in China, you first had to find the floor attendant. Guests were never given keys to their rooms. These attendants—always young women—were the key girls, the floor monitors, the gatekeepers. *Fuwuyuan* was one of the first Mandarin words Fanny learned. She'd shout, as she'd seen others do, *fuwuyuan, fuwuyuan*, down the echoing, dark hallways of whatever cheap guest-house, hotel, or hostel she'd checked into, and a surly young woman would eventually, later rather than sooner, come stomping, unlock the door, and slam it open. Fanny knew she'd been lucky to have spirited Daniel into her room at the hostel in Guangzhou without discovery by the *fuwuyuan*; guests were not allowed. Lucky, too, that a *fuwuyuan* had not barged in on them; the clerks habitually entered without knocking. Daniel represented so many kinds of getting lucky.

Wuzhou was awake and noisy when Fanny took a room at a dingy hotel overlooking the river. Her arrival interrupted the floor clerk's morning television program. Eye on the television, the clerk engaged in an exchange of deposits, chits, receipts. The Chinese had a passion for the small, complicated bureaucratic procedure. An elaborate ritual designed, perhaps, to occupy the clerk's time and to assign culpability in the event of petty crimes. If Fanny made off with one of the enormous quilts, or large flowered thermoses, the *fuwuyuan* would be held accountable. The clerk had flat cheeks, unwashed hair with white flakes sprinkled throughout, and a square figure. Not bothering to adjust her twisted skirt, she strode down the hall, unlocked and flung wide the door to Room Number 315, and hastened back to her television program.

Once, the room had been lovely but now the walls were peeling, the windows barely closed, the spittoon was full of brown water and floating cigarette butts, the chamber pot had dried lines of yellow, the sheets retained the indentation of a former tenant. What about communism as a communal consciousness, a sense of shared responsibility? The floor clerk opened the door again, snapped down a thermos of hot water, retreated. Fanny stood, unable to move. Travel was a return to a primary existence, in which your concerns were the acquisition of food and shelter and the delicate negotiation of contact with strangers who perceived you either as a possible threat or as competition for available resources. How to live an elemental life in the modern world: travel without reservations or plans, with few possessions, cheaply.

She set her bags on a chair and went down the hall. The bulb in the bathroom was out and there was no hot water in the trough-like sink. It would have been nice to wash her hair. She undid her braid, ran her hands under the cold water and wet her hair, then rebraided it.

Back in the clerk's cubbyhole, armed with the used chamber pot, the broken desk lamp, and a dirty sheet, Fanny performed a pantomime. On the television, a woman wept, hands folded over her face in the universal gesture of grief. The clerk, not looking away from the weeping woman on the screen, said, *mei you*. Don't have. Fanny had learned that in China no didn't mean never, or impossible. It was an answer of whim, of mood. It might mean that the person didn't want to do what you asked, find what you needed, sell what you wanted, just then. She heard mei you so often, it had become emblematic, the communist equivalent of a marketing slogan: don't have, don't have. A mantra, a philosophical metaphor, a religious precept. She thought that the phrase illustrated an essential difference between capitalism and communism: Communism = don't have; capitalism = have. Fanny took a chair to wait. The woman on the television began an argument with another woman.

Eventually, the clerk slammed through some cupboards and produced a clean chamber pot and a working lamp. No clean sheet, just so you knew that you couldn't have everything you desired.

Fanny opened the windows, spread her sleeping sheet on the bed, brushed her teeth without water, set out her clock, draped a bandanna over the pillow, and lay down on the bed. Buses rumbled up the street, the sounds of Chinese television barked from other rooms. *I am in Wuzhou, Guangxi Autonomous Region, People's Republic of China.* Early morning. She'd slept poorly on the boat. Disturbed by contemplating her lost family and her own lost way and now what better balm than this? Prone and still, awash in strangeness.

Wuzhou Steel Mills at Dawn: the caption on a postcard Fanny examined in the shop of the Beishan Hotel. The steel mills offered as an attraction. The black profile of factories in the postcard was spiked with smokestacks belching gray clouds into an apocalyptically lurid red sky. Funereal, a crematorium of molten products. Evidence of the Communist Party's adoration of production and industrialization, and a darkly comic photo of toxic pollution. Wasn't it also a photo of accomplishment and progress? The necessary hell a country must traverse in order to bring its people into the sweetness and light of modern middle-class life.

Fanny bought three of the cards from the shopgirl, yet another young woman who refused to meet her eye. The Chinese responded to Fanny in one of two styles. Sometimes she got the Frightened Gawk, which went something like this: open mouth covered with a hand, saucered eyes, body canted back and away, as if she were an animal apt to strike without warning. The other was She Doesn't Exist. The tall, large-eyed foreigner, the Big-Nosed Giantess, wasn't actually inches away, offering a crumpled wad of bills in her paw. Hard not to admire the severity of concentration required to ignore someone standing before you. It implied a Buddhist capacity for focus, or a practiced skill in tuning out the turmoil of being among a billion. The Frightened Gawk, at least, acknowledged your existence in the world; though an obviously invasive and disturbing presence, the Gawk confirmed your presence. She Doesn't Exist was an act of erasure. Fanny smiled at the girl who accepted her money as if it came from the air.

She settled into one of the shabby lobby chairs to read an outdated copy of the *China Daily*, China's English language paper. The Beishan was the nicest hotel in Wuzhou. The lobby featured a heavy chandelier, a curved staircase, wainscoting in Wedgwood blue with carved doves in the corners, their feet painted bright orange. Heavy, worn furniture recalled colonialism with an air of guilty charm. Such faint, battered whiffs of elegance in the staunch heart of communism gave off a reek of thrilling heresy. The amount of time she devoted to observing and considering the décor was an indication of something— she had nothing better to think about, she had worse things to think about, she hadn't had a real conversation in some time and was reduced to being interested in minutiae.

She would sit in the lobby but not stay at the nicest hotel. Not for Fanny the indulgent comforts of middle age. If you were going to leave behind a life of obligation and responsibility, you had to submit to other kinds of trouble. If your parents and brother were dead, you needed a concrete, tangible form of suffering. Grief had an irritatingly amorphous quality. You could not grapple with grief the way you could with a dirty hotel room. Bodily misery seemed fresh and nearly effortless; who wouldn't choose a bad meal over a dead brother, a stomachache over sorrow? Plus, long-term travel ought not to be treated like a vacation. Fanny believed that no traveler should be entirely comfortable in a third-world country. You had to experience the truth of where you were.

The *China Daily* had a cover story about the Beijing municipal government spending six million yuan on books for local schoolchildren. The books had been published, according to the paper, "in an attempt to wean children off pornographic novels and other low-quality reading matter." How Victorian. The article linked pornography to the pollution of bourgeois thinking. Each a product of the other.

People filled the sidewalks. She had a traveler's chores: change money, purchase an onward ticket, buy supplies. She must join that stream of Mao-jacketed strangers. Her stomach was empty, her mind lacy, full of a delicate mournfulness. She was older now than her parents had ever been. She would never know what they would have been like in their midforties. Her examples, her role models, were ghosts.

Thwarted. Fanny was an ant trying to get out of a tunnel, every turn a dead end. One bank claimed to have no money, even after she pointed to an open suitcase (a *suitcase?*) full of bundled hundred-yuan notes; another bank would only change $400. At the third bank, the clerk stared at Fanny in alarm for a long time. Finally, he said mei you repeatedly, folded his arms on his desk, and put his head on top of them. Astonished at this behavior, Fanny laughed, resisting the urge to poke him.

Banks seemed to be open, though not conducting the business of changing money. What *were* the business hours in the People's Republic? Sometimes it seemed that people worked every day of the week. Though often employees were at work without actually working; they knitted, talked, played checkers or card games. Happy socialist workers didn't have to care about their jobs (they couldn't be fired), or about the condition of public spaces, or about how they treated others. Neither hard work nor customer relations (what an alien concept it suddenly seemed) could affect their job status. What did Chinese workers care about? Not ideology, surely. Didn't life always come down to love and disappointment, meat and rice, a warm kitchen, dessert?

"Hello, do you speak English?"

"Fluently," Fanny said.

"I invite you to English corner please."

The young man wore thick glasses that magnified his eyes. "Sure," Fanny said. His name was Mr. Black, and the English corner, he explained as they walked toward it, met at noon in a nearby park. Wuzhou residents who wanted to practice English gathered there to speak to one another. They would be honored at her presence. He had an air that Fanny was beginning to recognize in the young men she'd met: earnest and naive, but not soft. You could imagine these thin, intense men cutting off their own fingers—or someone else's—for a cause. A kind of pristineness, a capacity for absolutism. He smiled as he talked, a wan smile. His teeth would make an orthodontist wealthy.

Mr. Black led her to a shady strip of park along the river where a milling group of people began pitching questions at her. What is life like in America? People work, buy things, read, go to movies, go for walks. Are there many Chinese people there? Yes. How much did your boots cost? Eighty dollars. How much money do you make? None, at the moment. Do you have children? Are you married? Do you have a boyfriend? No, no, and no. How much do you weigh? Fanny balked.

The crowd grew—ten people, twenty, thirty. She was like a talk show host without a microphone, or an evangelist preaching for converts. Converts to what? Capitalism? The American way of life? A phrase that made her cringe. Are you afraid? Of what? Why do Americans think they can tell Chinese what to do with Tibet? Because the American government has a habit of telling other countries what to do. Or, maybe it was because the Chinese treated the Tibetans badly. Fanny didn't say that. What is the average income in America? How do you get a green card? The crowd laughed uneasily whenever Fanny said, "I don't know." They behaved as if that answer were a tasteless joke.

Bloated with opinions, making pronouncements and assertions, she felt fake. Any minute, a real American (her image was the same as the audience's: a hard-jawed, blond, blue-eyed man in a dark suit and tie) was going to appear and uncover her charade. Not truly American! The crowd would part like the Red Sea and she would exit down the tunnel of her own embarrassment. The Russian corner, across the path, had only five or six people. Lonely, unpopular Russian speakers.

Two toddlers darted forward now and then to cast rapt, frightened glances up at Fanny. Fanny noticed their small figures and thought, yes, *that's what I need*. A child. *If I had a child, he could run around with these kids, pick up Mandarin phrases quickly, be my companion*, she thought. *I could be of some use to a child*, she thought.

Why do black men get killed in America? Why do Americans treat Indians poorly? Which do you prefer, socialism or capitalism? *Oh.* She was in a country where the answer to such a question was meaningful. One person stood out in the crowd: a strong, stern woman— twenty-five or forty-five—who asked questions about women. Is it hard for a woman with a lot of education to find a husband? No, Fanny said (but she herself had never tried to find a husband). How many women go to university? Do women make the same money as men? Is it hard for women to get choice assignments and positions? The woman's severe expression passed judgment: how could Fanny not know the answers to these questions? How could she squander her opportunities and rights?

After an hour, Fanny excused herself. Three men trailed after her: Mr. Black; Wang Dong, a stoop-shouldered young man with a long, wispy mustache and the burdened air of someone three times his age; and a third man wearing tinted aviator glasses slipping down a bridgeless nose. They accompanied her out of the park. Mr. Black offered that he, like Fanny, was unmarried. Wang Dong was married, but he and his wife didn't have children. The one with the tinted glasses interjected at frequent intervals in the vicinity of her ear, "You are very beautiful." They passed concrete high-rise apartment buildings. "You are very beautiful," Tinted Glasses whispered. He hinted that he needed hard currency to go to Australia next year.

Setting a stiff pace, Fanny hoped they'd peel off and attend to their own business. Mr. Black talked about his job. He worked at a liquid-glass factory, six days a week, one week of each shift. He spent his day off at the English corner. He didn't like his job. Fanny had met many Chinese who didn't like their jobs, or didn't like where they lived, but were unable to change the parameters—set by the government—of their lives. "We Chinese have to struggle to be happy." How fond the Chinese were of that word *struggle*. It defeated and enlivened them. Struggle was their true love. "You are very beautiful," Mr. Obsequious whispered in a soft hiss, followed by the word *dollars*.

Overhead, small lettuces like rows of ruffled baby hats hung on laundry lines. The fuzziness of urban China: no skyline was clear in this season of mist and pollution.

The young men accompanied her to the bus station where at last Mr. Obsequious gave up his quest for dollars via flattery and left. Mr. Black and Wang Dong watched her buy a ticket to Yangshuo. "Very bad road," they told her. "It should take very long. It's dangerous."

"Okay," she said. What could she do about the conditions of travel? She was not taking their advice to travel comfortably, as a foreigner ought, in a hired car under the watchful eye of the state-run China Travel Service.

Mr. Black and Wang Dong watched her longingly and said, "We'll miss you when you're gone."

Wary at this undeserved emotion, she still felt her breathing catch in her throat.

Chapter 10

The four men set out on a Wednesday, the trunk full of luggage, bottles of beer, a thermos of boiled water, sacks of peanuts and oranges,
motor oil, a tire-repair kit, some wrenches. Zhou had washed the car
inside and out, sweeping out Liu's peanut mess, cleaning the windows.
He'd arranged the plastic flowers, repaired the glove box, tucked the
protective Buddha into a corner. It was a day of gray glare and fumy
heat, the citizens of Guangzhou shining with sweat. To Zhou, the
graceless skyline, the buildings being torn apart or built new so that
you couldn't exactly tell which was happening to which, the milky-
tea-colored river, the packs of bicyclists and the tense scrum at intersections, all seemed achingly familiar and he felt a twinge of nostalgia
as he worked the car to the outskirts of the city. He'd come home after
Yuyi's accident and now he was leaving. Even as he went soft for the
way the heat and pollution formed their noxious alchemy, he felt the
punch and clench of adrenaline: he was leaving! To shed the familiar,
to wipe it like sweat off a palm, to toss it away for the unknown. The
sticky notes of Hong Kong pop music mixed with the honking of
horns was their exit sound track. Nervous and elated, he drove hor-
ribly.

Liu said that if Zhou didn't stop jabbing the brake, he was going
to abandon him to his solitary fate with the foreign devils. Or, maybe
he'd throw up all over Zhou's precious floor. Liu lit a cigarette, hooked

his elbow out the window, and squinted into the luminous haze. Going away! He smiled at Zhou. This is freedom, he pronounced.

Yevgo wore baggy pants that gathered in folds at his ankles because he pushed the waistband below the bulge of his belly. His purple and red batik shirt, which he'd bought in Bali, matched the plastic lilacs on the shelf above the rear seat. He sat behind Zhou so he could keep an eye on the road, give advice as needed. His chest felt a little tight and he tried to breathe lightly. Air pollution. He thought about the day in Bali he'd gone on a long swim with a too-young-for-him English girl he'd taken up with. After hours in the ocean, they'd gotten high on the beach under the powerful sun. Yevgo was too dark to sunburn easily but the English girl had taken it into her head that he might so she lay herself atop him. Her weight pressed him into the sand. The sensation of being buried, of suffocation, made him think about his uncle Viktor, shot and tossed into a mass grave, smothered under the weight of bodies. It was 1941 and his uncle had chosen not to come to Tashkent when Yevgo's family had moved west in 1939. Viktor had been courting a girl in another town and was unlucky—unlucky Uncle Viktor, the poor soul—to be there, in a town not even his own, when the Nazis arrived. Uncle Viktor—his prowess as a powerful and cunning soccer player, his charm, his tragic death—was the absent hero of Yevgo's youth. The English girl's breasts, soft and damp, sent streams of sweat onto Yevgo. Images jumped through his mind: a photo of his uncles as teenagers, standing straight and solemn in deep snow beside a sleigh; a cracked green glass bowl his grandmother kept on a sideboard; his mother's tiny stale-smelling kitchen in Tashkent. The past pressed him down. After flying around the world, peeling himself free of daily patterns and obligations, he felt as if he was falling backward into his life, falling deeper. Tears flowed like sweat into his ears. When the English girl lifted herself off him, he saw how like a baby she was, without corruption or complication. Her soft pink skin, her well-cared-for hair and fingernails, her round cheeks. "I want to go home," she said. She was on the verge of hysteria, having had too much sun and too much pot. He laughed. She had left England a week earlier. "You just arrived. Nothing's happened. You can't go home." Even while Yevgo comforted her, he'd felt indifferent. This was her first time away from Europe and she was homesick after a week.

Fiera would never have given up like that.

Before they had turned two corners, he was imagining the streets of Tashkent. The long avenues of plane trees flickering the light into gauzy shadows, the ocean of blue sky overhead, men playing dominoes in the shade while the yellow afternoon heat pounded the dust. Mutton kebabs sold on the streets of Tashkent, tender and juicy, grilled on a stick with plenty of salt and chili pepper flakes. The preserved tart cherries and pickled cabbage salads—finely shredded, in a pungent sweet-tart brine—his mother used to put up. Yevgo would see his aunt, if she was still alive, and his two best friends from university, whom he'd not heard from in years.

Daniel sat behind Liu. He fiddled with his shoulder bag, arranging it first down by his feet, then on the seat, then back on the floor. He was in a car, with a driver! Not for him the puny hassles of public transportation. (If Vivian could see him now!) How smart he'd been to make a Chinese connection, forgetting that it had been accidental. He liked Joe, not just because he was Chinese, but because he seemed both innocent and world-weary. It mattered to Daniel that Joe was *real*, not one of those fake locals, one of those huckster types who duped tourists with whipped-up charm. Of course Daniel was teaching Joe to see tourists as income. He was corrupting this innocent socialist with a capitalist scheme. Well, if communists *were* corruptible, then he wasn't entirely responsible. In any case, he, Daniel, knew the true Joe. He envisioned hours in which he might quiz Joe about life in China. He thought about the China of the British Museum, and the China of history books. Now he was going to see the real China. He was proving to be a better traveler than he'd imagined. An image of Fanny came to mind: the feel of her skin, the grip of her legs, the hot, shadowy room with the fan sweeping across his bare back, the prickly feeling that at any minute a floor clerk—a naive young woman— might enter to find his naked self on the edge of pleasure. He broke into song, drumming the top of the front seat to keep time. *I've been to Hong Kong, I've been to Canton, I hitched a ride down a lonely road, and discovered gold.* Then there was Yevgo: his rumpled shirt buttoned askew, crumbs in his lap. The old man, what a champ.

Chapter 11

Fanny held her place against a heaving press of people in line to buy tickets into Jiangshan Buddhist temple in Yangshuo. Someone had told her there was no word in Chinese for irony. Perhaps irony was a concept so embedded in everyday life it didn't require comment: the way the Chinese government seemed bent on profiting (that capitalist activity) from even the smallest opportunity, the way that materialism flourished in a communist country. She thought of People's Park in Shanghai with its entrance fee. Shouldn't a park for the people in a communist country be free?

The temple grounds had a carnival atmosphere. A man foot-pedaled a candy machine, and a long line of people waited for something advertised as "COMPUTER." The result was your photo hot-pressed onto a piece of cotton with one of two images surrounding it: Chinese characters, or a thousand-dollar bill that read "Reserve of the United States." Families were in the midst of picnics; children ran around as if at a playground. The grounds were littered with piles of pink incense powder and shreds of red paper. Carp, banana peels, and biscuit packets floated in a large pond. Each person stared at Fanny once, then again, and a space cleared as she walked the grounds. She held herself straighter, unabashedly tall. She was the white elephant. She was the queen feared by her subjects. If only she had been able to wash her hair. The buildings were ancient and beautiful; Jiangshan was the oldest temple in Guangxi.

At last she came upon a room where people were praying, bowing with bundles of incense in their hands, and laying their foreheads on small red cushions. Fanny stood against the back wall, considering potential prayers, her mind a tangled mess. She ought to have brought Bruno's ashes, so she could drop some into the cauldrons of incense ash. A piece of him would live in a Buddhist temple in China. She broke into a sweat and her legs started to shake. The smell of incense seemed suddenly sickening. Unsteadily she retraced her path through courtyards and halls, Buddhas above seeming to admonish her for thinking so often of herself, her needs and mistakes, petty moods and losses.

Once free of the temple and its crowds, Fanny walked slowly, past shops: the Rich Shop, a women's clothing store, Satisfaction Bakery, a cart of oranges run by a man with a cigar clamped between his jaws. She hadn't had a conversation since she'd said goodbye to Mr. Black and his friends two days before in Wuzhou. Yesterday had been spent on the bus to Yangshuo and now she was attempting to act like a proper tourist, seeing the sights: Buddhist temple, karst formations, the Li River. No one she knew, knew where she was.

When she saw Daniel he was walking away from her, across a street. It *was* him: tall, curly brown hair, a shirt with a collar, his walk which was determined and a little deferential. She ran into the street, causing a bike to swerve, the rider cursing in Chinese. "Hey, Daniel!" she called, flooded with happiness. The day was saved. People stared, but the object of her attention didn't waver. She pursued. He turned down an alley and she saw that it wasn't Daniel. It wasn't even a man. It was a tall woman, with permed, dyed hair. Fanny put her hands on her knees, breathing hard, filled with a loneliness so intense it brought tears to her eyes.

She dragged back to the hotel, wishing that someone would offer her sympathy. The floor clerk wouldn't even look at her. Under Fanny's self-pitying gaze, the room was a punishment. Thinking she'd return to the temple, she searched her bag and could not find the ash baggies. She rifled the side pockets: nail clippers, a rock, a sewing kit, a drain stopper, a length of rope, a bunch of safety pins. Finding only one baggie of Bruno, she tore through her things and burst into tears. Her irreplaceable brother was dead; her parents were dead. Sunlight barely penetrated the dust layered on the windows. The only people Fanny had come to know in China were clerks and ticket sellers, fruit vendors and waiters. But who did she think she'd befriend if she didn't speak Chinese? As soon as she had the chance, Fanny determined to disperse some of Bruno's ashes before she lost all of them.

By evening, Fanny understood she was ill. This realization came slowly and it surprised her; she was strong and rarely sickened. She walked to a pharmacy, stepping gingerly, as if the world's surface were delicate and could not properly handle her weight. A Chinese medicine doctor held office hours at a desk placed a few shallow steps up from the sidewalk. He was listening to a woman who sat on a narrow bench before him. They talked on and on. Fanny found the words for headache, nausea, fever in the health section of her phrasebook and marked the pages. She sat on a bench and dropped her head between her knees.

At last it was Fanny's turn to place her hand on the small white pillow with the red cross sewn onto it. The man's long fingers were cool against her wrist. She broke into a sweat and thought she might vomit and faint. Immediately, he set into action, rubbing tiger balm onto her upper lip and vigorously massaging the area between her thumb and forefinger. A woman in a blue smock took over while he made a phone call. Fanny, longing to drift away, was picked up and carried down the street. Four people, each holding a limb, the blue woman trotting behind shouting commands, Fanny like a large doll.

They laid her on a bench in a courtyard and a new set of inquisitive faces peered at her with curiosity. Images and ideas flitted through her head, a swirl of disturbances. She had failed by becoming ill; the unpleasantness of being tall. Lilliputians shouldering a giant. Fanny an oversized float in a parade, pink and puffy, spectators gazing at her in wonder. Someone folded and tucked her sweatshirt beneath her head, gently placed her braid out of the way, and put her bag at her feet, book and pen inside. Her temperature and blood pressure were taken and a series of questions asked of her in Chinese, patiently asked, over and over. Fanny eventually understood they were asking if she had a friend. Mei you, don't have, she said. There followed a chorus of sympathetic echoes, *ta mei you pengyou, ta mei you pengyou*. She doesn't have a friend, she doesn't have a friend. What, Fanny wondered, would her parents think of her if they could see her now? Alone in the world. She thought she'd come to terms with her parents' death, as if she'd closed the door on a room full of things she didn't need, was weary of, but could not part with. Saying to herself, only I am left, shocked her as if she'd just discovered this fact, much bigger than not having a friend in Yangshuo.

A cheerful woman doctor, who spoke a little English with the tone and manner of a kindergarten teacher, appeared. She told Fanny that she would take her to the hospital. "No," Fanny said. She probably only had the flu, needed rest and liquids. They went back and forth between yes and no until Fanny realized that the doctor would wait until Fanny said yes. Fanny said yes.

An ambulance arrived. A rusted vehicle, inside and out. Fanny hadn't fainted and now she didn't feel like fainting. She didn't want to go to the hospital but she was being taken to the hospital. How often while traveling she found herself in positions of enforced passivity. This would never happen in America, where she could exert her will. Here, in a foreign country, with imprecise communication and confusing cultural signals, she was always the passenger, never the driver. She could not make China bend to her will; she could not bend to China's will.

In the emergency ward, more doctors appeared; more poking of her stomach. They wanted her to have a blood test but when she saw that it entailed standing in line at a window that was closed, and then in another line down the hall, she couldn't do it. Did she want medicine? "No," she said, "just tea." Tea: her fallback. At this they laughed and she felt confused—why was it funny?—though pleased that she had made the Chinese laugh.

In her dream she was swimming in a large blue pool. The pool changed shape, sections of the floor sinking and filling with water. Fanny swam lap after lap and then jumped on the diving board, higher and higher. *I am frightened to death*, she thought in the dream. I don't like to swim; I don't like to jump off diving boards. People were in stands set up along one side of the pool, watching. She searched for Bruno. The dream changed abruptly and she was sick in her childhood bed, though she was her present age. She and Bruno had painted her room, and then his. Hers was blue and yellow, his was gray with red trim. Bruno was settled into the armchair, which he'd pulled close to her bed, studying Sanskrit. Periodically he patted her sweaty face with a cold washcloth and made her drink tepid water. She tried to say his name but her voice wouldn't work. That house in Albuquerque, on Idlewilde, they'd sold it long ago. They: she and Bruno, a family of two.

A yellow dawn filtered into the room. She'd been up and down the hall all night to and from the toilets. From her medical kit, she swallowed the first dose of antibiotics with cold tea, then returned to bed. Each ziplock baggie of ashes was nestled together in a corner of her bag; Bruno's ashes were not lost. She ought to find something sturdier than a plastic baggie to carry them in. No. She would scatter them, never mind the anniversary of his death, or Tibet. She had imagined every location: a temple, a river, a lake, the ocean, a mountainside, a meadow. Nothing seemed right. Nothing. She curled into the fluttery softness of her sleeping sheet, her bones within their armature of muscle, the dull daylight sliding into the room. Her preoccupation with the ashes—was it real, metaphorical, weird, or comical?

Chapter 12

At the beginning, it was the creamy romance of the road. While the car huffed up and down mountainsides, skirted rivers, snaked through patched fields, the passengers sank into troughs of silence. Chinese speakers in front; English speakers in back. Daniel initiated conversation. "Bloody miserable weather, isn't it?" he said. Heat and humidity pressed like a damp gag over one's nose and mouth. Exactly like summers in Houston with which he was intimately familiar though he didn't share that thought.

As a former cab driver, Yevgo knew that weather was everyone's default topic and introductory gambit.

"It's like an animal panting on you," Daniel said.

Until his mother died, Yevgo had called her, San Francisco to Tashkent, every Thursday night for ten minutes. The connections were usually terrible. Occasionally his mother's voice came through clearly, tracing the curve of the earth to arrive in his ear, so close he imagined her breath touching him. Natalia Lerman Velasquez. Every week she said, "Are you working? Do you have friends?" She'd launch into details of her health. Which he would attempt to derail. "I haven't called halfway across the world to hear about your constipation," he'd say.

"It's not easy getting old, you have no idea . . ."

Yevgo knew about her heart condition, the way her legs cramped at night, the pains in her stomach, what her friends said, what the doctors said. Yet she was, according to what he heard from others, healthy and uncomplaining. It was only to Yevgo that she presented a beleaguered version of her life.

"It makes one long for the sea, doesn't it?" Daniel was exuberant. "Have you been to Africa?" Without waiting for an answer, Daniel talked on. He'd read somewhere that hunting at the full moon was ideal. Wild creatures were unsettled by brightness in the dark. Just as if someone had flashed a torch in their faces. He didn't confess that he liked television nature programs. He made as if he'd done real research on the subject. He wasn't even getting the nature program facts right. It didn't matter. Nobody was listening. That didn't matter either; he was used to talking without his audience paying close attention. He'd been nicknamed The Radio by his friends. Daniel fell silent. Three minutes later, he began again.

Don't try to tell me there isn't something wrong with him, Liu said. He talks more than a girl.

Don't eat peanuts while I'm driving, Zhou said. He glanced down at Liu's feet. He wanted to listen closely to Daniel, pick up phrases and expressions, but he had to drive.

A peaceful trip we'd be having without him, Liu said.

If you eat peanuts, the foreigners will start to eat them. The car will be a disaster. Zhou could never tell Yevgo and Daniel to clean up or eat neatly. In honor of Yuyi, Zhou pleaded. Zhou wondered how his brother had tolerated Liu's slobby habits.

Liu snorted. The imperialist running dogs in the backseat cared about talking, not eating. He crushed a peanut into his cupped palm, shelling it with one hand, then ostentatiously threw the shell out the window. See? No mess.

"Do you find Chinese women beautiful?" Daniel asked Yevgo. He'd been catching sight of the petite but shapeless figures of peasant women beside the road: flat black slippers, loose blue pants. He'd never dated an Asian girl.

"Women are beautiful," Yevgo said.

"Right-o," Daniel said. Landscape ticked past, trees, pigs, rice fields, water buffalo, trees, pigs. He must stop saying *right-o*. Now that he was committed to being wholly English, he was anxious that American phrases would pop out. It was making him squirm, though, the way he was overplaying his Englishness. English, American; how could it matter? "Why did you get divorced?"

Yevgo shrugged. His divorce—three years later—was still a fiery ball in his gut.

"What happened?" Daniel mused. "I mean, it's a question I ask myself. I recently split up with a girlfriend. We'd been together a long time." Ten years. The breakup wasn't *that* recent, but never mind, it remained vivid, from their first meeting at a wedding in a Scottish castle. Daniel had just dropped out of Oxford—preempting an expected expulsion—and he hadn't yet told anybody, not even his best friend, Simon. Late one night, Daniel was playing billiards with Vivian, the last two of a rowdy gathering. Earlier, they'd been dancing and so had the feel, the shape, of each other's bodies in their fingertips. When she bent for a shot, he sensed the strength of her long waist. Amidst the click and thud of balls, he'd mostly told the truth, confessed that he was dropping out of Oxford, giving some story about wanting to do good in the world, not just become a flipping intellectual but actually become *a better person*. He'd seen the way her eyes lit at the idea of a promising young man throwing away an advantage like Oxford. He'd been after a weekend romp but his confession to her that night, the fact that he'd told her about dropping out before he'd told anyone else, forged a connection. Vivian's parents didn't approve of him (she was a lady, he was half-Texan, half-Jewish, and an Oxford dropout). Ten years passed, suddenly she was gone. He was ashamed at the degree to which it had taken him by surprise.

To compound his suffering, he'd found out while at his father's. Vivian had called to say that she wasn't coming out to Houston after all. She'd met a Nigel something-something. Daniel was on the telephone with her receiving this information while his father walked in from the pool, barefoot, a towel around his waist, empty drink in hand. Where, Vivian was asking, did he want his things sent? At the bar, his father tossed the dregs from his glass, refreshed the ice, and poured himself another Bloody Mary from a pitcher. When Daniel hung up, his father said, "The Royal Darling"—that's what he called Vivian—"isn't coming?" Daniel saw no way to evade.

"She's breaking up with me," he said, the statement hitting him like an electric current.

"You'll survive," his father said, not glancing at Daniel. He threw himself into the Eames chair by the big window facing the pool and flipped through a *Sports Illustrated*. After a few minutes of silence he said to Daniel, "Don't just stand there, get yourself a drink."

"I suppose we weren't well suited." Daniel cleared his throat. He'd thought he and Vivian very well suited to each other. "Or, something like that." The weather, so much like Houston, unnerved him.

Tell him to shut up, Liu said to Zhou.

You don't understand it, don't pay attention, Zhou said. If I find *one* shred of peanut shell, one fluttery peanut skin. He pointed at Liu's feet.

Liu chewed noisily. Why fight over peanuts? We're in this together. Communists against capitalists! We're a team.

What about Yevgo? Zhou said. He was from the Soviet Union. Whose team was he on?

Liu considered. Once a communist, always a communist. The English fool was the evil capitalist in the car. Communists united together would surely win! He beat his chest and laughed, then coughed on half-chewed peanuts and had to gulp tea, cough, clear his throat.

Why you shouldn't eat peanuts in a car and talk, Zhou said. He paused, then added, Besides, I thought you wanted to *be* a capitalist. You're always talking about making money.

Even though it was 1989, Zhou was still taken aback when someone talked about making money; it seemed brazen and risky. In the past Liu had done things—he'd never told Zhou—that haunted him still, things that had made him reckless. Now Liu disregarded politics. Would the government proclaim "to get rich is glorious"? Or, "money is dirty"? From one week to the next, no one could be certain what to pursue or to avoid but Liu lived as if he had nothing to lose.

Liu snorted. I'm still a socialist.

I like Daniel, Zhou said. Liu could learn to like him, too.

"There are always hard feelings." Yevgo wiped sweat from beneath his eyes.

"Traveling solo," Daniel said, "is truest to the spirit of travel. You can immerse yourself in the culture, meet locals like Joe and Leeyou." He thought, *immersion*, imagining photo paper soaking in a developing bath, and a clear image materializing, one that had not been there before.

Yevgo let his head tip back. He was practiced at listening while daydreaming. His mind, unaccounted for, drifting between past, present, and future. Yevgo assumed that a person's version of his or her life wasn't precisely accurate, though Yevgo rarely cared if someone lied to make themselves appear better in their own eyes or in the eyes of others. The truth was a malleable, shifting thing. Besides, to understand who a person would like to be, that was useful, too.

"What did you think of Fanny?" Daniel asked. He felt invigorated. He loved everything about the journey—the rusty, tidy car, his Chinese friends, the old man, the rice fields out the window, the muddy roads, the smell of burning coal. Fanny in his future. He sang a few bars of "Ruby Tuesday."

"Who?"

"Fanny. You know, she sat next to you in the taxi, on the sofa. Tall, long plait."

"Mmmm," Yevgo said. Then, after a moment, "Did you tell her about your scam?"

"Come on," Daniel said. "It's not a *scam*."

Yevgo looked amused.

"We're meeting in Emei Shan," Daniel said. "Did you like her?"

Yevgo shrugged.

Daniel turned to Zhou. "What did you think of the tall woman at the first performance?"

After a moment's pause, Zhou said, "Excessively amiable."

Daniel laughed. "*Man*, who taught you English?"

There were the small incidents of life on the road: finding places to sleep and eat, plotting the route, asking directions. The men settled into the routines and intimacies of travel. They soon knew that Zhou was garrulous after lunch and Liu could not be approached before he'd smoked several cigarettes and finished at least one jar of tea. Daniel began each morning with a comment about the weather, hummed or sang bits of songs throughout the day, talked a great deal. Yevgo and Zhou learned Daniel's version of "Out on the Weekend" and sang along with him. *"Think I'll toss my stuff into a taxi . . . Pray for the lonely boys, taking the low road."* Daniel drummed the back of the front seats. Liu didn't join in the singing.

Daniel talked about Fanny and the others offered opinions: she seemed very smart, very lovely, very very. Tofu gave Yevgo such appalling gas that he was forbidden from eating it. Daniel snored, Yevgo suffered from insomnia, Zhou and Liu slept in the car to guard it and Yevgo could not talk them out of their mistrust of their countrymen. First thing every morning, Zhou swept out the taxi, cleaned the windows, adjusted his mirrors. Sometimes he stared into the engine. He didn't know what he was seeing, but he was reassured by its mechanical appearance: the black tangle of hoses, the engine's imposing bulk. Liu ate peanuts and smoked all day. When he wasn't eating peanuts, he slept. Zhou clutched the steering wheel so hard he developed cramps in his hands.

Only when Daniel and Liu shared the back seat was there tension. Liu sat stiffly, head turned away from Daniel, examining the passing landscape as if looking for a means of escape. Daniel slouched against his door like a boy punished for bad behavior. Liu never imitated Daniel affectionately the way he did Yevgo; never tried to tease him or make him eat the best bits of food the way he did Yevgo. Daniel felt certain that if Liu had reason to value his presence, Liu would begin to like him. One more reason Daniel was eager for future episodes of Escaped Democracy Demonstrator. Despite his efforts to influence the route, they were nowhere near tourist destinations. Emei Shan held all of his hopes.

At one of their frequent stops for Yevgo to piss, Daniel noticed a plant along the roadside that resembled marijuana. He picked a few leafy branches and tucked the leaves into a pocket of his bag, thinking they would dry. Stoned in China.

Back in the car, Daniel asked Yevgo, "Where did you go to university?"

"In Tashkent. Think you'll have heard of it?"

"I dropped out of Oxford before I got expelled," Daniel said.

Yevgo had been noticing how adaptable the Chinese were in their agriculture; there were large fields, but also patches hewn from steep hillsides, or vegetable plots tucked into rectangles along the road or in triangles between buildings.

"I'd been studying Chinese history, and revolutions. I couldn't take the jolly English chap nonsense of the place and I needed extra cash so I started an opium den in my room," Daniel continued. "It actually sort of meshed with my studies. You know, the whole opium war thing. It was wild." He shook his head and laughed.

Yevgo grunted.

"The opium came in from Birmingham by courier every Thursday. First six, then twelve blokes would come over. For awhile it was perfection: illegal *and* I was making money." He sighed. "But then, well, stuff happened. I knew I was going to get tossed." Daniel checked Yevgo for his reaction. "I'm well educated sans degree, if you know what I mean." He leaned closer to Yevgo; yeah, he'd fallen asleep. What was he thinking, wasting the opium stories on an old man? He stared out the window before he leaned forward and asked Zhou, "Is this farmland state owned? Cooperatives?" They were on a road between fields of rapeseed.

"Indeed. The land is that for . . . pardon me, is the belonging of the government. Farmers sell the fruits of their labors to the government. Nowadays, in the new free economy, farmers may also sell their fruits in private markets. The farmer possess little education but they are exceedingly rich," Zhou said. Liu had been trying to capitalize on this new wealth by serving as a middleman for a small group of farmers.

"Are you a party member?" Daniel asked.

Zhou shook his head.

"Mr. Liu?" Daniel gestured at Liu.

Zhou shook his head again.

"Why not?"

"Too many elaborate. You process among many mountain of document. At principal you commit application and at second, you should excavate people to speech on your behest in present to officials. In short, I venture to implore, devotion are requisite."

"Devotion? To what?"

"Precisely." Zhou downshifted, a bit jerkily, a driving technique Yevgo had recently taught him.

"Do you believe in communism?" Odd, this. He would not ask, do you believe in capitalism, do you believe in democracy? Some political systems demanded an almost religious commitment. As if to account for the trouble you would be asked to endure.

"Our leaders wish to aid the people," Zhou said. He glanced at

Liu, grateful that he didn't understand English. He would have been irritated by Daniel's questions. He would have made fun of Zhou's answers. Zhou felt self-conscious, talking about China in this way to foreigners. He should always present China as excellent; it was not right to be critical. Zhou imagined living in a place where the government was not a constant presence in one's life, like loud parents, hovering, judging, correcting, scolding, punishing. Embracing to the death. Might he ever become a teacher of English literature? He swerved suddenly into bushes along the road, scraping the car, branches scratching at the windows. Turning the wheel sharply to prevent the car from diving into a ditch, he braked and killed the engine.

Yevgo snapped awake. A moment of silence. The car was in the road crosswise, everyone gripping a seat back or door handle.

Zhou had been imagining himself in a classroom, standing before a chalkboard, piece of chalk in hand. He watched a few leaves drift through the air. One, two, three leaves falling as if they had a century to reach the ground. His trouble, he now saw, was that his own desires were hidden behind his country's and the party's. In China, the question of individual desire was a problem. It was hard to be Chinese.

"First, the clutch, then start the car. Turn the wheel before you engage the clutch." Yevgo's calm voice from the backseat. "Check your mirrors. The left leg up, the right down at the same time. Slowly. Don't forget to breathe."

Daniel questioned Zhou in bursts: Was it possible to get rich in China? Did China supply all its own food? Was it hard to get a girlfriend? Was he in favor of revolution? What had Zhou done during the Cultural Revolution? Did he think Mao a favorable figure from China's history?

These question and answer sessions slaked Zhou's passion to practice English with an Englishman. Daniel's accent was clear and Zhou tried his best to imitate it. But when he grew tired, his brain shut down. To his frustration, he would find himself suddenly unable to understand the simplest English sentence. He could not tell Daniel this or ask for a rest, so he nodded, or smiled and said yes. What's the most lucrative crop? Yes. What would you most like to do in the future? Yes. He wanted to ask questions of Daniel, but there seemed never to be an opening.

Daniel wanted to stay in a village so rural it lacked a hotel. When they had first broken free of the tangle of the city, Daniel thought: *peasants*: China's peasants dressed in navy blue and gray, trousers folded above their knees, shirtless men exposing their bony torsos. The famous peasants who had risen up with Mao and changed life in China; the formerly oppressed, the freshly liberated, those for whom life under communism was meant to be better. It seemed magical that after reading about them at university here they were. Men and women in the fields. Were they pulling weeds or planting seedlings? Something as apparently basic as peasant life could appear, to the unpracticed eye, exotic, even strangely hard to comprehend. What exactly did a peasant do all day? Daniel recalled the feeling that had run through him in the library the day he read the Draft Agrarian Law written in 1947 and came across the sentence: *Landownership rights of all landlords are abolished.* Electrifying. The idea that a privileged way of life could be snatched, could be toppled with a sentence. All debts were abolished, all land was turned over to village peasant associations. Of course, it hadn't actually happened like that, with a single linguistic hatchet stroke. Battles ensued; people struggled, suffered, and died. And yet.

Here was a fantasy of Daniel's: he would, in one of the villages they visited, meet a peasant, a man who had worked in the fields his entire life, who possessed a sense of history, politics, and economics, *and* who spoke English. Someone like Zhou, except he planted rice and could drive a water buffalo. Not much from Mao's Little Red Book had stayed in Daniel's memory, just the odd word or phrase. *The masses. Enthusiasm for socialism.* With this ideal peasant, Daniel would discuss Chinese Marxist theory, agrarian politics, land reform, the efficacy of cooperatives, the history of famines in China. He'd move into the village, marry a beautiful—the most beautiful—local girl, become the admired and respected advisor to the villagers. He'd write a history, or a combination memoir–anthropological study. It would be intellectual with a compelling story which would make it a success. Or, he might start a vineyard, get into wine production. Cheap labor, an untapped market. He was trained: he knew wines, and he was already making money in China which was giving him a sense of the opportunities. Here in China lay his destiny.

One warm mid-afternoon, cicadas screeching in the trees, they stopped in a village. Zhou and Liu refueled the car while Daniel and Yevgo strolled the one muddy road. "Opium came to China in the Middle Ages as medicine, brought by Arab traders," Daniel said. "But its use as a recreational drug took off and by the time of the two wars with the English—in the 1800s, roughly a decade apart—large numbers of Chinese were addicted. Think of the Opium Wars as a conflict of addictions—the English to tea and the Chinese to opium." He paused. "The Addiction Wars."

Yevgo gazed into a small steaming cauldron with eggs bubbling in brown liquid. The proprietor of this streetside enterprise wasn't around. On a corner, a man had set out a cloth on which were arranged dead mice and one large, stiff rat corpse. Beside his specimens were traps and boxes of poison. A handful of men were gathering behind Yevgo and Daniel, watching their every move.

"I believe," Daniel said, "that Emperor Qin Shi Huangdi—you know, the chap who did the Terracotta Army—was a sort of template for Chinese rulers." He wanted to shape a mini-history lesson to impress Fanny with his knowledge of Chinese history. The Opium Wars or Emperor Qin?

Even with their shuttered walls open to the street, the small shops were dark. One shop had tools, wrenches, screwdrivers, two-handed saws. Another, baskets of brown, wrinkled roots, long and thin, bulbous and shriveled. A vegetable shop offered white onions with green tops, bundles of greens, small brown bananas. Yevgo examined the produce—the bruised bananas, the dirt clumped on the onion roots. The number of men following Yevgo and Daniel grew into a crowd.

When Yevgo and Daniel stopped, the locals surrounded each of them. Daniel watched in fascination as a man picked his nose, rotating a finger deep into the cavern of a nostril. When another man stepped forward to pull Daniel's arm hair, Daniel pushed him away. "Hey, back off." Once the offender disappeared into the crowd, Daniel couldn't tell which man had touched him. He liked the Chinese. Hadn't he studied their history? Before him was an array of flat faces framed in straight black hair, their skin not yellow, not red, not white, but some indeterminate tone, sand mixed with clay. Did they really look alike? Their pants and shirts were worn and dirty, their hands rough, their smell unwashed and garlicky. They were all, down to the last body at the ruffled hem of the crowd, men. Daniel was aware of his own fastidiousness, the effort he exerted to keep his nails clean, hair combed, shirt tucked in. He had no spots on his shirt (unlike each of his traveling companions). His Italian hiking shoes had probably cost as much as the annual salary of one of these men, possibly more. He stepped back. His personal crowd stepped forward. They were too close. His breathing tightened.

"Look at you skinny motherfuckers," Yevgo teased. He squeezed one man's bicep. "You're strong, but you boys need some flesh. Ever heard of a toothbrush? Somebody around here has bad breath." It amused Yevgo to be in a country where the men were sloppier than he was. A few of the men laughed, they didn't know at what. He took out his camera, which had no film in it, and pretended to snap photos. The men moved closer.

Murmuring rippled through Daniel's crowd and panic tightened in his chest. "Hey," he shouted over at Yevgo. "These blokes aren't friendly. What do you reckon?" He heard Yevgo laugh. Was he laughing at *him*, Daniel? He could barely see Yevgo in the throng. Daniel wiped sweat off his forehead. The men were talking about him and he had no idea what they were saying. He ought to have applied himself in studying Mandarin. For chrissake, where was Joe? The men edged closer. He stuck out an elbow, then swept his other arm, trying to clear a space. He didn't mind being stared at, but a crowd, and close, that was the thing that got to him. There were too many of them. His arm swung in a stiff flail, hitting shoulders, chests, someone's chin. The men pushed into him. He felt something near his waist and dropped his hands to protect his belt. Of course, they were after his money! He shoved, jabbing his elbows into ribs and stomachs.

Yevgo's camera was being handed around, each man examining it, looking through the viewfinder, snapping the shutter. They wanted to be amazed by it, but it didn't produce anything except a mild clicking sound.

Yevgo pulled his toothbrush out of his daypack and demonstrated brushing his teeth. He was proud of his teeth, which were white and strong. Tashkent water had contained fluoride, so he had no cavities.

The men stared at the foreigner brushing his teeth.

There were fifty-some men around Daniel and Yevgo—nearly the entire male population of the village. Zhou and Liu were a quarter mile away, discussing the cost of gas with the man filling their gas tank from plastic jugs, unaware of the commotion their charges were creating.

Daniel shouted, "They're after my money."

Yevgo turned and saw a pile of Chinese men lumped like a cluster of bees over a hive. He threw his arms into the air, toothbrush in one hand, tube of paste in the other and shouted, "Make way, make way." Was Daniel being attacked?

A woman bulldozed into the crowd, her shrill voice cutting through the commotion. She pulled men away by their shirtsleeves. Built low to the ground, she had skinny legs and a powerful body. Didn't they have more important things to do than bother foreigners? She addressed the men as if they were children caught in a playground scrape. The townsmen should act honorably. Go back to work.

Grumbling, the men drifted away. The woman marched back down the street and disappeared around a corner. The whole thing had taken ten minutes. "Where the hell is Joe when we need him?" Daniel said. He'd narrowly escaped being shaken down by a mob.

"He's a driver, not a bodyguard," Yevgo said evenly.

"I was worried about *you*." Daniel's tone was snappish. More quietly, he added, "They were after my money." He touched his belt, its soft leather. Trying to calm himself, Daniel admired the operatic snarl of clouds overhead. *Clouds.* The word evoked a particular memory. On one of his trips to Houston, he must've been about thirteen, his father wasn't at the airport to meet him. The woman from United Airlines kept saying, violently cheerful, "Don't you worry, honey, we'll get you fixed right up." Daniel hadn't been worried. Someone from his father's staff would appear to collect him and later his father would tease him about it, or say nothing at all, forgetting that Daniel had been forgotten. But it took nearly all day, because, as he later discovered, his father had been indicted for fraud. It was the summer his father lost everything—house in River Oaks, second wife. Though the losses proved to be temporary. By the following summer Daniel's father had another house, a new girlfriend. On that particular day at the airport, Daniel declined to wait in a windowless room and instead settled in a quiet corner of the terminal beside a wall of windows. He spent hours watching white and gray clouds build and disperse. Massive puffing creamy mounds, heavy and weightless, boiling up then oozing flat. The sky a painting, an entire world, the clouds unexpected comfort.

The taxi coughed into sight and Daniel and Yevgo slid into the backseat, slamming the doors shut. Daniel steered his gaze upward; the clouds, flat and gray, thinned at the horizon.

Chapter 13

Fanny met Tayama at a cave. She was standing at the kiosk trying to sort out the ticket situation, having determined that there were multiple options for viewing the cave. Tayama stepped up and translated: one could see the cave with music, with lights, with commentary, with any combination of music, lights, and commentary. He laughed when he finished translating; the laugh of someone capable of being entertained by almost anything. Fanny considered. "Could one see a cave without lights?" she said. And if you didn't pay for music, but someone else paid for music, didn't you hear the music, free of charge? She felt dubious about the nature of the commentary and paid for lights only. Tayama was a short, stocky Japanese man with a wispy mustache and an energetic expression of mischief. He purchased the same kind of ticket and they joined three young Hong Kongers, immaculately dressed in white polo shirts and pressed jeans. Fanny and Tayama were scruffier, and this, as well as being from elsewhere, turned them into a pair.

The lighting was a complicated system of garishly colored lights—red, green, pink, blue, orange—which, as they were turned on and off by the ticket vendor–guide, let off sparks and small popping sounds. The stalactite and stalagmite formations had names like Turtle and Elephant Eat Dinner Together. Tayama translated some of the commentary, which had been paid for by the Hong Kongers. They all stood patiently while the guide dashed back and forth, manipulating the lights, working himself into a sweat even in the cool of the cave. He switched the lights off (explosive spark) where they were standing, plunging them into deep black, and then ran forward with his flashlight to flick on the next set of lights (explosive spark), turning the darkness ahead into a startling kaleidoscope. The lights made the place cheesy and ugly, but not unappealing. Fanny and Tayama exchanged glances. He had elegant, narrow eyes, clean forearms, grease-rimmed fingernails. His name was Koji Tayama. When the tour ended and they emerged into brilliant sunlight, Fanny and Tayama walked back into Yangshuo together. A single shared odd experience in a foreign country was equivalent to years of ordinary life.

The cave was a practice outing for Fanny, to see if she was well enough to move onward from Yangshuo. She'd been taking the antibiotics she'd brought with her. She didn't know what it was she'd had, or where she'd gotten it, but she was improving.

"Your Chinese is very good," she said.

"No, no," Tayama said. "Not so. A little bit good. Listen, I say the same thing again and again."

They talked about languages, then about Japan. He was entertained by her stories of hitchhiking. "Japanese people could never do that. No Japanese driver would give rides to a Japanese person." Fanny listed the places she'd been and delivered the phrases she'd learned, which made him laugh. "Your Japanese is very good." This was certainly an exaggeration. They ate dinner together and Fanny filled pages of her notebook with useful Chinese phrases offered by Tayama. *Bu yao wei jing*: don't want MSG. *Wo yao yige pijiu*: I'd like a beer. He was a photographer, traveling around China on his Honda motorcycle. Japanese people loved photographs of China. Fanny told him that she was following, imprecisely, in her dead brother's footsteps.

"Oh." Tayama nodded. "Sad," he said. "Sad trip."

Fanny's eyes watered but she also felt like laughing. Sad Trip! Sad Sad Trip.

"I can give you a ride, okay?" he offered.

She agreed, first thinking that she could make up time lost being sick. Two weeks until her meeting with Daniel. Sex on her horizon, and something else—his singing? His wit? No, more basic: she wanted to follow her sense that there was more to him. She had to get moving; days had passed and she was barely free of Guang-zhou. Maybe Daniel was running into glitches in his travels, too. But mostly she said yes to Tayama because her first transcendent experi-ence of long-distance travel had happened on a motorcycle. During Fanny's last year of high school, Bruno worked construction and as an aide in a nursing home, something he had an uncanny aptitude for, as if he could tolerate other people's aging parents because he would never have his own. With his earnings, he bought a Harley Sportster which they took to Baja over Christmas, scandalizing relatives (they were not close) who expected them to come to New Jersey and disap-pointing friends in Albuquerque. Instead, they'd put over 3,000 miles on the bike in three weeks, slept on beaches, eaten tacos every meal. People were touched by a brother and sister traveling together. And because everyone loved Bruno, they were invited to fiestas, permit-ted to camp in special out-of-the-way places, treated to groceries or gasoline. On a motorcycle, on the road in a foreign country, Bruno was more than his usual self. More magnetic, more alive. He loved the traveling life and it loved him back. Among his other magical talents: he could get people to tell him anything. Fanny listened with amaze-ment to extraordinary tales—the fisherman who survived being lost at sea for two weeks—and ordinary tales, of heartbreak or untimely death (Bruno and Fanny would carefully avoid eye contact during tales of untimely death). People asked about their parents and Bruno had an assortment of answers, from *Our parents are too large to ride a motorcycle*, to *Our parents are in Africa adopting a little sister*, to the breathtakingly blunt, *We're orphans.* That statement always produced a flood of offerings. And Fanny? She was the sidekick, of course, though not infrequently left to her own devices, to which she was already accustomed. The trip allowed her to perfect her skill at being the observer, the noticer. Also, her Spanish was better than Bruno's.

They spent Christmas with a trio from Tasmania—a brother and sister and the sister's boyfriend. The Tazzies had driven an old van, outfitted with surfboards and a windsurfing kit, down from Seattle. They'd taught Fanny to surf. They'd say, *Whadiya reckin, Fen?*

It seemed to be that trip to Baja that had saved Bruno and Fanny.

Tayama was saying he'd come by her hotel at 7:30 in the morning. He bowed.

She bowed in return. Tayama was good company, cheerful and up-beat, full of quick smiling energy, and here was an offer of adventure she could not decline. A lucky break.

Near midnight, Fanny woke with a furious headache and worried that she might be getting sick with something else. Opening the bath-room window, she stood on a stool and stuck her head outside. The sky twirled high and away, sprayed with the glitter of stars. The wind licked through skinny pines and the air had a soft smell, relieved of its weight of decay. Here was the nature of travel: it whirled you about, taking you places you hadn't planned, like a dance partner leading you on a wild waltz. Was the world her friend or her enemy, a balm to her suffering or alcohol scouring a wound? Couldn't it, at least, send her a sign? Nothing fancy, rather something small yet definite, ordinary as a piece of overripe fruit falling from a tree. She shut the window, leaned her back against the wall. First her parents, almost thirty years ago. Now her brother. Dry-eyed, she stared at the cracked concrete floor.

Using her headlamp, she found the letters Wen Li had written to Bruno and paged through the flimsy rice paper. The subject mat-ters were ordinary: weather, a daughter at school, a grandmother she takes care of, the rare apologetic mention of a man who seemed to be an absent estranged husband. And this: "Hard life to me but to my LaoLao in past, so harder, many harder times. How to chose the future?" Fanny liked the way the past and present tenses appeared in the same sentences, putting all of time together. Wen Li's English did not seem accomplished, though in the letters she reports studying a grammar book that Bruno had sent her. Here was another sentence Fanny often reread: "I understand you say compassion to self is to make happy." It was not the meaning of the sentence that caught her attention, but the glimpse it provided into what Bruno might have been writing in his letters to Wen Li. Though reading them made her uncomfortable, she was drawn to the letters, even if it meant she felt that she was sneaking through someone's closet. What was here, in these letters? Every time she read, "Very dear Bruno" and "Always your Wen Li," it gave her pause, as if she'd just heard a secret.

The morning was warm and overcast. Tayama lashed one of her bags to the rear rack; she would wear the smaller knapsack. It was travel on a motorcycle that had taught Fanny to pack light and she was pleased to note the tidiness of her bags. Zipping himself into a shining, puffy silver suit, buckling black boots, Tayama was becoming someone else. Fanny straddled the souped-up Honda with red and blue racing stripes and fat, angled shining exhaust pipes. A different species of bike from the Sportster. How had he managed to get it into China? Tayama smiled, refreshingly unashamed to show his pleasure at her presence. Casually, but sincerely, he apologized that he did not have a helmet for her. He said that he was a very good driver. She was wearing jeans, hiking boots, a T-shirt with a windbreaker tied around her waist. The consequences of this decision, putting herself on this bike, were beginning to dawn on her. Her breathing tightened. Disappearing into his helmet, he became a character from a science fiction movie. Too late to break free, the situation beyond repair, her fate about to unfurl, Fanny put her hands lightly on his waist and wondered how to occupy her mind. He grasped her hands, pulled her forward and locked her fingers around his stomach, so that her chest was against his back, her legs gripping his hips. The engine revved, and they were off in a blast of acceleration and a rush of warm air.

After an overnight rain, the road was winding and wet. The bike moved very fast, leaning into the curves, the wind a tuneless whir, the blurred green foliage close. It was familiar and strange, terrible and exhilarating. Shutting her eyes gave her vertigo, so she kept them open, watching the edge of the road peel past, an endless rope curling away and away. She chanted to herself: think nothing, think nothing. Unbidden, images snapped in and out, a themeless slide show: skiing fast through steep powder just past the edge of control, tree trunks too close; having sex with an old boyfriend in an apple tree, both of them laughing at the absurd discomfort; a print of Jesus Christ hanging above the kitchen table of a house in Baja, Jesus's neck tilted as if broken, the colors a muted green except for the drops of blood-red; her father's hands demonstrating the proper way to hold a hammer. *Tacos.* Her mind flashing through the Baja trip. A different life, a different grief. Her cheek felt damp against the silver of Tayama's suit. The slick material was making her sweat. There had been one odd thing on the Baja trip. The day after Christmas the Tazzies were gone.

Christmas had been a "barbie on the beach"—grilled fish tacos and beer. When Fanny awoke the next morning, shaking sand from her sleeping bag, expecting an early morning surf with the older brother of the trio, she saw a rectangle of clean sand where the van had been parked. They'd cleared out in the middle of the night without saying goodbye or making a sound; a stealth departure. Fanny was hurt and confused but Bruno had shrugged. "People get to do what they want, Fan." But why, she'd wanted to know, why had they left like that? He'd let her ask a few times, without answering—one of his modes, just say nothing—and then he said, "Do not tangle with me, my hands are lethal weapons," which was a favorite phrase of theirs from *A Shot in the Dark*, a movie they watched a couple of times a year. He crouched and launched a Kato-style karate attack and they were off, laughing and fake fighting on the beach. Later—she'd been so innocent—it was clear: Bruno had been flirting too successfully with the woman of the trio. Her boyfriend and brother right there all the time. Later still, Fanny realized that was not the first nor the last time Bruno had wreaked some behind-the-scenes havoc.

When they slowed or stopped Tayama said, "Toilet? Tea? Beer?" Finally, the engine downshifted in smooth strokes and they came to a halt in a landscape of terraced hills, elegantly precise lines carved into the earth. The terraces were a luminous pale green, with hints of gold. Fanny cracked herself free of Tayama's back, then of the bike seat, and stood, legs shaking. Here she was, perfectly fine, which seemed both miraculous and unexceptional; smiling and giddy, filled with relief and surprise. Sad Trip by Motorcycle! Tayama doffed his helmet. Fanny bounced up and down, loosening her limbs. "It's so beautiful," she said. She'd hardly noticed anything about the countryside they'd been moving through.

"Longsheng Rice Terraces." He began extracting camera, tripod, and other gear from his saddlebags. "Now I photograph. We meet here at . . ." He checked his watch. "Two hours? One o'clock?" He hired a young man to watch over the bike. Still wearing her daypack, Fanny set out on the stone stairways that climbed through the terraces, and then across the narrow paths that traversed the edges of the paddies. She passed bony-hipped cows and stood aside for a man with a pole over his shoulder from which hung a large snake braided back on itself. People—men and women—stooped in the paddies, shaping the ditches, handling the rice plants. She had no idea what they were doing, the way she'd had no idea about the parts of a ship. When you traveled you were always meeting your own ignorance. These people were working and Fanny was not working and she felt more keenly her uselessness. This was another odd feature of travel: it was a kind of work but not actual work, it demanded intention and focus but it was not in itself a noble occupation. Not the way that growing rice was noble.

It was lovely not to be on a bus, to be here and able to wander around in this place that was not a tourist destination. She was free of a fixed route and schedule and with her was Tayama, who could order decent food, supply drinks and snacks. But riding on the back of a motorcycle, which she used to love, or at least not think about, now felt akin to standing blindfolded in the middle of a firing range.

A handful of years after the Baja trip, maybe 1971, she and Bruno were on a loose wander through South America—hitchhiking, taking buses, sometimes trains. In Bariloche, a guy Bruno met—she couldn't remember him at all—sold Bruno a Triumph Bonneville. They took that modest-looking, indestructible machine south and then west on a bad dirt road over the spine of the Andes, crossing into Chile, their passports examined and stamped by a couple of border guards who looked as if they hadn't showered or seen anyone in weeks. Fanny and Bruno joined them for dominoes and maté before continuing on into Chile, following a series of rough roads more or less along the Futaleufú River, a wild churn of tourmaline water. They arrived in a strange and magical landscape where the Andes met the sea: dense and lush and misty, or tumbled with massive gray boulders cradling dirty white tongues of glaciers that sent forth milky blue rivers. The trip had no through-line; they went wherever they encountered a road, or what Bruno took to calling "an imitation of a road."

It was the season of the *nalcas*, large leathery plants with leaves the size of umbrellas or truck tires. Darwin had called them noble. The sound of moving water, ever in the background, never ceased: rivers, waterfalls, lapping inlets. They stayed in fishing villages or camped. One night they'd found a mushroom growing through the wooden floor of the second-floor room in a house where they were spending the night and they started to laugh so hard—later they didn't know why that mushroom was so funny—laughing until they were near tears. If Bruno were here right now and she said "mushroom," they'd both burst into laughter. At a hot springs, they met a young man in training to become a shaman. While soaking in hot water to their necks and chatting, he became transfixed by Bruno and Fanny, especially Bruno. Afterward when they'd moved on to a meal and beers in a room that smelled of moss and pine, the young man said their auras revealed that tragedy was their destiny. Bruno had laughed, shoved a fresh beer into the young man's hands, and told him to stop nosing around their auras.

Sometimes Bruno would disappear overnight, leaving her alone. Usually she'd meet the women Bruno picked up, and most of them she liked. On that trip, Fanny, too, had an adventure, with a slightly manic, neurotic Argentinian who traveled parallel with them for a week. She could tell that he drove Bruno crazy, but Bruno was tolerant. Mostly, it was Bruno and Fanny and what Fanny liked best was the familial ease between them: grumpiness tolerated, irritations that didn't blow up into anything serious, the teasing, the easy laughter, the honesty. Everybody could see that they were siblings; Bruno and she looked alike, shared characteristics, intonations, and gestures, spoke in shorthand. It was this siblingness that she valued. They didn't have to look nice, be in a good mood, take care of each other's feelings. She relied upon the uncomplicated, undemanding comfort of their intimacy, the effortless access to their collection of shared experiences.

South America was their last trip together, and the last time she'd traveled by motorcycle. When she visited Bruno in Berkeley, they'd ride his Norton Commando to parties or to the movies, but that was mere transportation. After the South America trip, Bruno moved to Lake Tahoe, following a woman he'd fallen in love with, and worked at a casino and in one of the ski areas, and when that life fell apart he moved to the Bay Area and pursued his Buddhist practice more seriously. Fanny embarked upon her aimless work life in Santa Fe, interspersed with her own, solitary travels—to Ecuador and Guatemala, to Greece and Egypt and Turkey. She and Bruno talked about traveling together—they'd talked about going to Tibet together—but they never managed it. The future had felt expansive, a vast country where they might yet do any number of things. About which, it turned out, they were wrong.

She realized she was alone, an occurrence she hadn't thought possible in China. She sat on one of the stone steps flanked by rice plants and flooded paddies, nobody around, tiny figures in the distance far below. Rummaging in her bag, she extracted one of the baggies with Bruno's ashes and fingered it, idly looking for the hole that had leaked at lunch with Daniel. Maybe Bruno had been in the mood for a little risk on that day. Maybe he wanted to feel the wind on his bald head. How was riding a motorcycle without a helmet different than rock climbing? Nobody called rock climbing suicide. Fanny refused to use the euphemisms for death—passed on, crossed over—which seemed to her self-deluding. As if Bruno had passed her in a hallway or crossed a room. She was too literal-minded: Bruno was dead. She remembered something someone had told her at his funeral: a Zen student who has left his teacher was considered a *rōnin*, a masterless samurai. *Rōnin* meant "drifting person." Bruno had not told her about leaving his teacher and Zen; he'd said nothing of his experiments with traditionless Buddhism. Everybody had secrets. Fanny had always thought she and Bruno shared more than most people. But she could not align what she thought she knew about Bruno and what she'd apparently not known about him.

She held the baggie of ashes, thinking she ought to perform a ritual or say something. But she couldn't think beyond the imperative to release some of his ashes. She opened the baggie and let the ashes fall into the watery paddy. Much of the white gray ash sank, some floated on the surface. "Goodbye," she said. "Bye, Bruno." Her mind turned violently blank as if an enormous wind had blown through her, erasing thought. She felt queasy and stared fixedly over the layers of green below, blurred together. Standing, she dropped her sunglasses into the rice plants, picked them up, turned, and continued climbing the stone stairway in a kind of frantic half-jog. But she didn't get far before she stopped and sat down again.

She sat for a long time, the humidity soft on her skin, listening to her own breathing, inhaling the wet earth plant smells, a rich muddy, root scent. She exhaled, permitting her solitude to overwhelm her. Strangeness, unfamiliarity, distance, loneliness—these seemed to come from the landscape and she let them press against her eyelids, her mouth, her chest, until she felt herself succumb. Feeling released, from what she couldn't say, she stood and continued walking.

After an hour she arrived in a village high and deep in the middle of the terraces. She looked back to see how far she'd walked; Tayama and his motorcycle were lost to sight. The village was a quick jumble of dark wooden houses with one dirt road down the middle. Fanny walked down the eerily deserted street. Laundry hung from lines. A woman, then a man, emerged from the shadows and coldly observed her progress. She felt she was playing a role in a western: the unwelcome stranger come to town, ominous background music playing. *I'll just get through the village and bolt down the terraces.*

Once free of the village, she jogged down a stairway. She was breathing more easily—nothing had happened, only a weird, pressurized vibe of unfriendliness—when a man appeared and began to talk to her in a language that was not Chinese. She tried to act not unfriendly yet not overly friendly. He talked on, crowding beside her on the stairway that was too narrow for two. Then he took a ten-yuan note out of his pocket and held it out to her. She stared at the money. The creepy feeling she'd had in the village jolted back into her gut. What was going on? What was he offering her money *for*? She had two options for saying no—a smiling, friendly no, or a stern furious no. She went for angry with a tinge of righteousness; the tone of the village had been stern, this might be in their communication repertoire. He followed her for a time, making her back twitch and her neck tighten, then he vanished into the terraces. She continued, quickly for awhile, eventually slowing down when she felt she was out of range. The encounter with the man had been disturbing but she understood that she'd been more unsettled by that chilling village full of unsmiling people. What had happened there?

People told Fanny that she hadn't smiled for almost a year after her parents died. Never smiled; rarely seemed animated. It wasn't until she and Bruno began traveling that her sorrow over their parents' deaths eased. Those trips weren't easy or comfortable. The kind of travel she loved required her to make her way across unfamiliar terrain in another language among strangers; it required her to pay attention to the world outside the dark tunnel of her own thoughts and obsessions.

Bruno once described Buddhist beliefs this way: you're not going to survive life; you're never going to get your emotional needs met; there is no one to be. What, Fanny wanted to know, happened to the intervening years, between birth and death, if you weren't someone, trying to get your emotional needs met? If Bruno had been suffering, would he have accepted it? Tolerated it without asking for the participation of those he loved? Fanny didn't believe Bruno was capable of ordinary misery; he was cheerful, if tormented. Maybe she hadn't seen his misery because she saw Bruno in her mind as she wanted to see him. Maybe he understood this about her; and maybe he'd used her own narrow vision to sneak away while she wasn't paying attention. But this made him seem calculating, which she was sure he had not been.

Nick and Maria Molinari's will stated that Bruno and Fanny were to be left in charge of their own lives, with a guardian for advice and assistance. (There'd been a period in her twenties when this had infuriated her: Nick and Maria's will, her sense that they—the dead—were fine, in part because they were together. But what about Bruno? What about Fanny?) Ted was an unmarried family friend who lived on their street. He was good with practicalities, explaining the house mortgage, the way their investments worked, how to think about future expenses. He took them to dinner, or the movies, or skiing; he made them laugh and he made them feel capable. With his help, Bruno and Fanny took over care of the house and yard, paid bills, kept the car running. They cooked meals, drove themselves to school, got their teeth cleaned, even went on vacations. It wasn't all smooth. They had their period when neither of them washed dishes regularly, when they would eat huge bowls of chocolate pudding for dinner, when they would stay up late on weeknights, watching television. Their friends would show up with six-packs and pot, expecting their parentless house to be the party pad, and Bruno shouldered the unpopular chore of sending them off. They sorted it out eventually with what they used to call "division of labor" and two unspoken agreements: no fights (disagreement and discussion were acceptable) and Bruno was the leader, Fanny the follower. Their self-sufficiency buoyed them. Fanny learned that if you fed grief difficulty, it tasted milder. But then, she'd had someone beside her with the same grief; they could flail it together.

Fanny did not expect that she, like characters in certain kinds of novels, would uncover the truth about Bruno's death. She wasn't going to discover an unpleasant knot of family secrets leading to that solitary moment on his Norton Commando. Yet she would pluck and scrabble for the thread that might unravel the events. Like the stitching that sewed a sack of grain closed. If you found the right thread, the whole unraveled beautifully, in one pleasing movement. If you didn't find that thread, you had to pick at every stitch, and you ended with a pile of bits of string, irritated. Her family secret? That she was the only one left.

Perhaps she wasn't going to understand something about his death, but what about his life? Who was Bruno? The question embarrassed her because she thought he was the one person she truly knew. The more she questioned what she imagined she knew about him, the worse she felt. One thing was undeniable: she'd not reciprocated the gift of deep, complex understanding which he had given to her, and she wondered how she was going to digest that failure, along with all of her other failures.

She paused in her walking to bend close and examine the green stalks of rice in their bed of still water, considering the elaborate process necessary to grow this essential food. Such a beautiful, delicate plant, such an architectural arrangement of terraced earth, making art out of food. The Sad Traveler on her Sad Trip wanders through some rice terraces. Not everything, she thought, was meant to be understood, an idea to which she nonetheless lived in fierce opposition.

Chapter 14

When they stopped traveling for the day, Daniel and Yevgo would check into whatever cheap accommodation Zhou found. They'd fill out the forms with their passport and visa numbers, their occupations and reasons for visiting China. Yevgo dropped his bag on a bed, peed in the toilets that were down the hall, on another floor, or outside across a courtyard, and then he'd go for a walk. He never walked far. His need was for solitude, even if it was public solitude. Often he found a park and did some mild stretches for his back, the tepid evening air washing over him.

Meanwhile, Daniel familiarized himself with the contents of Yevgo's pack. He found where Yevgo kept his camera and film, medications, condoms, address book, dirty socks, travelers checks, and cash. Not that Yevgo had a system, everything was mixed up—Yevgo was not an organized packer. Also, no zipper was locked, which wouldn't have stymied Daniel, who could pick simple locks. Yevgo was relaxed about money. Daniel had seen the money belt he wore, but he kept thick wads of yuan in various semi-secret niches of his pack. Out of curiosity and to satisfy his restlessness, Daniel began going through Yevgo's pack. He discovered Yevgo's supply of butterscotch candies. He'd unwrap one, pop it into his mouth, and let it dissolve while he idly sifted through Yevgo's possessions. The butterscotch candies and the activity of checking on Yevgo's stash became a habit. Yevgo went for a walk; Daniel went through Yevgo's pack. Daniel wasn't after anything particular and he didn't intend to take anything—the butterscotches didn't count.

The evening after the incident with the crowd of men in the village, Daniel threw himself into a chair in their hotel room and fiddled with a tea bag, impatient for Yevgo to leave. He could taste butterscotch. Yevgo was in no hurry. "My mother was a real beauty," he said, sitting on the edge of his bed, foot propped on a chair, socks off, trimming his toenails. "She had dark hair, a strong face. She was warm, but savvy. Nobody got much past her. I think she had an affair a few years after my father's death, with Igor, a younger married man who lived in the next block of apartments and helped my mother with odd jobs." Yevgo paused. "Sometimes when I stopped in, I felt a breeze through her apartment, like someone had just left the room." He shook his head. "I was proud that she could get a good-looking guy like Igor. I can't remember his wife. Maybe she was asthmatic or had tuberculosis. Maybe she was fine, with a chest like a set of basketballs." He laughed.

Daniel thought about his own mother. She was pretty, and he'd seen men flirt with her, but he knew nothing of her love affairs. Quite the opposite from his father, whose girlfriends and wives were impossible to avoid. He could remember one day when he'd come out of school—he was seven or eight—his mother was waiting to walk him home, as usual. Her light brown hair was pulled back into a loose roll and she had on red lipstick; he could see it from where he was standing. A man he'd never seen was talking to her. He could tell they knew each other. He'd slipped back into the crowd of students, down hallways, across a field, and through a hole in a rear fence. Back and forth and around Oxford, he walked farther than he'd ever walked by himself. What had he told his mother, when he finally arrived home? He remembered her grave demeanor, her effort not to be sad. He remembered feeling that he didn't want to be taken care of, he wanted to be left alone. He understood that he could fool her if he wanted to and that she wouldn't stand in his way. He had an urge to share this memory with Yevgo, about his pretty mother waiting for him. He felt himself flush and dropped his head so Yevgo wouldn't see. "You going for a walk?" he said.

Yevgo threw the clippers into the mess of his pack. "Vodka! Why is there no vodka in this godforsaken country. No vodka, no coffee." He cursed in exasperation.

After Yevgo left, Daniel rifled Yevgo's bag, which Yevgo had left wide open, found a butterscotch, unwrapped the candy, and slipped it onto his tongue. Disappointment weighed on him. He wished he'd been calm in the village that afternoon. He should have sung to the men! Why hadn't he thought of that? Why couldn't he tell Yevgo stories about his past, the way Yevgo told him stories? He shook his head, muttering to himself, shoving Yevgo's mess of clothing around. When he found a bundle of bills stuffed into a sock, he took twenty yuan. He found a pill bottle with a blurred, scratched label. He put the pills in his pack and the money in his pocket. It gave him a rousing jolt. He told himself he'd return everything. Later.

Guangdong, Guangxi, Guizhou. Yevgo was not in a hurry. In America, on well-paved fast American highways, they'd be halfway to the border. This was China, and nothing was predictable. In small towns and villages, Zhou and Liu were asked by people staring at the foreigners in the backseat, what were they doing so far from home? Zhou rubbed his hands over the steering wheel, while Liu spun tales. They were driving foreign experts to Xinjiang to taste the world famous Xinjiang melons. They were escorting geologists to new oil fields in the west. The Communist Party was sponsoring a global children's storytelling festival and they were traveling around China collecting stories written by children. They were part of an international investigation into the kidnapping and selling of women as brides. Every time, Liu told a different story.

Zhou, preoccupied with his expectation of disaster, hardly noticed anything outside the taxi: he took no note of crops, people, animals, topography, dialects, food. The days passed in a series of stomach cramps and headaches; in his routines of care for the car, his sweeping out and wiping down. He took pleasure in his conversations—or question and answer sessions—with Daniel. He was practicing English every day; he was making a small fortune. He was taking his chance.

Yevgo chose the route and nobody questioned his decisions. Though Zhou was the driver, Yevgo was the leader. They deferred to him because the trip was his, and he was the elder.

It happened that between Xuyong and Luzhou, on the southern end of Sichuan Province, on an angled route Yevgo had chosen, they got stuck in a rut on a gash of dirt pretending to be a road. Zhou had become—with Yevgo's steady tutoring—a decent driver. It wasn't his fault. The ditch was unavoidable.

Three peasants popped out of the foliage and stared at the taxi and the four travelers. Look, foreign devils, one said loudly.

Yevgo and Daniel positioned themselves behind the car, while Liu took up the passenger side with his door open. Zhou stood on the driver's side, his right hand on the steering wheel, his shoulder against the car. They tried to push the taxi out of the rut.

Don't just stand there like soggy dumplings, help us! Liu said.

One hundred yuan.

"Fuck you," Liu said in English, though it sounded like "fookyo."

We've got a tractor. The spokesman of the trio, a stocky man with a large, bony face, pointed up the road to a piece of machinery half-hidden in the bushes.

Zhou and Liu conferred. Sichuan dialect is hard to understand, Zhou complained.

Yeah, but we understand numbers, Liu said. A hundred kuai? They think city people are fools. If they wanted to see fools they should look in a mirror.

Zhou agreed. We'll extract the car ourselves.

This time, Yevgo took the driver's seat while the others got the car rocking. They grunted and heaved. The peasants squatted on the muddy verge, smoking and spitting, impervious to the hovering mosquitoes. They appeared bored. The car remained stuck.

Yevgo got out and stood with the others eyeing their mired vehicle. Cicadas screeched, mosquitoes whined.

Zhou told Liu that he thought they should have stayed on the major road. Yevgo's route was too wild. Why, Zhou asked, was Liu not planning the route—why had it been left to Yevgo, a person who knew nothing about China?

Liu lit a cigarette. We're here now, he snapped. You always want to go back and change the way things have happened.

I'm talking about the future, too. How to prevent this happening again.

Liu sucked in his cheeks.

Daniel swatted mosquitoes. Yevgo walked off to take a piss. Spilling onto the road, the damp foliage exhaled a sweet, fetid breath.

They said they had a tractor, right? Zhou said.

They can't even speak *putonghua*, Liu said. Uneducated farmers.

We have to use their tractor, Zhou said.

Liu threw his cigarette onto the ground and crushed it with his heel.

"Son of a bitch," Liu said. "Motherfuckers." This was the English he'd learned from Yevgo. Liu, an admirer of all things Yevgo, mimicked the feeling behind the words. *Sunuvabeech. Muthurfoockurs.*

Twenty kuai, Zhou offered the peasants.

Eighty.

They went back and forth, using hand gestures to confirm the numbers, and finally agreed on fifty. The peasants backed the tractor—a rototiller motor attached to a long, bare chassis with a seat—in front of the car, hooked it up, and hauled the car free. Zhou bent to see if any damage had been done to the front bumper. There was a scratch and a small dent. He collected money from Yevgo and handed the cash to the leader, the man with the big, bony face.

Zhou hadn't driven far, around one curve in the road, when Yevgo said he had to take a piss.

What the hell is wrong with the Russian, Liu said. We stop three hundred times a day.

It's an old man thing, Zhou said. Have sympathy.

Liu glanced in the rearview mirror. Where's he going?

Yevgo was walking back down the road. He disappeared around the curve.

The screech of cicadas, like a blade scraping bone, continued. Yevgo returned, waving his arms.

What now, Liu grumbled. All three slid from the car and walked toward Yevgo, who put a finger to his lips. At the curve, the four men peered down the road through some branches. There were the peasants, digging the rut deeper.

"What are they saying?" Yevgo whispered to Zhou.

Zhou listened. "I am not one hundred percent. They are conducting disagreement of money. Big Face says they need received more money due to foreign presence."

"Son of a bitch," Yevgo and Liu cursed in tandem.

"How did you know?" Daniel asked Yevgo.

"I saw their shovels hidden in the bushes."

"Christ, you've got a nose for it." Daniel clapped him on the back. Zhou was laughing.

This isn't funny, Liu told Zhou. He was puffed with fury.

Zhou didn't know why he was laughing but he couldn't stop himself. Zhou had been afraid of trouble on the trip, but not peasants cheating them. It was funny and it was not *that* serious.

Not funny. Money is always serious, Liu said.

Okay, relax. We shall manufacture sublime plan. Zhou said this first in Chinese, then in English.

Beat them up, Liu said.

"Get our money back," Yevgo said.

"Get our money back, plus extra for our suffering and trouble," Daniel said. After a moment, he added, "Look, we're four, they're three. Here's what we do." The others were listening intently, even though Liu couldn't understand. "We'll divide into pairs on either side of the road, then, on a signal, jump into the road and tackle them. Yevgo and Liu, you'll get Big Face. Joe, you take the chap with the little ears, and I'll take the other one, the bloke with bad skin. Right?"

"Right-o." Zhou had taken to this word of Daniel's.

When Liu heard the plan, he snorted. Did the Englishman imagine they were in a Hong Kong movie? How were they to coordinate? Zhou didn't wear a watch and the capitalist pigs would fight for themselves and their little individual needs.

It was their money, Zhou pointed out.

A fight might wrinkle the Englishman's pants, or get his fancy shoes muddy.

It's his idea. Anyway, remember that article we saw in the paper, Zhou said.

What article?

Now that living standards have improved, Zhou intoned, we must be brave and encourage comrades to introduce elegance into their lives. Elegance is a mark of socialist civilization. Remember?

Liu laughed. Right, if Mao were chairman now he'd have to get new socks—no holes allowed.

Zhou fetched the car. He thought that Liu would benefit from emulating some of Daniel's habits of dress and hygiene, but he didn't say this to Liu. He backed the car up to the curve in the road and parked it out of sight. Yevgo and Liu entered the brush on the east side of the road and Daniel and Zhou on the west; they were to flap a handkerchief when they were in place. After the second pair had flapped a handkerchief, they would count to three and launch. The peasants stood idly in the road, propped on their shovels, smoking and talking.

It worked, more or less. Except at the last minute Daniel got knocked back by a branch he didn't see and landed on his back. He righted himself, chased down his peasant and tackled him in the damp dirt. There were shouts, scuffling, heavy breathing. Liu had grabbed the strand of plastic lilacs from the car and was using it to tie Big Face's wrists. Yevgo had him in a headlock. Liu berated him. Lowdown criminals. They should cut off their fingers! Turn them in to the PSB and then they'd see what happened to thieves. And so on.

Yevgo was breathing hard and motioned to Liu that he was going to let go of the man's arm. He had to stand up, ease the tightness in his chest. He stepped away, massaged a hand over his chest, shook out his arm. Liu, preoccupied, wasn't paying attention. The plastic lilacs were not an effective restraining device and Liu ripped them free and threw them into the mud. When Yevgo let go, the man twisted around, grabbed Liu's head with his newly freed arm, and bit Liu's ear. Not off, just a set of teeth marks in the lobe. Liu howled. Yevgo stepped heavily on Big Face's stomach. Big Face doubled over, groaning. For a few minutes the cicadas were drowned out by Liu's cursing and Big Face's groans. Blood dripped onto Liu's shiny polyester shirt and Big Face's blue work pants. Zhou and Daniel, with a tight grip on each of their peasants, were shouting, Are you all right? What's going on? The one in Chinese, the other in English.

Things settled, and the travelers whooped and clapped each other on the back as they sat the peasants down in their own ditch. "Way to go, lads." Daniel shook everyone's hand. Even Liu, pinching a handkerchief to his bleeding ear, shook Daniel's hand. Daniel began to sing to "Under My Thumb": ". . . *the peasants who thought they had us down, the sods who tried to push us around.*"

Zhou rifled their pockets and pulled out quite a bit of cash, more than their fifty yuan. The peasants sat with their shoulders collapsed, looking churlish. The sun, directly overhead, bathed the road in bright, shadowless light. Yevgo, quiet and gray, was feeling queasy. He should start taking those pills again.

How much do you make at this illegal venture? Liu demanded.

More than we did working the fields, Big Face said. He whined that, in fact, they *had* pulled them free and therefore had earned their pay.

We're not going to steal from you, Zhou said.

Even though you've stolen all this from innocent travelers, Liu said. He flapped the bills with one hand, holding his ear with the other.

Let's go, Zhou said.

Liu wanted to take the shovels.

Zhou shook his head. He spotted the plastic lilacs trampled in the mud and gave Liu a look.

It scratched our necks, Liu said. Just in the way.

Zhou passed Yevgo's money back to him and returned the remainder to the peasants. The men piled into the taxi. Daniel launched what was becoming their totem tune: "*Now let's toss our stuff into Joe's taxi, drive it out to Tashkent . . .*" Windows open, they sang loudly, even Liu. The sky filled with floating white hills of clouds. The weather was changing. *Soon*, Zhou thought, *it would be fall.*

Chapter 15

At dawn, the street lamps snapped off, though it was still dark when Fanny left her hotel. Her hair was clean and in a fresh braid. She walked briskly to the bus station inhaling the smell of China: vinegar, vegetable peelings, garlic, drains. This, now, was her life: walking to a bus station through a half-lit world in a strange place where she barely spoke the language. Her job was to put herself into the hands of an unknown driver, sit on a bus all day, move from one unfamiliar place to another. She'd been riding buses for a couple of days. They were uncomfortable and she was both relieved and regretful to be off the motorcycle. She missed Tayama's company and with him she'd eaten better and stayed in cleaner hotel rooms. He'd even extracted candles (to augment weak electricity) and a smile from a floor clerk. He could make things happen in China that seemed impossible.

A bus attendant stamped, tore, and punched her ticket. This was a two-day ride to Chengdu, moving her closer to her meeting with Wen Li, and with Daniel. About Wen Li she was tentative in her imagination, a little wary of what she might discover. Fanny put her larger bag up front where she could keep an eye on it and took a seat. She watched the complicated arrangements and rearrangements of the luggage piled into the space beside the driver. She only half-believed she'd see Daniel again, but she held him in her mind, a warm spot of possibility, a place to daydream. Her imagination moved from Daniel to a child, someone who would return home with her from this trip. She'd never before seriously considered a child so it was a little odd that it now seemed both imperative and obvious. A small Molinari—of course! If she had a child it would clarify everything, even what she should do next: find a job that was perfect for a single parent.

"Do you speak English?" asked the man sitting across the aisle.

She hesitated, in the mood for the silence of traveling without language. In the mood to daydream about Daniel, the child, the perfect job. "I do." She blew her nose.

"Today is my lucky day," he said with such clear delight that Fanny found herself smiling back at him.

His name was Mr. Wu and he was a judicial official investigating cases in small towns around Sichuan Province. He launched a vigorous conversation as the other passengers dropped into sleep. Of course he asked if she was married, but he didn't ask how much money she made or what life in America was like. He asked what kind of work she did (another thing to like about China: her ordinary, unimpressive job as a clerk in a hospital was nothing to be ashamed of), what she liked to do when she wasn't working, and if her parents were alive (a blunt question that surprised her). Mr. Wu became grave when she said, no, her parents were not alive. Neither were his. "We are both homeless fellows." After a pause he smiled. "Fortunately, everyone in the world shall be homeless at least for a period of time in life."

Fanny nodded.

Mr. Wu revealed that he was an accomplished mah-jongg player, liked American movies, and didn't smoke but liked to drink. A little, he said. He lived in a single room assigned to him by his work unit and ate his meals in the communal cafeteria. His sisters and brothers were farmers (all married with lots of children) in a distant province. He read books in English—this was how he improved his English. His English name was William, after William Shakespeare, whose work he admired. He'd just finished reading an English translation of *Crime and Punishment*.

"I have a strong interest in world literature," he said. "Unfortunately, I'm not qualified to engage in a discussion in such a field. Two reasons account for my failure."

Fanny leaned across the aisle, charmed by the formality of his English and the occasional odd grammatical construction.

"I've to spend most of the time studying the law science, and I'm ill informed about the world trend. I admire very much the novels of Dostoyevsky, especially *Crime and Punishment*. What do you think of him?"

"I love to read but you may know more than I," she said. "Strangely, I've never read anything by Dostoyevsky." She saw that screen of sadness and disappointment cross his face. To be a traveler was to be made repeatedly aware of the privileges one squandered, the seemingly endless numbers of opportunities one did not grab hold of, that others would count the best things in their lives. "I do love Tolstoy," she said, to compensate. "*War and Peace* is one of my favorite books."

"*Crime and Punishment* is a very tension book." Mr. Wu grabbed hold of the seat back in front of him as the bus bounced over a rutted section of road.

"I'm thirty-five years old," he said and gave an embarrassed laugh. "For a Chinese, a man over thirty is never young. He should have completed some career by making some notable contributions to the society or the country. For me, it's really a long sigh. I'm still wondering what I should do as my final goal. Usually speaking, a man of more than thirty is married. This is a social pattern. For you, maybe it's not the same. You would receive much pressure if you would live in our country." He ran his hand repeatedly through his hair, two, three, five times, leaving it sticking up in different directions. "The U.S.A. is freer than China. It's a fact." He stared straight ahead, suddenly looking bereft. He turned to speak with his colleague, an officious man in a stiff green uniform. Then Mr. Wu turned back to Fanny, leaning across the aisle. "Here's a joke for you. I have a friend studying journalism in Tashkent," he said.

"Do they teach them to write propaganda?"

"Sure, that's journalism," Mr. Wu said. "But that's not the joke. So Reagan, Gorbachev, and Deng Xiaoping are all in front of God. Reagan asks: God, when will communism come to my country? Three hundred years, God answers. Deng says, God, when will communism come to my country? Six hundred years, says God. Then it's Gorbachev's turn and he asks the same question. God says, Oh no, I don't see communism ever coming to your country."

Fanny laughed.

They talked until two men at the back of the bus complained, their voices rising up from the silent rows of passengers. "Why are they objecting?" Fanny whispered. "Because we're speaking English?"

"I wonder," Mr. Wu said, wary. He specialized in economic law though he also did the occasional criminal case. "I'm supposed to be in uniform, like my colleague." His colleague had a bland, pudgy face perched like a dumpling atop his thick neck. His uniform pants had red stripes along the seams and the jacket, tight around his neck, had gold-colored buttons. He wore a rigid hat squeezed onto his head, with a black patent leather brim. He never removed his enormous square sunglasses. "If I was in uniform, no one would have the nerve to bully me," Mr. Wu said. Mr. Wu was scruffy, in a spotted gray sweatshirt beneath a rumpled suit jacket.

"Do you think they understand English?" she asked.

Mr. Wu shrugged, his expression somber.

When they stopped talking, the bus was silent. The driver negotiated the road's winding, uneven surface crowded with trucks, carts, bicyclists, pedestrians, and pigs—enormous, hairy, snorting pink and black pigs hauling their owners forward on rope leashes. Sichuan Province was heavily cultivated: rice fields, vegetable patches, apple, plum, cherry trees. Narrow strips of cabbages grew alongside the road, and small clusters of fruit trees were crammed in between houses and rice terraces. People, pants rolled to mid-thigh, calf deep in water, planted rice seedlings. A man and a buffalo plowed through mud; two men sawed fat rounds off a huge carrot of a tree trunk with a handmade two-handed saw.

At the lunch stop, one of the passengers wanted to talk to Fanny; Mr. Wu translated. There were the usual questions about age and marriage and then the woman wanted to know what Fanny thought of Chinese toilets. Fanny and the woman both burst into laughter. "They're awful," Fanny said. The woman was pleased at the frankness of this answer. She was thirty-two years old with a ten-year-old son; she wore gray slacks and a blue blouse. She apologized for not speaking English, then explained wistfully that she had lost her chance to study English because of the Cultural Revolution.

In China, Fanny thought, people suffered on a grand scale at the hands of rulers, governments, and policies; industrial-grade greed and ambition. Her own suffering had been familial or personal—some of it, but not all, caused by herself. She thought of that word *struggle* that the Chongqing boys had used so frequently. The Cultural Revolution had elevated struggle to a kind of torture. People were tormented into suicide, hounded to death. She looked into the sad eyes of this woman whose name she did not know. Perhaps here was another unexpected balm offered by China: every person had suffered. Fanny was among people who had endured the unendurable.

Fanny and Mr. Wu ate thin soup in a restaurant with posters on opposing walls, one of Deng Xiaoping, his torso emerging from a froth of pink flowers, the other of Sylvester Stallone as Rocky. Mr. Wu wanted to know if she'd seen that movie and what she thought of it.

"It's the only movie I've ever liked Stallone in," she said. Mr. Wu was delighted with this opinion. They discussed the movie, the costumes, the direction, the acting.

"I am pleased that the comments I hold on world films can be shared by another," Mr. Wu said. "You are an expert critic, so my comments can be more authoritative."

She protested that she was an ordinary critic, not an expert.

Two young men arm wrestled at a nearby table; Fanny and Mr. Wu exchanged glances. It was as if they'd known one another for a long time.

Outside in the dust beside the bus, Mr. Wu said, "As a friend." He stared above the tops of the buildings across the road. "When you return to America I think you should get married." He spoke softly, finishing the sentence in a burst.

He had a fresh grease spot on his sweatshirt and his cheap suit jacket was so crumpled she imagined it had been rolled into a ball and stored beneath his bed. She had always liked shabbily dressed men.

"We cannot live without love."

"Mmm." Fanny made a sound of mild agreement. *Here we go again.* She had come to understand that in China the absence of a mate was interpreted as evidence of some drastic undesirability. Daniel came to mind, sex came to mind, a child came to mind, but not marriage.

"I," Mr. Wu began. He fell silent.

"Do you know about what happened in Tiananmen Square last month?" Fanny said and immediately felt that it was a question she should not have asked.

Mr. Wu straightened. His long animated face with its slightly puffy cheeks and narrow forehead slowly leached of expression. "Some people," his voice trailed off. Relief at the return of the bus driver flooded his features.

Fanny wondered in what ways Mr. Wu had suffered. She wouldn't ask.

They stayed overnight in a small town, and Fanny, the sole foreign passenger, was put in a room at the bus-stop hotel by herself, apart from the others. Mr. Wu had to eat dinner with his colleague.

Fanny filled out the usual hotel registration form, which was in Chinese and English. She paused at the box labeled *Reason for Visit*: what to write? This box on these forms, which she filled out every time she stayed in a hotel, had become a game. Reason for Visit: morbid restlessness. Reason for Visit: love of discomfort. Reason for Visit: failure to thrive in ordinary life. That was what she wrote in the blank space now. She followed a floor clerk down a hallway sprinkled with broken window glass and dropped her bags on one of the four beds in the room.

An hour after arrival, a man from Switzerland with curly red hair, escorted by the staff, burst through the door. Fanny, who had been stretched out fully clothed on the bed, doing nothing, stood. Confusion upon confusion ensued. Did they want Fanny to change rooms? Or had they decided to put two foreigners together, even if they were not the same gender? He was a tall, thin man with lively eyes. "Do you want me in this one?" he shouted and pointed to one bed, interrogating the hotel clerks who hovered, frightened and amused, in the doorway. "Do you want me in this one?" He flopped onto Fanny's bed. The women covered their mouths and laughed nervously. Finally, he threw his bag with a flourish on an empty bed across the room from Fanny's.

Fanny clapped.

"What an *irritating* place," he said. The clerks had gone. His name was George. "I tried to buy a pack of cigarettes. *One* pack I wanted, but the girl would only sell me two. I didn't want two. Why two, why not one?" He pulled at his hair. "In China, there is no logic!" He paced up and down. "They make me stand downstairs for half an hour while they decide to put me in one room, then another room, then another room. Every room is like every other room; what difference it makes, I don't know."

It was a relief for Fanny to see someone else tormented by China's impenetrable systems. After he calmed down, he told her about Emei Shan, where he'd been the previous week. He said, if she liked to hike, Emei was the place. You could escape from the noise and stress of cities. Hearing this made her glad that it happened to be her immediate destination. He said the only peace to be found in China was at Buddhist sites, even though the Chinese didn't appear the least bit spiritual. She'd thought she could only get to Emei via Chengdu but he showed her on a map a couple of towns where she could catch a minibus to Emei.

Fanny loaned him her clock so he could get up at 5:30 to catch his bus. She didn't hear him set the clock near her head when he left before dawn.

In the cool, foggy morning the passengers on Fanny's bus stood for forty-five minutes awaiting the arrival of their driver, who didn't like to get up early.

"I'm sorry for improper remarks I made yesterday," Mr. Wu said.

"That's okay," Fanny said. What about her question regarding Tiananmen Square? She didn't apologize. Mist settled along the rooftops and dipped down onto the dark earth. It was too early for conversation. Her stomach was upset.

"I want that for myself, you see, and I hope you will agree with my thinking."

The passengers shuffled like cows waiting to be led to pasture. They had grown accustomed to the sounds of Mr. Wu and Fanny speaking English.

"I understand. Only, I can't think of marriage in the abstract. Maybe I would want to marry someone *particular*." Funny how you could sound reasonable without being reasonable at all. The idea of marriage panicked her, filled her with sadness. Someone spat behind her. Every passenger except Mr. Wu and Fanny hacked in long ragged notes, then spat forcefully. It was a small town and its citizens clustered around the communal spigot across the road, brushing their teeth. Watching the bus passengers, the townspeople also spat with vigor, enamel cups held in their hands. Mornings in China were rough: so much expectoration to tolerate.

Mr. Wu nodded. "I wish to marry," he said. He sounded tentative and firm.

The day had barely started, the light still unfolding from the night. *I'm in the middle of China, talking about marriage*, Fanny thought.

Mr. Wu's colleague, stern and dull, interrupted, wanting to know where Fanny had been in China. He admonished her for not visiting Beijing and the Great Wall. "Beijing is China's treasure," Mr. Wu translated his colleague's tepid conversation.

Fanny yawned.

"No one in my small circle can communicate with me in English," Mr. Wu said.

Mr. Wu obediently translated his colleague's prim approval of the Chinese government policy of charging foreigners twice as much as locals for tickets and hotel rooms. Then Mr. Wu said, gesturing to Fanny, "When we're together, we can talk. We are both of us talkative."

"Yes," she said.

"You are my first American."

His colleague said that the proposed Yangtze River dam would place China among the world's great powers. Mr. Wu translated.

"It seems that I'm in the dark about my future," Mr. Wu said. "Presently, I don't have a long-term program to work for. Numerous variables are influencing my life."

Mr. Wu translated his colleague's advice that Fanny visit Dujiangyan, famous for its ancient irrigation system. Across the road, the town's citizens left the water spigot and dispersed to their tasks. The light turned yellow, the sun climbing a low hill at the edge of the town.

The driver, rumpled and sleepy, opened the bus. So began another day of traveling past villages from the Middle Ages: dark doorways, long dark tables set up outside. Everything happened beside the road: women cooked over coal braziers, men stood with bowls of noodles or rice, chopsticks working mechanically, eyes on the passing traffic. A woman kneaded a massive mound of dough on a stone slab in front of a thatch-roofed house. The Middle Ages, when people died from small cuts and persistent coughs.

"Do you know the word *castrato*?" Mr. Wu said. The bus had stopped for a break.

"Yes."

"There was a time when boys were castrated to retain their high voices, for singing."

She nodded. *I'm in the middle of China, talking about eunuchs.*

"There's a film from Beijing about eunuchs who attended princesses and empresses, do you know it?"

Fanny shook her head.

"They posed no threat to the women."

She bent and retied her boot laces. They were awaiting the driver again.

"I imagine," Mr. Wu said, leaning close to her. "I imagine us having a comic dialogue. I'm teaching you Chinese but all you remember are the swear words."

She laughed.

They reboarded the bus and the driver passed the keys to his assistant. The driver sat beside Fanny. She liked this driver. He had messy hair, thick fingers, long legs. His teeth were tea-stained and his eyelids slightly swollen, giving him a sultry aspect.

The bus stopped to let someone off and Mr. Wu herded Fanny outside to take photos. She saw his hands trembling and he was talking so fast she could hardly understand him. "I haven't paid any attention to my rhetoric," he said at one point. Then he chopped his hand through his hair, leaving it sticking up in all directions. "I will be working my long-term temporary job in the cage-like cabin. I don't know when I will be promoted." Wistfully, he continued, "You're learning how round the earth is on your global journey, at a real cost. I can only visualize it with the help of a map costing few dimes. I'm indebted to you. You are so frank and you have shared with me the down-to-earth English language."

Half an hour later, Mr. Wu and his colleague disembarked at the edge of a cramped town. Fanny stood at the bottom of the bus steps, shook his hand, and told him that she was very pleased to have met him. "Here," she said, handing him the last, fat novel that she hadn't yet read, *A House for Mr. Biswas*. "I think you'll like this book very much. It's sad but it's also funny." For the first time Mr. Wu was without words and for a long, excruciating moment Fanny thought he might cry. She turned quickly. Mr. Wu stood in the dust of the road, watching the bus move away. *The young men of China are sad*, Fanny thought, and she felt as if something was brushing past her, something she felt but did not understand.

She curled into her seat next to the driver and stared at the floor littered with eggshells, sunflower seed husks, tea leaves, letting her mind jostle through subjects. Giving away *Mr. Biswas* would mean she'd be rereading the books she had with her. She thought that Mr. Wu would keep the book for years and that it would sustain his imagination. Was she more interested in the world outside her self, or the world of her self? Something had occurred in her encounter with Mr. Wu and she had missed it. She'd had a life in Mr. Wu's mind. She was too old for him, and she had ignored the possibility that he might be attracted to her. Maybe meeting her made him sad to be alone. Was there any reason, any reason at all, for her to feel responsible for Bruno's death? Was he dead because of something she'd done or not done? She fell into a fitful sleep. Sometimes she forgot about Bruno, forgot to think of him as dead.

The driver touched her shoulder. He stood with her—he was as tall as she was and self-contained, like one of those dogs who appreciated its owner's affection but could live fine without it. Fanny regarded him with fondness. In fact, she liked nearly everyone on this bus and felt a spasm of regret at leaving them. The driver watched her hoist her bag, as if he were worried about what would happen to her once she left the safety of his bus and the haven of his careful driving.

The Sad Traveler on her Sad Trip in the middle of China. Against the washed-out blue sky she discerned a faint bulky image. It might have been masses of cloud, it might have been a mountain. The afternoon light was long, the air soft, the chance of rain lingered, like potential.

Chapter 16

On a steamy afternoon eighteen days out from Guangzhou, Yevgo, Daniel, Zhou, and Liu pulled into the town at the base of Emei Shan. Yevgo was planning to get a massage for his aching back. Zhou insisted that Liu get his ear looked after, its bandage now dirty and ragged, while Liu refused to discuss his injury or its care; he intended to go out drinking. He suggested that Zhou was ready to handle his freight solo, and he, Liu, once they arrived in Chengdu, would return to Guangzhou and his own life. This possibility alarmed Zhou but he had not yet formed a counterargument. Daniel made no claims for his time at Emei. His traveling companions assumed that he would climb the mountain, rustle up some Escaped Democracy Demonstrator action, and, above all and before anything else, find Fanny. They were taking several days of rest before resuming the journey west.

In Room 412 of the Number Two Guesthouse for Foreigners, Yevgo lay on his back on the hard mattress with his knees bent, wriggling his toes to loosen his tired feet, watching Daniel, who sat on the bed opposite, trying to both hide and count his yuan. Yevgo had surmised that Daniel had plenty of money and that he wasn't as economically desperate as he sometimes made himself out to be. Daniel liked to hold on to money; he didn't like to spend it. To Yevgo, money seemed as insubstantial and ephemeral as salvation or disappointment. Real was the flavor of lamb shanks cooked until the meat fell from the bone, or the feel of a woman's hip beneath his palm. Money was less than a game; it was a concept, inflated with air.

"You going for a walk?" Daniel said. Now that they'd arrived where he thought he'd meet up with Fanny, the imperative to find her had receded, sustaining what had begun to feel like a natural distance between his ardor and the object of his ardor.

Yevgo sighed. He took the matryoshka doll out of his pocket. Every day, male topics of conversation: business, money, girls, politics. He missed Fiera, even sometimes their marriage, which had been like a clash of dictators, but certainly Fiera herself. Her strong opinions, her complaints and generous laughter. Her talk of meals and clothes and beauty treatments; her appreciation for the details and disasters of other people's lives. He rubbed the doll's round wooden waist with his thumb. The women he'd tried out since Fiera—how flimsy they seemed. The thrill of unfamiliar flesh was not, in the end, compelling. He put the doll back in his pocket and rolled onto his side.

Daniel gave up his counting efforts. He picked up a packet of biscuits, extracted two, checked his watch. Should he go out now? Wait until Yevgo left? Go with Yevgo? He lounged back on the bed, offering the biscuits to Yevgo, who waved no.

"When I was in Bali I met an English woman—she talked like you," Yevgo said. "In one village, we stayed in a hut on stilts, which shook like crazy if you even rolled over in bed." Yevgo paused and stretched. "We got it moving pretty good and then I jumped around for some extra rocking and the next day the owner comes by and wants to know what I use, so much vigor at my age. I grab the first thing, which turns out to be herbal pills she brought for digestive problems. Umi balls, they're called. Little black balls. I'm not kidding. Next day, a young guy knocks, wanting some of the love pills. He's been trying to seduce a village girl for two years and the owner's walking around like he's been dipped in gold." Yevgo laughed. "I gave him a few pills and then I told him if he wanted a girl he had to brush his teeth and comb his hair. Personal hygiene. Her comb was handy, so I demonstrated what I was talking about. By the next day it was completely out of hand—the kid got his girl and I had a lineup of men at the door. The English woman found out the whole village was talking about me and my love pills. Ooh, she was pissed."

"She didn't want to be locally famous?" Daniel said, letting a Texan twang into his speech.

Yevgo flipped his hand as if it had gotten burnt. "Those villagers hadn't had sex like that in decades." He was pleased. "With little black balls meant to soothe digestion. It doesn't take much."

They were silent for a few minutes.

"You're off to find the fabulous Fanny." Yevgo gave him a measuring look. "No doubt."

"How'd you lose your fingertip?" Daniel indicated Yevgo's shortened finger.

"Run over by a motorcycle."

"Come. On. I'm not stupid."

"My dog ate it. No, I ate it."

Daniel shook his head.

"I've gotta piss."

"Every five minutes."

"It'll happen to you." Yevgo put his shoes on, stood. "Oh, my back!" A walk would be good. He touched his hand lightly to his chest and inhaled slowly. "A few years ago I went to the doctor and said, 'What the hell is going on, I can hardly work I spend so much time jumping in and out of the car to piss." They walked down the hall to the bathroom.

Daniel checked himself in the mirror and hummed "Everybody Knows This Is Nowhere."

At the hall counter, Yevgo handed the key to the floor clerk with a bow and a flourish. She covered her smile with her hand. "They ran some test," Yevgo continued. "When he called with the results, it was my prostate. I don't even know where the damn thing is. I went back to his office. He said I might want surgery and he put me in a room with a video and left. Son of a bitch. It showed someone sticking a knife up some guy's dick, digging out his prostate. I turned it off and wrote a note: *Before seeing this movie there was a slight chance I might have had this surgery but now? Never.* I stuck it on the television and walked out."

"Enough!" Daniel held up a hand.

Within ten minutes they reached the outskirts of town and found themselves on a dirt road that smelled of pigs. They paused at the entrance to a yard with racks of noodles hung like laundry. Three people worked two deafening machines: roll, cut, roll, cut. It was a noodle factory. The rich floury smell of dough filled the air. A man stepped out of one of the buildings and beckoned them into the courtyard. Yevgo followed him into a timbered house at the rear of the courtyard. Daniel hesitated, studying his surroundings. Carved wooden doors, folded back, opened the front wall of the house. Inside was a packed-earth floor and a poster of Mao tacked on a wall. A bent, wrinkled man sat drinking tea. The bulky shapes of beds draped with mosquito netting lurked in the corners of the cavernous space. There was a Ping-Pong table with tobacco leaves drying atop it. An old woman with a solitary front tooth brought sesame biscuits and tea. She pointed Yevgo and Daniel into a couple of bamboo chairs, then she squatted on a stool and yawned. Her feet were child-sized in flat black cotton shoes. Yevgo and Daniel sipped tea with the two old people. The noodle machine in the courtyard stopped. Silence ballooned. Swallows flew back and forth between the glaring light outside and the darkness within. The noodles flickered the sunlight into splintery shadows.

Yevgo relaxed, as if settling into a bath. China was an old country and the Chinese seemed to have no illusions about the promise of life. There was no pressure to speak as he had no shared language with his hosts. He held the teacup, occasionally bringing his lips to the rim, letting the steam bathe his face. He remembered the day he'd translated for an eye doctor performing surgery on his aunt at the medical college in Tashkent. The doctor, from Spain, had been invited to give a series of lectures and annotated procedures. Yevgo's father's sister had been visiting from Cuba. Yevgo was to translate for the medical students, who spoke Russian. In the barren lecture hall, seats rose in a half-moon of graduated rows, and one wall of windows opened onto a small garden with a few stunted pines and dusty bushes. The students were from Africa, Asia, Russia. His Aunt Carmela was voluptuous and bossy. She adored Tashkent's white snow, cold, dry air, and men. She said, "Russian men, they're like mastodons, powerful, very sexy." She loved their light skin covered in hair and wanted a Russian man of her own. Yevgo must've been around sixteen. Why was his aunt the patient? What had been wrong with her eye? Perhaps the regular translator had been sick and Yevgo's father couldn't get out of work. Yevgo had no memory of the circumstances, but the scene rested with perfect clarity in a small cave of memory: the petite doctor perched on a tall stool, his aunt rigid in a reclining chair, tipped slightly back, her eye propped open with tiny stretchers, the rapt rows of medical students. The doctor described each step of the process in a measured voice and Yevgo stood, translating from Spanish into Russian. He observed the doctor prep the eye, irrigating it with a solution. There were the doctor's clean fingers, ringless. There was the staring eye. There were details of procedure, anatomy, disease, to translate. All went smoothly until the moment the doctor inserted a thin drill into the eye. Yevgo fainted in a crash, tipping a stool, spilling a glass of water. The doctor leaned above him, a precise man, his face grave. Yevgo had fallen into a hot clammy dream that seemed to be unfolding in a deep pit. The doctor pinched Yevgo's cheek, drifted a vial of ammonia beneath his nostrils, and Yevgo lurched awake, his nose fiery, no memory of where he'd been in the dream or where he now found himself. The doctor drew up a chair, turned it toward the garden, and pushed Yevgo into it, calling for a glass of tea and making Yevgo translate the request. An assistant held a bandage over the half-started eye. Yevgo, sweating and nauseated, resumed translating, sentence by sentence, seeing and not-seeing the shriveled garden, his own eyes watering, his stomach sour. His aunt had not married a Russian. She'd returned to Cuba, contracted diabetes, and died of its complications, he couldn't remember when. So much was forgotten.

Thoughts circulated in Daniel's head. He could learn to play mahjongg, play for money, and win. He was good at games. He might take a run at learning Chinese again; he'd been lazy about it at Oxford. How could he get into a rice field? He wanted to be in the tourist part of town. Whatever he was expecting to find, this old house with its old people wasn't it. The tea was warm and bitter.

It's going to rain, Yevgo thought. He noticed a woman standing at the entrance to the courtyard like a figure in a painting, tall, graceful, her eyes—so large—gazing about with a leisurely curiosity. The quiet lengthened, as if there was a vacant, airy space between one moment and the next. He snapped out of his reverie; the woman was Fanny.

She would not be able to see them sitting inside the dark room. He stood. "Hey," he said, about to call her name.

Daniel grabbed his arm, pulled him back. "Shh."

Yevgo queried him with a look.

Daniel shook his head.

The two men stood silently. Fanny glanced at her watch, turned, and disappeared.

With a half hour before she had to be at the café, Fanny paced the backstreets, checking her watch. Following Wen Li's instructions, she'd left a message with the proprietor of the Teddy Bear the previous day. Now she was to be in the café by 1:30, and if Wen Li didn't show by 2:30, Fanny was to try the next day. No telephone calls, no confirmation. It was all rather espionage-like but she supposed Wen Li didn't have a telephone. At the café, she'd checked the message board near the entrance for a note from Daniel; nothing with her name on it and she had not left a note for him. She wasn't actually in the town of Emei Shan; she was in a smaller town called Baguo, at the base of the mountain. If Wen Li didn't show and there was no message from Daniel, should she climb the mountain by herself? Find a better hotel room? Bruno hadn't written in his journal where he'd stayed; she was without her ghostly guide.

The Teddy Bear Café was narrow, with seven carved wooden tables and carved square stools, fluorescent lighting, white formica floors, as if the Qing dynasty had mated with 1950. On the white walls, stuffed teddy bears, some rather worn, were hung, by their necks, or an arm, or a leg. It was either weird art or a twisted joke. Near the entrance, walking sticks were propped against the wall in a messy pile. At 1:30 the café was empty except for a French couple sitting with the owner who was explaining how to manage the monkeys on the mountain and making recommendations about monastery accommodations.

Fanny took a table near the entrance. "Banana pancake?" asked the waiter, a bored young man with a shaved head. Banana pancakes appeared on menus at every café catering to individual travelers; Fanny didn't like them. Tea, she said. Two people. A piece of communication she could conduct in Mandarin, which made her feel momentarily pleased. She eavesdropped on the French couple and owner while rifling her bag. She had Bruno's journal, but not Wen Li's letters. While waiting, she reread the entries that referred to Wen Li in the journal, marveling at their obscurity and brevity.

Under W: *bags of black & green wholesale tea, translation task. Best tea ever. Wen Li . . .*
Under E: *here I met WL, soft days, soft nights.*

That's all. Wen Li's letters implied that the entries were woefully inadequate to the experience. The remainder of Bruno's ashes were also in her bag. She recalled lunch with Daniel when she'd dropped the leaking baggie onto the linen tablecloth. Oh god. Worried that something might happen to them if she left them behind, she carried the ashes with her. What difference would it make if something happened to them? Who would steal a baggie of ashes? This was what she was thinking when she noticed a beautiful, petite woman standing beside her table. Fanny jumped up, they almost shook hands, almost hugged, did neither, sat down, and plunged into an awkward silence. Fanny tried not to stare, Wen Li tried not to stare, they didn't know where to look. Now that the real Wen Li was across from her, Fanny saw how wrong she had been to expect a plump, matronly woman, unhappy, with a sense of humor. This delicately lovely person, tiny and self-possessed, erased Fanny's preconceptions. She tried to manage her face, hoping not to reveal her surprise. "Thank you for coming. I'm so happy to meet you," Fanny said.

"Thank you thank you," Wen Li said, the words run together. Her voice was light and a little musical. "I apologize my English. Not good."

Fanny smiled. "Your English *is* good. I'm grateful because I speak very little Chinese." Her tone was too upbeat.

They nodded at each other. Silence settled down, not an easy silence. Fanny was trying to decide if they should talk about something else before discussing Bruno, and if so, what? The surprise of Wen Li's beauty made Fanny hesitant about asking personal questions. She was trying not to gape at the fine translucent skin and softly rounded face. Her shoulder-length hair was unpretentious and perfect. She was not conscious of her beauty or her effect on people. She wore no makeup, no clothes that enhanced her figure. Just the boxy, plain clothing common to Chinese women living in out-of-the-way places. Her appearance was simple and without an agenda. Of course Bruno would correspond with a beautiful woman. How could she ever have thought otherwise? Fanny blurted, "You have a child?"

Wen Li was staring at Fanny too, fixedly and carefully. "Yes. Girl, four years old."

"A lovely age." Fanny paused. "You live with your grandmother?"

"Yes. Grandmother have, excuse, *has*, eighty-five years. I take care of him and of my daughter. I work for a tea . . ." she paused. "Tea shop. And I have drawings."

"You're busy!"

Wen Li nodded. "I hear to you Fanny. You work in hospital."

Her pronunciation turned Fanny's name into *funny*. Call me Funny.

Wen Li smoothed her hand over the table as if Fanny had made it. "Very kind, I hear to."

"I have a good job." Simple sentences, Fanny told herself, keep it simple. "What kind of drawings?"

"Pen, and, how to say? Ash?"

"Charcoal?" Fanny said.

"Oh, very good." Wen Li nodded. "My grandfather was very talent calligraphy but now he is died."

At this, they both stared at the table, a somber quiet stretching between them. Fanny glanced up at the row of teddy bears hanging from the wall, mocking and amused, a speechless audience. She was aware of a gap: Bruno had spoken, or written, to Wen Li about Fanny but he had not spoken to Fanny about Wen Li. What Fanny knew about her was a result of her nosing through letters, reading Wen Li's sentences meant only for Bruno. Of course Wen Li couldn't know this. She would imagine Bruno had told Fanny about her.

The waiter brought the tea and Wen Li engaged him in a rapid exchange. Soon, food appeared: a small dish of stir-fried peanuts with chili peppers and another of pickled cucumbers.

"Eat, please." Wen Li smiled. "Bruno love it very much."

The first mention of his name broke the stiffness between them. "You very look like Bruno," Wen Li said, staring into Fanny's face as if she were trying to see behind her. Fanny had taken their resem-

blance for granted—a visual analogue to their invisible connection—
but it turned strange after Bruno's death. Seeing her either disturbed
or soothed Bruno's friends. Not only did they look alike, but their
voices, their gestures, their facial expressions were hauntingly similar. His friends wanted to be near her, or they wanted to stay away
from her. At his memorial service, strangers had stared at her. When
she smiled, talked with her hands, or laughed, the similarity could be
overwhelming. Even Fanny had occasionally been startled when, for
example, in a phone conversation, Bruno laughed and she felt as if she
were hearing a recording of her own laughter.

"How did you meet?" Fanny asked. "You and Bruno."

"At tea company I work," Wen Li said. Bruno had been lost, had
gotten off a minibus at the wrong place. Wen Li was in the shop by
herself and they'd had tea and talked for what turned into the rest of
the day. Bruno helped with her work, translating text for a brochure.
They'd traveled home together, first to his hostel, then to her house
where he'd met her grandmother and daughter. For two weeks they
saw as much of each other as possible. "I believe him, I don't know,"
Wen Li said. After two weeks, he'd traveled onward but had stayed
away only five days before returning to Emei. He began to make
friends in town and to learn Chinese.

Fanny listened without interrupting.

Then Bruno left, traveled to Chengdu, and Wen Li never saw him
again. He wrote weekly letters up until the month before his death.

When he left, Wen Li had been sad though not without hope for
his return. She was married, divorce was unlikely; she hadn't seen her
husband in over a year. She said no more about that. When Bruno's
letters stopped, she couldn't sleep or draw and had trouble working.
Then she received Fanny's letter and plunged into deep misery. Her
voice grew quieter and slowed. Wen Li didn't cry, she sat very still,
gazing at the dish of cucumbers. Many of Bruno's friends had been
devastated by his death, but Fanny was moved by the sorrow of this
stranger in a far-off country.

It took a long time for this tale to come out in Wen Li's bumpy
English. Fanny was grateful for the slow unfolding which gave her
time to absorb what was said. Neither of them ate the peanuts or
cucumbers; the tea grew cold. Wen Li regarded Fanny expectantly.

It was her turn: Fanny related how Bruno had died, telling a version without ambiguity or nuance. A simple, comprehensible story about a motorcycle accident. She didn't mention the helmet not worn, nor any of the minute details that cast, in Fanny's imagination, a shadow over the accident. Another silence followed. Wen Li put her bag on the table and pulled out an envelope carefully folded around a few photographs. "He send me," she said and handed them to Fanny.

Bruno with Wen Li's adorable daughter, with her adorable grandmother, then between them, the old woman under one of his arms, the little girl under his other, on a blue sofa surrounded by potted plants. A close-up of Bruno, gazing tenderly into the camera lens. Then Bruno and Wen Li—who had taken the photograph?—in a warm embrace. "Beautiful photographs," she whispered, returning them to Wen Li. "I'm glad you have them."

They sat without speaking for a few minutes, then pulled out money to pay. Fanny pushed Wen Li's money away, and Wen Li pushed Fanny's money away. Wen Li said, "Please, you come far. Far." Wen Li paid for the food and tea they had not consumed. Fanny thanked her and they rose. Fanny wanted to hug Wen Li but there was something formal about her, something that held off ordinary comfort. They grasped hands. Fanny considered another meeting, but for what? It was too painful, too difficult in language and loss for either of them, Fanny guessed, to really want to get together again. Fanny might easily have never known about Wen Li. Her discovery of the letters, the fact that she'd made this trip and they'd managed to meet, it all seemed random. Lucky or not, she couldn't tell.

Walking back through town Fanny thought, yes, coming to see Wen Li had provided answers. Except with Bruno, every answer provoked fresh questions. Why had he left Emei Shan abruptly? Why had he stopped writing to Wen Li a month before he died? She paused in the shade, breathing in cloying, moist air. There was Bruno's image: good-looking, charming, serene, together. And there were the facts: Buddhism abandoned, woman he seemed to have fallen in love with, abandoned. Then, dead. There was something she was missing. She was desperate to understand, but why? Why the drive to understand? Maybe it wasn't about Bruno. If not Bruno, what?

Chapter 17

The restaurant was crowded, which Yevgo hoped was a good sign. Chinese food tried his patience. No spice except garlic and chili, every dish in a pool of oil. The other day he'd sent Joe on an expedition to find lemons to cut the grease. Lemons were not to be found. No coffee, no lemons. No Coke, not that Yevgo cared about Coke but it told you something about a place when it was unavailable. Yevgo was hungry, had out his own fork and spoon. With his fingers, he drummed the table, which was covered in white plastic imitation lace. A simple meal, eggs and potatoes (what he wouldn't give for an omelet). He was sick of white rice. He couldn't stomach another dish with pork and greasy cabbage. Was cabbage the sole vegetable grown in China? It was a sturdy vegetable, but pale and gassy. Was there not an animal apart from the pig that would give its life for the Chinese table?

"You think all these people are here to climb the mountain?" Daniel asked.

Yevgo was trying to catch the waiter's attention. There was one waiter, moving about the crowded restaurant at a leisurely pace. Yevgo had lost weight since he'd been in China; his baggy pants were baggier. He felt thin inside, depleted. His appetite was unreliable and there were the twinges in his chest that *might* be—how was he to know?—something serious or merely heartburn. His burning heart. He should take his medication. For a start, he might find the pills.

Whenever he thought of the pills, like now, he was in no position to search for them and when he could look for the pills, he didn't think of it. "We'd like some tea," he shouted at the waiter.

"I guess I'll climb it tomorrow," Daniel said.

"What about Fanny?"

The waiter's eyes skipped over the foreigners. He bellowed into the kitchen that they had two capitalist running dogs on the premises. The other diners stood to gawk at Yevgo and Daniel. A few laughed. The waiter attended to a group that had just arrived.

"What is *wrong* with this country? I know this routine. The Soviets were the same. I *know*: nobody gives a shit. Throw your food down like it's slop and it *was* slop. Make you wait for everything—an hour for a pair of soggy blintzes, days for a fucking ten-part form." The waiter moved between tables. Yevgo slapped his hand on his knee.

"Take it easy, old man."

Yevgo glanced at Daniel. He was *not* an old man, goddammit. "It's been Emei Shan, Fanny, Fanny, Fanny and now we're here and you're acting like someone died. We've seen her! *Por qué* have we endured a thousand hours of Fanny?" Three waitresses joined the waiter, each serving diners who had arrived after Yevgo and Daniel. "That's it." Yevgo rose. His shirt was buttoned unevenly; his sunglasses, dangling from a strap, hung on his chest, a small load of crumbs trapped in the shelf of the lenses. He charged across the dining room, slammed through the double doors into the kitchen, and lifted his arms wide as if he were making a distress signal. "We're hungry and we want to eat," he shouted.

Kitchen activity halted. The waiter, a flat round nose and small mouth giving his face a pugnacious aspect, leaned against a counter.

Yevgo pointed at the waiter. "This how you treat guests in your country? Ignore them?" Yevgo strode to one of the cooks, who stood over a boiling wok. Yevgo waved his arm as if in blessing over the piles of cabbage, garlic, and meat on the counter and mimed stir-frying. He pointed at some potatoes. Then he stood back, crossed his arms over his chest, and fixed his gaze on the cook's face.

The hot kitchen grew still, the sound of the bubbling wok like a soft breeze. The waiter tapped the row of orders lined up on the wooden chopping block.

Yevgo swept them aside. "We are next."

The waiter told the cook he should prepare food for the foreign devil before there was trouble.

Someone remarked that *this* was trouble.

The waiter grasped Yevgo's arm.

Yevgo shook him off.

The waiter took his arm again.

"Don't touch me." Yevgo yanked free.

The waiter shrugged and returned to the dining room.

Yevgo leaned against a counter.

The cooks prepared two dishes, one of dried bits of stir-fried pork and another of julienned potatoes with chili sauce. The appearance of the prepared food didn't inspire optimism. Yevgo wanted eggs, but there apparently were none. He didn't believe this and was tempted to overturn the kitchen to discover where they were hidden. Hold on or let go? This was always the choice. He returned to the dining room behind a kitchen worker carrying the two dishes and a bowl of rice. Fanny was sitting with Daniel, three beers on the table. Yevgo leaned over and kissed Fanny's cheek, as if they were old friends. He sat and winked at Daniel. "You should have seen them in there." He tilted his head in the direction of the kitchen. "Poor slobs, they didn't know what to do with a hungry, pissed-off foreigner." In fact, his outburst had left him feeling chagrined. He sighed. Yevgo barely remembered Fanny's broad, clear forehead, the pattern of light freckles across the tops of her cheekbones, the dark circles beneath her eyes which made her appear haunted and weary, as if the world were too much for her. She possessed an attractive air of self-sufficiency. Her chopsticks came in their own carrying case. "I stayed until they'd cooked our food." Yevgo nodded at Fanny. "Eat, eat. Where'd the beers come from?"

"Fanny got them."

"From the waiter?"

"Waitress." Daniel grinned at Yevgo as if to say, See? It can be done without getting all worked up. "Fanny and I are discussing the assault on the mountain." Daniel tapped Fanny's wrist lightly with a chopstick but addressed Yevgo. "You coming?"

Yevgo made a face.

"A Swiss guy I met says you can hike it in a day, but it's better to stay overnight," Fanny said. "If you're thinking about it."

"I'm not thinking about it," Yevgo said.

Daniel tapped his chopsticks against a bowl. "I didn't realize there were hotels."

"One or two at the top, but all along the way there are monasteries which have dorm rooms. Some are nicer than others, I've heard." Fanny selected bits of food with her chopsticks. At the entrance to the restaurant when she'd spotted Daniel she thought, *of course*. Of course she would run into him in this effortless manner, of course they would not miss each other. It seemed not magical but inevitable. The world of travelers was filled with barely credible coincidences. Now here she was eating with two strangers who were, by default, also her friends. A particular category of connection: stranger-friends. She was conscious of a line of sweat on her upper lip and wished her braid was not full of dust and that she was cleaner. Daniel continued to be unaffected by the bad-food-poor-sleep-no-shower aspect of travel, which was irksome.

"You sure you don't want to come?" Daniel asked Yevgo.

"No mountain for me."

"It's supposed to increase longevity, write you in the book of life for the next year." Yevgo snorted a laugh. "You don't believe that." He felt defeated; the food was abysmal, greasy and salty. All that anger and effort for this?

"But I'd *like* to. If I were older I'd be open to influencing fate with a little magical walkabout." He smiled slyly at Yevgo.

"Here," Fanny held aloft her chopsticks. Daniel's chopstick skills were terrible, and watching him try to bring food to his mouth, most of it falling back into the bowl, was exasperating. "Hold the bottom one like so, and the top one like this. The bottom is fixed, the top moves."

"Nietzsche says that fate is the force of opposition against free will." He noticed her chopsticks raised. "What?"

"Come on, you'll be able to quote Nietzsche *and* use China's national utensil."

"There's no fate without free will, no free will without fate. Hiking the mountain is the perfect action, the intersection of free will and fate." Daniel nodded at Fanny, attempting to wield the chopsticks in the manner of her demonstration.

"Fuck Nietzsche," Yevgo said. "He died like everyone else."

Daniel flushed.

"Live more, think less," Yevgo said.

"Master the chopstick," Fanny said.

Fanny and Yevgo were laughing. After a stiff minute, Daniel said, "Read Nietzsche, understand yourself!" and joined in the laughter.

"You must've had a real education if you can quote Nietzsche," Fanny said.

"Yeah, well, I got *kicked out* of Oxford." Daniel sounded sheepish.

"For?" Fanny said.

"Opium." He shook his head. "It's not what you think. It came out of my getting rather obsessed with the opium wars."

"Mmm," Fanny said.

The other diners had finished and the restaurant emptied. Employees closed the pink curtains and locked the doors. Yevgo, Fanny, and Daniel were the only remaining diners. The staff sat down to a meal at an adjacent table. One of the waitresses began to harangue one of the men.

"I started an opium den, didn't I tell you this? I thought I had. All rather louche and recherché and massively successful, which was, alas, its downfall."

Yevgo rolled his eyes.

"You got caught and they booted you?"

"Technically, I dropped out before they dispatched a letter of expulsion."

At the staff table, the waitress broke into sobs, her ribcage heaving, her head bent so low her forehead almost touched the food.

"The thing about the opium wars," Daniel began, then stopped himself.

"How is it that you two are traveling together?" Fanny asked, distracted by the woman's distress.

"Joe's taxi," Yevgo said.

"The Tiananmen guy? The one who escaped arrest?" Fanny said. The sobbing went on and on.

Yevgo didn't answer.

"Joe's the translator," Daniel said. "Liu's the one you're thinking of." He was flipping a single chopstick between the fingers of one hand, tipping his chair back and drinking beer.

"Oh."

"Liu is with us, too." The chopstick flipped between Daniel's fingers. "Yevgo's going home."

"Still raising money for democracy in China?"

"Liu had a profound experience at the demonstrations."

A moment of silence followed. The woman at the workers' table wept.

Fanny turned to Yevgo. "Where's home?"

"Tashkent." Their voices had dropped; they were almost whispering. Finally they stopped talking altogether and the silence magnified the sounds of weeping. The waitress sobbed on and the man she'd been addressing pushed clear of the table, leaned back in his chair, and lit a cigarette. Smoke hung in the air. The setting sun cast a rosy glow through the pink curtains.

"What's going on?" Fanny whispered, fingering the plastic fake-lace tablecloth, her eyes on the workers.

"Love trouble," said Yevgo, also watching the workers.

Daniel started to hum a Stones song and broke into the lyrics.

Fanny tried not to smile. "You are going to get us in trouble." She turned to Yevgo. "Don't laugh."

Yevgo didn't feel like laughing.

"No way do they speak English," Daniel said and sang in a soft falsetto to "Play with Fire," "*If you sing to me, you'll be singed by fire.*"

"You know all the Stones and you always make up your own lyrics?"

"They've got a song for every occasion; I like to make up my own lyrics. Keeping it fresh." At last the sobbing ebbed and a tense quiet took its place. "What time should we meet in the morning?" Daniel said. They worked out a plan: at 5:30 in the morning they'd catch a bus to an entrance point. After climbing to the top, they'd descend partway to the monastery which Fanny had overheard the owner of the Teddy Bear recommend to the French couple. There, they would spend the night.

"Anyway, we shouldn't carry anything except money and an umbrella or rain parka. Especially don't bring anything that might appeal to monkeys."

"Monkeys?" Daniel said.

"They can be aggressive. Maybe *assertive* is a better word. If you don't have food, they leave you alone."

Daniel was bending one of his chopsticks into a half-moon.

"Look, it's only monkeys. Not grizzlies or mountain lions," Fanny said.

The waitress scraped back her chair, clattered across the dining room, and slammed through the blue double doors into the kitchen, sending them thumping back and forth, cutting the tension in the room. A couple of men spoke to the cigarette smoker, who maintained a studied indifference. Yevgo rinsed his utensils in a cup of tea.

Fanny pulled out money. Yevgo put up a hand to stop her. "Daniel's turn."

"Ahh," Fanny said.

The woman blasted into the dining room, meat cleaver in hand, lunging at the object of her ire and source of her tears. He jumped, knocking over a chair. She threw the cleaver, nicking the forearm of the man next to her intended target. The man howled, drops of blood dotted the white plastic tablecloth, and he tipped onto the table in a faint. The cleaver hit the floor with a clang. One of the men grabbed the shrieking woman and hauled her back into the kitchen. Someone wrapped a towel around the man's small wound and slapped his cheek; someone else poured him a drink. The cigarette smoker doused his cigarette in his tea with a soft hiss.

"Shit," Fanny said.

"*Did I ever love her, 'cause it's forgotten now,*" Daniel sang to "It's All Over Now."

In the kitchen, the woman wept. Then, as if a faucet had been shut off, the sobbing ceased. Once again, silence bloomed through the room. From the street, horns honked and a couple walked by talking in amiable tones.

"Now what?" Fanny whispered. They waited.

A crashing sound, followed by a knife hurtling through the window glass in one of the kitchen doors, spraying the floor with glass. Spinning across the room, the knife slid to a stop at Daniel's feet. Its wide long blade showed signs of having been often sharpened.

"We better get out of here before our fate is decided," Daniel said.

"Our fate *is* decided," Yevgo said.

"I mean our present fate, not our future fate."

One of the women rose to sweep the glass. In the kitchen, the crying resumed. Nobody spoke, only sounds filled the room: swish of broom, delicate tinkling of glass shards, and wracking sobs.

"The door's locked," Yevgo said.

Fanny pushed back her chair and approached the woman sweeping up the broken glass, spoke a few quiet words, gestured toward the door, and pulled money from her pocket. A minute later they were on the street.

"Another clean escape." Daniel moved a strand of Fanny's hair out of her face, tucking it behind her ear.

She froze.

"Sorry," he said. "You probably don't fancy someone pawing your hair."

She didn't say anything. Her hair wasn't clean enough to be touched.

Yevgo watched to see if Daniel would reimburse Fanny for the meal. He didn't.

Chapter 18

While waiting for Daniel at the bus stop in the gray dawn, Fanny flipped through Bruno's journal, rereading his entries about the mountain, which were detailed, ranging from a mini-geology lesson (where had he gotten his information?) to the political, to the lyrical-spiritual. Crammed under the letter *E*:

200 million yrs ago
marine sediments in limestone
on the sea bottom
& something happens, always
something happens
the sea bottom bucks & kicks limestone out of the water,
streaming in a lava sweat
or, limestone crumples & heaves & shreds
letting loose heavy basalt.
here's something else: mountains are made
deformation pushes earth up, erosion shapes
dough rising, punched down, separated, rolled, braided, loafed
& so: valleys, ravines, crags, hills, peaks.
E-shan is a limestone mtn with a cap of basalt,
a stony sharp thing under its padding of foliage.

He'd stayed near the mountain for weeks, not, she thought, because of the mountain, but he'd written more about this mountain than he had about Wen Li. His entries suggested that he'd been thinking about his connection to the earth and also about the expansiveness of time—in millions of years. In the margin of another page, in tiny print:

obstacles to overland travel,
a place for grand views
connecting man to an unreachable heaven
an emissary between the seen and the unseen
to climb into the blank slate of cloud
& pass through the eternity of white mist
assail the unassailable

And then, under *C*, she found this:

Communism: a course in bullying
where o where is the sacred on Emei Shan?
entrance fees, funicular, karaoke bars, merchandise
gold and red plastic trinkets & bobble-headed Buddhas
shrieking with laughter.
temples w/ dart games
monks glued to tvs
the CCP a block-headed monster crushing 2000 yrs of culture
in a matter of decades
oh what fine work do those zealous soldiers of socialism
in the shadows buddhism plays dead
waiting for the big red boots to quit their stomping
Where is hidden China's sacred soul?

Daniel materialized out of the mist, thin walking stick in hand. "Monkey protection." He brandished the stick.

"Hey." Fanny shut the journal, shoved it into her pack. No mention of monkeys in Bruno's journal.

"A chap at the hotel gave it to me, said it was just the thing." He'd bought it, after querying everyone. "Did we miss the bus? Am I late?"

He was late, but at six in the morning there was no one on the bus and no one on the path except Fanny and Daniel. They paid an inflated-for-foreigners trail entrance fee to a sleepy attendant in a kiosk and walked through dense patches of bamboo bent over their heads as if to keep an eye on them. The only sound was trickling water from a creek. For a time the stone path, slicing through a narrow valley, was mostly flat. At a wooden bridge, a pack of monkeys blinked sleepily and picked at their fur. As soon as Fanny and Daniel set foot on the bridge, every set of monkey eyes focused on them. Fanny strode forward. "Hold your palms out. That way they know you don't have anything," she said.

Daniel was close on Fanny's heels, trying to keep an eye on the monkeys without letting them notice. Animals could smell fear. *What*, Daniel wondered, *did fear smell like? Relax*, he told himself; the monkeys were nothing to get worked up over. He was climbing a mountain in China with an attractive woman of substance. In front of him, tall and sturdy, Fanny's body was like a farm implement, an asset to arable land, something to be relied upon. He talked. About Joe and Liu, about what it was like to travel in a taxi. He talked as if Joe and Liu were his close friends, and Yevgo the perfect sidekick. To him, the journey sounded impressive. All true. More or less.

Fanny half-listened. It was too early for conversation and she wasn't fond of talking while hiking. But she liked Daniel's voice and found herself imitating him. *Democracy*, she whispered to herself in an English accent. *Chap. Splendid old chap.* The path turned steep, a staircase twisting up, the stone steps worn smooth by thousands of footfalls, slippery with the mist that dropped and lifted. One minute it was hot and humid and sunny with blue skies and little puffs of white steam rising like breath. The next minute it was gray; scarves of mist laced through the foliage, wrapping Fanny and Daniel in a cloak of white.

"Did you meet your brother's friend?" Daniel said.

She let five, then ten steps pass before she said, "Yes."

"And?"

If she were going to give a report, she'd say that Wen Li was not Bruno's type, though what did Fanny know anymore? His former girlfriends had tended to be tall—like he was—and tomboys. But girlfriends were among the many things he'd stopped sharing with

Fanny. Wen Li was both more delicate and more steely than the girl-friends Fanny had met.

"It's true, for a communist country, it's remarkably easy to make money here," Daniel was saying. He didn't wait for answers. "I can't *believe* how eager people are to do business. Or, rather, I guess I can believe it. If you go back to the 1800s, when China was supplying England with twenty to thirty *million* pounds of tea per year . . ."

She could imagine what had attracted Bruno to Wen Li, notwith-standing her beauty. It had to do with the trouble she'd lived through and the way she had no expectation of getting what she wanted, of de-serving more than what she had. He would have admired her matter-of-fact resilience; suffering taken for granted, an approach to life that seemed to issue from another era when people suited themselves to the world they lived in rather than trying to arrange the world to suit them. In Wen Li's letters to Bruno, there'd been no mention of divorce; why discuss something that was never going to happen?

". . . before the opium wars." The trees dripped, the air smelled of wet plants and soaked earth. Daniel talked: opium, tea, prices, gaso-line, rice, oranges. "Capitalism is natural. It's the best fit to human nature. This is what we like: we like to buy and we like to sell," Daniel said. "Even communists like to buy and sell."

Fanny had sensed that something of import took place on Bru-no's trip to Asia though she hadn't asked. When had putting direct questions to Bruno begun to seem invasive? Years ago, and gradu-ally. At first, he'd deftly sidestep instead of answering her questions and Fanny accommodated, editing herself, staying within the range of what he was willing to talk about until she knew little of what was really going on with him. Thinking this—an awareness she'd hidden from herself—made her restless and sad. She wanted to go back, talk to him, ask him the questions she'd held back. They were each other's only family. She kept telling herself that she wasn't looking for an-swers about Bruno, but what was this trip—meeting Wen Li, follow-ing in Bruno's path—if not a search for answers? Who was she kid-ding except herself? Wrong about Bruno, wrong about herself. The question that she should be asking, the one she had a chance of find-ing an answer to: how had she fooled herself into thinking that she knew her brother, that they were very close and vital to one another?

Hiking uphill and crying didn't mix well; her breath felt trapped in her throat. She stopped, turned to face Daniel, who, when she focused in on his talk, was delivering another Chinese history lesson.

"Emperor Qin Shi Huangdi—the chap who built the Terracotta Army and the Great Wall—well, he didn't build them of course, he made hundreds of thousands of blokes like these," Daniel gestured to a group of porters on the trail, "do all the work. While he was having that wall built, he was creating China, the *idea* of China as a united country. He was the one who set a style for ruling China. He used peasant labor for his projects to the detriment of everything else. Land was left untended and famines were rampant during his reign." Daniel began to enliven his story, happy to be talking to Fanny's face instead of to the knapsack hanging from her back.

Here was Fanny's love interest blessedly distracting her. Or, maybe he was a lust interest, or merely an interest. Could she have a crush like a normal person without worrying that if she cared about a person she had to find a way to feel indifferent to the loss of that person? "Go on, tell me everything." She poked him lightly. She felt so grateful for his nonstop talking that she almost laughed.

"His projects," Daniel continued, "didn't, of course, benefit the people who were building them. He had a prime minister, called Li Shi, who helped to create a totalitarian state where they eventually tried to control the thoughts of the population—by burning entire libraries. Sound familiar?" Daniel was nodding. "I *know*. Hundreds of years later, like an echo, the Cultural Revolution."

The climb grew steeper. Fanny's thoughts drifted to Mr. Wu saying, *we cannot live without love*. Was love always a gift and an affliction? A gift that might undo you, an affliction from which you might never recover. Any kind of love, not only romantic love. Brotherly love.

Daniel discerned that he was failing to hold Fanny's full attention. What next? He hadn't earned his nickname—The Radio—for nothing. He liked a conversational challenge. A woman to flirt with, to charm, to seduce. Nothing better. He could always sing. They detoured through temples: old wooden buildings, chipped Buddhas, monks in dirty robes, monkeys stalking the rooflines. "All the pilgrims are women. Old women," Daniel whispered. "Are the men working? Are they nonbelievers?" The old women wore worn Mao jackets and thin-soled sneakers. They knelt on round cushions, held bundles of incense to their foreheads, and prayed. "Or, are they dead?" Once the old women were off the cushions, their laughter and conversation was lively and boisterous. "It's not all reverence. I mean, socializing seems key."

"I know," Fanny agreed. In spite of having read about the sad state of Buddhism on the mountain in Bruno's journals, Fanny was taken aback by the air of neglect, perfume of apathy, atmosphere of triviality. The monks! They slouched on stools, staring blankly into space, radios blaring nearby. It seemed as if they had jobs they didn't like but couldn't quit, jobs with costumes. They eyed Fanny and Daniel with envy and longing, as if the foreigners might prove to be a means of escape from the dripping trees and gray mist, from the devout women and the pacing monkeys. Fanny stood at the entrance to one of the courtyards, monks in a corner watching television. She felt hollow and agitated. *What am I doing here*, she thought in a kind of panic, feeling abruptly that she'd traveled a great distance under false pretenses. *Take a trip, Fanny*, indeed.

Rain started to fall. They paused under a sheltered platform to regroup. Fanny stared out into the density of wet greenery. It had taken her far too long to understand an obvious, simple fact: she and Bruno were not close. They'd been drifting apart for years and she'd failed to recognize it. To live without the idea—the fantasy—that they were close, a family of two, each other's distant but necessary counterpart—how was she going to manage that? If only she hadn't taken this trip, she could have maintained the illusion of their closeness indefinitely. She'd always thought she was a maniac for the truth but it seemed she'd been avoiding the truth for years. Fanny extracted an umbrella from her pack.

Daniel donned a flimsy poncho, a billowing yellow plastic cape with a hood, something a child would wear. "It was the only thing I could find," he said. "I look ridiculous."

"Yellow is your color," she said.

"You think?" Daniel struck a pose and sang to "Waiting on a Friend," "*I'm just waiting for a windfall . . .*" He paused. "You're so together. You're fit and competent and smart and funny."

"If we're insulting each other: you're freshly washed, unstained, and unwrinkled." She was a roiling, desperate, sad mess inside and not that sparkling outside. "Even your fingernails are clean. How do you do it?"

"It's nothing." He flapped a hand. "Truly nothing."

They met a group of porters hiking down the mountain with heavy loads tied onto their backs, negotiating the slick steps in rope sandals or bare feet. One of the porters, his face half-obscured by a shabby hat, hissed and imitated a monkey, then burst into raucous laughter. Soon Fanny and Daniel came to a sign that read: *Monkeys Ahead. Be Aware*. Sure enough, around a corner a cluster of large male monkeys perched close to the path. Fanny was remembering what the man from Switzerland had told her: the monkeys don't bother Chinese people, only foreign tourists. That's what a Chinese man had told him. She watched the eyes of the monkeys, held her palms open, and walked up the path.

Behind her, Daniel cried out. Spinning around, Fanny saw a large monkey straddling his shoulders. The creature pushed off the hood of Daniel's poncho and grabbed curls of his hair. A second monkey pulled at his backpack from the bottom. He flailed his arms, trying to keep his balance and shake the monkeys loose.

Fanny closed her umbrella and ran back. She aimed at the face of the monkey on his shoulders and pulled the triggered snap to open the umbrella. Startled by the unfurling umbrella, the creature leapt to the ground. Fanny repeated the action for the second monkey. It also retreated. "Quick, quick. Use the stick," she said.

Chaotically Daniel waved the stick in the faces of the monkeys. Their hissing made him sick to his stomach. Things had just started to move in his favor. Why did he want to impress Fanny? Only, he did, he did. He thought of Yevgo, getting a massage.

Lunch was bowls of noodles from a trailside food stall. Fanny's lower back was tight, water had started to seep through her boots to her socks. She put her face close to the bowl to feel the steam. When they finished poking their chopsticks through the noodles, neither of them eating much, Daniel rose and said he'd be back. Becalmed in this dank hut, on a wooden bench in the gloom, a deep sadness came into her. Rain splashed onto the stone path. After awhile, she wondered if Daniel was escaping without paying. When he reappeared, he said, "Good thing lunch was cheap, since it was inedible."

They resumed the climb, through a couple of turns in the path, and quickly encountered another pack of monkeys crowding the trail. Daniel put his arm out, halting Fanny. "Wait." He leaned close and whispered, "Let's sing." She felt his warm breath against her ear. "What?" she whispered back, watching the monkeys creep closer out of the corner of her eye. He started to hum the first few bars of "As Tears Go By," then sang, "*We stalk the earth as monkeys fly . . .*" Fanny joined in. Daniel took her in his arms and, in a smooth set of waltzing moves, twirled her through the monkeys, singing. Their voices rose into the mist; Fanny's voice cracked. The monkeys sat on their haunches, their eyes following them. When they were in the clear, Fanny said, "That was brilliant. They were *mesmerized.*"

"Entranced. Chinese monkeys love Mick and Keith!" He pulled a couple of butterscotch candies from his pocket and offered her one. "Want one?"

She took a candy, paused, and gazed at it. "Wait. You've had *candies* in your pocket?"

"Hmmm. I guess." He unwrapped one and popped it in his mouth.

"Maybe that's what the monkeys were after."

"Can't be. So small, only two, and wrapped."

"No doubt." Fanny nodded, restraining herself from saying more. "Anyway, here." She gave the butterscotch back to him. "I don't like butterscotch."

They continued higher, the rain grew heavier, their feet were wet, their pants were soaked to the knee. The path was deserted, pilgrims escaping the rain and the slick stairs to hunker down in temples and nap, knit, or chat in dorm rooms. Soon, even the monkeys abandoned the trail.

"We aren't going to be able see anything when we get to the top," Fanny said. There was something in the thwarting of intention, by weather and circumstance, that suited her mood. They turned back to find the monastery where they intended to spend the night. Shortly they encountered the only other hikers on the path, a pair of men striding swiftly through the rain. Daniel quizzed the men. "Are you going to the top?"

"Of course."

"You won't be able to see anything."

The men shrugged. "Rain is nothing."

"Where are you from?"

"Austria." They shifted from one foot to another like racehorses behind a gate.

"Did you meet the monkeys?" Daniel asked. "Giant monkeys. Very aggressive."

"Monkeys are no problem," one said. "Just small creatures," the other said.

Daniel and Fanny moved aside and the men sprinted off.

"Bloody hell," Daniel muttered. He and Fanny burst out laughing. "You should join us in the car. We'll give you a lift to Chengdu. Farther even, if you'd like."

"Okay," Fanny said. It was what she wanted. Companionship. She wanted to travel with Daniel. She wanted to get to know Joe and Liu, and she liked what she'd seen of Yevgo. Maybe she would actually make it to Tibet and then home at the end of October in time for her friend Cora's daughter's wedding. They turned off the main path and reached the monastery, pausing at the gates. "Maybe the others won't like the idea of an additional person," she said. She pictured Yevgo, his shirt askew, his appetite, his intelligent, humorous face, the missing tip of his finger.

"The others are no problem," he said, doing a good imitation of the Austrians.

Checking in at the monastery, Daniel said, yes, we're together. Fanny admired the dark wood of the counter. Monasteries were places of spiritual practice, they were hotels and restaurants, they were tourist spectacles. Such a complicated combination of purposes.

The monk assigned them a room with three beds, the third bed unoccupied. Fanny felt suddenly self-conscious. It was one thing to hike up a mountain with a strange man, or sneak him into a hotel room for a couple of hours, but it was something else to check into a room with said strange man, as a couple. She liked to manage the degree of closeness—come here, now go away. She took her umbrella and toilet kit and pretended she was going out to wash. Keep it simple: traverse the fields of fate, stumble on happiness, and she might yet extract comfort from this trip. Mistakes and suffering were part of the package. You left home, you tore the fabric of your life. Through the holes you surveyed the world.

Her things tucked under her arm, she set out to explore the overgrown patches of garden and the old buildings where monks strode about. This monastery had a completely different atmosphere from the others on the mountain. Here, the monks wore clean robes, were energetic and serious. In a courtyard near the back reaches of the monastery, she came upon a monk sweeping a portico, bent over a soft, short-handled broom. The broom's susurrus, the monk's dreamy rhythmic movement, filled her with a shadowy pleasant feeling, the distant echo of a sound you once loved.

She knew what produced that softening sensation. Since around the time she was a teenager, Fanny had drawn on a particular image to calm herself: a robed monk sweeping a rice-grass broom as he walked, to avoid stepping on and killing insects. The robes were sometimes purple, sometimes orange or gray, always an elaborate voluminous wrapping. A year or so before their parents died, Bruno had read a book about Jainism with such a monk in it. He told Fanny that here was the thing for him. With such a careful, reverent regard for all living creatures was how he wanted to live. The way to liberation of the soul was a life of harmlessness and renunciation. Bruno habitually relocated spiders, wasps, ants, careful not to kill. He was already a vegetarian. From Jainism, his interest slid into Buddhism. The figure of the monk fixed in Fanny's imagination, and over time, the monk became Bruno. The shape of his back bent over, the length of his arm sweeping. She never saw the face of the imagined monk; she could only follow behind his sweeping figure, able to move blithely through the world thanks to his careful sweeping.

The rain stopped and a purple dusk filtered through the trees. Fanny and Daniel ate four-season beans, old lady tofu, spinach with garlic, and rice under a portico along one side of the courtyard, the only diners as night fell. The food was good. Sipping small cups of jasmine tea, unable to see each other's faces, they lingered in the dark.

"A Riesling or a Sauvignon Blanc," Daniel said, "would go well with this meal. Something precise, but not floral. More," he paused, "autumnal and arctic." Daniel had begun his life in wine, as he referred to it, working in a high-end restaurant as an assistant to the sommelier. Eventually he'd done an official training course and presently, or before he left to travel, worked in a Notting Hill wine shop. He'd grown up in Oxford, his parents were divorced. His mother was a math teacher, his father a lawyer. Fanny listened, waiting for that piece of information that would unlock his secrets, let her glimpse his inner workings.

"You're not like a Singing Sommelier or anything like that?" The darkness made it seem as if they were the only people on the mountain.

"Shit, no."

"You're such a good singer, I can't believe you aren't trying to make something of it."

"Not good enough. Anyway, I only sing Neil Young and the Stones. You should hear me try an aria."

"Bad?"

"A*bys*mal. Tell me about *your* work."

"Oh no, don't ask. I'm sorry I brought up the subject. I don't have real work, only a job. I'm always thinking about doing something else."

"Such as?"

"I took a woodworking class in the spring."

"Woodworking?"

"I'd like to make stools, chairs, shelves. No drawers; I don't believe in drawers."

"Who could object to the innocent, useful drawer? The perfect place to hide things."

"Yeah, in Japan I liked *tansu* and they have drawers." Temple bells clanged through the trees, briefly drowning the constant scraping of cicadas. The moon was up, casting shadows of the rooflines onto the courtyard. Musingly, Fanny said, "I can't figure you out—Chinese history at Oxford, sommelier, rock 'n' roll singer . . . What aren't you good at?"

"Chopsticks?" Daniel held them like a cross.

"Pretty bad." Fanny laughed. "Do you regret dropping out of Oxford?"

"You mean, did it change my life for the worse? I don't know. I don't mind upheaval, you know what I mean? It has a certain je ne sais quoi."

"You and French." Fanny rolled her eyes. After a minute she said, "Inoculated by chaos. I do know what you mean."

"In the aftermath, you think you'll survive anything."

The waiter appeared holding aloft a short fat candle. With him was the cook swaddled in a filthy apron, carrying a plate on which rested a small flower-shaped yellow cake. They broke into a song that sounded like it might be "Happy Birthday," in Sichuanese. Fanny was amused and then startled when they set the cake in front of her. She kept a frozen smile. They finished singing, put the candle before her, and stood back, expectantly.

"What's going on?"

"Make a wish," Daniel said.

She looked dubious.

"Blow out the candle."

She hesitated, inhaled, blew.

The cook and waiter bobbed with pleasure. Daniel leaned over and kissed her on each cheek.

"It's not my birthday."

"Cut the cake," Daniel said.

"You told them it was my birthday."

He shrugged.

Using a chopstick, she split the spongy cake in half, thanked the waiter and the cook who, somewhat reluctantly, retreated. The cake was tasteless and rubbery and they laughed at how awful it was. "What did you wish for?" Daniel asked.

"None of your business."

The black night was warm, streaks of filmy clouds laced among the stars. *There goes a day*, Fanny thought, *sliding from the clamp of memory*.

Daniel paid for dinner, saying, "Do you reckon this makes us even?"

She couldn't think in terms of what was owed.

The night was still, the mattress thin and the sheets damp. They were on Daniel's bed, making out. Daniel raised Fanny's shirt. She whispered, "We're in a monastery." The sounds of boisterous Chinese voices filtered through the walls. Doors slammed, laughter followed. People were having a good time. It didn't seem like a monastery yet it didn't seem right to have sex here.

Daniel's hands were on her bare waist. "Sacred sex." He wasn't whispering. He stroked her ribs.

She stilled his hands. "This place is a noise sieve. Everyone can hear."

"Fine." He ran a finger along her collarbone. "We'll be quiet."

Images from the day clicked through her mind: puffs of incense mixing with puffs of mist, the slap of rain on large leaves, Daniel in his yellow poncho, singing in the rain. She had understood something about herself, what was it? The waiter and cook with the cake and candle. It moved her to think that someone would pretend it was her birthday and create a tiny celebration in the middle of China. She hadn't made a wish—not even for a child—before she blew out the candle. To make a wish, even under such a silly circumstance, one has to feel hopeful. Instead, her mind had emptied in one sweeping flush. She became aware that they weren't going to have sex after all.

Daniel stood up and pulled on shorts and a T-shirt.

"Thank you," she said. He'd changed his mind.

"It sounds like the room is full of pilgrims."

"I know," Fanny agreed. "Maybe it's Buddhist juju. No sex in the Monastery of Ten Thousand Years." She moved to her own bed. "We have Chengdu," she said, cheerfully. "And beyond." She cringed internally at that plural pronoun. They were not a *we*, she and Daniel.

As soon as she stopped thinking about Daniel, the question the day had produced entered her mind: how was she going to live without her fantasy that she and Bruno had been close, vital family to each other?

Daniel felt sick with dismay. He'd spent the day working to get her attention and he'd won it and she was willing to have sex with him even though she didn't want to—she hadn't said that, but he guessed—and now, he couldn't follow through and there was no faking that. This had happened to him three times before. Today made four. Once, during the opium days, once with Vivian when things were very bad between them, recently with a whore in the Philippines whom he hadn't wanted to get into bed with in the first place.

Each offered an explanation: opium, relationship trouble, not wanting sex . . . but here and now? *Why?* His mind veered and flipped and rolled to avoid the word *impotence*. He couldn't forget the feeling of monkey fingers in his hair, touching his scalp. What if the beast had given him fleas, or lice? He ran his fingers through his hair, scratched the back of his neck. Was it Fanny? Maybe she wasn't the right person for him after all. He thought of Yevgo's "love" pills. He could find them in Yevgo's pack, try them. Maybe they were the pills in the bottle he'd taken a week or so ago and not bothered to look at, in which case they were in the bag he'd left in town. No, they weren't love pills, they were for digestion, and they weren't Yevgo's either, they'd belonged to the girl he'd been with at the time. Maybe it was something about Fanny. *I'm not in love*, he thought.

Chapter 19

Do you think she's sexy? Liu asked.

Zhou couldn't tell. What do you mean by sexy? he said. He didn't want to think of her that way. It seemed rude. To him, it was obvious that she did not invite that kind of thinking.

Okay, beautiful, Liu tried. Did Zhou think she was beautiful?

Zhou glanced at Fanny in the rearview mirror. Maybe. She was tall. She had large eyes. She had pale skin. Her pieces, when you set them out one by one, ought to add up to beautiful but Zhou wasn't certain. What did Liu think? Zhou jerked the steering wheel, downshifted, and pulled out to pass a donkey cart loaded with saplings. He accelerated and shifted higher, then turned quickly back into the line of traffic.

First, Liu thought that Zhou was indecisive to his own detriment. Didn't Zhou know his own taste? Second, Liu thought she was beautiful. He thought she was sexy. He thought she would be well worth the effort. *Dream of the Red Chamber* with a *waiguoren* twist. International sex. Liu smiled, made a soft kissing sound with his lips.

Zhou said there was one thing Liu wasn't considering.

What?

Her own people. Daniel and Yevgo. She'd go for one of them first.

That was where Zhou was foolish, Liu said. She was traveling alone in China; she must, therefore, be interested in something different.

Liu knew about women, he had experience. He tapped his forefinger on his nose. He was married, plus he'd had girlfriends, a lot of girlfriends. Why would she come all the way to China if not to try out its men?

Women weren't just after sex, Zhou said, trailing a little too close to a truck in front of him. He jabbed the brake. They might want to get to know this woman, learn something.

Everything you needed to know about American women was in the movies. American women had sex with men right away. Sometimes they got divorced, sometimes they never even got married. Was she married? If she had a husband she wouldn't be traveling alone. The most interesting fact about her was that she was alone far from her home.

How had she become so brave, Zhou wondered to himself. He couldn't manage this trip alone, without Liu. A thought came to him. *Hey, where had Liu seen American movies?*

Fanny was the only one to get mail.

She and Daniel ran into Yevgo at the entrance to the Chengdu main post office. They stood in line together: nothing for Yevgeny Velasquez or Daniel Lowe. "Motherfuckers," Yevgo said.

Daniel wondered who he expected to hear from. Vivian? He was not that delusional. His mother? Never his father. Simon, then. Apparently, no one had thought to write him.

Yevgo squeezed Fanny's arm. "Somebody loves *you*," he said. He and Daniel tried not to hover over the single thick envelope she held.

Fanny didn't want to open the heavy embossed envelope, her name and address in calligraphy, but the boys were standing expectantly. She struggled with the seal until Yevgo took it from her and slit it open with a penknife. Daniel picked up the pink squares of rice paper that fluttered onto the cement steps. Charmaine Tarkanian's wedding invitation. *Please join us to celebrate . . . Saturday, the twenty-first of October, nineteen hundred and eighty-nine, at one o'clock in the afternoon at the home of . . .* Charmaine's mother, Fanny's friend Cora, had jotted a note on the bottom: *Fanny, I miss you! The arrangements are driving me mad! Come home soon! We can't wait to see you! Soon!* Cora herself was an exclamation point. In metallic gold ink and elegant cursive.

"Someone sent you a *wedding* invitation, poste restante, to China?" Yevgo laughed.

"She's got a wacky sense of humor." It was the middle of September. Before she'd left Santa Fe, the wedding had seemed a real reason to return but from the middle of China, the view had changed. Her life in Santa Fe was like the theory of a life. She tossed the invitation with its many bits and squares of paper into a trash bin.

"You're throwing it away?" Daniel said. He fished the envelope and its contents out of the trash bin. Even unwanted mail, even somebody else's mail, seemed valuable.

The invitation agitated Fanny. She'd started to consider crossing Tibet into Nepal, traveling into India afterward. Or she'd cross China into Pakistan. She could fly home from Kathmandu, Delhi, or Islamabad. The trip had its own momentum and what was at home to draw her back? Fanny considered Daniel and Yevgo: *my pals.* A couple of guys she didn't know: one with a missing fingertip who cared about food, the other . . .

Fanny had just finished blowing her nose and was refolding her blue-checked handkerchief when Daniel kissed her. She was thinking of the muffled, thick feeling in her head as if her brains were sunk in plush carpeting, of the cold she was coming down with. They were standing on the third-floor landing of the Black Coffee Hotel, the squat, gold spittoon, with its aroma of soggy cigarette butts, their only witness. The lower half of the walls was painted the familiar unattractive green which she saw everywhere in China and the top half was a muddy white. For once it was fortuitous that the floor clerk was not where she was supposed to be. Early afternoon in China: naptime. In a blurry corner of her mind Fanny found herself once again thinking about a child. No need to mention it; Daniel could accidentally participate. She was probably too old, her parents dead, her brother dead. Best to act without thinking.

Daniel took her elbow and led her into his dorm room with its fifteen beds. He was explaining how he managed access to his room without the floor clerks: he chatted them up and then persuaded them to close the door without the latch catching. "I could pick those locks, if I had to," he said. He'd taught himself to pick simple locks when he was a teenager. Daniel sat Fanny down on his bed with a crisp manner, as if they were going to have a chat about her recent job performance. She pointed to the other beds.

"Yevgo, Hong Kong Chinese, German, German." He identified each bed's occupant and moved closer to her on the mattress, the length of his thigh warm against the length of hers.

How well they knew each other was up for debate, but for a time their bodies acted like old friends. Kissing as if they'd been apart for weeks. Soon they were cooperatively out of their clothing. Fanny's mind happily retreated and she sank into the feel of skin until things inexplicably came to a pause. Daniel scooted to the edge of the bed and they lay side by side, two naked strangers in a strange city. They had not quite worked up a sweat.

From the street rose sounds of bicycle bells and buses, the frothy tones of Sichuan dialect. The boom and wail of life in China made the big, square windows vibrate. How rare were these moments of undisturbed peace in China. The rows of empty beds, the ceiling high above, filled Fanny with an emotion she couldn't define. As if she were a stranger to herself. Reluctantly, she considered the man next to her, the full awkwardness of the present. In such situations, who was meant to make the first move, the first comment? They lay on their backs on the narrow bed, each of them flush on their respective borders, arms in close. Fanny was aware of his legs, the dark hair on his arms, his broad chest. Her neck cramped. There were other more important things to fret over than unconsummated sex; it was a fluke, temporary. There would be another chance. Suddenly conscious of how little she knew Daniel, she could not speak, afraid of saying the wrong thing. *No big deal*, but it might be a big deal to him. *It's okay* sounded patronizing. *It doesn't matter* could be construed as a lack of investment in what had seemed to be a deepening intimacy. *How about those crazy communists?* Nope. What *was* there to say? There were, of course, other options. *Do something*, she thought. Anything would be better than nothing. Hey, what was a little impotence? Not fraud, embezzlement, rape, or murder. Never mind her daydreams of sex with Daniel, never mind her laughable, insane fantasy of a child (did she really imagine she'd get pregnant by accident at age forty-three?). She reached for his hand. Not looking, reaching in the direction where she imagined his hand would be, she lay her hand on his thigh. She withdrew as if she'd burnt her fingers.

Daniel swung off the bed and began to dress.

Fanny began to dress, too. She didn't want to be caught naked in the men's dorm by one of the dreaded floor clerks. She paused to gaze at her bare feet on the cool linoleum floor. Had other women had their feet on this floor in the men's dorm? Some subterranean emotion in the room: a plague of uneasiness.

Daniel was tucking in his shirt with quick jabs, buckling his belt.

Fanny laced her boots. He hadn't found her attractive enough to follow through. Once their clothes were off he'd changed his mind. The body does not lie, an ex-boyfriend had once said to Fanny. She was beginning to believe that anything and anybody might lie, that the truth was never pure.

"I've got to meet Joe. Best that we leave the room separately in any case." He smiled, a professional smile, the kind you would give to someone you don't want to know better.

Fanny watched him leave, his manner of clipped efficiency. She was alone in the middle of China; she could go where she wanted. She felt a simultaneous impulse to jump up and down for joy and hide under the covers and mope. Did she never have unmixed feelings? She studied the line where the two colors of paint met on the wall. Ever since she was a child, she could gaze at such distinctions with intense absorption, saying to herself: a blank wall, but this part is green and that part is white; two parts, one surface, and there is the line that makes of one surface, two parts. There must be some significance to these ordinary things, that became, in her mind, inexplicable, full of mystery. If she could make the parts seamless, she would understand something larger.

Later that afternoon, Daniel arranged a performance of Escaped Democracy Demonstrator in a strip of park along the Fu River. The audience was composed of three Israeli young women, freshly released from army service, giddy and boisterous. They wore long bright skirts and their hair was clumps of straggly dreadlocks. They laughed at everything Daniel said. He was animated, flirtatious, teasing. In the back of his mind he couldn't stop asking, why was he so *unlucky*?

He'd been wrong about Fanny. That was clear; she was not the right woman for him.

Zhou parked the taxi alongside a quiet stretch of the river and set out the stools. A few old people performed their exercises nearby, and a stray peasant wandering past stared at the girls. Liu wanted to know, was that real hair? Did they wash? Liu sweated through his account and Zhou did his part without enthusiasm. The girls leaned forward on their stools. The sounds of children singing a song came from across the river. Liu liked to alter his ending exhortations and Zhou wondered which he would use today. Down with Corrupt Officials! Give Me Democracy or Give Me Death! Democratic Revolution Now! Revolution Forever! Zhou's stomach felt unsettled.

Suddenly, three policemen were standing off to the side. At first, nobody noticed. When he saw the green uniforms, Zhou stumbled in his translation, his throat tightening. How long had they been listening, how much had they heard? It was damning merely to be speaking privately in this way, in a foreign language, with foreigners. Zhou thought if they were arrested, that was the end of the taxi, the end of his adventure. He felt awash with relief. Take this trip off his hands—make it end!

Noting Zhou's hesitation, Liu spun around and called out, "Welcome Comrades! Come tell the truth about life in China to these kind young capitalist roaders. They want to know about the *real* China. It is time—it is past time—don't you think, for the world to know how good life is in our great country?" The younger policeman seemed on the verge of hooting with laughter, but his colleagues pulled him away. They crossed the road and disappeared into a neighborhood.

Liu continued as if the policemen were still there: in this delicate time of national need, it was more important than ever that responsible, caring citizens take measures to ensure the stability of the party. Hadn't Mao said it was their duty to convert the imperialist running dogs to the true way of socialist thought? With Mao in mind he and Comrade Zhou had set out on their mission to . . .

Hey, Zhou said. They're gone.

Liu didn't pause: thus far they'd persuaded fifty-seven imperialist running dog foreign devils of the party's value to the world. Progress! Power to the People! They had traveled the richly productive countryside, visited China's prosperous cities, and delivered the truth! The world will know the great success of communism!

Shut up. Zhou took hold of Liu's arm. Enough.

Be enterprising in the name of the party. Entrepreneurs for socialism! Itinerant communists!

Liu, Zhou called directly into Liu's face.

Liu's eyes were unfocused, he was glazed in sweat.

Zhou said, It's okay. They left. We'll get in the car, we'll drive away.

Liu was breathing hard. Oh, he said.

We'll be gone before they can send anyone. Nobody can find us, Zhou said.

The Israeli girls had stood and were staring at Liu, awaiting Zhou's translation.

Victory is assured, Liu said. His voice was shaky.

Zhou nodded. That's right. Take some deep breaths.

Fanny sat on her bed painting her toenails. The shade was called Little Red Riding Hood. In Japan she'd met a beautician from Bakersfield, who'd made a gift of the nail polish, in the interest of inspiring Fanny toward some beautifying self-improvement. Fanny remembered the way Cheryl had squinted at her appraisingly. "You have very nice eyes. It's a feature and you owe it some attention. Love yourself and the world will love you." Which Fanny considered ridiculous. Not that Fanny was without vanity. She had good legs—long and shapely—though she hid them in pants. And her hair, long and straight, not a streak of gray. She wore it in a thick braid down her back, a rope that could save a person.

After she'd left Daniel's room, Fanny had gone straight to the bus station, bought a ticket, and returned to pack. She'd been unable to get a ticket to Golmud, the most direct route to Tibet. For her, then, a journey across western Sichuan into Tibet. To Tibet! She felt excited, intact, entire to herself. She didn't need anyone else. Happy Familiar Solitude.

A pair of her fellow dorm residents sat close, observing Fanny's every move. She stuck little wads of toilet paper between her toes, the way Cheryl had shown her. Knee bent, head close to her toes, she brushed the pungent red polish over each nail. The bus to Hongyuan left early the next morning.

"All right, you two, off with your shoes." Fanny motioned to the women to remove their battered black pumps and stubby nylon socks. She hesitated at the thought of touching the feet of strangers. They covered their mouths in embarrassment, then settled quietly like children, bursting murmurs of Mandarin bubbling up. Fanny began with the one dressed in flowers and plaid, her foot in Fanny's lap. Here was the virtue of human touch, Fanny thought. It put you in the lap of humanity. Maybe it was a good thing that . . . what? She pictured horses halting at a cattle guard set into a road. Maybe she and Daniel had arrived at a place they shouldn't cross. Maybe they were being saved from a future mortification or catastrophe. She dipped the little brush into the bottle and slopped polish on a toe. "Damn." Wiping the smear with her fingernail, she paused, holding the brush still. A shot at love exerted a pull beyond reason or logic. She was not intact, that was a lie she told herself; she was full of holes, a leaky vessel. If you believed in a lie, did that make it true? She resumed her task. A spectator would have thought Fanny was performing foot surgery. The women watched Fanny intently and talked to each other, the sounds warming, as if their voices were touch rather than words. Fanny let the peace of being without common language wash over her.

At dawn, Chengdu was brown and deserted, with a dense, pungent fog slumped over the river. Wrinkled leaves dangled from skinny trees like ill-fitting clothes. A few trucks rattled past, then two people on bicycles cycling lazily, chatting in desultory tones. When they saw Fanny, they stopped talking to stare, their bikes wobbling. A couple of sweepers worked against the curbs with their rice-grass brooms, bent over, mouths and noses covered with white masks. The cheerless deserted streets stretched into the foggy distance. Walking crippled sidewalks, she counted her steps in Mandarin—*yi, er, san, si, wu, liu, qi, ba, jiu, shi*—and peered into the steamed windows of parked cabs, in search of a driver who was awake.

Ejected into the unknown. She saw herself from the outside, a woman with one blue pear-shaped backpack, a small brown backpack, and a long braid. The Sad Traveler on her Sad Trip. She felt lost and determined. What did one *do* as a traveler? The expansive vacancy of the days. There was virtue to paring life down to a few possessions but this morning she had a falling-away feeling at the absence of so much. Her hold on purpose: catch the 6 A.M. bus to Hongyuan.

The taxi driver she found was unimpressive. He kept turning to inspect her.

"Let me drive. I'm from America, the land of the automobile, it's a way of life." She pleaded with him; he stared at her even more intently. "The road, you moron!" She waved her arms. She took a deep breath. Every task took longer than expected, was complicated in ways she could not anticipate. She had a driver who couldn't drive and he spoke a language she couldn't speak. She was in his country so the burden of communication was hers, at which she was failing. The cab drifted past a park where she and Daniel had walked, then it stopped at a stoplight beside a teahouse where they'd had tea. She and Daniel had returned to the hotel, snuck into his empty dorm room, Fanny had imagined pregnancy followed by a child, her very own child, which seemed absurdly, comically off-key, they'd taken off their clothes and . . . she did not know what had happened. Now she was getting on a bus instead of loading into the taxi with Daniel, Yevgo, Joe, and Liu. The teahouse was closed, chairs stacked into tottering thrones, tables covered in dry leaves.

The road followed the river. At an intersection, Fanny turned to see Yevgo strolling. "Hey," she called out without thinking.

"Fanny, darling!" Yevgo came over, leaned in the window and kissed each of her cheeks. "What're you doing in a stranger's taxi?" He looked confused.

"Catching a bus to Hongyuan."

"Why?"

Fanny didn't say anything.

"What did that motherfucker do?"

Fanny shook her head, held her hands up in a *who knows?* gesture. The light changed.

Yevgo stepped back onto the sidewalk, calling after her, "Hong-what? We'll meet you there!" The driver turned up the wide boulevard that split Chengdu down the middle. At the top was the monstrous statue of Mao, holding one concrete arm up in a weighty gesture of blessing, facing great squares of perfect lawn that no one was allowed to walk or sit on.

She wondered if it was possible to accidentally fall in love with someone, against one's will. Was an accident fate? For a moment her life in New Mexico rose up in Fanny's mind and seemed so close she could taste it: juniper and sage, roasted green chile, crackling dry air, the wedding she was supposed to attend in a matter of weeks. She thought of her friends, who were tolerant of her peripatetic habits though they might resist the scale. She didn't take vacations—two weeks in Mexico or Thailand. She put her life into storage, stopped working, and went away for half a year or more. People wanted to know why, and what was her itinerary? This hankering for reason and plans irked her. Why couldn't she go away *for no reason*? Why couldn't she up-end her life, *for no reason*? Wasn't upheaval an end in itself? This was one thing the culture of therapy had accomplished: seduced people into believing that there was logic behind every human action, that there were lines of cause and effect, responsibility and blame. If you dug far enough into someone, motive and desire would be revealed like fossils in a rock. Following this line, there must be a reason her brother was dead at forty-four. A reason she was in a taxi by herself. She wanted to live as if she had somewhere to go and someplace to be and people to be there with; she wanted to live as if she had nowhere to go and nowhere to be and only herself to think of.

Chapter 20

Zhou awoke before dawn in a sweat, his heart beating hard. The dream he'd been having hung in his mind, a dream he had often on this trip: he was admiring the branches of tall, grand trees, a shadowy spangled light blinking in his face, filling him with longing and nostalgia. The air smelled of the past, a lost smell he could almost place. The light gradually turned into a single white beam, piercing, hot, and uncomfortable. He tried to turn away but the light followed him, the beam widening. It turned pink, gradually deepening to red, and his face was bathed with what he took for water, then understood, by its thickness and warmth, was blood. He recoiled. In the background people were laughing or crying. Laughter or despair. How could they sound so similar? Agitated and despondent, he woke, flipped onto his back and flexed his legs, wiped sweat from his face and checked his hand to make sure it was really sweat. He occupied the backseat. Liu was in the passenger seat, tilted as far back as it would go; the seat back touched Zhou's legs. Zhou could see a clump of Liu's uncombed hair sticking up. The sight of that messy head of hair made him smile. They had plenty of money, enough to get beds in a dorm room, but Zhou was afraid to leave the car unattended. Liu grumbled and Zhou said go ahead, get a dorm bed, but Liu wouldn't. They parked in the lots of guesthouses, sleeping in the car and paying a small fee to use the facilities. Zhou looked down; the floor of the backseat was sprinkled with dried mud and tiny bits of peanut shell. They were collecting Yevgo, Daniel, and Fanny at six to drive north toward Lanzhou. He had no idea how many more days before they arrived at the western border. Then Zhou and Liu would return to Guangzhou. Such a long way.

The performances. He groaned. He wasn't cut out to go over and over the same material. He felt bad, taking foreigners' money. Liu said if they were foolish enough to believe the scam, they deserved to lose their money. Zhou found lying about politics nerve-racking. He was not political; he'd gotten through life by standing back, nodding but not speaking, agreeing without acting, slipping through crowds, turning corners, hiding indoors. He knew, of course—what every Chinese learned in school—enough Marxist theory and socialist rhetoric to survive. They were sentences he could repeat if necessary; they were not sentences that touched his heart. Maybe he didn't know exactly what had happened at Tiananmen Square—no ordinary person knew the truth in China. After a performance, he felt sad and anxious. This feeling had nothing to do with Chen.

Maybe he missed his job at the guesthouse in Hangzhou. The unsmiling Ailin whom he longed to make smile. The steady routine of his life which, before Yuyi's accident, had seemed dull and predictable. Awakening to an instrumental version of "Like a Bridge Over Troubled Water" every morning at six playing from the loudspeaker attached to the light pole near his dorm window followed by the news broadcast while he had his tea and rice soup. He rode his bicycle to work, chatted with the old man who worked as night guard, before checking the reports from the night shift. Yes, maybe he was homesick.

He shifted on the seat, curling up in the opposite direction. Homesickness was not responsible for the nightmares or his awareness of the potential for disaster.

Liu claimed that Zhou didn't need him on the trip any longer. He wanted to go home.

What, Zhou asked plaintively, was he going to do on the drive back, *by himself?* Nobody drove a car around China alone. He offered to teach Liu to drive, thinking that would be an incentive. Learn a new skill, improve his prospects.

Liu scoffed. His ambition was not to be a chauffeur.

Zhou unwound the window for a breath of warm rank Chengdu air. He could offer Liu a bigger cut of their earnings. He admired his new watch, pleased by the gold band, gold trim, gold numbers. Zhou had at last spent some of his money, purchasing this watch in a Chengdu market. He closed the window and tried to sleep. The days were long and he was always tired.

As the light turned from black to pale gray, Liu sat up and said *Zhou*. Foreigners. Zhou had finally fallen back to sleep.

Liu reached behind his seat, grabbed Zhou's knee and shook it. Wake up, lazy.

I don't know what they are saying, Zhou mumbled. It wasn't English, he decided. He could ignore it. No, it *was* English, with an accent. He wondered where they were from and felt embarrassed by the persistence of his curiosity. He didn't understand why he cared about foreigners.

Liu shouted at the men to go away, leave them alone.

They want a taxi, Zhou said. They think we're a real taxi.

Liu snorted. Foreigners always wanted something. "Fookoff," Liu shouted, then heaved onto his side, presenting his wide back to the window.

Zhou could make out their straight, thick, foreign legs, naked beneath shorts. Mei you, he whispered. Don't have. He waved his hand, shaking his head no. No eye contact. Mei you. He pretended to be sleeping. The foreigners pounded their fists on the car and shouted.

You're not doing anything, Liu said.

Go back to sleep, Zhou said.

In this racket?

The foreigners rocked the car back and forth. Then came a set of words Zhou understood perfectly. *Fucking stupid Chinese.* His stomach twisted. Zhou turned his nose into the vinyl of the seat. He crossed his arms over his chest. He might have explained to the men why his taxi wasn't for hire. Still, there were other taxis in Chengdu. They needn't have gotten angry. He checked his beautiful new watch. It was almost time to get up. He liked to be punctual. He would brush his teeth, fill his and Liu's tea jars with hot water, sweep out the car, once the foreigners were gone.

They took the main road north from Chengdu. After the incident with the peasants and the rut, Zhou had insisted that Liu confer with Yevgo over the map. They traced routes with their fingers and watched each other's expressions, nodding or shaking their heads. Yevgo told Liu he wanted to see a place called Hong-something, and after some searching, Liu found Hongyuan and said yes, that was a good route.

Even early in the morning, the road out of Chengdu was throttled with carts, pedestrians, bicycles, animals, buses. *You could not drive out of a city early enough*, Zhou thought, his shoulders tense. To his relief, Liu and Daniel fell instantly asleep. Easier to concentrate when those two slept. No Fanny. Zhou didn't know why and didn't ask.

Yevgo didn't nap in the car. He wasn't sleeping much at night either. His mind felt unusually alert though he wasn't necessarily alert to the present. The past and the present seemed to have melded into a seamless sensation of no-time. Out the window were bushes with purple flowers bending in a breeze, a bony-hipped cow in a field rimmed by a stone wall. He couldn't say where he was. California, Tashkent, China. No physical place seemed adequate to hold the layers of memory and experience which gathered into a single awareness. Despite his insomnia, despite the persistent tightness in his chest and periodic bouts of nausea, he felt clearheaded and calm. He was going home to Tashkent. Not since he'd married Fiera had he felt so certain about a course of action. He resisted the impulse to pull the matryoshka doll out of his pocket to stare at it. Foolishly he still felt married to Fiera, though she was married to someone else now. He'd had plenty of girlfriends since, but even after their divorce he felt that he was being unfaithful to Fiera. He would have no other wife than Fiera. In a way that he could not explain, he understood that he was going home to Tashkent because he was no longer married to Fiera. He could not have Fiera in his life, but he could have Tashkent. He touched his hand to his chest where it felt tight and tingling, surprised to realize the matryoshka doll was in his fist.

The car stalled three times before they reached the checkpoint at Mianyang. The first time, Zhou pumped the gas and turned the starter over and over again until Yevgo said, "Don't flood it." Leaning forward from the backseat.

"Flood?" Zhou pictured the Yangtze overflowing its banks.

Yevgo explained about gas pouring into the carburetor.

The third time the car died, it didn't restart. Zhou popped the hood. Daniel staggered out of the car and peeled off to wander the roadside, looking for marijuana plants. He was building a collection of flaccid plant leaves between the pages of his notebook (full of lists of ideas for making money in China) and the book he had not even begun to read, *Of Human Bondage*. He pulled the notebook out of his shoulder bag and opened it. Out fell bits of pink paper. The wedding invitation Fanny had collected at the Chengdu GPO. Christ. He shoved the bits of paper out of sight and focused on the plants at his feet. He was thinking of profit, more than personal use. Maybe the pills he'd taken from Yevgo would turn out to be something that would get him high. Perhaps he would become an international businessman; import-export. He stopped, staring sightlessly at a rangy bush with tiny purple flowers. He'd left Chengdu without seeing Fanny; he didn't want to see her. He felt betrayed.

Yevgo fingered belts, checked the battery and spark plugs, Zhou alongside him, trying unsuccessfully not to get in the way. Liu stumbled out of the car, his jar of tea in one hand, bottle of bai jiu in the other. He carried on a litany of complaints, yawning loudly between sentences. A sour alcohol smell rose off him like steam. He could be in Guangzhou becoming a Big Man. He drank some tea. Yawn. He was wasting his time, making no advancement in his life. Yawn. He, Liu Po, had ambitions. Yawn. He drank from the bottle. Those ambitions didn't involve driving through stupid small towns. Yawn. Babysitting capitalist dogs. Yawn. He could hop a bus and be back in Guangzhou by the end of the week. He stretched, drank from the bottle of bai jiu, then the jar of tea. What happened to their American Beauty? He wanted to travel with *her*.

"Start it," Yevgo said. The car coughed twice, then turned over. Zhou left the engine idling, took a rag from the trunk, and watched the various whirrings and vibratings in the engine beside Yevgo. Yevgo wasn't certain what had solved the problem, but he knew it would be temporary.

Get in, Zhou said to Liu. Zhou dropped the hood, pushed on it until it clicked. He and Liu exchanged a look over the front end of the car while Zhou took a rag to the spattering of dead insects across the hood.

Liu hacked and spat before he threw himself into the front seat and slammed the door.

Zhou spoke through the open window. You're traveling with two capitalists—you could collect tips about being an entrepreneur. They're businessmen, right?

One is a fool, Liu said, and the other is a former communist. Would you trust a former communist?

You talk of ambition, Zhou snorted. Your ambition seems to be to get drunk. Go ahead, return to Guangzhou and be a Big Drunk Man.

Yevgo shut his door carefully. He had a bad feeling about the state of the car. "We need to find a mechanic in the next town."

It was noon when they joined the line at the checkpoint at Mianyang. The sun flared overhead, a naked bulb in the sky. The Min River ran beside the road, a fast-moving blue-green churn of water. Where were they, Liu asked, sitting up.

Mianyang, checkpoint, Zhou whispered. The word *checkpoint* stuck in his throat. What were PLA soldiers doing out here in the middle of Sichuan Province? They inched forward, a motorcycle with sidecar in front of them, a truck behind them.

Liu rubbed his cheeks vigorously, waking himself up.

When they finally reached the head of the line, a soldier leaned companionably into Zhou's window. He had a soft puffy face, sleepy and fresh. Barely interested, he asked for Zhou's papers. His gaze settled on the foreigners in the backseat, one asleep, one awake. He smiled. Are they *real*? Where'd you get the exotic cargo?

Liu leaned across Zhou, grinning up at the soldier. We're taking foreign experts on a tour of cooperatives: Purple Moon Harvest Cooperative. Peonies and Pandas in the Motherland. Honorable visitors, Chinese farming techniques, means of production . . .

Zhou tried to catch Liu's eye, get him to stop babbling. Sweat dripped down Liu's temples, his hands shook, and he stank of alcohol. To the soldier, Zhou said softly, He's not feeling well. Zhou felt surprisingly calm.

Not to mention rice fields, Liu continued. China has the best rice fields in the world! A beautiful word, isn't it? *Mi fan*. Rice. Every day mi fan, mi fan.

The soldier stood in the white noon light, laughing. Your friend's a real joker, he said to Zhou. Come on, show us their papers.

Zhou hesitated.

Help us out, comrade, nothing happens here.

The line's so long, Zhou protested and gestured to the line of vehicles stretching behind them.

They can wait, the soldier said. We never see foreigners. If they come this way, they're guarded by CTS people, locked into special vans. Wait'll my pals hear about this.

What are you doing out here anyway? It gave Zhou a twitch of adrenaline to ask this question.

Oh, the dam. The soldier gestured behind him. And other stuff, but trust me, nothing ever happens. He rolled his eyes.

Zhou turned to the backseat. "Please to convey identification."

Daniel came awake noisily. He straightened his pants and adjusted his shirt collar. "What's happening? Where are we?" Silence. "Who's the bossy bloke?"

"Papers," Zhou said.

"What's going on? Should we call someone?"

Just who, Yevgo thought, did Daniel imagine he might call? The Queen of England? The thought made Yevgo smile. "Checkpoint," he said. "The guy in uniform wants to see our passports." He pulled his out of his shoulder bag.

Daniel protested. "This isn't a border crossing."

Yevgo handed his passport to the soldier through the window.

"What are you *doing*?" Daniel bugged his eyes at Yevgo. "Tell me what this is about, Joe. Why does he want our passports?"

The soldier was staring at Daniel with intense curiosity. He reached into the car and lifted up one of Daniel's curls and pulled his arm hair. "*Hey!*" Daniel recoiled.

"There's nothing to be discovered from giving over a passport." Yevgo had little faith in papers which might, in his experience, be both useful and obstructive. His identity was too tangled to be easily reinforced by citizenship in a single country. This didn't confuse or interest him. He switched languages blithely, he thought like a Slav, felt like a Latin, had passing moments of belief in communism, socialism, democracy, capitalism.

The soldier leaned against the car, deeply engrossed in the pages of Yevgo's passport. Another soldier came over and soon the two were poring over each page, turning the little booklet upside down and sideways.

Their soldier bent down to examine Daniel while he spoke to Zhou and Liu. What's his problem?

You don't have time to hear all of his problems, Liu said.

The soldier laughed. Tell me one.

He lost a woman. Liu was enjoying himself.

A foreign woman? You had a foreign woman in this car? The soldier sounded crushed. He handed back Yevgo's passport, smiled at Daniel.

"What are they talking about?" Daniel asked.

"No interesting," Zhou said. "Only Chinese things."

Liu said, "Oh ho, a real American beauty."

Missing an American beauty, the soldier groaned. How had he lost her?

Liu eyed Daniel, shrugged, and said, He's an idiot, that's how.

I want to see his papers, the soldier said, holding out his hand. Hey, nice watch there, buddy.

Zhou noted the time on the watch he'd just bought in Chengdu, amazed and pleased with its shiny glitter. He turned to the backseat. "Please, Mr. Soldier supplicates your papers."

"Okay, okay! No big deal." Humming "Under My Thumb," Daniel untucked his shirt, reached into his pants for his hidden security belt, unzipped the main compartment, extracted a blue passport, and held it out to the soldier.

Behind them, the truck driver tooted his horn.

You better move. The soldier didn't take Daniel's passport. He stood back and waved them forward. Thank you! Thank you! Next time, don't lose the beauty!

Once they were under way, Liu said, Come on, ask him what happened to the American woman. Liu had really liked her.

Zhou threw out his arms in a Yevgo-gesture. Liu hadn't spoken three words with her and didn't know one thing about her. What was he talking about, *liked* her? Anyway, foreigners were independent and free. They did what they felt like. Probably she wanted to go someplace else.

Liu shook his head. That was certainly false. Anyway, if *he'd* talked to her, she'd still be in the car with them, that was certain.

Sure, if she wanted to talk to a drunk, Zhou muttered.

Never underestimate the party, Zhou's father used to say. Best to be unimportant. Do nothing to attract notice. Driving his brother's taxi across China with two foreigners in the backseat was no way to evade attention. Any self-respecting Chinese knew that from one province to another, from one town to another, the rules changed, under the control of local officials. Yet no one could ever shake the sense that the government, clairvoyant and omnipresent, could accomplish anything it desired. What was he doing: driving, eating, buying petrol . . . showing strangers his country? Why were these ordinary activities illegal? He glanced over at Liu, dirty and sweaty, slumped and snoring in his seat. Zhou had never seen him like this. Liu was indestructible, resilient, inventive, with a capacity, that had once seemed endless, to extract joy from life.

Chapter 21

Fanny Molinari boarded the bus to Hongyuan at 5:45 A.M., her insides under siege, the final assault an argument with the taxi driver. He'd overcharged her (she suspected). She'd slammed the door to the cab, furious and aware of the impression she was leaving when she behaved badly: rude, stingy foreigner. The taxi driver, a puffy-eyed, slack-jawed pinhead who could barely manage to shift, brake, and turn a corner at the same time, *pretended* to misunderstand her when she'd told him, firmly, that it was too expensive. Too expensive! He'd looked shocked and uncomprehending. She called him a *huai dan*—a bad egg—which sounds comical, a fake insult in English, but which was the Chinese equivalent of saying *you evil fuckhead*.

She cased the bus bays, ticket in hand, until she found characters that matched: Hongyuan. The bus was beige and white with a red stripe, its surface scratched and dented but without rust. It had squared edges, a luggage rack, and a cracked front grille. The tires were worn but not bald. It wasn't the worst-looking vehicle she'd ever boarded. The driver sported a thin mustache (notable due to its rarity in China) beneath which were lips lush as a woman's. His eyes were cool and secretive. He wore white gloves. He was drinking tea and smoking out the window, one white glove draped over his knee. When Fanny handed him her ticket, he gave her a look, as if he'd never seen her species before. She snapped the ticket out of his hand—white gloves, ha! If he only knew what she'd gone through to get that ticket, he might show a little respect. The lines she'd stood in, the ticket clerks she'd battled. Her seat, the window slot of a bench seat covered in stained, beige fabric, was surely too small for three people.

A short, stocky middle-aged woman hurried across the Chengdu West bus station waiting room, sweating through her gray, shimmery city blouse and into her quilted Mao jacket; she tried not to fall behind her father who was charging ahead, admonishing her in a voice loud enough for others to hear. She saw heads turning and dropped her eyes as if that might render her invisible. The speckled yellow linoleum was swept clean except around one bench where there was a clump of sticky red candies, the kind she liked. Hurry, her father shouted. His hearing wasn't good anymore. She felt a trickle of sweat between her breasts. Thinking about the red candies made her salivate; they were a little sour. She wanted to stop and rehoist her load: the new television in a box tied up with a string carrier, a small plastic satchel with the zipper pinned closed holding some clothes, and the net bag of snacks for the journey—oranges, small cakes, tea, hard-boiled eggs, sugarcane—slung over her shoulder. Though not young, she was stronger than her father. He carried his own satchel in a trembling hand; a hand that could no longer open the lid to a jar of peaches or of tea. Her father needed her; he had no one else. She had no one else, but . . . If we miss the bus! her father warned. She wished she'd bought some of those red candies.

They were the last to board. Her father supervised the tying of the television on top of the bus. He wanted to be an entrepreneur in his old age, now that the economy was opening, so they had made the two-day journey from Hongyuan to Chengdu to buy the television. His plan was to charge neighbors to watch the nightly news and other television programs. His daughter suspected this would be a failure—anyone could watch the news at the local restaurant for the price of a few dumplings.

She saw that many passengers were already sleeping, as if the uncomfortable bench seats were like the beds they'd just left. Others sat stiffly, bags in their laps, jars of tea steeping in one hand. Shuffling down the aisle to their seats, she glanced around for someone they might know returning to Hongyuan; nobody. After three short, anonymous days in Chengdu, these would be her last hours among strangers. Her father loudly castigated her for not getting a window seat. I'll ask the person who has the window to trade with me, she said. She wanted to explain to the other passengers that her father was a nice man, only traveling made him nervous. They never left Hongyuan and in Chengdu they had gotten lost, and city people were hard to understand and her father feared they'd overpaid for the television. When she saw that the window seat was occupied by a foreigner, she hesitated before squeezing into the middle with her bundles. Her armpits were damp. It was better to wear plain blouses which didn't make her sweat.

As soon as she was settled, Fanny's seatmate launched a complicated, urgent communiqué which Fanny pretended not to understand even though she surmised the meaning. The woman wanted to trade seats. In no way did Fanny relish the prospect of being smashed between the bulky duo, nor did she want to lose precious access to fresh air. The reason behind her seat negotiations? Ahh, she was a barfer. Fanny understood the demonstration the woman gave of throwing up. *Great.*

The woman's voice grew shrill, and other passengers glared at Fanny, upstart foreigner. The bus hadn't left and already Fanny was a pariah. If other passengers felt bad for the woman, one of them could give up a window seat. Fanny felt her stubbornness dig in its claws; now she could never give up her seat. She wondered, what did these people care about? Companionship or solitude; the cracked pavements of this city or the muddy paths between rice fields? She blew her nose. She didn't care if everyone on this bus disliked her, if the entire population of China decided she was selfish and unfeeling. Their opinions meant nothing to her.

Out the window, a man stood on top of the adjacent bus, tying down a bicycle. Fanny's bus, full and loaded, pulled out of the station. China, the only country in the world where transportation didn't leave on time—it left early.

Next to the driver, atop a pile of luggage, perched a slab of meat partially wrapped in a shroud of newspaper. Jammed into the aisle was a large basket of chicks, chirping ceaselessly, a bundle of spinach leaves, and a sack of rice. While working the crowded streets, blasting the horn, braking and accelerating, the driver adjudicated a fracas over seats between an elegant, well-dressed man and a man with greasy, slicked hair and a sly look. Voices rose. Mr. Sly stood and clenched his fists, Mr. Elegant unbuttoned his jacket. The bus driver waved his white-gloved hand and pointed Mr. Sly to a seat in the third row. Mr. Sly turned to the bus driver and puffed his chest. The driver braked sharply and Mr. Sly stumbled into the pile of luggage, his hand slapping onto the meat. He righted himself, wiped his bloodied hand on his pants, and took his new seat.

Fanny admired the way the driver dealt firmly with the seat argument, his calm management of the road chaos. She was in good hands. Along the road people brushed their teeth, children walked to school, vendors jogged under the bouncing weight of shoulder poles with baskets of apples on the ends. These ordinary, now-familiar sights calmed her. As Fanny relaxed, she realized that what she had been saying to the taxi driver was not *too expensive*, but *too oily, too oily*! She cringed in dismay. Foreigner Acts Badly, as expected. She could not keep count of the number of blunders she'd made on this trip, the number of cultural misunderstandings she'd perpetrated or participated in. Too numerous to count. She'd said the wrong thing, no doubt she'd been wrong about the overcharge.

And now she could add Daniel to the tally of mistakes and failures. She hugged her bag on her lap. Sing the failure song. Wrong about Daniel. She wished she could explain herself. No, she wished she understood herself. Even if she did understand herself, which she did not, it wouldn't mean she would act differently or behave better. Over and over again, wrong about herself. How she hated the particular kind of suffering from dashed hopes in love. She hated to think that their starter sex, attraction-escapade hadn't worked out because of her. Her fault, herself to blame. Because she didn't take love seriously, because her motives were muddled, because she seemed indifferent when she wasn't. Her hands were too dirty to rub her eyes.

The plump, middle-aged woman squeezed between her father and the foreigner, peeled an orange, and ate it. Then she peeled a second orange. She was worried about not having the window seat and she'd made a scene which left her feeling hot and embarrassed. She spent much of her life feeling embarrassed. Why did she feel ashamed? The oranges were sweet; she ate another. Within an hour, she began groaning and clutching her stomach. She looked helplessly at the foreign woman in the window seat.

Now that she was feeling sick, the woman sitting beside Fanny was willing to make eye contact, a pleading, comically morose look. Fanny slammed the window open and pressed back while the woman leaned across her and was sick out the window. Fanny caught a flashing glimpse of surprised, horrified expressions on the faces of some bicyclists.

The woman wiped her mouth with the back of her hand and moaned, slowly opening a bag of little, star-shaped cakes.

Fanny left the window open, cold gusts of air slapping her cheek. She shook her head at her seatmate. "Honey," she said, "stop eating." They were destined to become well acquainted. My name is Fanny, Fanny said in Mandarin. The woman's face broke into a heartbreakingly happy smile and Fanny had a glimpse of the shyness behind the disturbance over the seat arrangements. Her name was Liping. Lu Liping. Fanny Molinari. The star-shaped cakes, Fanny noted, were like the one served at the monastery for her faux-birthday. With, she thought wryly, her faux-friend, Daniel.

At the morning break Fanny took a book and a small sack of peanuts and sat on a bench. The air smelled like New Mexico—cool and dry with a sharp edge. It was so quiet she could hear the ring of a distant ax. On the end of the bench lay a large white pig with a red bullet hole in its neck. She bent back the spine of *The Ballad of the Sad Café* and read. *The town itself is dreary; not much is there except . . . a miserable main street only a hundred yards long.* Not unlike China. The physical discomforts of the bus and her solitude eased Fanny's mind. Alone in China. She couldn't think of anything she wanted that she didn't have in this precise moment.

A group of passengers and locals stood off to one side, watching her. One man with a wide mouth and wildly uncombed hair separated himself from the group and, as if he were the brave one, leaned over her to peer at the pages of the book. She smelled garlic, cigarettes, sweat. She cracked a peanut; he grabbed the book from her and waved it at the group, shouting in Chinese. Everyone gathered close.

The thin paperback was passed from hand to hand, each person murmuring over it. Fanny waited, amused and resigned. There seemed at times in China no barrier between people, no natural separation. She had passed from being a disease, a quarantine danger, to being examined as if she were a prize horse. They were talking about her.

She's French.

No, German.

Swiss, I think.

She is French. The man advocating this, the same man who had grabbed the book from her, was not a passenger, but a local. Now he demanded, You're French, right?

His face was so eager, so sure. Correct, she said.

He turned in triumph. I told you, she's French.

What difference did it make? She was different, she was not-Chinese. The passengers regarded her with respect, not, she thought, because she was French, but because knowing that fact made her from somewhere. Contact had been made. Why hadn't she offered information about herself? She wished she were more spontaneous, one of those people who threw themselves into embraces with strangers, freely told details of her life without confessional remorse, slid into and out of bed with men. An actor not an observer. She wished she were more like Bruno. The crowd dispersed to buy tea and snacks, returning her book with humility, beholden to her for being strange and for reading something they could not comprehend.

. . . *the town is lonesome, sad, and like a place that is far off and estranged from all other places in the world.* A dirt courtyard in the middle of China, vast blue plate of sky overhead, smells of dust, cigarettes, diesel. Two Tibetan monks paused at the entrance to the courtyard, their red robes distinct against the yellow earth. They stared at Fanny and she looked up from her book to stare back at their scarlet wind-chapped faces, the cracked skin of their ankle bones, the glossy beads wrapped around their wrists.

On the bus, now that they knew who she was—a Frenchwoman—the passengers befriended Fanny. They ran through the usual batch of questions and a puzzled silence descended. Passengers leaned forward and turned around to stare. What was wrong with this foreign woman, old and unmarried and childless? Liping felt protective of

Fanny. When Fanny reported her age, Liping coughed. They were the same age. Foreigners looked younger; Fanny's hair was shiny and liquid while Liping's was coarse. Then when Fanny said, no, she wasn't married, Liping dropped her head. Liping wasn't married either; she was fat and dark and nobody had ever wanted her. She flushed with embarrassment as if everyone on the bus had suddenly discovered *she* was unmarried and she thought of going back to Hongyuan where everyone did know she was unmarried. Where they felt sorry for her, where she was merely the person who took care of her father. There were so many questions Liping wished to ask the foreign woman: How could she leave her parents alone? How could she go so far away, by herself? Liping stared at Fanny's pack with its zipper that was not broken, that was as wide and strong as a set of railroad tracks. Liping peeled an egg and popped it whole into her mouth.

The passengers began to behave like relatives, telling Fanny what to do and how to live. She felt simultaneously relieved to be included and resentful at their bossy advice, not that she understood the particulars, but the tone was unmistakable. From connection they had zapped right through intimacy to invasion. They didn't really *see* her, only their image of *foreigner*. They were wrong about her.

Fanny brought out her phrasebook and dictionary, and slow, halting conversations unfolded. Liping's father insisted on extracting Fanny's itinerary from her and admonishing her for missing Beijing, the Great Wall, the terracotta soldiers in Xi'an, just as Mr. Wu's sanctimonious colleague had done. And like Mr. Wu's colleague, the sly, slick-haired man who'd been forced to change seats told her that she had made a great mistake by not visiting the Dujiangyan Irrigation Project, the most famous in the world. The Way of the Good Tourist. A way she failed to master. Conversations were glacial, the books passed from hand to hand, everyone who got hold of one dreamily leafing through the pages. Nobody seemed to notice that the books were English-Chinese, not French-Chinese. Nobody seemed dismayed that these conversational stabs were not actually puncturing the surface.

Mr. Sly was gung ho to talk, but Fanny couldn't make sense of the characters his fingers pointed to in the dictionary: cow and cowboy; now sink, now emerge, drift along; honeymoon; to have no illusions. As if she were on a television game show, she tried to construct sentences from these cryptic clues. He wanted to be a cowboy; he liked cows? He sank and emerged; for this, she pictured him thrashing in quicksand. His honeymoon left him with no illusions? He was a cowboy drifting on a honeymoon of illusion? She smiled and shrugged, wishing he'd quit trying so hard so she might distance herself from his bad breath, understanding now how incomparable had been her encounter with Mr. Wu.

The bus climbed into the mountains; the river turned from a sea-green to a deep aquamarine; the roadside grasses bent and writhed in a bitter wind. There were wild lilacs on the hillsides and goats among stiff bushes. Mountains loomed above the river, scrubbed with snow. Fanny blew her nose and stared out the window; a harsh and beautiful landscape. For that matter, New Mexico was beautiful. She'd left a daily life of books and movies and friends and a decent, if not compelling, job for this: petty, half-understood conversations with people who thought she was a freak in a place that was no more beautiful than her home. She could blame Bruno, make him responsible for this trip. Thinking this she felt a weight momentarily lift from her chest. It was all his fault. *Fanny, take a trip.* A dead person could not argue back or deny the charges.

Lixian had one restaurant on its one street. Fanny ate by herself, hidden behind two pink curtains at a round table with fifteen vacant chairs. As the foreigner, she'd been sequestered in a separate building of the bus station hotel, everything—room, hallway, building—to herself. The minute passengers unloaded from the bus, she ceased to exist. Now that they were in a town with officials, the foreigner was potential trouble. Before going out she'd opened all the windows in her room and inhaled the cold piney air.

She ordered spinach soup and rice. A few diners peered through the curtains to see the foreigner eating by herself and she felt a twinge of shame. To be alone was pristine; to be with others, affirming. To be alone was to be utterly exposed. The tap of the porcelain spoon against the porcelain bowl made a thin sound. What was it about Daniel? She had the feeling that she was missing something obvious. All day she had swung between indifferent resentment (she was not to blame for the failure . . .) and sad self-critique (it was all her fault);

between, *it doesn't matter, I don't need anybody* and, *I would give anything to be squashed in that taxi between Daniel and Yevgo.* The hot soup made sweat break out below her eyes. She spooned the clear, fragrant broth and swallowed its warm saltiness.

After eating, in a gloomy shop, she ran into Liping. Seeing the stubby, thick figure of her seatmate in that small room, Fanny felt disproportionately happy. She smiled and said, "You eat when you're nervous; I eat when I'm unhappy." She pulled out her dictionary and found the word, hoping she pronounced it with the correct tones—*bukuailede*—aware that she would never say to a stranger in America, hey, I bet you're unhappy! Liping flushed and Fanny wondered if there was anywhere in the world where being unhappy was acceptable. The soft click of abacus beads played in the background as the shopkeeper totted up Liping's biscuits and peanuts. Fanny touched the edge of the nicked wooden counter. She saw herself from a distance, as if she were looking down at the globe, her figure like a stickpin in the giant slab of land that was Asia, oceans swirling far off, the deep swoosh of air massing around her. Together, Fanny and Liping walked silently through the dark to the hotel and Fanny thought that you *could* communicate without language.

Liping longed to tell Fanny that she, too, was unmarried and childless. The weight of the unsaid made her stomach ache and she pushed her fingers into the bag of peanuts, touching the dry, dusty shells.

"China: land of leaks." Yevgo tightened the taps on the sink, which increased the drip rate, and jiggled the handle of the toilet flushing ceaseless as a waterfall. Bad plumbing was a signature of communism. Hasty, sloppy construction. Poor function, no finesse. It was all familiar to Yevgo.

Yevgo sat in one chair and put his feet up on the other. He'd adopted the American habit—unacceptable in so many cultures—of putting one's feet up on furniture. He took an orange out of his bag and began to peel it.

Daniel was pacing. He picked up a spoon from the tea tray and slapped it into his palm.

"I thought Fanny was going to travel with us for awhile," Yevgo said. "What happened?"

"Where *are* we? Why can't Joe find us a good hotel, for once."

"You scared her off," Yevgo teased. He wasn't interested in Fanny—not sexually. He wasn't, he realized with surprise, interested in sex. Had he finally been released from the tyranny of sexual desire? Would it come back to him when he got home to Tashkent?

"I'd expect a man of your age to want a better hotel room."

Man of your age. Yevgo shoved the chair his feet were on back into place. "Teach me some British slang for sex."

"Aren't you going for a walk?" Thwack, thwack went the spoon into his palm.

"What's up with you? You've been in a mood all day." Daniel was as volatile and temperamental as Yevgo's daughters had been as teenagers.

Daniel paced the width of the room, taking four strides to cross it, then four back, stepping over Yevgo's feet, slapping the spoon against his thigh. He paused to flick the light switch. The filament in the single dangling lightbulb turned a faint orange, casting no light whatsoever. "Christ, what a pathetic country."

"Take it easy." Yevgo laughed, stretching his legs into Daniel's path.

"Right, of course you're right," Daniel said, bristling at Yevgo's laughter.

"She's a good person, a good traveler. What'd she see in you?" Yevgo had resisted his friend Edwin's claim that between every unrelated man and woman there existed the potential for sex. Edwin had said this over and over to Yevgo in a warning tone around the time that Fiera had become "friends" with her gym trainer.

"What kind of a comment is that?" Daniel stopped pacing and stared at Yevgo.

"You need to raise your game, to play in her league."

Daniel ran his hands through his hair. "Why would you say a thing like that?"

Because it's true. Daniel's aggrieved expression gave Yevgo an uncharacteristic satisfaction. It came to him: he disliked Daniel. At first, he'd neither liked nor disliked Daniel. He'd barely registered who Daniel was, despite the whole democracy demonstrator scam, the voluminous chatter, but here it was: he was traveling with someone he didn't like or respect and he'd been pretending to like Daniel because it was easier to act like he liked someone than to manage troublesome feelings of dislike. Another one of Fiera's complaints about him: that he would be friendly and talk to people he disliked, or that he never knew how he felt about someone.

"What're we waiting for anyway?" Daniel asked.

"Just waiting." Yevgo wished that he were a reader. It was the perfect time to pull out a book, but reading was hard on his eyes, it made him sleepy, and what language would he read in? He spoke English fluently, but read it slowly and without pleasure. His Russian was stiff and plodding. He had never read anything except children's books in Spanish. What Yevgo liked to do was study maps. The map was in the car. He considered the dented aluminum ashtray on the table between the two chairs with longing. If only he still smoked. He offered Daniel sections of the orange.

Daniel waved off the fruit.

"Settle down for chrissake." Yevgo began to peel another orange. He'd had enough of Daniel. "Tell me something interesting or funny." How could he get Daniel off the trip? Fiera was the schemer, the one who planned and plotted. How had he managed to live for more than six decades and still find himself in situations which, if he'd been able to sufficiently imagine the future, he would have avoided? His inability to imagine the future: another reason Fiera had left him.

With a heavy sigh, Daniel threw himself into the chair and dropped his head into his hands. "All over the earth sit men who are waiting, scarcely knowing in what way they are waiting, much less that they are waiting in vain," Daniel recited.

"You're an uplifting motherfucker," Yevgo said.

"Nietzsche."

"So? Waiting is a gift. That's what we taxi drivers say. You need to fucking learn to relax."

"Let's eat," Daniel said. A sentence he knew Yevgo was always happy to hear. Daniel stood, tucking in his shirt. The thing was, he'd had hopes for Fanny.

Dinner was bowls of dumplings and bottles of beer in a noisy restaurant. Liu drank two beers quickly. Zhou twirled his bottle and picked at the label, glancing at his watch now and then, for the jolt of pleasure it gave him. At the next table a group of girls could not keep their eyes off Daniel. They laughed and covered their mouths when he mugged for them by putting dumplings into his mouth whole. "I've discovered the key to the Chinese heart," Daniel said to Yevgo. Yevgo raised an eyebrow. "Make a fool of yourself." Daniel finished his second beer, keeping pace with Liu.

"For you, shouldn't be difficult," Yevgo murmured. He, too, was drinking with an unusual seriousness of purpose.

"I'm going to get myself a beautiful Chinese girlfriend," Daniel said.

Yevgo reached into Daniel's bowl with his spoon and took the last dumpling, blocking Daniel's chopsticks with his forearm. "Last week you were on your way to having a beautiful girlfriend," Yevgo said. He turned to Zhou. "Will you ask them," he said, nodding at a young couple at another nearby table, "if they are married, or on a date."

The girl covered her mouth when Zhou put the question to them. They were not married. More questions from Yevgo followed. Of course, the young man answered, she thinks I'm handsome. The young man hesitated before he said, yes, he thought she was beautiful.

To Yevgo, she was lovely, with glasses too big for her small face, and a shy smile. Watching them, he felt a comforting melancholy. The angle of the woman's head as she listened to the man, the nervous flickering of his fingers moving his chopsticks one way, then another. The clatter of dishes behind them, the waiters slamming bowls and bottles onto tables, blue evening light filling the windows. As soon as Yevgo finished a beer, Liu had the waiter at his elbow, opening a fresh one. Yevgo began to feel blurry and soppy. Why hadn't he been drinking more? It made things so much more . . . pleasant. He lifted his beer in a toast. "Here's to," Yevgo paused, "the confusion of our enemies!" They clinked bottles and drank.

Zhou was too tired to try to make sense of Yevgo's toast. Weary, eating slowly, he was off-duty. The tension he carried during the day abated. Observing the couple Yevgo had queried, Zhou recognized a pattern; they encountered people, conversation bloomed, small inter-actions took place which interested or amused him and he discovered that he was curious about what they would find, who they would meet, where they would arrive. This, he was beginning to understand, was the appeal of travel. This curiosity, these small encounters, were what made the onerous, tiring work of moving from one place to another, never getting a decent night's sleep, eating strange food that upset your stomach, worth it. He was becoming a person he would not have recognized, a man of the world. It seemed barely credible.

On the way back to the hotel, Daniel began singing a Stones tune, really belting it. Liu competed with a Chinese song, loud and enthusiastic, but not melodious. They were weaving down an empty street, Yevgo flanked by Daniel and Liu. Yevgo tried to keep each of the singers at a safe distance. Now and then Liu would hang back, reach behind Yevgo, and slug Daniel in the arm in a quasi-friendly manner. It was not yet nine o'clock; they'd shut down the restaurant. Zhou had left hours before, missing out on rounds of beer and games of rock, paper, scissors. Liu talked ceaselessly in Chinese, unconcerned that his companions didn't understand. They paused at a corner, scanning a side street lined with shade trees casting moonlit shadows. Daniel linked his arm through Yevgo's and leaned into him. "Thank you for letting me come on your trip. Thank you thank you thank you. It's been . . ." He freed his arm only to throw it around Yevgo's shoulders. "The best experience of my life. The best!"

"Forget it." Yevgo slipped free and stepped sideways. He was not as drunk as either Daniel or Liu. Still, he'd had to drink quite a few beers before he began to feel almost comradely toward Daniel, though that didn't mean he was willing to be pressed up against him.

"The truth is," Daniel whispered. He hiccuped, lurched close to Yevgo. "The truth is."

Liu, behind them, pulled Daniel's belt. Daniel whirled and pushed Liu. Liu shoved back.

"Hands off my belt, *asshole*."

"Whoa, whoa," Yevgo said. "Calm down, boys." He put a hand on each of them.

Liu was hooting with laughter. Daniel scowled, which made Liu laugh harder.

A bicycle cart came slowly along the street and Liu flagged it over. He made an elaborate gesture of invitation for Daniel to be the first to sit on the cart bed. All three men sat, their legs dangling. The cyclist pedaled, turning to query Liu and stare at Daniel and Yevgo.

"Trouble with women," Daniel slurred. "I fuck it up, they leave, then I miss her," Daniel confided in a choked voice, so close his breath puffed hot and beery into Yevgo's face. "I'm so sorry, my mistakes, my ex . . . it was my . . ." Daniel's words slipped. "I'm so sorry . . . always . . ."

Yevgo turned away. Only to meet, on the other side, Liu's beery breath and identical drunken confidential tone. Yevgo didn't want to listen to self-pitying confessions.

"Never mind, never mind," Yevgo said, hoping at least to cut off Daniel, who seemed on the verge of tears. Yevgo threw an elbow out to keep Liu from collapsing onto his lap.

At the hotel, Yevgo peeled bills from a roll, handed them to Liu, who handed them to the cyclist. Before staggering away to find the taxi, Liu enveloped Yevgo in a damp hug. Yevgo patted Liu's back and extricated himself saying, "Good night, you crazy loser. Sweet dreams."

Back in the room with the dripping sink, the perpetually flushing toilet, Yevgo took two aspirin and sat in a chair holding a cup of hot water. Daniel stretched out fully clothed on one of the beds and commenced snoring. Sounds of doors slamming and televisions in distant rooms echoed down the corridors, Chinese voices rumbling and receding. Yevgo's mind was full of wispy threads of conversation. He felt so tired, so deeply weary.

Chapter 22

On the final day of the two-day journey between Chengdu and Hongyuan, the bus climbed a high plateau, following the surge and ebb of a thin road. There were few trees, no fences, steep drops. By mid-morning most of the passengers collapsed into sleep, including Liping and her father. Liping pressed heavily against Fanny, who tried to accept the Chinese indifference about physical space. She longed to shove Liping and her father away.

Out the window, the land was emptier and emptier, massive and stripped down. Fanny felt her life boiled down to this road and this bus, its engine grinding, cold air through the window, grasses bending in a wind, her back tight, her seatmate soft and warm against her shoulder. They passed into Tibetan territory, a cluster of wooden houses with carved and painted window trim and Buddhist symbols in goldenrod and red. Yaks with long morose faces raised their heads. Pussy willows stood in rows. The road climbed higher, leaving houses and villages behind. It seemed as if the bus was rising above the clouds, banked in rows of creamy white against a wall of blue. Swelling waves of land unfurled and fanned wide as the sea. This must have been what Bruno had in mind when he told her to take a trip: this loneliness. The truest thing was the inescapability of solitude.

The passengers slept, Fanny stared out the window, the bus driver drove. Then the bus fell from the road like a marble down an incline, without impediment, without hesitation, as if it were made for this purpose: to roll off a mountainside. Silence like a vacuum, all noise sucked away by the shock of falling. For a second, before gravity entered the equation, the bus floated like a feather in the air below the road. It lifted everyone as if to imply that their troubles would disappear. Even a bus could fly. The prosaic and the concrete, the downtrodden and neglected, they too were allotted their airborne moment; their lives drifting as carefree and light, as purposeful, random, and delicate as spores on a breeze.

The bus driver and Fanny were the only two awake; their eyes met for a second in the mirror.

Fanny wondered: was the driver hungover? An insomniac? Here, she thought, was the random come to twist her fate. She gave in to the banging, syncopated sounds, gave in to the twirling and spinning, like a carnival ride. Nothing was in her control, why struggle? She wrapped her head in her arms, curled up, and rolled with the falling bus.

Gravity asserted its pedestrian grip, the bus bounced in a clattering, menacing jab against the earth, rolled, stopped. Passengers awoke to being hit on the head: chicks, the slab of meat, the sack of rice, satchels of clothing, parcels of oranges and bananas, jars of tea. The bus hissed into a terrible silence at the bottom of the ravine. Her moments of detached ease gone, as if she'd never had them, Fanny was trying, in her fixed, narrow view, to open her window. Escape, that was what she wanted to do. Get out of the bus, open the window, hold on to her seat. Stay put, move, get away. Trying three things at once.

There had been no premonition, no early warning system. One moment your life was fine to the point of seeming dull, your fate soft and innocuous. The next moment you were wedged beneath a seat with rice in your ear and a dead chick in your line of sight, your body bruised and the blood on your hands was your own. How quickly the bottom could fall from a solid-seeming life.

First aid. Lie down for shock, or elevate? Abruptly, the silence was replaced by noise, cries and moans, the squawk of chicks. Bits of light yellow fluff floated in the air.

Slowly Fanny extracted herself from beneath the seat. The bus was on its side and she crawled toward what had become the ceiling to open a window. The window was jammed. Determined, focused, she stood on a jumbled pile, grunting and pushing. Finally it gave but only opened part way. Her head fit, but not her shoulders. Break the glass, no, find an already broken window. She felt calm and practical: get out of the bus. She felt completely hysterical. Bus accident! Bus accident! Her mind full of jagged images of the fuel line trickling, an explosion imminent. Her parents were dead. Her brother was dead. Accidents had killed everyone in her immediate family. She saw, as if it were within reach, her brother's motorcycle helmet on the bench in his entryway, and she thought that everyone should wear a helmet, all the time.

She found a shattered window and tapped it with her elbow, the pane caving in a shower of tinkling glass, a shockingly pretty sound. She vaulted out, cutting her hand on a shard, and stood on the bus's side, then jumped to the ground. She felt better immediately, bruised and cut but unbroken. *Flee. Now.*

A few passengers stood atop the bus, pulling people up through broken windows. Fanny was nervous. *Nobody smoke, please nobody smoke.* It was potentially valiant to die helping others; it was inglorious to die trying to recover possessions. She hoped to recover her two packs. She wanted her things and she wanted to get away from these people, as if going through this accident together was a contamination.

Fanny got her bags, though not without seeing the three figures who could not be helped out of the bus. One of them was the elegantly dressed man who had argued over his wife's seat, his body twisted, his oiled hair disheveled. People were dead. Bruno's absence hovered in the shadows of her mind; she'd never argue with him again about where to set up the tent; she'd never marshal evidence to prove that he was more stubborn. She felt as if a fist were lodged in her throat, stuffing an indigestible mass down, slamming closed a lid. Bags in hand, she looked for Lu Liping and her father.

Liping knelt in the grass, bent over her father. Fanny didn't want to see what had happened, but she made herself approach. Liping was arranging her father's hands, laying them alongside his body with the palms facing up, pulling on the fingers so they would lie straight. Fanny crouched on the other side of Liping's father's body. Liping grabbed Fanny's hand and squeezed it. Fanny squeezed back then tried to pull her hand away, but Liping gripped it harder. Fanny began to stand, but Liping yanked her back down. Fanny was holding hands with a stranger over a dead body. His Mao jacket was buttoned under his chin. He looked like someone who had once worked hard, his body sturdy and soft, its edges no longer distinct. She thought of the pig on the bench yesterday, the heavy slackness of death. Fanny's hand began to sweat. *Settle down*, she told herself. The air smelled of gasoline, no, it was an amorphous engine smell of burnt rubber and dripping fluid. Liping had tears in her eyes and an indecipherable expression—dread? Relief? Her blouse front was printed with blood. Speaking in an urgent whisper, she began shaking Fanny's hand. *What was going on?* Fanny wondered. Liping let go abruptly and Fanny had a clear image of something she'd never seen: Bruno skidding and spinning on Highway 1.

Liping watched Fanny rise, take her bags, and walk away. She should look for the television. How upset her father would be to discover that, after all their effort, the television had disappeared; maybe it was broken, maybe someone was taking it away. Fanny's back was receding. *Away, go away*, Liping murmured, watching Fanny, thinking of her father, thinking of herself.

Fanny sat on a rock beside the driver and they stared at the bus as if the world were suddenly reduced to this one thing. The bus was not going to explode; there wasn't going to be a purifying, hellish conflagration to send smoke signals for assistance. People were lying on the stiff, scrubby grass, among the rocks, moaning. The Chinese suffered with a humility that impressed Fanny. As if they did not expect rescue. They were far from anywhere; where would rescue come from? The blue sky was swept clean of clouds. Fanny wondered about the driver, what kind of trouble he would be in now. She imagined him, a good person, with a wife and sweet-faced baby girl. One of the few men in China happy to have a daughter. He did the cooking at home, his wife . . . Fanny stopped. She knew nothing. The driver could be arrogant, dishonest, manic-depressive. She was always imputing either very good qualities or very bad behavior onto perfect strangers. No doubt she was wrong. Wrong about strangers.

One afternoon in Chengdu, Fanny had stopped at an electronics shop to see the news on the display televisions in the window. She stood on the sidewalk watching, in a crowd of others, a mountain blown apart in a town that needed an airport. Authorities were eliminating the mountain for an airstrip. The shop window displayed three televisions tuned to the same station. Nobody watching looked as if they could afford to buy any electronics. The explosion and the ensuing massive, booming collapse of earth played again and again. She was mesmerized by the repeated crash in triplicate and felt that it was telling her something about China. Here was a place where upheaval and chaos were ordinary, almost planned everyday occurrences.

The road which they had been inexplicably thrown from was out of sight, the ravine deep, the rim of the earth in the realm of the sky. Mr. Sly stood over Fanny, talking, though she didn't understand anything he said. His pants and shirt were streaked with dirt. She surmised that he was proposing they climb up to the road and catch a ride. On what? They hadn't seen another vehicle all day. Oh, why not. Bad things had already happened: her parents were dead, her brother was dead, others were dead. What further disaster could occur? She had survived a bus accident in the middle of China.

When Fanny bent to pick up her bags the driver touched her arm, shaking his head vigorously.

He wanted her to do something, or not to do something? They weren't going to get a ride? There were no rides to get? She shrugged.

The last thing the driver said sounded vaguely familiar but Fanny couldn't find its meaning in her jumbled brain. She hoisted her bags and glanced at the bus; they were rescuing chicks now, and the slab of meat, dirty and torn, was resting on one of the tires which spun slowly in the air, presenting the raw, battered meat like a pie on a pie tray.

On the steep climb to the road Fanny's legs trembled, blood slamming through her veins, gushing like water loosened from a dam. The orb of blue overhead pressed down and receded as if it were breathing. From it, glittering flakes of snow formed midair, drifting and disappearing before reaching the ground. Cryptic messages from heaven. Fanny watched the icy bits of white materialize and dematerialize; the freakish whimsy of it startled her, as if she were witnessing a kind of celestial game.

They were not lucky. It was two hours before a truck passed and by then there were other passengers on the road and Mr. Sly practically got into a fight in order to procure them seats. The truck driver ignored the pleas of the others; money was what he wanted and Fanny and Mr. Sly paid up.

Fanny pulled herself painfully into the cab of the truck, eyeing this new driver, his face placid and impassive. Then she realized she was going to be in the middle, trapped between two men she didn't know.

"It's a communist party." Daniel laughed at his own pun. The taxi was slowed to a crawl in a small town. It was near noon. Daniel and Liu were waking from sleeping off their hangovers. Through the morning, Yevgo had been consuming so much tea, Zhou had to stop constantly for him to pee.

They were in the foothills of Sichuan's mountainous periphery, amidst pine trees, narrow terraced fields of wheat, patches of cabbages, high snowy peaks. The street was crammed with people on foot or on bicycles with a few cars and tractors jockeying for space. It was a mild day, the taxi windows were rolled down. Everyone in their best clothes—clean navy blue Mao jackets, flowered blouses—and Tibetans in robes, jackets, and beads strolled up and down the main street. A child clad in yellow silk stood on the back of a bicycle, imperiously steering his mother's shoulders. A man walked a monkey, dressed up in a Mao suit, on a leash. Another man used a hand-cranked contraption to spin caramelized sugar into great spider-webbed shapes—lions, camels, parasols—for a line of children. A swaybacked horse patiently walked in circles with a child close to tears on its back.

The town festival, Zhou said. At the end of the street stood a statue of an oversized figure on a golden buffalo. Zhou and Liu discussed who it might be. A military hero wouldn't be on a buffalo. What political figure would sit astride a buffalo? None. Lao Tzu, Zhou guessed. Nearby was a sacred Taoist mountain. Communism hadn't succeeded in wiping religion from everyone's minds. Maybe this was a Taoist festival. Is that Lao Tzu? Zhou asked a peasant.

No. He died last year, the man said.

Lao Tzu? Zhou said. Died last year?

During the second harvest, the man said.

Zhou waved his thanks and when the man disappeared into the crowd, he and Liu burst into laughter. Peasants, Liu said, shaking his head and snorting.

"Nothing," Zhou said in answer to Daniel's question. They were laughing at nothing.

"Let's play," Daniel said, and jumped out of the car. "Come on, old man."

"I'm *not* an old man, goddammit," Yevgo muttered. He got stiffly out of the car, leaned in at Zhou's window. "Meet at the golden buffalo?"

The first game involved tossing wooden disks over a stake driven into the ground. The distance was ten yards or so. It cost twenty *mao* for a set of six rings. Daniel landed half the rings in his first batch. A crowd gathered. In his first round, Yevgo hooked one out of six. Daniel bought a double batch the second time and hooked nine out of twelve disks, raising his arms in victory as each disk thunked over the stake. The crowd grew. With every round the rings piled on Daniel's stake, until he tossed a perfect set of twelve. The crowd cheered. Daniel bowed. Yevgo never hooked more than two. Within ten minutes, Daniel and Yevgo had become celebrities: Daniel for his prowess, Yevgo for his good-natured losing.

Except today Yevgo was not a good-natured loser. Only someone who knew him well would have recognized signs of a grudge building, the rigid smile, the averted gaze. He smiled as Daniel collected his prize, some small enameled pins. He smiled as Daniel passed out the pins to girls in the crowd. Whatever thin, fleeting affection he'd felt for Daniel the previous night under the sway of beer had vanished. Daniel clapped Yevgo on the back, grinning into his face and talking about how good it was to do something physical, something besides sitting in the car. Yevgo compressed his irritation and dislike into a tight ball rolling around his gut.

"I feel doggedly topping," Daniel pronounced and cracked up. "Get it?"

Yevgo said nothing. Was the guy an imbecile?

"My version of Joe's English. Not bad, eh?"

The crowd, clamorous and festive, trailed after them.

The objective of their next competition was to shoot balloons nailed to a board using an ancient BB gun. Daniel had trouble with the gun. The stone-faced proprietor made adjustments. Daniel sighted and shot. Loud pops as the gun fired, but the balloons were still inflated, pinned to the board. Yevgo took up the gun. He knew how to shoot. He didn't know why he hadn't been good at the ring toss. He shot the board free of balloons, each small explosion followed by the percussive pop of a balloon. The crowd clapped enthusiastically over murmurs of appreciation. Yevgo held the gun over his head and hammed for the crowd. They cheered: the underdog had prevailed.

The proprietor, a thin man with an expression of unshakable apathy (even Mao Tse-tung shooting his balloons would be unremarkable to him), took fresh balloons from a bin of already blown-up balloons and attached them to the board. Reloading the gun, he handed it to Daniel, who raised the gun to his shoulder and sighted down the barrel. A tense silence fell. He pulled the trigger and the barrel of the gun bucked and wavered. Not a single balloon. An entire round of shot. Nothing. The crowd groaned delicately. Daniel inspected the gun as if it were the problem, then he returned the gun to Mr. Impassive.

No balloons to replace, the proprietor reloaded and collected Yevgo's money. Yevgo held the gun casually. The weather was perfect, sunny with clear skies—such a rarity in China it was enough to fill you with a sense of unearned happiness, the best kind of happiness. A light breeze tousled everyone's hair. The crowd waited patiently. The particular charms of this day: luck and loss, triumph and foolishness. He recalled the soft aftertaste of sorrow he'd felt in the restaurant the night before which had precipitated his consumption of many beers. He'd been lonely since Fiera left him. He'd filled his life with girls and work and travel but there it was, at the bottom of his being: the clarity of loneliness. He wished for an interesting complicated woman. Someone his age, with a past. With a waist that went in and hips that went out. He touched the matryoshka doll in his pocket. He'd felt privileged to witness Fiera's grooming procedures—like seeing the toilette of a bird species. Private, petty, expansive. Maybe, in Tashkent, he would meet someone. Was there another woman in the world like Fiera? Yevgo lifted the gun and aimed. Working from the center out, he cleared the board. How lovely it would be to return to a hotel room and find a woman putting on lotion or filing her fingernails. Anybody, really, besides Daniel, farting and surreptitiously counting his money.

Gravely, the crowd watched and cheered the winner, but not too boisterously so as not to offend the loser. Then from back in the crowd violent shouts of "Halloo, Halloo, Halloo." The crowd split, people standing near the shouter jostling to move away.

Daniel took the gun a third time, his lips waxy. The voice continued shouting "Halloo," an innocent word delivered as an unmistakable insult. Daniel stared into the crowd, as if he would shoot the voice, puncture that halloo, then turned back to the balloons. He fired. Nothing. Wearily, he offered the gun to the proprietor. "I'm still hungover. We should catch our ride, what do you reckon?"

"We're just warming up." Yevgo adjusted his hat. The sun was high. "How about a round of pool? You call it billiards, right?" He'd thought of something, a way to flick Daniel off him like a fly.

The crowd leaned close, listening to the words they didn't understand. They were entranced. Barbarians playing games. There were those in the crowd who favored the old one, those who sided with the young one. Discussion of the men ran through the crowd: the thick hair on their arms, their prowess, their clumsiness. Where had they come from, how had they gotten here? The shouter resumed shouting, "Bye-bye" which sounded like "Baybee, baybee." His voice rose: "Baybee, baybee, baybee."

Daniel scanned the crowd.

"Leave it," Yevgo said. They walked down the street, the river of people streaming in their wake. Four pool tables were set up in a row. Players had to be careful not to jab pedestrians with their cues. A table was quickly made available. The crowd formed a shell around the table. Yevgo set a fifty kuai note on the table's edge. A murmur rippled through the crowd. Less than five dollars in U.S. currency, it was a lot of money by Chinese standards.

"I don't want to take your money, old man," Daniel demurred.

Yevgo had considered the sum. He guessed that Daniel wouldn't be able to resist fifty kuai. Anything less wouldn't be sufficient enticement. By the time Daniel realized that he wasn't going to win anything off Yevgo, it would be too late to lower the bet or back out. He would have to embarrass himself or lose money. True, in yuan, which didn't have high value, but fifty yuan went a long way in China.

Play me! A Chinese! I'll win your money! the shouter yelled. His friends laughed. The crowd shushed them.

Daniel had put in his time in pubs, playing plenty of billiards. He could knock balls about. He put a fifty kuai note on the table and smiled. Yevgo would be playing to win, unbeknownst to him, his own money. He liked the symmetry, the neatness.

For years Yevgo played pool three nights a week at The Crooked Cue with his friends. That was when he was still married with domestic responsibilities. After his divorce, he played daily. He had his own cue. He played for money, he played for fun. He disliked losing and rarely did.

They lagged for the break and Yevgo lost. He racked, Daniel broke. They were playing stripes and solids. Daniel chose stripes and quickly dropped three balls. Yevgo stared intently at the table, acting for the audience. It felt as if all of China was at his back. Not just audience, *witnesses*, Yevgo thought. For the crowd, he smiled nervously. As if he was worried that he would lose his money. The game, the audience, the prospects before him—he was enjoying himself.

Fat Foreigners, Rich Foreigners, Stupid Foreigners, the shouter yelled with a lack of imagination. Send them back to where they came from! We don't need them! The crowd began to surge and push, some people trying to get away from the hecklers, some trying to get the hecklers away from them.

At last Daniel flubbed a shot. It was Yevgo's turn. Daniel, solicitous, gestured for people to back away, give Yevgo space. Yevgo sensed a change of tone in the crowd—they were restive. He circled the table once, appearing uncertain. He knocked in one ball and missed his second. Daniel cleared two. Yevgo hit one and missed one. It went like this until Daniel won. Yevgo looked chagrined. He lost the second game as well and acted more worried. He was down a hundred kuai.

On the brink of another loss in the third game, Yevgo cleared his remaining balls slowly, as if it were difficult. From the start, he'd been controlling the table, setting Daniel up for shots and then taking them away. For the audience, for Daniel, Yevgo acted surprised and pleased at his sudden success. Handily, he won game after game, knocking the balls into the pockets with loud thwacks, thinking, *old man, old man*? Daniel remained cheerful and even-tempered, humming snatches of songs, though his play went to hell. He played badly, and then he played worse. He milked the crowd for sympathy, waving his arms like a conductor when he missed a shot so they would groan more loudly. It seemed impossible to humiliate him.

The crowd leaned in so close Yevgo could feel them holding their breath, then releasing it into a cheer when the shot was successful. They wanted to be on the side of a winner. They liked the triumph of the old over the young. But they did not abandon their support of Daniel. Yevgo began to notice the audience's attention shift to the back of the crowd, away from the game. He could hear the hecklers. The audience grew chaotic, spilling forward as if shoved from behind, growing loud though not in response to the game. Yevgo noted the yuan piling up on the side of the table. Suddenly, shoving broke out in the crowd.

Daniel scooped up the cash. "Follow me." They ducked behind the kiosk on the other side of the table and wove down the street toward the golden buffalo. Shouts echoed after them. "What was that about?" Daniel said. It was an inglorious departure; they'd been made into local celebrities and then abruptly were fleeing like criminals.

When they found Zhou and Liu slouched against the taxi waiting for them, Yevgo held a hand out to Daniel.

"Good play, old man. Jolly good." Daniel clapped Yevgo's back.

Yevgo made a "give me the cash" gesture, smiling.

Zhou watched his two charges. What had happened?

A splayed yak carcass lay abandoned in the landscape like a rotting ship. Where was Hongyuan? They'd been driving for what seemed a long time, though Fanny's watch had stopped working in the accident and she had no accurate sense of time. There was no sign of a town; no thickening of traffic, no crossroads, no people waiting for rides by the roadside. There was the rare nomad's tent, herds of ponies and yaks. The truck driver stopped frequently to fiddle with the engine. At one of the stops, Mr. Sly got out and turned to pee with the wind. Fanny walked into the landscape. This was where Liping lived: China's middle of nowhere, 360 degrees of geography devoid of human life or many signs of it. A hawk flew past, the blue truck crouched, small and enfeebled, against the enormous surge of surrounding hills. There were no fences, gas stations, rest areas, snack bars. There was no National Park, National Scenic Highway. There were no guardrails, roadside trash bins, signs prohibiting littering. There were no signs. They had seen no other vehicles. Nothing but yaks, an eagle, a vulture. The wind whistled through her earrings.

She took stock. Her hands and an elbow were crisscrossed with scratches. Her hip hurt badly. A sickening headache pounded through her. She rolled her shoulders and wrists, shook out her arms, bent her knees, rocked her hips. She did not like to turn her head or neck. Here she was, alive, alone, female, with all of her possessions in a parked truck a quarter mile from where she was standing. In a money belt, warm against her belly, was about four hundred dollars in yuan and more than that in U.S. dollars. Thinking of her unattended bags made her uneasy; she shouldn't have left them in the truck—though really, what could happen? These guys were not going to fire up that beast of a vehicle and hightail away with her modest haul of clothes and books and toiletries and Bruno's remaining ashes.

The men stopped talking as Fanny approached the truck, dusk drifting down behind them. Before her these two men, strangers who did not speak her language. If the driver or Mr. Sly decided to rob her, rape her, kill her, or leave her out here, nobody would ever know. She thought of the Canadian woman thrown overboard into the South China Sea. What if Fanny hadn't been an inadvertent witness? Mr. Sly took her arm to help her into the truck. She shook free.

Without language you relied on facial expression and gesture, though gesture might be dicey—in some countries *go away* meant *come here*. A few gestures were universal, like the one Mr. Sly was now making, finger of one hand jabbing in and out of the slightly opened fist of the other. Considering a response, she shifted her eyes and gazed into the calm sea of softening sky. *Oh.* The bus driver had been saying: *huai dan*, bad egg. Mr. Sly was *an evil fuckhead*.

Mr. Sly reached for her a second time.

Chapter 23

Just as Zhou was becoming comfortable with travel, there was this: a terrifying road. Narrow, with sheer drop-offs, twisting up-and-down passes—three in one day. Yevgo said he was frying the brakes and took over the driving. There were no officials to fret about in this remote place; there was no one at all. Flooding and frying? Zhou could not make sense of the language of driving. He sat in the front seat, gripping the dash, his eyes closed as they hurtled off a pass at a ferocious speed. Yevgo pulled over twice for Zhou. He threw up onto the ground beside the car, the dry cold stinging his eyes.

Now he missed traffic. He felt lost beneath a sky that was more vacant than the ocean. With islands, boats, waves, the ocean gave signs of life. Something soothing and alive in its surges and movements. At the top of one pass, Yevgo stopped the car. Zhou looked out from the relative safety of his seat; there was only the thin ribbon of road curving into the distance. The silence pressed against his eardrums. Not a cloud, tree, or bush. Not a human being. All was still. A single hawk dipped in the updrafts, as if it were the sole survivor in this harsh and lonely land. The loneliness! From the backseat, Liu's yammering soothed Zhou. Liu was bored. There was nothing to see. And no women. He was tired of sleeping in the car. He drank from his tea jar, spiked with bai jiu. No women either. Had he mentioned that?

The second night out from Chengdu, the men stayed in an adobe compound: dorm rooms around a courtyard. They ate dinner in the kitchen with a couple of truckers. The manager tied an apron across his thick waist and prepared pork with scallions and cabbage. There were a pair of deer legs with small sharp hooves sticking out of a trash can in the corner. Zhou and Liu talked with the truckers. One, middle-aged, winced when he said yes, he was married. He peeled garlic cloves with a penknife and ate them whole, grimacing as he chewed. Dressed in a dusty black suit, he slouched, smoked, chomped garlic, never smiled. His hitched-up pants revealed pale shanks of calf. Explaining the garlic, he said he had a bad stomach. The other trucker, cigarette lit, pouring his own drinks one after the other, said that he drank, gambled, smoked, and had too many girlfriends to get married. He wore army pants, thin transparent socks, tennis shoes.

The truckers wanted to know if the foreigners were married. Yevgo and Daniel sat at opposite ends of the table. The young one, Zhou indicated, was supposed to marry but it didn't work out. A sad story. This was a story Zhou thought Daniel had told him; had he misunderstood? Daniel didn't behave as if he were sad. The older foreigner's wife had died, Zhou answered. Zhou lied to protect Yevgo. Better to have a dead wife than an ex-wife. Very sad, Zhou said. Love was sad.

One trucker chewed garlic, the other threw back a shot of liquor. Liu emptied his shot glass and put his head in his hands. He said nothing about his estranged wife, his numerous girlfriends. Zhou took a garlic clove to peel himself; maybe it would help him, too.

The best wife, the cook said, was a distant wife. He lit a cigarette from the hot coals beneath the wok. His wife lived in a province north of Beijing. They saw each other twice a year and everything was fine—no squabbles. The truckers nodded. Nice watch, the cook said, pointing his cigarette at Zhou's wrist.

Zhou thought, *why be married if you're only going to see each other twice a year?* He chewed the garlic clove; it stung his throat. He thought he would never get married. Then he scrutinized Liu, his rumpled, stained clothes, his crushed hair, the dirty bandage on his ear, his stink of alcohol. Even the irritating, foolish, and unkempt found mates. Even the unattractive and the poor. He must try harder, Zhou decided.

Liu drank two beers and offered to help with the meal. The enormous cleaver appeared a featherweight in his hands, peeling potatoes. Working rapidly, he julienned the potatoes and stir-fried them with chilis and salt. Liu quizzed the truckers about their knowledge of the student demonstrations in Beijing.

They had heard some things . . . Sure, officials were corrupt. Act against the government? They shook their heads. What could ordinary workers do? They had their deliveries to make, their trucks to maintain—no time for politics. Liu and Zhou nodded. The men drank.

Daniel ate little and left the kitchen before the others. He stood outside in the shadows. Mud flakes spilled from the pocked whitewashed wall, the flap of wings audible from the darkening sky. He'd replayed and replayed his time with Fanny to no conclusion. He leaned against the wall, a cascade of dust falling around his ankles. The temperature was dropping. Falling night, moonless night. He turned sharply toward a shadowy movement but saw nothing. He padded to the taxi, carefully opened the front passenger door. The interior light didn't go on. How sweet the reliable malfunction of everything Chinese. He felt under the seat, flinching when his fingers encountered bits of something. Oh, crushed peanut shells. He reached across and from beneath the driver's seat grasped Joe's bag. Only a toothbrush. Poor bugger didn't own a single thing of value except the watch he'd just bought and couldn't stop mooning over. He pushed the bag under the seat and drew out Liu's bag from the passenger seat, shedding peanut shells. More nothing. These chaps were traveling with a change of underwear, a washcloth, a toothbrush, and a tea jar. He wasn't in the market for anything particular, nor was he in need. Unless you counted a vague yearning that no object in all of China would satisfy; a restless hankering for a roll in the hay with risk, chance, opportunity. The seatback collapsed with a snap that rang in the silent courtyard. If he could get his hands on Liu's tea jar, Liu would be like a baby without his bottle; the thought made Daniel smile. But Liu was never more than an arm's length from his jar. Daniel shut the car door and brushed off peanut chaff, feeling itchy, looking around. What else?

In the room he shared with Yevgo, he left the light off, retrieved his torch, and set to rifling Yevgo's bag. He found a butterscotch, the sound of its wrapper loud in the deep quiet. Yevgo would go for his walk after eating. Although the money Daniel had lost playing pool had technically been Yevgo's, Daniel had come to think of it as money he'd earned through his own resourcefulness. If Yevgo was going to leave cash around, someone was going to pick it up. Daniel would know in an instant if someone were dipping into his supply. Not that anybody could steal from him; his money wasn't here and there and everywhere in his bags. It was compact and very hidden within his belt that appeared to be an ordinary belt. When he heard a sound from outside, he paused and listened. The door didn't lock from the inside. He turned to his own bag and found the unmarked pill bottle he'd taken from Yevgo: oblong blue pills. Not the love pills, he knew that much. Maybe these would get him high, make him feel good. Daniel shook one into his palm and swallowed it dry. Scritch scritch. The crunch of footsteps. He snapped off the flashlight, stuffed the pill bottle back into his bag, and lay down.

Yevgo entered, fumbled, and flicked on the dim light, surprised to find Daniel prone on a bed. "Asleep already?" Yevgo said.

"Meditating. Clearing my head."

Head full of crap, Yevgo thought. *Nothing a lobotomy wouldn't remedy.* The thought made him smile.

Daniel saw the smile. It didn't matter what the blue pills were for, did it? Yevgo hadn't been taking them and wasn't going to as long as Daniel had them.

Fanny slapped Mr. Sly. He stumbled, held a hand to his cheek. They stood in the embrace of the open truck door. Fanny was aware of the three of them—the driver poised at the hood of the truck, Mr. Sly with his hand on his cheek, and herself—small figures in a massive landscape, enacting an ancient contest. The strong advancing on the weak. She would not be the weak. She shoved Mr. Sly aside to grab her bags from the cab.

Mr. Sly fell backwards and sideways, his head scraping the edge of the truck door. The heavy sound of his body hitting the ground, as of two dense, solid objects meeting. He did not move. He made no sound.

Bags in hand, Fanny turned to find Mr. Sly on the ground. She wasn't a flimsy person but she didn't think herself capable of flattening a man. She and the driver stared at Mr. Sly lying, slightly twisted, eyes closed. The driver bent, shook Mr. Sly, spoke some words, then shouted and rolled him onto his back. Mr. Sly groaned. His left temple was bleeding. The driver continued to shout at Mr. Sly as if by shouting he would eventually be heard.

Fanny held up her hand. "Stop. We have to get to town, take him to a clinic." The driver stared at her. With trembling hands, she fumbled through her bag for her phrasebook. Hospital, she said, after leafing through it. The driver's blank stare didn't change. Hospital, she said again, trying to get the tones right. And again, and again.

Finally, the driver said, okay, okay. He found a couple of rags, one to tie around Mr. Sly's bleeding temple, and the other to cover the front seat. He hauled Mr. Sly to a standing position and, holding him like a drunk, helped him into the cab, where Mr. Sly collapsed across the seat.

Fanny stood back, not helping. She used the tire as a step and swung her leg over the side of the truck bed. The truck was loaded with lengths of wide plastic piping covered with a tarpaulin. Fanny dropped her bags and lowered herself. The canvas-covered pipes were slippery. It was impossible to stand so she crouched, gripping the side of the truck.

The driver followed after her, waving his arms, talking frantically. He squinted up at her—her head just visible above the rim of the truck bed—with a fretful expression.

Was he admonishing her, or giving advice, or suggesting that she disappear? He didn't want her in the bed of the truck? His cargo was precious? Always guessing, never entirely certain. An affliction of misunderstandings though she had not misunderstood the initial gesture. She set her bags so that she leaned against one and used the other as cushioning between her body and the side of the truck. She heard the driver get in the cab and close his door. The engine started and they lurched forward. Fanny released her breath. She would be fine. Could she jump down? Mr. Sly was only injured; it had been an accident. She must have surprised him; he hadn't expected her to push him. Would she be taken in for questioning, charged? Charged with what? The crime of misunderstanding, of rash action. She could not fool herself into believing that in China, between a man and a woman, between a foreigner and a local, her version of events would prevail. She stared at the stained tarp covering the long pipes.

It was a miserable ride. She tried to hold herself steady as the truck pitched and rolled. She should have paid attention. Go off with a sleazy man? What was happening to her? The wind picked up, and she tried to keep her head low. He should be ashamed of himself. Harassing a solitary woman, a guest in his country. The driver, too. A pathetic, desperate pair of preying men. As for herself, how easily her tolerance for other cultures and her effort to appreciate and accommodate difference had left her. The more she tried to focus on the truth, the more impenetrable it seemed. The wind whipped strands of hair loose from her braid. She scrunched against her bags to keep from bouncing on the pipes and pressed her forehead against one of her bent knees, closing her eyes.

In her mind was Daniel in a comfortable car with his Chinese escorts to negotiate every cultural exchange. No accidents for Daniel. No confusion. No injured man drooped across the seat, bleeding as a result of your own actions. As for her? No friend as shield and cohort. You could laugh at disaster with someone else. Disappointment welled in her, that feeling of hopes so crushed the color of the world changed.

She scanned the landscape and suddenly joy took her by surprise. Above lay a curved dome of flawless blue. She'd survived a bus accident and now found herself in an expanse of stillness lapping up to the sharp line of the horizon in the far, far distance, beneath it the earth laid out, a curl of exquisite green. She had the entire truck bed to herself and the air she was breathing was cold and clean. What a strange kind of luck it was, to be alone in the world.

The driver turned the truck off the road, weaving over a barely visible track out into the grass. *Now what?* They bumped wildly for ten minutes before the truck rocked to a halt and the driver got out. Fanny stood, her tailbone and back aching, swung her leg over with difficulty—this ride might have been fine when she was twenty-eight, but at forty-three, my god—and climbed down the tire to find the driver trying to haul Mr. Sly from the front seat.

"What the hell?" Fanny said. "He's injured, he needs to go to a hospital, a clinic." Once again, she'd left her bag with her phrasebook out of reach. She shouted in English, trying to get him to leave Mr. Sly in the truck. Maybe he needed stitches, maybe he had a concussion.

The driver waved her off, arguing in Chinese. His apparent objective: drag Mr. Sly from the truck, dump him, drive away. Leave Mr. Sly to whatever fate might await him. Not a happy one. Fanny found herself throwing a tantrum, in lieu of language, reason, argument. She couldn't debate, she couldn't make herself understood except by stamping her feet and pushing Mr. Sly back in the truck. Mr. Sly moaned and flopped about in an almost comical representation of a helpless person. Fanny and the driver stood facing each other, breathing hard. What idiocy! Turning an accident into a crime. Bad thinking, bad thinking. The driver stood poised to reach around her and yank Mr. Sly out of the truck's cab. She slapped him across the cheek.

When Mr. Sly was restored to his former position slumped in the passenger seat, Fanny ordered the driver, her finger pointing to the road, to drive straight to Hongyuan, dogging him into his seat, doing a creditable imitation of a bossy Chinese woman. She retrieved her bags and watched as he laboriously turned the big truck and headed toward the road. Good riddance. She fervently hoped never to see those two again, one with his bleeding temple, the other with his stupid schemes. She shook her stinging hand; she'd never hit anybody before. It had felt good, slapping the driver. She had no idea how far she was from Hongyuan but she'd had enough of being at the mercy of others. She would take care of herself. Intact, she was, after all, intact.

Chapter 24

Hongyuan had dirt streets, adobe buildings, dark brown balls of peat stacked in piles. After walking for three hours through waves of grassland, the town was the only thing that did not shimmer on Fanny's horizon. She paused at the end of one of Hongyuan's two streets, taking in its echoing, dusty length. It felt as if two nails, one above each eye, were being pounded, with measured, regular strokes, into her forehead. At 11,000 feet every movement required effort. The light was tempered and hard as a blade. The accident, the two foolish, predatory men, the exhausting walk with a sore hip across the high plains, and this is where she had landed? Where was the warm bed with clean sheets; where was the hot shower and good soup? Safe bet: not here.

Fanny entered a dusty courtyard: the bus station. Where she would have been delivered had her bus not rolled off the side of a mountain. It seemed incredible that she was still in the same day that had begun in the misty dawn of Lixian, when her failure with Daniel was her most recent trouble. Which now seemed proportionately less significant.

Tibetans appeared from the shadows to examine her, as if she were the exotic species. She examined them in turn, their high-heeled boots and tall hats with fur visors, the women with stacks of cloth on their heads over which were flung their braids. Then she went to the ticket window, asked about a hotel, and was given complicated directions. Left at (she thought) a tree, then right at a sign—a red sign?—then something about water or bread? Even if by some slim chance she'd actually understood the directions, could she find the tree, the sign, the water, the bread? A Tibetan rode into the courtyard on horseback, wheeled his horse in a cloud of dust, and galloped out. A white van with a red cross drove through the dust and was soon being loaded with crates of vegetables, meat, eggs. The young man supervising the proceedings addressed Fanny in English. "Hotel?"

"Yes."

He gestured for her to take a seat in the van and introduced himself: Dr. Tang, Hongyuan's doctor.

"There was a bus accident," she said. Where? "On the road to Lixian."

"How far?"

She didn't know.

"Serious?"

She nodded.

Dr. Tang barked at his driver, then hustled Fanny into the van. They would drop her first, then the food supplies, then see what they could find out about the accident.

"Did you help a man with a cut?" She indicated her temple.

Dr. Tang braced himself against the crates of vegetables as the driver took a corner. "Yes. In the accident?"

Fanny shrugged. Fuck the truck driver *and* Mr. Sly. Of course they hadn't told the doctor about the accident. "Is he okay?" She wanted the answer to be yes.

"He is drunk." Dr. Tang shook his head, disgusted. "Some Chinese men drink very much." His tone was apologetic.

Mr. Sly a drunk. How had she missed it? She stared at the flats of brown eggs in little beds of straw and remembered the dead chicks from the bus. If only someone would swoop down and whip things in order for her: hot water, clean towels, a comfortable bed, warm food. Oh, to be taken care of.

"Here was much green, but now is brown." Dr. Tang told her he was halfway through a two-year stint at Hongyuan's hospital. When his time was up he was immediately returning to Chengdu. He steadied the eggs as the van jostled over potholes. They pulled into a courtyard; Dr. Tang opened the door and waved goodbye. The van disappeared. She walked around the silent dirt courtyard, then into another courtyard, and then another. Finally she found a room with a young man at a desk. She filled out the usual forms, leaving *Reason for Visit* blank. She was beyond reason and this felt more like punishment than a visit. Her room, two courtyards away from registration, was depressing; nevertheless she contemplated collapsing onto the bed. Instead she found the hotel's restaurant (which had no diners and featured a pile of stiffened, curled yak hides in a corner and a wall mural of frolicking yaks in lush grass) and ordered soup and dumplings. While she was eating the soup, which was hot but not delicious, a woman appeared, pulled a chair close, and said in English, "I am Wang Ping."

Fanny stared at her, speechless with surprise. Here she was in the middle of nowhere, greeted twice by English-speakers, as if she'd fallen into Alice in anti-Wonderland. After an awkward moment, Fanny offered her own name.

"Person alone, no good." Wang Ping wagged a finger. Not much happened in Hongyuan, Wang Ping told Fanny, staring at Fanny's boots under the table with an undisguised expression of disapproval. Fanny followed her gaze and noted Wang Ping's worn black pumps, thinking she would be better off with a pair of hiking boots, even if she found them ugly. The restaurant floor was littered with thread-like fish bones; fish from where? She had seen no rivers or lakes, and Hongyuan was far from an ocean. Wang Ping explained that the foreigners who came to Hongyuan were typically big men with huge backpacks and loud voices and she never wanted to practice English with them. "You are brave and foolish," she said.

"Thank you," Fanny said.

Wang Ping told Fanny that she'd lived in Hongyuan for two months, though it already felt like years. Her husband, an officer in the PLA, had been transferred from Chengdu. She had to leave their ten-year-old son with her parents in Chengdu because he had a heart condition and he could not tolerate the altitude. She thought about her son two hundred times a day. Glancing at her watch, she said, "Now he is go home." Her husband was always in the field, which left her alone in Hongyuan where she had no work, no child, no parents. She was bored. In fact, what she said was, "In Hongyuan, I am very boring."

Firmly grasping Fanny's elbow, Wang Ping pulled her from the table. She wanted Fanny to accompany her. This was not what Fanny had had in mind when she had wished for someone to take care of things. She meant, make arrangements and leave her be.

Sore, exhausted, and with a sickening headache, Fanny begged off in favor of a return to her room. Except there was no one to let her into the room. More absconded *fuwuyuans*. She gazed through the window at her bag sitting on the bed. *Take care of yourself, take care of yourself.* Wang Ping, eager to be useful, paced the courtyards with Fanny, calling out, *Fuwuyuan, fuwuyuan.* The clerks with the keys were nowhere and the silence was a weight against Fanny's ears. The irony of her situation was not lost on her: her capacity for autonomy, her vitality of self, had carried her to Hongyuan, alone, and here was a stranger stepping up to displace that autonomy. Always the passenger, never the driver.

Fanny, such a pretty name, like a Chinese name, Wang Ping chattered. Fanny agreed to go home with Wang Ping and they set out across fields dotted with grazing yaks. Fanny, her head throbbing, her neck so tight it felt like a board had been attached to it, stood listlessly outside a small shop while Wang Ping bought peanuts and a jar of pears. She lived in a compound with a dirt basketball court, the baskets without nets, and a row of identical, single-story two-room apartments in one long building.

It was the first Chinese apartment Fanny had been invited into and like most Chinese interiors, the walls were painted half-green and half-white, as if the Communist Party had approved only two shades of paint. There was an assortment of plastic and wooden chairs and stools, a stand for an enamel washbasin, a small wood-burning stove. Paper clips held a curtain over a cupboard door. Fifteen women in blue suits with red neckties and red hats stood in a line posed for a 1986 wall calendar, still hanging three years on.

Hours of tea drinking ensued with Fanny listening to Wang Ping's mix of English and Chinese. Trying to listen, her mind kept returning to the accident, to the events of the truck ride, to her exhausting though peacefully solitary walk into town. People came and went from the apartment, dusk fell. Fanny had been staring at a bucket of water on the concrete floor for a long time when she realized that the apartment had no plumbing. Finally, she extracted herself, insisting that she could find her way back to the hotel, of which she was not at all certain. She walked slowly, her limbs clenched and stiff. A birdcall and the thwack of a tool rang like church bells. The quiet pressed down, the darkening land and sky encircled her. The tumbling fall of the bus hadn't been like a carnival ride; there'd been no thrill.

An image came to her of Bruno's lit-up face, adrenalized, like he was high, as he told her about a near-miss bicycle accident. He'd been riding fast down a hill, too fast, but he'd kept the option of a stop in mind, his eye on the crosswalk signal of an intersection which, in the speed of the moment, he was trying to interpret. A white hand was lit. Red meant stop, a hand meant stop, what did a white hand mean? Trying to work it out. He didn't brake. A car squealed and fishtailed, laying a streak of rubber. Bruno managed to stop, too, without tossing himself from the bike. He and the driver stared at one another, what might have happened suspended between the car's front grille and Bruno's bike. The driver waved Bruno on. It would have been Bruno's fault; he would have been responsible for his own catastrophe. This happened around the time he was discovering Buddhism; their parents were still alive, though they would be dead within a year. He cycled home, lifting up each layer of understanding the moment had given him. Understanding the problem with the hand signal. Understanding that death could appear suddenly. Understanding that the possibility of death was always a surprise at the same time that it felt familiar. Familiar enough that you would find yourself giving in to it. "It was weird, Fan," Bruno said, staring out her bedroom window at the shivering aspen. "My life didn't flash before my eyes and I didn't feel afraid. I felt." He'd paused for a long time, comfortably stretched out on her bed. Fanny was sitting at her desk, flipping a pencil. "I can't explain it. I felt kind of happy. I mean, yeah, happy *not* to have gotten flattened by the car. But, I mean, just letting it go." He gazed up at the ceiling. Fanny listened to the rustling of leaves against the windowpane.

His story had frightened her. She hadn't comprehended what he was describing, except to feel that Bruno was out of her range. He was willing to leave her behind.

Now, after the bus accident, it did seem easy to give in to the possibility of death. Death as unavoidable and unthinkable to avoid. She didn't want *to die*, but being dead? Was there a difference? The verb involved engagement in the process of prevention. Yet, she'd been thoroughly absorbed in trying and hoping not to die. No parents, sibling, children, boyfriend; nothing tangible to live for. Only life itself.

The hotel staff was playing badminton without a net. The ratty shuttlecock rose into the air and seemed to hold still for a second before it dropped, back and forth. It was night in this remote small town on the edge of the Tibetan plateau and these workers were playing in the dark. Even the smallest things had begun to seem mysterious and significant.

Her longed-for room was very cold. Fanny stripped and crawled into her sleeping sheet, painfully weary. Trucks pulled into the courtyard until midnight when someone banged on a pot twelve times.

Out of a heavy troubled sleep, Fanny was awakened by voices and footsteps outside her room. She'd been dreaming of falling. Her right leg tensed as if pushing a brake to the floor. The footsteps stopped near her door. "Laydee, Amereecan Laydee." She awakened sharply, the dream shoved aside. The torn curtains were a sheer white; a pale beam of moonlight slanted into the room. "Laydee, Amereecan Laydee." High-pitched with a trace of menace. She held still, as if the man whose voice she could hear would see her if she moved. What did this voice want from her? To inform her that everyone in town knew there was a solitary American woman in a room in an empty courtyard. Whose voice? The young man who had taken the money she'd paid for the room and put it straight into his pocket? Or was it the guard with buck teeth and high heels who could never find the girls with the keys—that troop of women so bored, with so little to do, they were always absent. Or was it a trucker. *The* truck driver, *her* truck driver. Or Mr. Sly. She listened hard. She heard breathing. A mouth breather outside her room with its flimsy lock and cracked windows. Shoes scuffled in dirt and silence returned. She had no idea what had happened or what it meant. She inhaled and exhaled, her heart beating in heavy pulses. This was the way it was with traveling, the inscrutable mixed up with the confusing, the bland and the exotic humming together, as if the life you were living could reach inside you and touch, with long slender fingers, your soul.

Chapter 25

Scratchy news came over a loudspeaker at six in the morning—the time at which all of China was awakened. Birds sang. Despite her exhaustion, Fanny hadn't slept well. Behind the opening instrumental rendition of "Swanee River," beneath the announcer's voice reading the news, the town was quiet. She washed with freezing water and quickly packed. Her cold was gone, as if the accident had slammed it out of her system. The sun lit the dusty street into a soft yellow as she walked to the bus station. Boys uncovered outdoor billiard tables, streetside businesses were setting up: a woman with a crate of brown eggs, a man with a couple of baskets of greens, garlic, and ginger. On this bright, cold morning, nobody paid any attention to her.

There was nothing straightforward about buying bus tickets in China so Fanny was not surprised when the ticket clerk, with her lurid pink eyeshadow, informed her that there were three buses going to Zoigê—the next town—but foreigners were allowed to travel on only one of them and Fanny would be permitted to board only if there was a seat available. Foreigners were forbidden to stand. The clerk demanded proof of life insurance. Offering her driver's license, Fanny explained that it was American life insurance, good for any country or incident in the world, thinking that it had already passed through one accident, thinking how useless life insurance was for someone who had no family. The clerk examined the card with approval. The plastic driver's license had Fanny's picture on it and announced across the top, *State of New Mexico Driver's License.*

In the courtyard, Fanny sat on an overturned crate, joining five Tibetan monks, a bony dog, and the bus station staff. Her job for the day: waiting. At noon, she discovered that the bus she might be allowed to board, if there was a seat, ought to have arrived at eleven but now was not expected until two. Her feet were cold. How was she going to get out of this town? A spasm of urgency gripped her. She didn't have time to get stuck in an obscure town in the middle of China. Notes of a Gershwin tune drifted into the courtyard. *Summertime . . .*

Wang Ping appeared and tried to persuade Fanny to wait in the waiting room—the proper waiting location—where no one was waiting because the room was dark and cold and had a view of absolutely nothing. A tractor barreled up and down the street at intervals, hauling dirt. A Tibetan man in a torn jacket picked up stray scraps of newspaper on his way to the toilets behind the station courtyard. Huge clouds slid across the sky casting giant amoebic shadows. The bus to Barkam arrived and two Tibetans in thick yak-skin boots stepped down, gaped at Fanny, and sauntered out of the courtyard. The five monks who'd been waiting boarded and the bus left with a shudder, emitting a gust of greasy smoke into the pristine air. The quotidian life of Hongyuan—was it Wednesday or Thursday?— passed in and out of the courtyard and across the view provided by its entrance. Something like watching an unedited movie, an art movie in which everyone acted either with predictable and ordinary motives, or with motives so hidden they seemed ominous and magical. Either way, the meaning wouldn't become clear until weeks or months or years later.

Fanny wondered what had happened to the survivors of the bus accident. If they had been rescued. She thought of Lu Liping; was she at home? She pictured her in an apartment like Wang Ping's, with her father stretched out on one of the narrow beds she'd seen at the back of the apartment, his hands crossed over his chest like Mao lying in state. The thing about waiting was that you never knew at the outset that you would wait eight hours. It was always just an hour or an hour and a half, and then another forty-five minutes, and so on until you'd spent an entire day without a thought in your head more complex than, *Will the bus come? Will it come soon?*

The familiar battered taxi pulled into the courtyard and coughed to a halt. Yevgo rocked his hips back and forth, Zhou and Liu shook their pant legs. Daniel rolled down the sleeves of his shirt and buttoned the cuffs. Even while Fanny thought, *oh no*, she was not surprised. China was large, the world larger still, and she was fated to run into the same people over and over. As if there were only the five of them in all of China. She restrained herself from running over and embracing each one of them. Friends had arrived! She was rescued.

Yevgo noticed her first. "There you are," he shouted. He grabbed a crate and set it down next to hers, then eased onto it, leaned over, and kissed her cheeks. "I knew we'd find you. I knew it." He smiled broadly. "Spectacular countryside! Fantastic!"

Fanny laughed at his exuberance.

Wang Ping arrived with lunch: *bao zi*, stuffed steamed buns. She sent a boy out for more at the sight of Fanny with foreigners.

Yevgo split a bun and offered Fanny half. "I like this part of China best," Yevgo said between mouthfuls. "Reminds me of home. Outside Tashkent it's empty like this." He swept his arm toward Hongyuan's outskirts, a slice of which was visible.

"You left Tashkent."

"My wife's dream. *Ex*-wife. She didn't respect the government." He snorted a laugh. "Okay, the government was lousy. What government isn't? We had our friends, family, our whole lives. Fiera is impatient. Life should be perfect and she will make it so." He made a chopping motion with one of his hands.

"Where'd you go?" She thought Daniel had told her while they were climbing the mountain, but she hadn't been paying attention.

"San Francisco."

"San Francisco?"

"Crazy, no? Nobody would choose Tashkent over San Francisco." He took a bite of bun. "My daughters got a good education and now they have good jobs. My wife, too. We made friends—a lot of Russians in San Francisco. But life in America is too complicated. There's no time. It's work, work, and papers. Insurance! Health insurance, house insurance, car insurance, life insurance. So much fucking insurance. Americans expect something bad to happen so they can get some money." He shook his head. "Why I became a taxi driver."

Because he hated insurance?

"I was an engineer and my skills were desirable in America at that time. I had a job offer with a company in San Francisco. Also, we are Jews. Well, I'm half. Not religious. Anyway, that's why we could come to America. But I was bored; I didn't want to be an engineer." He wiped his fingers on his socks. "I love maps. I love navigation: from point A to point B you can take five, eight different routes. I love to drive. I started sharing a taxi with a friend, some weekend and night shifts, and finally I quit engineering to drive a taxi full-time." His smile was mischievous and rueful. "Fiera was not happy."

"Your marriage ended because you became a taxi driver." Fanny found herself smiling. Yevgo made his story into a comic soap opera with a Russian accent.

He threw his arms out. "In America everyone makes themselves happy. Happiness like a punishment." He laughed. "Fiera left me for a dentist. A *Russian* dentist." He paused as if it were a punch line. "We became true Americans: we divorced." He sighed. "How about you?"

"No," Fanny said. Was he asking if she was divorced, or married? Either way, the answer was no. "What do you miss about Tashkent?"

"Life was simple. Absolutely, the Soviet bureaucracy was *not* simple." He rolled his eyes. "There was very little to buy which is, you know, a relief. People talked. That's what I miss. Conversation. We told stories, played cards, laughed, listened, talked." He sounded as if he might cry. "And snow crunches in the eyes, innocent, like clean bread." He wiped his eyes. "From a Mandelstam poem. Enough. Tell me something about you."

"I was in a bus accident. Yesterday."

"What?"

Accident prone, she was thinking, imagining her family members lying prone.

"Son of a bitch," Yevgo said. "You okay?" He looked her over. "I see it now." Lightly he touched a bruise high on a cheekbone.

"I'm fine," Fanny said cheerfully. "I've got a bruise on my hip and these scratches." She pushed up a sleeve to show a scratched-up elbow.

"What happened?"

She shrugged. "Dunno. The bus rolled off the road, down a . ." She paused. "It was pretty bad actually."

More *bao zi* arrived. Zhou and Liu ate standing in the sun. Daniel walked to the courtyard entrance. Fanny tried not to watch him.

Yevgo said quietly, "He's not as good a pool player as he thinks he is."

She cut a sideways glance at him and caught his sly smile.

"He's good-looking and he can sing, but he's no bargain."

Fanny burst out laughing.

Daniel strolled over, half-eaten bun in hand. "Good trip?" he asked Fanny.

Yevgo offered his crate to Daniel. "Sit, sit."

"Not exactly." She glanced at his face, as if checking its temperature, then flicked her gaze to the bun in her hand, the sky visible over his shoulder, settling on his shoes. Astonished at that still-dust-free leather.

"I've been sitting all day, old man. Thanks anyway."

"How about you?" Fanny said.

"Excellent. I mean, grotty hotel rooms, but that's . . . you know." He shrugged. "Thought you'd make straight for Lhasa."

"Impossible. You have to go through Golmud and I couldn't get a ticket." She watched Yevgo cross the courtyard.

"Couldn't?"

"Buying a bus ticket in China, it's so, you have no idea . . . the lines, the petty ticket clerks, the endless mistakes, the perseverance called for . . . I'll spare you the gory details." She lifted her chin at the taxi. "You won't have to experience it yourself."

"The middle of fucking nowhere." Daniel frowned at the desolate courtyard. "Not much of a town."

Having spent all day here, the courtyard felt homey to Fanny. She thought of some of the distant corners of New Mexico.

"About the other day," he said.

"We don't have to talk about it," she said quickly.

"It's just, I've got . . ."

"It's my fault." She spoke at the same time he did.

"I don't want you to get the wrong idea," he said.

"No matter." What idea would that be? She had a hundred wrong ideas.

"It's, you know . . ." He patted his stomach. "I think an alien has taken up residence in my digestive system."

Christ, not excuses. She picked at a flake of skin peeling from her lip.

He moved closer. "Are you okay?" He was looking at her with an expression of slightly confused concern.

She sighed. Another guy baffled by her not-weeping, not acting coy or crushed or angry or resentful. Bruno sometimes called her the Anti-Drama Queen. "Yeah, I'm fine."

"Brilliant." He lifted his dumpling in a toast. "Fantastic dumplings."

She almost laughed. He was an asshole. Okay, maybe a lightweight asshole. No, midweight. She felt the strain; avoiding the truth was delicate work, especially when you weren't certain what the truth was. He probably had no idea what to say. *Cue a song, here it comes*, she thought. But Daniel didn't sing.

"I missed you," he said. "All the guys did. In the car."

"No doubt." Her tone sarcastic.

He seemed about to protest but Wang Ping plopped onto Fanny's crate and grabbed her free hand. "Why you go bus?" she demanded.

Fanny took a bite of dumpling. Miss out on Liping throwing up across her lap, the resentment, followed by the friendly bossiness of the other passengers, the accident?

"You go for car," Wang Ping ordered.

Resistance was Fanny's typical response to being directed. But here was this kind, if bossy, woman, who had taken Fanny in when she'd been locked out of her hotel room. Plus, how else was she going to get out of Hongyuan? "Yes," she said, imagining the relief she was going to feel to pull out of this courtyard.

Wang Ping circulated back to the guys. Fanny watched Liu's face for signs of annoyance but he looked unfocused. He touched a hand to his left ear, a raw thing, lumpy and misshapen. Joe listened to Wang Ping attentively, drinking his tea in gulps, taking small bites of dumpling. What a delicate, polite man he seemed.

Zhou, Liu, and Wang Ping approached. "You are convicted to persevere," Zhou said.

Fanny hesitated, considering possible meanings. She chose an innocuous reply. "I'm all right, thank you." She tilted her head to feel her neck, which was tight and sore. In fact, the day after rolling off a cliff in a bus in the middle of China, she was fine. She'd always thought that it was easy to die in an accident, but maybe it was more a matter of luck or intention. How does one arrange an accidental death?

Liu leaned ceremonially forward, offering her a dumpling as if it were different from the others she'd eaten. Her gaze fixed on his grimy hand; she declined with a smile. Zhou said, "We implore you approbate our invitation sincerely traveling to wit our humble transport." This statement was followed by much back-and-forth between Zhou and Liu, Wang Ping interjecting commentary.

Zhou held open the front passenger door for Fanny. "Please, we sally forth."

She hesitated. Another vehicle full of men, one of whom she'd slept with, then fallen out with. *Be neutral*, she thought, *not neutered, neutral*. She set her bags on the floor and slid into the seat.

The following morning, in a cool gray dawn, Fanny watched the woman who ran the kitchen at the Zoigê bus-and-truck stop clean scallions. Small, with her hair pulled into a tidy ponytail, she efficiently smashed and minced a garlic clove, then chopped pork, the sound of the cleaver hitting wood. She wiped the blade with a towel, uncovered a mound of dough, punched and kneaded it, then began dividing it into small balls which she slapped flat between her palms. Mixing the pork, garlic, and scallions in a bowl, she filled her flats of dough, folding them into buns and placing them on the stackable slatted trays of a bamboo steamer. She worked steadily, stopping now and then to check the fire in the woodstove. When the steamer racks were full, she set the whole structure on the stove and wiped her hands.

A round-cheeked girl in a yellow jacket blew into the kitchen with her brother on their way to school. Fanny asked their ages—among her repertoire of Mandarin sentences. Seventeen and thirteen, though they looked younger. Hovering around Fanny, they tried to squeeze out a few English sentences they'd learned in school. Laughing, hesitating, turning away, touching her arms. The girl stroked Fanny's braid. Finally, the girl pronounced a complete English sentence. "Do you have a Mama?"

To these children, Fanny realized, she was an alien. Perhaps her arrival in this remote place was a token of something, full of meaning and import.

She said, yes, she had a mother, a father, a brother. If chance hadn't turned its sinister key, she *would* have a mother, father, and brother. She did not want these two children to think that she was entirely alone in the world. She glanced past the girl and boy into the courtyard washed in oyster shadows. Packed dirt, rusting oil drums, some bent tire rims in a pile. A cold draft blew into the kitchen. She zipped up her jacket.

"Morning," Yevgo said, setting his bag on the floor in the corner of the kitchen. He was unshaven, sleepy-eyed, with rumpled hair and a sweater he'd pulled on inside out. The girl watched Fanny and Yevgo, her eyes moving back and forth. "Sleep okay?" Yevgo asked, yawning.

"Not especially." Fanny saw the inside of his mouth, his teeth lined with gold and silver fillings. It was an astonishing sight, like looking into the earth, a cavern glinting with fine metals. "I couldn't sleep trying to figure out how to beat your slippery soul at cards." She sighed. "A good person like you, cheating—what is the world coming to?" They'd arrived in the dark and Fanny and Yevgo had stayed up late playing gin in the kitchen. Every time Fanny called gin Yevgo would be holding a perfect hand, or he'd have seven extra cards, or he'd be five cards short.

Yevgo smiled and rubbed his eyes. "The problem with China is tea." He looked woefully at the thermos, hissing steam, standing on the floor. "What I would give for a cup of strong, sweet coffee."

The girl leaned into Fanny. The cook spoke to her in Chinese and the girl backed off. She conferred with her brother over their next English sentence. Which was delivered as a single word. "Husband?" the girl said. She knocked her two index fingers together.

In a flash, Mr. Sly's gesture came to mind. Had it only been two days ago? "No," Fanny said to the girl. "*Pengyou.*" Friend. Fanny looked at Yevgo, pouring hot water for tea. She wasn't after a husband but he would make an excellent relative, and for a moment she wished he was related to her. The girl and her brother gathered their book bags and waved goodbye.

"I haven't been home in twenty-five years." Yevgo stared abstractedly out the doorway. "What's a few more months? My father is dead. My mother is dead. I'll find out when I get there who else is dead." The lines in his unshaven face were deep. "Nothing to rush for." His voice was low. He drank tea and grimaced at the watery green liquid in his cup.

They strolled out of the courtyard into a land as pure as a peeled peach. The crunch of their boots made the only sound. The sky grew lighter, the sun squinting a yellow eye along the mascaraed line of horizon.

Yevgo's sentences echoed in Fanny's head: *my father is dead, my mother is dead, and who else?* Yevgo, Mr. Wu, Liping, herself. Everyone had their dead.

Yevgo stopped and touched her arm. Fanny turned. Three ravens hunched against the wind like judges, looking stern and cold, as if they would welcome a cup of tea. Farther along they spotted an eagle, huge wings spread, lazily cruising on the wind, head swinging back and forth.

Driving north to the boundary between Sichuan and Gansu Provinces, they passed yaks, skinny-necked sheep with curling horns, rows of gleaming white stupas, a black tent in the middle of nothing, not even a nearby source of water. A pair of egrets flew overhead. No sound but for the wind. There was the rare person: a shepherd lying on the ground; four riders abreast on horse and yak, rifles slung over their shoulders, sleeves down to the ground, daggers in their sash belts, strings of heavy beads around their necks. Grand men, riding out of a different century. Fanny felt a tug of nostalgia at the sight of a town with a windswept dirt basketball court, the rims bent and rusted, the posts crooked, like towns in northern New Mexico.

Zhou, gripping the steering wheel, craved the distraction of conversation. He tried to take as little note of the landscape as possible. He surveyed the stretch of dirt road in front of the car's hood and he checked the rearview mirror and the ribbon of dust trailing behind. Both views made him feel unaccountably sad. "What is your vocation, if you kindly oblige my inquisition?" Zhou asked Fanny. It was her turn in the front passenger seat.

She told him that she worked in a hospital, not saying that she was thinking of doing something else because it was practically impossible—so it seemed to her—for a Chinese person to change jobs and she didn't want to make Joe feel badly.

Zhou told her about his guesthouse job, about his brother and his injuries, and about how he, Zhou, had become a taxi driver. Zhou tapped his forefinger on his nose. "My brother image is precisely me." He paused. "We are . . ."

"Twins."

Zhou nodded.

"Identical twins?"

Indeed, he said. Zhou was enjoying himself. Fanny's face was in shadow and she seemed, in Zhou's peripheral vision, a listener without prejudice or judgment. A perfect listener. After a few minutes Zhou asked if, in Fanny's family, there were brothers and sisters. Where rested the home of her parents?

She hesitated, staring out the windshield. Twice in one day. You could learn to hide your losses within yourself but when you had to reveal them to others, their ugliness was unmistakable. The fact that her family was dead and she wasn't seemed somehow suspect; how had *she* survived? What made her so special? On the other hand, she was bored with grief. It clamored for her attention in an irritating manner. Didn't she have enough to cope with? She couldn't pet her grief every ten minutes, too. "My parents died when I was a teenager, in an airplane accident. My brother died last year. In a motorcycle accident."

"Uh," Zhou grunted.

The Chinese expressed agreement with a deep grunt.

"Please accept my deep congratulations," he said, with a sigh and a mournful bow of his head. He downshifted as they approached a slope. The engine whined.

Fanny stifled a laugh, coughed. She must not laugh. She'd told him her family was dead; it would be bad behavior of the highest order to burst into laughter. His tone was perfectly pitched to express sympathy. She felt so grateful for his mistake she wished she could hug him. *Please accept my deepest congratulations on the loss of your entire family.* She leaned over and pulled her water bottle from her pack to hide her smile, her overwhelming desire to laugh and laugh.

Zhou felt he was beginning to understand something about how the rest of the world thought. This foreign woman had lost her parents and her brother and had come to China, far from her home. When people suffered, they went away, they embarked upon a journey. Perhaps this was what he was doing, too.

Fanny drifted into a doze. She had not known Bruno; he had known her. To be known was a gift and an oppression. Maybe she had both failed him and granted him a certain freedom, by being wrong about him. She shifted in the seat, trying to get comfortable. It seemed as if she'd been sprinting across Asia to arrive here in this lumpy car seat, with this noisy engine playing in the background, to listen to Joe's sweetly antiquated British English spoken with a Chinese accent. It was never too late to arrive, even if it was not at your desired destination.

Chapter 26

In Gansu Province the road was paved and there were signs in three scripts: Chinese, Tibetan, and Arabic. On the other side of a pass, trees for the first time in days: tall dark pines. Daniel had kept everyone singing through the morning. A few old blues tunes and then, "*In the jungle, the mighty jungle,*" which he split into parts, giving the front seat one part, and the back another. The music did its work. They rolled down the windows and sang into the surrounding emptiness. In a village where they stopped for lunch, Zhou ordered a feast: yak, pork and onions, pork and peppers, eggs, fried potatoes, rice, soup, and steamed buns followed by cups of tea with cardamom balls and rock sugar.

A couple of hours after dark they pulled into the courtyard of a guesthouse on the outskirts of Xiahe, a small town with a large Tibetan Buddhist monastery. The guesthouse had once been the summer residence for the monks. Every inch of exterior wall was painted in a crowded pattern of blues, reds, yellows. A woman with her hair wrapped in a white towel dreamily mopped the corridor around the inner courtyard in the dim light provided by two bulbs. Birds chirped in the dark. Yevgo and Fanny played gin on the bed in Fanny's room. The only sound was Yevgo's breathing and the snap of cards, the occasional sentence spoken by Yevgo—"Give me something I need"—and the occasional curse from Fanny.

Daniel strolled the perimeter of the courtyard, zipping his jacket against the cold. All he'd gotten out of the blue pill was a crushing headache and an uneasy stomach; not fun pills. He stopped across from a room where he could see the silhouettes of Fanny and Yevgo. He'd spied them late the previous night playing cards, and here they were again. Cards, not sex. He turned away and walked out of the courtyard to the edge of a large fallow field, lumpy and churned up, ghostly with the bent stalks of its former crop. When he was younger, he'd longed for a brother or sister. Later, there were step-siblings, his father's kids, but Daniel wasn't close to them. Yevgo had gotten a room of his own, possibly because at this guesthouse it was possible. The game day rankled still in Daniel; he *hated* to lose. He shoved his hands into his pockets and buttoned the top button of his jacket. Beneath the sky rolling its freight of stars, a half-moon hung near the horizon; the cold and dark and silence gradually seeped into him.

In Fanny's dream, her parents, who had lived to grow old, had come to China to visit her. One night her father ate too much and died. Fanny felt responsible. If she hadn't invited them to China, her father would still be alive. Her mother was angry at her father; she'd told him that he couldn't eat like that at his age. Fanny was desolate and knew that Bruno would be furious with her for letting it happen. Then a Chinese woman tried to get Fanny to join in a game of flag football being played in a huge field. She told the woman that she knew how to play but it was unfashionable, nobody played flag football anymore. Fanny sagged onto the ground weeping. She said, "My father died, I can't play." When she awoke, she thought she'd had the dream because she'd eaten too much at lunch and because, well . . .

It was still early when she stepped into the courtyard to find Yevgo closing the door to his room. They set out across the fields into town. Fields that resembled the one in her dream.

"Do you always cheat at cards?" Fanny asked.

"Sometimes always," Yevgo said.

A woman wrapped to the eyelids in a scarf topped by a broad-brimmed hat joined them. She asked for Fanny's boots, and then for her shirt. Fanny gave her a battered pear she'd bought in Chengdu. The pear had traveled some eight hundred kilometers. The monastery gleamed golden above the town in the morning sun. Old men in round sunglasses with flat crystal lenses watched passing traffic. Monks in red robes were everywhere laughing and talking; men in long black coats and white cotton skull caps strolled the streets. Xiahe had a mixed population of Tibetans, Hui, and Han.

Pilgrims circumnavigated the monastery buildings, prostrating themselves, some with knee and hand pads of wood or cloth. Others spun the giant prayer wheels set into a long row. Behind the incessant clicking of the prayer wheels was the low hum of chanting. Fanny and Yevgo entered the shadowy rooms of the monastery. It smelled of dust, feet, and yak butter lamps. Threadbare *thangkas* hung on the walls, and every surface was covered in colored rugs, hangings, and cushions. A monk pointed out the Living Buddha, dressed in a wide, finely pleated red wool robe, a magnificent mohawk of a yellow hat on his head. A pigeon flapped through sparkling dust high overhead.

At noon, several hundred monks gathered outside the main hall. White smoke poured into the air from an urn filled with burning juniper. The monks sat on the steps, horsing around and laughing while removing their boots. They trod barefoot into the hall, leaving behind rows of identical felt and leather boots. Fanny and Yevgo peered into the great hall; sunlight cast bars of yellow through the dark room. "Life elsewhere," Fanny whispered. After awhile they sat on the cold concrete steps and listened to the chanting coming from inside. Yevgo shifted, straightened, and bent his legs. His back was stiff.

"What is it about life elsewhere?" Fanny said. "Why do we go to so much trouble? Why is the life we know not enough?"

"Curiosity, restlessness." Yevgo said. "Longing."

"Longing." Fanny mused. "The romance of the world." They began to walk back to town. "Travel is everything: beauty, confusion, failure, adventure, risk."

"Love," Yevgo said.

Death, Fanny thought but did not say. She made a face. "Not love!"

They strolled down a street of shops selling pink and orange flowered bedspreads, plastic flowers, and Tibetan things: harnesses set with coral and turquoise, bracelets, heavy necklaces, rope, saddles. "You ever ride horses, fish, go camping, anything like that?" she asked.

"Hell, no."

"But here you are, in the middle of China's outback."

He shrugged. "For some things, there are no explanations."

She regarded him thoughtfully. "At least you have a destination. I guess I've got an objective."

"An objective? You mean like: 'find yourself' or 'lose yourself'?"

"No." She punched his arm. "Like: disperse Bruno's ashes. Free myself of grief."

"My Russian grandmother used to say that you can have as much joy in your life as the grief you absorb."

"Then I should be ecstatic."

"Maybe you are."

"You think?" Fanny laughed. She hopped up and down. "Maybe I am. Maybe I am."

The white minarets of the mosque rose into the sky above the town like a pair of baby pagodas. Dogs slept in the streets. Children chased after Fanny and Yevgo, shrieking, "Hello hello bye bye," shrill and relentless. A regal woman sitting against a mud wall yelled at the children, who instantly shut up. Fanny thanked her and, unsmiling, the woman bowed.

"Good comes of trouble; trouble is good. Wait, wait." Yevgo halted at a bakery. "Bread! We haven't seen bread in weeks." He bought a small brown loaf and they walked to the river where monks sat on the grass blowing long horns. Lengthy, deep mournful notes split the quiet. Fanny and Yevgo settled nearby and had a picnic of bread and oranges, Yevgo saying that some cheese would be nice. No cheese in China. Fanny noticed how beautiful the monks were—perfect rosy skin, hazel eyes, straight white teeth. Not a cloudy, depressed countenance among them. A notable difference, she thought, from the monks she'd seen on Emei Shan. She lay back, the cool earth hard against her head. *Basking in ease, that's what I'm doing*, she thought.

Daniel had awakened feeling refreshed and energetic, psyched to be in a town with tourists, ready for the next episode of Escaped Democracy Demonstrator. First he found Dar, an American with two earrings and blond curls that hung in his eyes. Dar was on leave from Stanford where he'd been studying philosophy. "Stanford's cool, man. A good place to lie in the sun and party." He announced that he thought the Chinese the ugliest people in the world and the Tibetans the coolest, though they should consider taking more showers. Daniel noted Dar's unwashed hair, his stained T-shirt, his saggy streaked jeans, and shook his head. They walked around for awhile, Dar talking nonstop, Daniel keeping an eye out for other tourists. "They know nothing about sex," Dar said.

"Impossible," Daniel said. "The population is growing."

"I'm not kidding. A nation of virgins. A billion people who haven't had sex before they're married."

"You do recognize the illogic of that statement." Daniel was pretty certain that the two Chinese guys he knew—Joe and Liu—were not virgins.

"I met this guy on Hainan Island. He was twenty-three years old and had been up all night thinking about some girl. He couldn't sleep and when I said, sure I've had sex, he acted like I was some kind of god. It was weird, man." Dar shook his head.

Although now that Daniel thought about it, had Joe mentioned girls? Still, he thought Dar was deluded. He watched the entrance to the monastery. Two tall blonde women emerged and looked around hesitantly. He said to Dar, "Wait here."

Shortly, Daniel led his three recruits to the river where he was to meet Zhou and Liu. Daniel introduced Dar, then Jetta and Anna from Amsterdam.

Liu drank from his jar while the foreigners settled on the dry grass along the river, which was little more than a narrow ribbon of clear water. He twisted the lid on and off his tea jar, sipped the tea, twisted the lid. He began his tale, his voice shaking. While he spoke, monks, in groups of three or four, drifted near, appearing at the lip of the road above Liu. Gradually the red robed figures moved closer. They listened, leaning against each other, examining the faces of the foreigners. Zhou caught Liu's attention, but what could they do? Besides, it wasn't as if Buddhist monks were a threat.

Fanny and Yevgo strolled along the road that ran parallel to and above the river. The weather was clear and cool. Fanny was thinking that friendship was less likely with age, less of a happy accident. Yevgo was such good company. What a piece of luck to make a new friend. "There's Joe." Fanny pointed. They spied their traveling companions plus three blonde westerners. Liu drank from his jar, swiped his mouth with his sleeve, coughed, spat. Monks stood around, their arms draped over each other's shoulders.

"It's not real, you know," Yevgo said.

"What happened to Liu?"

"Bingo."

Fanny didn't say anything.

"It's Daniel's scheme—he won't call it a *scam*."

Fanny remained silent.

"You knew, right?" Yevgo said, watching her.

"Not for sure." She remembered thinking that Daniel was being duped, fleeced by Joe and Liu. Wrong again.

"Joe wouldn't do anything to take advantage of anybody," Yevgo said.

Fanny nodded.

"What's that look on your face about?" Yevgo said.

"The money," she said.

"Three-way split." Yevgo linked her arm through his and turned them toward the edge of town. "Joe bought a watch in Chengdu and you'd think it was the fucking Hope diamond." He shook his head. "They've been wearing the same clothes the entire trip. They don't have a suitcase or duffel between them."

"You mean, at least they're earning money," Fanny said.

"I'm paying Joe too."

"Maybe he's getting rich."

"By Chinese standards."

Suddenly, a girl's voice called out from amidst the knot of monks. She pushed to the front, shouting, Lies, lies. They are telling lies! Pointing at Zhou and Liu.

A peaceful, dazed smile came over Liu's face. He turned to Zhou and they nodded in understanding: caught at last.

The young woman faced them. It's not true! Nobody who was arrested has escaped or been released. She stared down Liu, who gazed blearily back at her, his head bobbing loosely. He held out his tea jar, proffering a swig of his special tea. She brushed his hand aside. Her voice trembled with emotion; flushed mottled patches appeared on her cheeks. You don't know what you're talking about, she said.

That's right, Liu said and snorted a laugh. We don't know what we're talking about! He raised his jar high. In China, nobody knows what they're talking about! His face streamed with sweat though it was cool by the river. Jar aloft, he continued shouting, Here's to lies and misinformation! Here's to doing wrong for the wrong reason!

Zhou tried to wrest the tea jar from him but Liu crammed it under his arm and turned away, mumbling, Can't have, can't have.

Zhou said to the young woman, Were you at Tiananmen Square? He spoke very softly, hoping the monks, who were crowding close, wouldn't hear. What he'd been expecting all along was happening and it was not as he had expected.

"What's all this about, Joe?" Daniel called out. Dar and the Dutch girls watched, riveted and bemused.

The girl said to Zhou, My brother and my cousin have not come home from Beijing. They went to support the students. I don't know what has happened to them. I don't know where they are.

Zhou could see that she might cry, or maybe she would punch him. He said, I'm sorry. Please accept our deepest apologies. It's a mistake, this thing that you've heard. Our mistake. We do not wish to hurt. We respect the demonstrators. Please forgive us. He bowed his head. I only wish we could help you. He looked around for Liu to agree but Liu was nowhere in sight. Oh, he exclaimed. I must . . . He set out down the riverbank, calling out Liu's name.

The monks jostled each other, the young woman walked back up to the road. A couple of passing policemen paused and the monks dispersed. In a matter of minutes, Daniel was left alone on the riverbank with his recruits. "Let's get some beers," he suggested.

Zhou found Liu stretched out in the grass a quarter mile down the river. He sat and awkwardly patted Liu's shoulder. After a moment he suggested that they get back to the taxi and did Liu think it might help if he drank less?

No, no. I have to.

Have to?

Drink.

Why?

In answer, Liu rolled over and covered his face with his hands.

Okay, okay, Zhou said. Let's go, come on. He helped Liu stand, led him up to the road, and flagged a donkey cart. They clopped slowly out of town; Zhou saw Fanny and Yevgo crossing the field toward the guesthouse. At the guesthouse, Zhou made Liu drink tea while he packed the car. Fanny and Yevgo arrived and threw their gear into the trunk. "Where is Daniel?" Zhou asked. Zhou was beginning to have doubts about Daniel, to feel a stain on his judgment of him.

Fanny and Yevgo glanced at each other and shrugged. They'd witnessed the scene down by the river from a distance.

"What's our next stop?" Yevgo said. He and Liu had sorted out the rest of the route, all the way to the town of Ghulja at the western border. It's not as if the route was complicated; there was only one road that cut west across the expanse of Xinjiang.

"Xining," Zhou said.

"One of those towns transliterated into English with an *X*, but pronounced like *sh*," Fanny said. "*X-i-n* is *shin*. *X-i-a* is *shia*. Xining, Xiahe, Xinjiang."

Yevgo rolled his eyes. "Why so fucking complicated."

Liu was trying to insist that Fanny sit in the back with him. His face was dirty and smeared, as if it had gotten wet and he'd half-swiped at his cheeks and mouth. Fanny smiled and stepped back. He smelled powerfully of alcohol.

Daniel blew into the courtyard, full of energy, his bag over his shoulder. "Thanks for waiting." He put an arm around Zhou's shoulder and squeezed. "Whoa, that was weird. What *happened?*" He shook his head, grinning. "I thought you guys might be in trouble."

Liu lurched forward, grabbed Daniel's belt.

Daniel jerked back. "Leave my belt the fuck alone!" Immediately he resumed his wide, giddy smiling. "Y'all ready? Let's blow this candle out." He shoved his bag into the trunk and popped into the back seat, scooting to the middle and singing, "*Let's load up the car and buy a camel . . .*"

Chapter 27

Dawn came like the exhalation of a deity. Zhou shivered in the icy light and watched the slice of moon fade on the horizon. After a long drive and a poor night's sleep at a truck stop, Zhou had awakened everyone early and they set out for Xining. Once they left Xining, they had 2,500 kilometers of mostly empty desert to the border. The car was in desperate need of repairs. They stopped often for Yevgo to tweak and fiddle in the engine. Zhou drove with urgency. He felt their luck was leaking away.

In the gray morning, plush as a blanket, Liu argued that they should take a Qinghai license plate to make the trip easier on themselves. In the dark, they'd crossed into Qinghai without fanfare or a sign. A plate from Qinghai Province wouldn't stand out in Xinjiang, Qinghai Province's neighbor. Not the way a Guangzhou plate stuck out.

Take, Zhou said. You mean *steal*. He couldn't handle more lies.

It is the difference, Liu said, between getting caught and having to lie, or not getting caught and not having to lie.

I should think you've had enough of lying, he said to Liu. He hated the word *lie*. After a few minutes of silence, Zhou glanced at Liu to see tears streaking his cheeks. What *is* it, Zhou said.

Liu swiped his cheeks. You know, he said.

Zhou sighed, exasperated. I do *not* know. I cannot read your soul.

By late morning, on the outskirts of Xining, they found a repair shop. The mechanic was Hui and wore a white crocheted skullcap, torn along its hem. His shop was on a narrow backstreet littered with cabbage leaves and puddles of oil. He had grease-blackened hands and a prominent nose. As they discussed the car and its troubles, his eyes slid over the car's plates. He avoided eye contact, stuck his head under the hood, and mumbled that he'd be finished in three hours.

The others left and Zhou sat on a steel drum at the entrance to the shop, watching children in the street kick a homemade toy, a ball made of rubber bands with feathers attached, like a rooster's tail. He held the small wooden Buddha that lived in the glovebox, which he was surprised to realize he'd taken out. Men came and went. Some lingered and chatted with the mechanic, his body half-hidden beneath the car. When the shop emptied, the mechanic grew talkative. He asked Zhou about jobs in Guangzhou, the weather, the proximity to Hong Kong. Could you see it? His voice came from underneath the car. He'd heard that the buildings in Hong Kong were so high they were always in the clouds. Like mountains.

Zhou answered politely, inserting a mild joke here and there. Nothing wrong with being amiable to the mechanic. He'd never been to Hong Kong and merely repeated rumors. He could smell his own sweat. They were far from the area proscribed by the car registration. Anyone might hand them over to authorities and Zhou was beginning to see Liu's point about the license plate.

The mechanic slid free of the car to show Zhou a worn part, caked in oil and grime. Be careful, the mechanic said quietly. The policemen in Gansu were suspicious of cars from other provinces.

Thoughts inside Zhou's head turned to static. He felt a horrible satisfaction: his nightmare would come true. The sun was a harsh glare in the street. A man pedaled slowly past on a bicycle, the chain clicking. Was the mechanic going to turn them in, or not turn them in, Zhou asked.

Not turn them in, the mechanic said, shaking his head.

The way he said it, Zhou surmised that he had been in trouble himself once. Qinghai Province was known for its prisons and labor camps. Prisoners, political or common criminals, were released into the province because they were not given resident permits to return to their former homes. There were outlaws of all kinds out here. Zhou felt himself relax. At least he was in good company. He used to believe that it was best to act correctly, to fit in with the right way of life in China. He was beginning to think it was better to be outside and to be amongst outsiders.

The mechanic resumed his friendly interrogation. Was it good money, driving a taxi in Guangzhou? A big city. Who, he wanted to know, had the money to take a taxi? How long had it taken them, from Guangzhou to Xining?

It felt like it had taken years of his life, Zhou thought. They'd driven some 1,000 kilometers since Chengdu, and to Chengdu? Fifteen hundred kilometers, at least. Zhou had never traveled such a distance. To think that he'd driven it and that they were only halfway to their destination! Zhou paid for the repairs from a thick roll of bills he carried split into two pads in each front pocket. Do you think, he asked the mechanic, you could get us a Qinghai license plate?

An expired one, the mechanic said.

Zhou peeled off a few more bills.

The mechanic said it would take another hour.

Fanny yawned for the third or fourth time in ten minutes.

"Goddammit, you're making me tired, stop yawning," Yevgo said in a mock-aggrieved tone.

"Should we try these?" She held up a packet of what appeared, from the photo, to be sesame crackers. She turned the package over. "Only eight months past the expiration date."

The shop where Fanny and Yevgo were purchasing supplies for the next leg of the journey—up onto the Tibetan plateau and across the edge of the Taklamakan Desert to China's western border—was divided into counters, each with its specialty: needles and thread at one; open bins of crumbled, dry cookies behind another; cans of processed meats at a third; and so on. The counters were each staffed by one or two uniformed clerks, tired and bored. A few slept. Some drank tea, staring into space. The rest gossiped with the focus of a survival tactic. Fanny described the shopping process to Yevgo: the purchase of an item involved going back and forth between clerk and cashier to exchange rice-paper chits for rice-paper receipts, which were then

stamped, punched, initialed. "I can only think it's a method for employing as many people as possible. People are assigned these jobs
but the work has little to do with what a person might be interested
in or good at. See how bored everyone is? They can't change jobs or
be fired," Fanny said. "Hence the fathomless, ubiquitous surliness. I
mean, who wouldn't be ill-tempered with jobs like these?"

"You don't have the right attitude," Yevgo said

Fanny raised an eyebrow. "No doubt."

"In your country, the value is always with the individual. 'Am I
satisfied?' Americans ask. 'Do I like my work? Am I making enough
money to buy the things I want?' The central question is always: 'what
do *I* want, what are *my* needs?' In a communist, or socialist, country,
the issue is the group. Is the work you're doing important for everyone, helpful to the family, neighborhood, town, country? If so, then it
is meaningful to you."

"That assumes that human beings aren't, by nature, selfish creatures."

Yevgo picked up a can. He glanced at the drawing of a pig on the
label and put it back on the shelf.

"The good of the group is not persuasive for long." Fanny prodded
Yevgo's bicep.

"Here we are." Yevgo opened his arms. "The crater of communism."

She shook her head. "I'm disappointed. I haven't noticed any *feeling*
for communality. If that's even a word. We need tea."

"Americans are raised from the time they're babies to focus on
themselves," Yevgo said.

"Black or green? In China, black is for men, green tea for women,"
Fanny said.

"Get both."

"Here's what everyone cares about: material comfort, which trans-
lates to money and the ability to buy things. For yourself, your family,"
Fanny said.

"But *you* don't buy things," he said.

"I don't want to have to carry it." She didn't have a family. She selected a box of jasmine tea and a box of green tea. "The material world
is irresistible. I'm not saying this is a good thing. Come on, who could
construe being a clerk as important to the country, the community?

Retail has no meaning because *stuff* is essentially meaningless and the selling of stuff?" Fanny pointed to a brown item with a red ribbon tied around it. *Yak penis*, the box read. "Poor yak."

Yevgo cringed.

"What does one do with a yak penis? Put it on a mantel? Boil it for tea?" She turned the box over. "Hey, did you say *crater* of communism?"

"Put that back." Yevgo waved at the box.

She laughed. "I love that—crater of communism. Where communism comes to die." She shook her head. "I know nothing. Not that my ignorance is going to stop me from forming an opinion." She smiled. "The flaw in capitalism is its overdependence on materialism and the flaw in communism is its overdetermination of people's lives. You're screwed one way or the other. Let's split up and meet back here in . . ." Fanny checked Yevgo's watch. They were at the cashier counter. "Ten minutes?"

Fanny shopped for plain white T-shirts. An extra T-shirt would extend the number of days she could go without doing a handwash. After making her choice, she turned to discover five employees close behind her. She said in Mandarin, Five Chinese people, one foreigner. Why? She made a funny face and the women laughed.

Yevgo found the games section and bought tips for cue sticks and chalk, which came in pink cubes rather than blue. He inspected the cue sticks, not well made, not expensive either, but didn't buy one.

Ferrying their bits of rice paper across the store, Fanny and Yevgo crossed paths. "About how bored these women look," Fanny said. "If you take away incentive, which might seem like a good idea—the state makes all your decisions and you follow along—it proves to be intolerably dull." They packed their purchases into their bags. "It's a mistake to undervalue independent thinking. To erase autonomy."

"Work hard, be happy." Yevgo arranged his bags on his shoulder. "A communist system aims to give people a sense of community, by force, by example. It gives a nod to proportion—family life, social life, work life. Not too much of one over the others. Communism should, at its best, create happy people who work just hard enough," Yevgo said.

Fanny looked skeptical. "Is that what happens?"

"In my dreams. Let's get breakfast."

Yevgo's life was a relay of meals, dinner handed off to breakfast, handed off to lunch, handed off to dinner.

"What?" Yevgo said, seeing Fanny's expression.

"I don't like Chinese breakfasts."

"You're a traveler, you'll eat anything."

"Breakfast is the most elemental meal. It's hard to give up your notion of what breakfast ought to be."

They joined the street crowds. The air smelled of coal fires.

"I want toast," Fanny said. "Anyway, I want to be clear that I'm not a fan of capitalism, which is all about shopping. Or, worse, marketing. Where's the soul in that?" She was beginning to sound a little wound up.

"What about Daniel?" Yevgo said.

"What about Daniel?" Fanny was startled at the change of subject.

"You can tell me." Yevgo tapped an elbow into her ribs.

"What?"

"What happened."

"I wish I knew." She adjusted one of the bags hooked over her shoulder. As they'd driven away from Xiahe, Daniel had made everybody laugh even though nobody felt like laughing. That was his gift. He could soften resentments and tensions. She'd felt his charm working on her. He *might* be a bad person—what to make of the democracy scam?—but his charisma and warmth made her like him and wonder if she was responsible for things going off between them. Also there was something, something that she couldn't put her finger on, that made her question her assumptions about him. She could hear him saying yesterday, *y'all ready*. Perfectly natural.

They were at a row of snack kiosks. "Let's get these," Yevgo said, pointing to slabs of fried bread with a thin filling of vegetables. He bought two slices, trying to make the proprietress laugh as she slipped the slices into folded sheets of newspaper. "Not even a smile," Yevgo said. He handed Fanny one of the breads. "Nobody ever tried to marry you?" Yevgo asked. They sat on a low concrete wall and ate their breakfast.

"Nope." Fanny chewed. "Yuck. Too greasy." She made a face and offered him the bread.

"Eat, don't whine." He patted her knee. "You can do it: chew, swallow. Keep your strength up."

The car wasn't ready. A chill wind pushed clouds around the sky. Across the street from the mechanic's, a man banged on a bicycle tire rim. They were waiting on the borrowed license plate. Borrowed: Zhou preferred to think of it that way. He'd offered to return it to the mechanic on his way back to Guangzhou, but the mechanic said, Keep it. A souvenir. He laughed.

Yevgo leaned against a wall. The wind made him cough and coughing hurt his chest. He felt unwell. The shriek of buses, blaring of horns, all that brushing up against strangers, it tired him. Fanny had been right, that bread was too greasy; he had a stomachache, maybe heartburn. He said he'd wait with Joe, pack the provisions in the car, refine their route. A second meeting time was set.

"Fancy lunch?" Daniel said to Fanny.

"I've eaten, but I'll walk with you." They turned onto one of Xining's central streets, shoulder to shoulder in the crowd.

"Where are your parents? I don't think I've heard you speak of them," Daniel said.

"Dead."

"*Both?*"

"Together."

"No shit." He stopped in the middle of the sidewalk, people bumping and jostling them. "Did I know this?"

She shrugged.

"When?"

"Ages ago." Fanny avoided his gaze.

Suddenly Daniel wrapped her in an embrace. "An orphan," he said into her hair.

She pulled away. "Yup, just like in Dickens."

"What did they do?" They resumed walking.

"They traveled: Mexico, Central America. Import business. They'd started going to India."

"So it runs in the family, this . . ." he gestured at the street.

Yes, travel ran in her family, not that it had done them any good. *You'd think we—or anyway, I—would never go anywhere,* Fanny thought. "Definitely my favorite part of China out here."

"Too brown. Too desolate. I miss green. Trees! Where are the forests?"

"I can almost imagine staying here, crazy as that sounds." It was comical to travel around the world to discover that your favorite place was very like where you lived. There was a symmetry to it: same kind of place, possibility of a different, fresh life. "It reminds me of New Mexico."

"I know what you mean," Daniel said.

"You *do?*"

He blushed. "No, not really."

She was surprised to recognize that he was lying. She didn't know what he was lying about, or why.

"Molinari's Italian? You Catholic?"

"Atheist Catholics. My parents didn't take us to mass. And you, what's Lowe?"

"Lithuanian Jew. An altered name."

A bus blasted past. "I reckon you . . . wish . . . traveling you . . . together," Daniel said.

"*What?*" They parted for a woman walking with her son.

"Your brother!" Daniel shouted. "You must miss him!"

Fanny stared. Jesus, enough already about her dead family. She covered her mouth as great black puffs of exhaust spewed from a van. She was not watching where she was going and knocked square into an old woman. Daniel tried to pull her out of the woman's path. Fanny reached for the woman so she wouldn't fall. I'm sorry, I'm sorry, Fanny said in Chinese. The woman glared.

"I am such an idiot," Fanny said.

"You okay?"

"Yeah, fine."

They walked in silence, Daniel keeping hold of her arm.

"You've traveled in the U.S., I bet," she said. "New York? No, Vegas. Everybody goes to Vegas."

He smiled at her, sheepish. "Promise you won't laugh?"

"No."

"Texas."

She laughed. "Do me a Texan."

"I can't," he demurred.

"But why didn't you say you'd been in Texas? It's practically my backyard. Come on, give me an Englishman's version of *y'all.*" Oh, right, she could say, I heard you say a perfect Texas *y'all* yesterday, a sound so unexpected she was still wondering over it.

They stopped where a market intersected the street, a bustle of people and food stalls. "Duck in here and get something to eat," Daniel said.

"I'll see you back at the mechanic's," she said. They were standing close and she was aware of the air against her bare neck, her own dry and cracked lips, his blue eyes which in this light were the color of the sky, and the shape of his mouth, at which she was failing to not stare.

He leaned near and they kissed, not moving closer and not lingering. Fanny had never seen anybody in China kiss in public.

She continued walking, then turned around and walked back. This was the way to see life elsewhere—on foot, insignificant street by insignificant street. Xining was the capital city of Qinghai Province, but it seemed merely an overgrown town. You could sense the unsettled expanse of the Tibetan plateau to the south and the basin of desolate desert to the north, Xining like a stone in a lake of emptiness. The area was considered the birthplace of China. A conundrum, because it did not feel Chinese. Apart from prisoners of all ethnic groups, the province was populated with Tibetan nomads, Hui, and Kazakhs. At a fruit stall, an elderly woman commented on Fanny's chapped lips and offered her a cup of tea. What would happen to China when its old people were gone—the people who had lived through its troubles? The men and their birds, the women and their Buddhism? Would it become a soulless place? What would be lost when their perseverance and suffering were forgotten, the knowledge and experience in their cell structure buried with them? Bruno had not been here. There were no entries in his journal under the letter *X*. Did that mean she was on her own trip now? Finally.

Fanny scanned a long avenue leading to the bony mountains surrounding the city, a cold wind sliding down off the plateau. The kiss had calmed her, lightened her mood. Even as an adult you wanted to feel anticipation and pleasure at a birthday, or Christmas. Her life felt mostly bleached of anticipatory pleasures. If she kept Daniel in her imagination, he was possibility—a doorway, a horizon, a corner. No doubt it was a mistake, to open that door. He was a scam artist of a kind (at least his scam was benefiting Joe and Liu); he was unpredictable. But she wasn't trying to spend the rest of her life with him, only . . . only what? It made her smile to think about. Failure was a kind of understanding.

Everybody except Liu was present. They stood around the mechanic's, waiting. Five minutes, ten, then twenty. Zhou checked his new watch every two minutes until finally he went in search of Liu. He searched restaurants—most were closed at this in-between hour—and walked through every shop that he thought Liu might enter. He skipped the shops selling pounded metal containers, the shop selling links of chain. As he searched he grew more and more angry. Liu was his assistant. He should be on time, responsible, helpful, thinking of what Zhou might need. When Zhou found Liu flirting with three blushing shop girls, he barely managed to resist putting his hands on his hips and berating him.

Liu saw Zhou, grabbed him by the shoulders, and told the girls, This is my driver. He's brilliant *and* he's single. He winked.

What the hell is going on, Zhou hissed.

Liu whispered in Zhou's ear that he was playing a government official come to the provinces to see how the new culture of luxury was catching on. Were people buying good quality shoes, perfume, nice soaps?

Zhou shook his head. Liu had lost his mind.

Liu patted Zhou's shoulder. Settle down. He said farewell to the girls, who giggled as he complimented them on their superior service, their dedication to the party's policy of bringing elegance into the lives of workers.

Zhou herded Liu in front of him like a prisoner. You stink, he said when they were on the street.

Liu laughed. A cocktail of perfumes he'd let the girls try on him.

Zhou couldn't believe those girls were so gullible they believed that load of crap Liu had shoveled about the party and luxury. Nobody in Guangzhou would have believed it for three seconds.

Liu nodded. It was true, he agreed. He was getting to like the provinces. Out here, people were still fresh. He shook his head. The good people of Xining weren't cynical.

Zhou stopped walking. Sometimes Liu's naïveté surprised him. They were only girls, he said. No doubt there was an abundance of savvy, cynical citizens in Xining. People who wouldn't believe Liu's nonsense. Those girls were young and foolish and they wanted to flirt. So who had been duped? Now Liu had to go through the rest of the day stinking like a courtesan. Maybe Zhou would buy him a flowered fan.

Where had Zhou's sense of fun gone, Liu wanted to know. This trip was turning him into a grouchy old cabbage.

What is happening to you, Zhou wanted to know. One minute Liu was weeping and despondent, the next he was happy like a crazy person.

Liu grew silent but Zhou could see that he was struggling to control his face. Perhaps, Zhou thought, it was the performances, or being away from home that was getting to Liu. They walked back to the mechanic's shop.

Liu broke the silence. I'm sitting in back with Fanny. *She* likes me.

As they were getting into the car, Liu reached out a hand to run his fingers along Daniel's belt. Daniel slapped at his hand and missed. Liu laughed heartily.

Chapter 28

Under *S* in Bruno's journal, Fanny found this:

A long ago story:
India on a solitary ocean voyage,
provoked by a trend of continental divorce
Africa from S America, Europe from N America
everyone from Antarctica.
One night India collides with Asia
& ensues a violent mixing of the two.
Asia fine bone porcelain, India grainy stoneware.
Still, offspring: the Tibetan Plateau
a table (plateau) & a bowl (basin)
highest table, deepest bowl
out of which flow the Indus Ganges Brahmaputra Yellow Yangtze
too cold dry high for agriculture
for centuries tents only—no vehicles appliances books
no stuff. but animals wool butter salt

Bruno had not talked about making it into Tibet so Fanny couldn't make sense of these entries. Had he gone there and never spoken of it to her? Another thing he'd not told her. She knew nothing! Nothing about Bruno. This thought was beginning to offer relief.

They took the road to Lhasa. The rusting Toyota skimmed along a river and then climbed the flank of the Tibetan plateau. Liu talked, his thick shoulder against Fanny's. Long rambling monologues, accompanied by gesture and expression, his voice rising and falling. Fanny smiled, nodded, looked baffled, amused, interested, though the content of Liu's conversation largely eluded her. She guessed, had the odd flash of insight, and covered her nose against the overpowering smell of perfume on top of alcohol. Several times she responded, but her grasp of Mandarin was so error-prone—she might have the right "word" but pronounce it with the wrong tone, in which case it became the wrong word—that she never knew if she was saying what she wanted to say. One thing was clear: Liu was flirting with her. A hazy, humorous, no-goal flirtation. Liu's clumped dirty hair, his rumpled stained clothes, his pudgy figure, his chewed earlobe, pretty much eliminated any chance of sex appeal. He had an air of innocence often imputed to round men, but there was something fixed in his self-interest, a ruthlessness underneath the charm.

At dusk, the sun slinking toward the horizon like a thief, they arrived at Qinghai Hu, a salt lake large as an inland sea in Qinghai Province. White caps dusted the water. Birds lifted in surges, their undersides burned white in the last light of day. The scale of the landscape was so vast, people looked like shrunken dolls. This austere landscape seemed to reflect some essential truth: the world was not made to coddle human beings. With a cold wind gusting, Fanny considered that here was a place, a whole part of the world, into which one might vanish. Maybe she was more like Bruno than she thought; if this were true, then to know herself would be to know Bruno.

The guesthouse at Qinghai Hu offered unheated dorm rooms in a concrete block. Temperatures inside were lower than outside. Fanny followed Yevgo, who did not look like himself. "Do you feel okay?" she said.

"Just a headache."

"You got aspirin or something?"

"I'll have some tea and rest."

Yevgo looked alarming, his color gray, his face sagging. Was it the altitude? "Shall I come get you for dinner?"

He was searching for his medications. How sweet to have a woman concerned about him. Temporarily, it made him feel better. "I've got snacks if I miss dinner."

Miss dinner? Everything she'd come to know about Yevgo indicated that missing a meal was a sign of trouble. "All right," she said reluctantly. "Let me know if you need anything." She started to walk away, then turned back. "I'll check on you after dinner, see if you want to lose to me at gin."

Yevgo sat on his bed and stared at a pile of dusty folded quilts and a stack of enamel washbasins, listening to the wind banging a window. His breathing was shallow, his chest tight. Back to sharing a room with Daniel. In his distant other life, the stable life which felt so far in the past that it might have belonged to someone else, his doctor had told him to watch for signs of pain down his left arm. He lifted his arm and gazed at it as if it might speak to him, inform him about what was going on inside his body, tell him what to do. It did not speak, and he had no arm pain. His chest felt under pressure, a kind of internal claustrophobia, as if his heart were slightly too big, too active, for its container.

When Yevgo's doctor had put him on medication, his blood pressure had been 180/130. His doctor, a second-generation Russian popular among émigrés, had told him to change his lifestyle: stop smoking, exercise, eat less meat, no fried food, more green leafy vegetables, lower his stress, take these pills. Yevgo *had* stopped smoking, kind of, for a time. He cut back, he stopped for a few weeks, began again, cut back again, stopped again. He'd tried the occasional game of soccer for exercise but he preferred his nightly pool games. Every now and then he gave himself two consecutive days off work. For a time, he took the pills regularly. At first they seemed to calm him and he felt good, but then the pills caused problems: insomnia, constipation, eventually what his doctor called "erectile dysfunction." Yevgo wasn't going to tolerate that. Why live if there was little to live for? The day after he'd arrived in Bangkok, he quit the pills. Traveling in Thailand and Bali was the easy life and he'd felt great. He ate fish and fresh fruit and swam almost every day. He hadn't smoked in months. Traveling was stress-free compared to driving a taxi in San Francisco and his whole family catastrophe: the loss of Fiera, the fury of

Fiera, the disappointment and anger of his daughters (somehow he was blamed for the fact that their mother had left him). Now he was rummaging through his pack, looking for those pills, which he should have restarted a couple of weeks ago when he first noticed symptoms. If he swallowed one immediately, maybe it would loosen the tight feeling in his chest and ease the sensation of air being squeezed through a too-narrow passageway.

The pills weren't in his toilet kit. He tried to remember when he'd seen them last. He stared into the kit: toothbrush, floss, razor, shaving soap, comb, a few loose Tylenol, other pills, a steroid ointment. He put a hand to his forehead. What else should be in here? The heart medication, butterscotches, some Chinese currency? Maybe two hundred kuai, a half-intentional emergency fund. No money, no medication, not even very many candies. Where had he put the pills? He sat back, closed his eyes. His heart beat against his chest like a fist pounding a wall. He took the matryoshka doll out of his pocket and set it on the bed. *Calmly, calmly*, he thought. Then he dumped the contents of his pack. He repacked, examining anything that might hold the pills. He found a pair of warm socks he could use, but no pills. Not as much money as he remembered though he was probably wrong about that. Definitely low on butterscotches. He put on the socks.

Yevgo disliked the business aspect of traveling: trips to banks, filling out forms, waiting in lines. He changed money in large amounts and hid the currency. There was something about foreign currency that never seemed real and he treated it like play money, protecting the real currency, American dollars, by carrying it in his money belt. Only Chinese currency was hidden in the pack. Probably he'd spent the yuan and forgotten. Possibly he'd lost the medication without noticing. In a tangle of clothes and receipts he found a card from Bliss Beer and Guesthouse in Bangkok. He'd give anything for a cup of that awful coffee the proprietress used to serve him every morning. He threw away assorted bits of paper and tickets. He took two Tylenol and drank several cups of plain hot water from the room thermos then stripped to his long underwear and slid under one of the big quilts. As he was falling asleep he saw on the floor under Daniel's bed a butterscotch wrapper. He turned over and fell into a restless doze.

The travelers, minus Yevgo, ate in a bare room that held six square Ming-replica tables and two benches. Fanny and Liu shared a bench, facing Zhou and Daniel. The food was delicious: fish from the lake, poached with chilis and garlic. Rice. The omnipresent cabbage but not too greasy. Fanny had come to rely on that cabbage. Its presence at every meal constituted the stabilizing familiarity of routine. She was eating greasy cabbage; she was in China.

Daniel ate heartily. "The end of the fucking world."

Liu snorted.

"In your wildest dreams, did you think you'd come here? This lake, these mountains?" Out the window waves churned the lake into a tousled gray bedspread.

"No," Zhou shook his head.

"What do you think of the trip so far?" Daniel asked.

Zhou was trying to be more forthcoming, but it didn't come easily, even in another language. "Perhaps," he began. He was beginning to like it out here and the realization surprised him. He felt safe among Tibetans and other minority people. Unimportant people. In such a landscape, how small and foolish his anxieties seemed. He shrugged, the way he'd seen Yevgo move his shoulders. He could not yet bring himself to say *I don't know* in answer to a question.

"What about your pal?" Daniel said. He hooked a thumb in Liu's direction.

Zhou asked the question of Liu.

Liu pursed his full lips as if he were blowing a kiss. The Prince of England wants to talk with me! Liu said.

Zhou groaned. *Please.*

Liu put on a thoughtful expression, tapping a forefinger on his nose. He smiled at Fanny out of the corner of his eye. Tell him this, he said to Zhou. I am most honored to have venerable foreigners provide the opportunity to see the greatness, no, make that *riches*, of my motherland. He bowed his head as if in reverence toward Daniel. What? he asked Zhou.

You are a pain in my ass, Zhou said, translating a Yevgo phrase into Chinese. He finds it beautiful, Zhou said.

Daniel turned to Fanny. "I know you love it out here." He paused in his eating. "But the loneliness of all this space, it makes you feel, no, it fills you with *longing*. For anything, for something missing. Don't you think? What do you long for?"

"Are you still working on that?" She was thinking of the cake and candle, of his desire to know what she'd wished for. The wish she hadn't made. "You first."

Without hesitation Daniel said, "Easy: fame and fortune."

"*Too* easy. I don't believe it."

He shrugged. "Your turn."

"No." She stared at the rice in her bowl. "I can't answer."

"Sorry, sorry," he murmured and reached for her hand.

Fanny let him take her hand for a moment.

Zhou had been roughly translating the conversation for Liu. He's trying to flirt with her, win her back, Liu said. Pathetic. Anyway, he's too fancy for her. She'd never resume with such a faker. His approach is too obvious, all wrong for her.

Do you want him to succeed? Because if you do, maybe you can advise him since you're the expert on how to charm foreign women. Zhou heard the sarcasm in his own voice with surprise. He was becoming like Liu.

It's simple, Liu said, undeterred. He should make her laugh. Was she laughing? Emphatically, no.

You make her laugh then, Zhou said.

No. She isn't right for me, Liu said. I respect her too much.

Fanny set down her chopsticks and asked Zhou, "Were you born in Guangzhou?"

"Yes."

"And Liu?"

"We are wholeheart friends."

"Do you live near each other?"

"To much grievous, we reside asunder."

Fanny managed not to laugh. She turned to Daniel, about to put a question to him.

"Look." Daniel pointed a chopstick. A man on horseback was galloping full speed toward the restaurant. He whirled the horse to a stop in a cloud of dust and clopped into the restaurant through the open door, past the diners to the kitchen. The travelers stared at the horse, breathing heavily and snorting two feet from their table, its flanks lined with lathered sweat. The rider called into the kitchen and a worker came out. They talked, the one on horseback, the other standing in a dirty apron with a ladle in his hand. The horse delicately lifted a hind hoof.

"What are they saying?" Daniel asked.

"It is not Chinese," Zhou said.

The rider finished his conversation, walked the horse past the table of transfixed travelers, and trotted away.

The four burst into laughter.

"Okay." Daniel held up one hand. "I, uh. I have wanted to say . . ." He paused. "For weeks." He kept his gaze fixed on the horse and rider diminishing in the distance.

Fanny and Zhou listened. Liu continued to eat, chopsticks scraping the bottom of his bowl.

"My dad's Texan." He grimaced. "Not for generations; his parents entered the U.S. through Galveston. I *am* English. My mum is and I went to school there. It's hard to explain." He fiddled with his chopsticks. "I knew you wouldn't . . . I don't know, it's not like *I'm* a Texan but my father lives in Houston. I've been to New Mexico." He coughed. "A few times. Not a big deal."

Silence followed this short speech.

Liu wanted to know what was going on. Zhou shook his head.

"You are American," Zhou said.

"Part."

What, what? Liu said.

He's American. English and American.

Twice the evil! Worse than I thought! Liu said. He socked Zhou's bicep. What have I been telling you from the start?

Be quiet, Zhou said. Later, he would taste the disappointment. He felt his pockets, suddenly fearing that he'd lost the small wooden Buddha. He didn't remember returning it to the glovebox. Had he left it at the mechanic's?

Fanny cleaned her chopsticks in her teacup and put them in their carrying case. "I need some sleep." Daniel was not who she'd thought him to be. He'd lied to her about the democracy performances and now this. But what difference did it make if he were a hundred percent English, or half-American? Besides, she felt she'd known something like this all along. How could she have so much trouble recognizing the truth? She slid off the bench. "Night, boys." Disappointment was not the same as regret, and it was the dry, stony landscape of disappointment where, out of familiarity or perversity, she felt at home.

She stopped at Daniel and Yevgo's room and peered in at the lump of Yevgo's body, tiptoed across to the bed, witnessed the rise and fall of his torso, and left.

In the middle of the night, Yevgo awoke. He was in a clammy sweat and felt as if his chest were in a vise grip. He was alone, Daniel's bed unoccupied. It was the altitude, it was the altitude, he repeated to himself as if it would make him more comfortable. Tomorrow they would drop down to sea level where he could get more oxygen out of each pump of his heart. So much work; why it was called "labored breathing." He took slow breaths. He didn't want to feel the pain in his own chest. He clenched the matryoshka doll in his sweaty hand.

The guesthouse had no locks on the doors and no floor clerks. The door to Fanny's room creaked open, sending in a blast of cold air. "That you?" she whispered and listened to his boots on the concrete floor. She didn't move, engaged in an internal skirmish about how much resentment to allow herself, but then she slid to the edge of the bed to make room. She shouldn't do what she was about to do but there was no one to stop her. The effort to arrive at bare skin was hampered by layers of clothing, her sleeping sheet (sized for one), and the enormous, weighty quilt, which was not unlike being pinned beneath an extra body. The clumsy, tangled maneuvering unfolded in silence, though at several points Fanny thought she might burst out laughing. She did not laugh, however, because they weren't on laughing-during-sex terms, but she imagined the two of them in a scene in a comedy. Sex in China was funny and this took the edge off her rancor. In the end, they managed without speaking a word and the effect was to unleash an unexpected tenderness, despite the window banging at their heads, the twisted mess of fabric, and the unholy discomfort of the narrow bed. After he left, she felt a relaxed, drifting, free-floating sadness. The Sad Traveler on her Sad Trip makes a Sad Mistake. A sad funny mistake.

Over tea and dumplings the next morning, only Fanny appeared rested. Zhou and Liu could hardly hold their heads up over breakfast. "Much strange noises in the night," Zhou said. Daniel, dark circles under his eyes and a yellowish cast to his skin, asked if anybody else had gotten sick. Something had kept him running to and from the toilets which were outside, across a dark, wind-whipped courtyard. It had been frosty and impenetrably dark. He'd nearly dropped his flashlight. Fanny announced that she'd slept beautifully. In the strident morning light, she couldn't make eye contact with Daniel but when she glanced at him out of the corner of her eye and saw that he was assiduously avoiding her, she felt galled at his presumption. She was the one making a mistake with him, not he with her. Avoidance was her prerogative.

"Don't gloat," Yevgo said to Fanny, about her good night of sleep. He had no appetite; he didn't know what was going on, but he understood the gravity of his situation. It felt as if his body had changed from automatic to manual. As if he would breathe only if he thought about each inhalation, each exhalation. In. Out. In. Out. There wasn't a hospital or a clinic for hundreds of kilometers. Where was Fiera when he needed her? If she hadn't insisted on leaving Tashkent, if he hadn't given in and let her win those arguments, if they hadn't left Tashkent, if they hadn't moved to San Francisco, if she hadn't abandoned him to his solitary fate, he would not be here now, having chest pain at twelve thousand feet on the Tibetan plateau, speaking a language he'd not grown up speaking, surrounded by a yet-more-foreign language. Alone. He would still be married to Fiera, living in Tashkent among friends, speaking Russian. He twirled his teacup, remembering the way Fiera cried when she was angry. Wept tears of rage and disappointment. Cried for what she wanted and what he hadn't wanted: to leave Tashkent forever. He'd given in, of course. What man could tolerate tears?

They were loading the car. "I'm worried about you," Fanny said.

"Don't worry."

"Your color isn't good."

Yevgo took hold of her arm. "We'll sit together in the back, with Liu." He winked. "And talk." A wave of nausea came over him. Her steady gaze regarded him without judgment or criticism, with a warmth that wasn't cloying, that had no underlying layer of resentment or anger, no ulterior motive. It was hard to lie to Fanny, who was his friend. He remembered the way that Fiera's concern for him had often been tinged with what she wanted and what she resented. He still didn't want to tell Fanny the truth about how he felt. The habit of not telling women the entire truth, of protecting himself from their small patting hands and prying minds, was too strong.

Zhou checked the glovebox: nothing but some rags and a pile of peanut shells. He'd lost the wooden Buddha.

Once they were under way, Yevgo said, "Tell me stories."

Quietly, Fanny talked. She told him about the trip she and Bruno had taken to South America: the list of countries they had visited, the motorcycle they'd ended up with, what kind of food they ate, what the people were like. On her other side, Liu was asleep, leaning warmly against her.

Yevgo's head tipped against the window. "My eyes are closed, but I'm listening." *Por favor, habla en español.*

Bueno . . . She continued in Spanish, talking about how she was never going to know if Bruno's death was intentional or accidental. Seeing in her mind the bus accident—her accident—the luggage and people scattered on the ground. Death could happen half-accidentally, almost-intentionally. What about fate? Was it the driver's fate, Liping's father's fate? Among so many other things she was fated to not understand, she could not understand the workings of fate. She glanced at Yevgo. "I don't know why death is less surprising when you're traveling." Beside her, Yevgo snored. She felt she'd been moving back and forth, closer to death one moment, closer to life the next. Liping's father's jacket buttoned to his chin, the Canadian woman tossed into the East China Sea like an emptied bag of chips. What was missing was the padding of the familiar, a kind of insulation. In a nontraveling life you could forget about death. Alone in the world, it was you, your self, your flaws, your life, your death. No safety net of friends and family, no protective circle of obligations and caretaking. Bruno had been her anchor to reality, to the present, and now that he was gone, what was there to hold her in place? She touched Yevgo's sweaty hand, the foreshortened index finger containing a story she didn't know. What was unknowable was at the center of life. Uncertainty could fill your whole consciousness.

A scattering of yaks in the distance, a Tibetan or two on horseback. Apart from these isolated dots, the plateau was a treeless expanse the size of a small country. Zhou relaxed. There was no traffic and he could think and daydream. Maybe he preferred this landscape to the heat and noise and crowds of southern cities. It still frightened him, but he could think. He thought about the trip, tried to anticipate problems, projecting his mind an hour or a day into the future, imagining solutions to possible trouble. It seemed to Zhou that he had thought, really *thought*, very little in his life.

He'd learned English, but that had required skills he already possessed, skills that every Chinese citizen refined: memorization and repetition. To survive in China meant to be silent or to parrot the correct line or phrase. Your memory must be precise, your repetition exact. The correct words had been sanctioned by the party and deviation was a sign of disloyalty. Studying English had been Zhou's single act of rebellion and it too required memorization and repetition. Little in his former life could be repeated on this trip; there was no way to memorize for the situations he found himself in every day. Now Zhou understood why Liu felt that anything was possible. If you could *imagine* opening a disco then you could do it. Why had Liu been able to think for himself, and Zhou had not? Liu's father had been a reactionary and gotten into trouble even before the Cultural Revolution. The entire family had suffered; maybe suffering had put Liu outside normal life. Through all of those difficult years, Zhou's parents had kept a low profile and Zhou had learned to blend in, to hide his thoughts even from himself. He had a shy mind. Maybe he *had* been thinking, only he hadn't noticed his own thinking. The pressures and unfamiliarity of travel were making him stronger. Maybe those same pressures were not working so well for Liu. Zhou checked his watch. Still the same time? A memory of the snowflakes he'd seen falling through the air somewhere on the road to Hongyuan came back to him. Very exciting; the only snowfall he'd ever seen. Mysteriously, the flakes hadn't reached the ground. They vanished in midair.

In Yevgo's dream he was trying to find a door that would open. First, he was in an apartment, not his old apartment in Tashkent, but nevertheless a Russian apartment. Then he was in a house like a Chinese hotel. Some of the doors had no handles. He pushed at them, felt for a secret handle. Other doors were locked. He bent down to examine the locks. He found a keyhole and looked through into a room full of tables covered in food. Coils of sausages, whole new potatoes shining with butter and sprinkled with parsley, thick-sliced bread, bowls of sour cream, a roast chicken, a tall yellow cake. He wasn't hungry. He stared through the keyhole and, aware that he was dreaming, wondered what he was after. Why was he trying to get into that room? There were no people and he was not hungry. Then he wondered if he was trying to get out of the room he was in, or get into the room he could see.

Zhou pulled off the road, sending a herd of yaks running. The men dispersed to pee. Fanny walked farther off and squatted, her skirt spread around her. Suddenly, the crisp horizon splintered; the men staggered, braced their legs.

Fanny felt the earth rise beneath her, shake her like a rug. A single vigorous thrash.

"Earthquake," Yevgo said. He had been in numerous earthquakes in both San Francisco and Tashkent, and one devastation: the 1966 Tashkent earthquake leveled the city, collapsed the apartment buildings of several aunts and uncles who, afterward, moved in with his family. Nobody died, but it changed the face of the city.

The travelers waited. The world was silent; even the wind died. There were no buildings to crumble and collapse, no volcanoes to erupt, no ocean to rise into a tsunami. The yaks fled in panic, halted, put their heads down, chewed a few tufts of grass, raised their heads, and stood still. The travelers got back into the car. The road had fresh cracks and lumps. Zhou drove more slowly. He felt a heady sense of release, as if the earth's sudden strong shaking had loosened something inside him. He looked at his watch, which was moving forward again. He smiled at Liu, who seemed unnerved. No big deal, Zhou said. This day we are lucky.

Chapter 29

They drove hard for two days, sleeping rough in a very cold truck stop. Fanny spelled Zhou since Yevgo was not feeling well enough to drive. She drove for a couple of hours at a stretch—once under a black sky full of stars, not a single light for miles; once through a cold, glaringly bright afternoon; and finally with a pink dawn in the rearview. They never saw more than three vehicles a day. On the afternoon of the second day they reached Dunhuang, a small dehydrated oasis town at the eastern edge of the Taklamakan Desert, bordered by mounds of sand dunes, smooth and warm as skin. A man squatted in the dirt beside the road, using a blowtorch to burn the hairs off a severed pig's head, the pig's four feet and shins beside him. "Welcome to Dunhuang," Fanny said. She gave Yevgo a measuring look.

"I'm fine," he said, glancing at her over the top of his sunglasses. "Don't put me in the grave yet." He cuffed her shoulder.

"You gonna eat?"

"Shit, don't worry about me."

"I'll worry about you if I want to."

Out the window, Yevgo saw a dusty lot with three billiard tables and men hanging around, games in progress. Every small town in western China offered outdoor pool tables.

"My generation are communists," Zhou said in answer to Fanny's question about religion. Fanny and Zhou were sitting on a stone wall in warm shade outside the entrance to the Mogao caves. After checking into the one hotel in Dunhuang that hosted foreigners, they had rushed to the caves, arriving ten minutes after closing so now they were gazing at an empty dirt lot instead of Buddhist temple carvings and wall paintings. Yevgo and Liu were back at the hotel sleeping. Nobody knew where Daniel was; he had been atypically quiet in the car and was often nowhere to be found after they arrived at their night's stop.

"My mother revised her attention for many years. I surmise that now and again, she beseeched privately. My parents are good communists. In that time, we had no shrine at home. Now my mother adheres to the temple near our home." Supplicating, he did not add, for his brother Yuyi's full recovery.

"Is it hard for her to have you far away?" Fanny asked.

Zhou gave one of Yevgo's shrugs. It still seemed strange that westerners expected their lives to go well. They thought life should be happy and fun; they sought to improve their circumstances and to succeed. They expected to get what they wanted and they believed in a better future. He had noted these qualities in the tourists he'd met through their performances. For a moment, he felt he was outside looking in at what it was like to be Chinese. His mother had been sad but not shocked when Yuyi was attacked and ended up in the hospital. His parents expected disaster to rain down upon them.

Momentarily stalled and idle, they sat swinging their legs. Zhou was trying out hopeful thoughts, rolling them around like a hard candy.

Fanny, who had been traveling for nearly six months, was thinking that after Yevgo was dropped at the border, she would turn around and make for Lhasa to disperse the remainder of Bruno's ashes. Maybe from there into Nepal. Never mind the wedding; she'd mail off a few apologetic postcards, which would take awhile to arrive. Never mind the problem of what to do with herself, with her life; the present was so dense there was no room for the future. The thousands of miles she had covered felt paltry. This was only beginning to be a substantial trip. Fleshy expanses of sand were visible beyond a hem of shade trees. In this part of China, the past felt close, as if it were resting barely beneath the surface. Perhaps because the towns were small, there were few roads, and not many people. Fanny turned her gaze toward the horizon, imagining travelers moving across this piece of geography for thousands of years, in every kind of weather, in every kind of mood. She was doing what humans always had done: countless travelers before her had made mistakes, worried, grieved, suffered, while on the move from one place to another, and then another. She was on an ancient route crossing difficult and dangerous terrain. It seemed most fitting.

"Shall we retire?" Zhou said. He looked at his watch: stopped again. This watch which he was so proud to have purchased was not a reliable keeper of time. He hated to admit it.

Evening light gathered and retreated. The orange ball of the sun bowled into the earth. The temperature began its plummet into cold. As they headed back to the hotel, Fanny felt a buoyant, vague hope though things did not obviously appear to be going well. Her confusion about Bruno and her behavior with Daniel were tangled up in the same chamber of her heart, as if there had occurred a mischievous conflation so that when she thought of the one grief, the other problem appeared, its hapless, less significant friend. She and Daniel had barely exchanged minor polite greetings since their silent grappling in that comically dreadful room at Qinghai Hu. Her attitude about him had shifted toward wariness and disbelief. It seemed more absurd than ever that she'd considered a child. Ha! But at least she was on the move in a foreign country and she liked most of her travelmates: Joe, Liu, Yevgo. Traveling made everything better, even suffering and stupidity.

Again, Yevgo searched for the pills. Why hadn't he made himself look for them weeks ago, when his symptoms first appeared? He was disorganized, of course. Inefficient, sloppy, careless. Careless about things, careless about others. Another reason Fiera had left him. She had complained for years that he did not take care of himself, his health, their lives, their possessions . . . She used to say that the reason they didn't have anything nice was because of him. He'd use one of her best towels to check the oil in his car. Once he brought three laying hens home and let them roam around the house. He lost jackets and umbrellas and sunglasses with such regularity that he bought only cheap versions and two at a time so he had a replacement ready. He left things behind. He counted his supply of yuan. As much yuan as last time. Was that right? An extravagant sunset played like an orchestra out the window and the echo of it reached Yevgo's room. Orange light streaked the beds and floor. Then the light turned blue, then there was no light. The vise grip that had clamped down on his chest had loosened its hold. Whatever was happening to him was either his fault or his fate. Technically, he felt better, in the way that the suffering of a hangover is a sort of cure for the chaos of drunkenness. He felt as if his muscles had been pummeled, his insides wrung dry.

At dawn, the travelers left Dunhuang in a dusty wake. Nobody had seen the famous Buddhist caves. Nobody had seen the great sand dunes. Five people in a hurry, tearing through Gansu Province on their way to Xinjiang. Gansu, rugged and barren, forgotten and poor, used to be the outer limit of the Chinese empire. The Great Wall ended there, in a feeble wobbling line of broken stones marking the end of the Han world. It was a conduit province through which for hundreds of years goods and ideas were carried into and out of China. Not the heart or lungs of the country, but an artery, a set of blood vessels. Now China's outer limit was the far side of Xinjiang, the border which Yevgo would cross and where the others would turn back. The adobe houses, the braids of red chilis, the sea of brown land evoked home for two of the car's passengers. Even the food was familiar to Yevgo: mutton kebabs, flat bread, thick noodle soup made with mutton. He was getting closer. Fanny decided that the light in Xinjiang was bigger, more diffuse, not as piercing as in New Mexico. It did not shine as fiercely into your soul.

Chapter 30

After the exposure of the open desert, Turpan was a respite of leafy trees, grapevine-covered arbors, and cool shadows. Bells tinkled from the necks of donkeys, and the wooden carts they slowly pulled creaked. From the highest plateau in the world, the travelers had arrived at the lowest point in China. They had been cold and now were hot. At twice the size of any town they'd passed through since Xining, Turpan was not large but felt to the travelers a metropolis. They planned to rest.

The inside of Daniel's nose was dry and cracked. He lay down on his bed at the Turpan Guesthouse, kicking his feet, which hung off the end, up and down, up and down. He was without access to butterscotch candies, Yevgo having gotten a single room. He sat up, flopped back down, unbuckled and rebuckled his belt. He'd recovered himself with Fanny, but he still felt jittery, uneasy in his skin. He hated the dust, the hammering of the sun, the fatty greasy meat, the oppressiveness of brown. Hellish. He wanted to break something, the monotony, the sunlight. He was aware, not a peripheral awareness, but a central awareness, that this journey had jumped its track of potential. His mission of self-improvement, his sense of passing tests and meeting challenges, compromised. In his mind, the image of his father's back. Stan Lowe liked to quiz Daniel while he was mixing himself a drink. Stirring and shaking a martini, his father speaking at the shaker, the bottles of gin and vermouth, the olives. Daniel would answer or evade, watching his father's wide shoulders encased in fine tailored cotton, usually white. If he was still wearing his jacket, the shoulders would be wider, clothed in soft gray lightweight wool. The back of his head communicated the focus he was giving his drink preparations: the arms lifting to shake, dropping to pour; the torso turning for a glass from the freezer or to spear an olive.

Cocktail hour was Daniel's restless time of day, the hour in which he was moved to grand designs. Restructuring, overhaul, upheaval. Of late, he'd fall into a reverie, imagining his next moves. He was considering New York or Chicago or Atlanta; his American passport the ticket to his next life. Then he'd crash back to the present, surprised to find himself in China, standing beside a billiard table in a dirt yard, or sitting in a deserted teahouse, or crouched in the dust by an irrigation canal, snapping a stick into smaller and smaller pieces.

"Sometimes this trip feels, briefly I admit, like a vacation." Fanny and Yevgo strolled through Turpan, past old men lined up in chairs against adobe walls. Streetside barbers wielded straight razors against scalps. In the market, piles of reddish spices, legumes, rice, melons, grapes, raisins, onion, garlic, squashes, bread, rope, hats.

Glancing down a side alley, Yevgo spotted a full-sized pool table. He went to investigate. Yes, a good table tucked into a narrow dirt side street. He made a note of the location, between a tea shop featuring a large poster of a kung fu movie and a metalworker's. The table was behind the kung fu movie poster.

When they ran into Daniel at an outdoor café, Yevgo thought, *We've become a family, stuck together, even though we don't like one another*. In his family, Yevgo was famous for joking and teasing a little too hard, too pointedly, even when nobody was laughing. There was the time he'd worked over Mischa, a good-for-nothing cousin, a minor hoodlum who thought he was dangerous though anyone could see he was lazy, coddled, not very smart. Mischa had curly black hair, big dark eyes, long eyelashes. Yevgo remembered laying into him, had it been someone's wedding? Anyaschka's? Or one of the Sunday dinners at his grandmother's? Ahh, this was what was fading, the particulars, the facts. There was no one else to remember. Fiera, that *puta*, refused, even when they'd still been married, to indulge in five minutes of nostalgia, five minutes of remembering. She left Tashkent and it was like she'd chopped the head off something. He respected her ruthlessness, but he resented it, too. The past, it seemed to Yevgo, was his richest material. His best daydreams were about the past. Sure, his worst, too. That only seemed fair. So he'd teased Mischa about his low-life friends, some black-market deal they'd supposedly been into, and everyone had laughed. The men slapping Yevgo on the back, happy to have Mischa get some of what he deserved. But Yevgo was too close to the truth and afterward, Mischa and one of his thug pals had grabbed Yevgo, pulled him down an alley, slammed him against a wall, held a knife to his throat. Nothing came of it. Still, damage had a habit of becoming two-way. Here he was, sitting down with Daniel, who resembled Mischa, come to think of it.

Daniel, sweaty, slightly breathless, jumped up and pulled out chairs. Fanny gazed at the blank postcards strewn on the table. A young boy arrived swinging a large aluminum teapot in one hand, balancing a stack of handleless cups in the other. He slapped down three cups, prefilled with tea leaves, and poured with a flourish, raising the teapot high and directing a fall of steaming water into the cups. Daniel handed the boy some bills.

"You treating?" Yevgo asked.

"You bet," Daniel said.

Fanny arranged the postcards so that they formed one large, discontinuous picture: sand dunes alongside a lake beneath palm trees beside a factory. Nobody said anything for awhile and they could hear the low burble of water in an irrigation ditch behind the café. The sun splintered through the grape arbor overhead.

Daniel broke the silence. "You're getting close to home. What's the visa situation?"

"Closer," Yevgo said. A thousand kilometers still to go.

"Maybe a former resident, you don't need a visa."

Yevgo shrugged. A philosophical movement between the shoulders and the neck. As if the head and the body, the mind and the heart, were attempting to reach an accord. "I'll finally get to have some fucking coffee."

The boy with the teakettle returned and splashed more hot water into each of their cups. "What if they won't let you cross the border?" Daniel said.

Yevgo smiled. "A chat, a little drink of something. Conversation can work like a piece of paper."

The air smelled of dust. The wooden table was scratched and nicked. Fanny wiped sweat from her palms. Why did people drink hot tea on a hot day? She was thinking about history again, and geography. They were at one edge of the Taklamakan Desert, a word which might mean, she'd read, *you go in, and you never come out.* Or it might mean *point of no return.* What to do about her own past, which felt both too far away and too close?

She hadn't had a chance to tell Yevgo that Daniel was half-American, that he was an ace liar. Probably Yevgo knew. It seemed not to matter who knew what about whom. The whole truth, a convenient truth, a half-truth, an accidental lie, a useful lie. She stared at her dirty fingernails. There was a blank space where her feelings, her attitude, about Daniel used to be.

"She never wilts, our Fanny, have you noticed?" Daniel reached out and tugged her braid fondly. "What's next for Fanny?"

"Not telling."

"What about the wedding?"

Wedding? Fanny stared at Daniel, those unsettling blue eyes. Of course, Cora's daughter's wedding. "What about you, where're you doing next?"

"Gonna stick with my buddy, Joe." Daniel shuffled the postcards into a pile. He asked Yevgo if he was interested in a friendly game of billiards.

Yevgo finished his tea. "I know the perfect place."

Fanny considered suggesting that Yevgo might not be well enough to spend time standing under a scorching sun, but she was only a friend.

As soon as the floor clerk opened the door to Fanny's room, Fanny forgot about her. The room had been sacked, her things scattered across the bed, onto the floor. It wasn't that there was anything of particular value, no electronic equipment, no cash. Ordinary things were the only things she had and their value in her mind was wildly inflated. She could be attached to a particular, unremarkable pen, or a paper clip might capture her affection. Bruno used to make relentless fun of her about this. She walked over to the bed, picked up a scarf, set aside the packet of Wen Li's letters. The silk fabric she'd bought in Shanghai, gone. The handmade wooden toys she'd bought from a street vendor, out of sympathy more than desire for the toys, gone. Photos, gone. Puffs of light powder floated into the air as she lifted a sandal, a book, a pair of socks. She moved away and sat on the empty bed. The sun shone through the window, a river of warm buttery yellow. Her left foot cramped and she took off her boot and sock and massaged her arch, surprised to see her red toenails; she'd forgotten that she'd painted them before leaving Chengdu. Shiny red toenails seemed an absurdity in western China. What was happening to her?

She put her sock and shoe back on and stood over her things, dusted in Bruno's ashes, wondering what to do. Bruno's remains covering her possessions, like a ghost's breath. She tried to scoop the ashes into a metal box she'd bought in Chengdu and which the thief thought too little of to steal, wondering what manner of thievery had occurred among the ancient caravans that rested in this town. The ashes rose into the dry air and drifted slowly back down. Her skin was powdered with ash. At first she felt light-headed, then she started to laugh. How weird and dark and comical. She heard her own laughter and recognized it: Bruno's laugh. Her laugh was Bruno's. And oh, how Bruno would laugh at this—his ashes all over her stuff. Her meaningless possessions about which she was always so particular. Bruno was with her in so many ways: the kinds of mistakes she made, her restlessness, her willingness to travel to the far edge of a distant place and slip from the seen to the unseen.

Zhou helped Fanny question the floor clerk, but they ended up spending most of the time reassuring the terrified girl, who went from hysterical weeping to fatal resignation in the space of three minutes. Fanny knew the *fuwuyuan* hadn't had anything to do with it. She only wanted to find out if she'd seen anything. Perhaps a tall, dark-haired, handsome foreigner fiddling with the door to Fanny's room? Hadn't Daniel told her that he had ways of getting into rooms without the floor clerks? The girl had been sound asleep, passed out in the half-dead semi-coma of the depressed. She sobbed and told Zhou that she couldn't lose her job even though she hated her job and was bored beyond tolerance by it. To be free of this floor! Its musty corners, the long dark hallway she gazed down every day until it seemed to her more like the inside of her own mind than an actual place. Fanny told Zhou to reassure the girl; they weren't going to report anything to anybody. Her job wasn't in danger. They only wanted information. If she had any. Which she didn't. Zhou and Fanny listened to the girl go on and on. *Oh hell*, Fanny thought, *probably it had been a stranger*. But if Daniel had done it—gone through her possessions, taken her photos, dumped Bruno's ashes over everything—it was personal.

Zhou, who was relishing his role as Inspector Bucket, repeated his question. Further supplemental query for the *fuwuyuan*?

Fanny stared at him blankly, then shook her head.

The felt on the table was dry, faded nearly white. There were two narrow strips of shade along two sides of the table; otherwise, the playing area was unshaded. A boy brushed the table and the cushions in preparation. From the teahouse, sounds of the advertised kung fu movie blared into the still afternoon. Though it was late September, it was over ninety degrees. A row of men sat on a bench against a wall beside the table: strong noses, wrinkled skin, shaved, capped heads, and long beards. Their hands rested on their knees or clasped the top of canes and their erect posture and serious expressions made them seem part of a court proceeding.

Daniel watched, with covert glee, Yevgo testing the cue sticks, sighting down their length as if they were shotgun barrels. Then, having chosen one, Yevgo replaced the tip, pulling a fresh tip out of his bag and performing a bit of transplant surgery with a penknife before placing a cube of pink chalk on the table and a hundred-yuan note.

"Nine-ball," Yevgo said. A fast game, a bettor's game. They lagged, Yevgo lost, Daniel racked.

The time Daniel had spent practicing was paying off. He felt confident and controlled. He glanced at Yevgo. Yes, the old man was taken by surprise.

When it was Yevgo's play, he flubbed in order to give Daniel the temporary illusion of a competition, then waited in the shade, listening to the sounds of kung fu mayhem from the movie next door. The air smelled slightly sweet with dust and manure and melon rinds.

Noting that Daniel's game had improved made Yevgo feel sorry for him. It dawned on him that when Daniel had been missing, he hadn't been out scouting for women, he'd been playing pool. Yevgo could see that the stakes were intangible, higher than he imagined. Daniel really, really wanted to beat him.

Yevgo won several games. The stack of bills on his side of the table thickened. Daniel had improved but not enough; he lacked strategic skills. He couldn't control placement of the cue ball to his own advantage or to thwart his opponent. Daniel racked. The heat intensified, lowering like a lid over the streets of Turpan. People disappeared indoors, the tinkle of bells and clop of donkey hoofs halted. The sounds of kung fu paused while the movie reels were changed. Yevgo leaned into the sudden quiet. The old men made for impassive witnesses, nodding sagely now and then. What, Yevgo wondered, did Daniel want from him? It couldn't be money. Money was such flimsy motivation. Yevgo could hear Fiera admonishing him for not knowing his opponent, for not gathering information that might be useful. According to Fiera, he foolishly assumed the best in others and did not pay sufficient attention to reality.

"I'm going to write a book about this trip." Daniel prepared to break, running the cue stick back and forth between his thumb and forefinger. The balls scattered. "You'll be in it." He smiled at Yevgo. "A supporting role." Pacing the table, he called the seven into a corner pocket. He stilled, bent at the waist, lined up the shot. His chest expanded as he inhaled and held his breath.

Yevgo coughed and spat into the dust.

The seven ball collided into Yevgo's three, popping it into a corner pocket. Daniel jabbed his stick in the dirt.

"Close," Yevgo said. He tapped his six into a side pocket, the four into a corner, the seven into another corner. The cue ball was spinning nicely, the balls meeting with a solid thunk.

Daniel shoved his shirttail into his khakis. "You'll be the aging man, just a tiny bit desperate. Just desperate enough to cheat."

Yevgo lifted his eyebrows.

The old men sent a boy for tea. They fanned themselves. Yevgo hadn't lost a game. Why dissemble? He took short breaks in the thin shade. His sweat dried before it had time to cool him, turning to salt crystals, a white powder dusting his temples and forehead. He felt light-headed with the occasional wave of nausea washing through him.

Daniel stalked the table, swinging his stick. A book about this trip was an excellent idea. He chose his shot, yanked his arm back, jabbed the cue ball; the balls slammed together.

Fanny came down the alley. "Hey," she said to Yevgo. "Have some water." She gave him her water bottle.

Yevgo drank in big gulps.

"Take it easy. You'll give yourself a cramp. Sip it, you ninny."

He stopped, gasped, dribbled some water into his palm, and splashed his forehead and the back of his neck.

"Here." Fanny handed him a bandanna and he worked it over his face and neck. She took out her book and fanned him. "Listen, it's enough."

Yevgo shook his head. "What snacks have you got?"

"Nothing."

"What, no food?"

"It's too hot to eat." She eyed him appraisingly. "Let's go."

Daniel continued to play, glancing up quickly when the three ball didn't quite make it into a pocket. He circled the table and kept playing as if he hadn't missed.

"How about you buy some peanuts, one of those bread things, an orange." Yevgo took up his cue stick.

"You won't eat," she said. His hands trembled gently. His skin was a translucent gray.

"Go," he said.

Fanny stayed. While Yevgo perused the table, Daniel came and draped his arm over her shoulder. "If you're going scavenging, I'd love a Coke. With ice."

She dipped her knees, slipped free of the weight of his arm. There wasn't a Coke to be had in all of western China. Nor ice. She noted a stiff plastic quality in his features. What *had* she seen in him? She wanted to say something explicit, bring the truth out. What truth would that be? Over his shoulder she gazed at the lineup of men against the wall, wearing clothes that looked like costumes from another era. Imagining other travelers who'd passed this way gave her the relief of a long view: even a glancing awareness of history made your problems small. She shook her head.

"What?"

"He's not well. He needs rest."

Daniel scratched his neck. "He's not complaining."

"Leave him be."

"My play." Daniel returned to the table and won that game, his first win. Some of the bills on the edge of the table were moved.

Yevgo made for the shade, coughing delicately.

The Hong Kong movie ended and a stream of men came blinking into the bright afternoon light. Liu could be heard before he was seen, his voice loud, jagged—sounding, even to those who couldn't understand him, wild and revved. He staggered around the corner and swayed to a halt. What have we got here, he crowed, belching. Zhou stepped around Liu and stood near Fanny. Liu drained his bottle of bai jiu, slinging the empty bottle by its neck. He reeled, regained his balance, his gaze settling on Daniel. He erupted in laughter, a raunchy, hacking sound. Liu raised his arms, backed up, and ran full tilt at the pool table, arms outstretched, hands hitting the edge as he vaulted himself onto the tabletop. It was not neatly done. Liu was pudgy, unfit and drunk. He sprawled across the table with a shudder, billiard balls careening against cushions and popping into the dust. He made one of those preposterously quick recoveries, the way drunks can assemble their bodies into configurations that would be impossible for them to manage sober. He shot to his feet on the table and began to do a creditable drunken imitation of John Travolta in *Saturday Night Fever*.

Zhou crossed his arms over his chest. Fanny was laughing. "Where the hell did he learn that?"

"What is it?" Zhou asked.

Fanny described the film.

"I fail to comprehend Liu," Zhou said with a sigh.

The old men were openmouthed with astonishment; the tea boy had an ecstatic grin on his face.

Daniel dropped his cue stick, reached up, and grabbed Liu's knees, toppling him. With a shrill yodeling cry, as if he were on an ancient battlefield, Liu fell with Daniel. A dense thud, a mess of limbs, Daniel and Liu down in the dirt. Daniel leapt to his feet, brushing his pants. Cursing, flailing in a swirl of dust, Liu lunged, grasped Daniel's belt buckle, and used it to haul himself to a standing position, pulling Daniel into a hot embrace. Liu wrapped an arm snugly around Daniel's torso and put his mouth up against Daniel's ear, whispering drunkenly. One hand worked loose the belt buckle, the other locked around Daniel's chest. Twisting, Daniel tried to break free but Liu held on. The buckle unleashed, Liu slid the belt from Daniel's waist as he shoved Daniel, turning him as if they were in a dance.

The audience to this strange spectacle—the moviegoers, the bench of judges, the tea boy—were transfixed. Fanny wanted to applaud. Liu lifted the belt like a prize snakeskin. Crowing and dancing, he lassoed the belt over his head. Daniel lunged, trying to recover the belt and tackle Liu. Liu spun away in comically mincing steps, took the belt between his spread hands, and, bowing, presented it to Yevgo—who was standing apart from everyone else—as if it were Daniel's head on a platter. Leaning wearily in the shadows, Yevgo waved Liu off.

Down the alley came slowly a policeman on a motorcycle with a sidecar.

Yevgo saw, astride the seat, in cap and goggles, his uncle. Not Uncle Viktor who died in a mass grave during World War II, but Viktor's brother, Joseph, who had played soccer, the village's legendary forward, and who used to tell Yevgo stories of how they cheated by throwing pepper into their opponents' eyes. The perfect defense, better than dirt or ash. Yevgo began to laugh. Quietly at first, but then it took hold of him, like a spasm, like relief. He laughed because he saw himself in a long line of men in his family who played games for profit they didn't care about, who cheated not for gain but for fun. The men of his family were jokesters, irresistibly, even when it landed them in trouble. He laughed because his uncles were dead and could no longer tell him about their tricks and mistakes. He laughed because he was in a far corner of a far country, because he was playing pool with someone whom he didn't like enough to want to cheat. The motorcycle engine revved, then went silent, and a cloud of dust drifted over the pool table. Yevgo sank down, laughing and coughing and laughing. In the dirt, near where Daniel and Liu had grappled, he saw two butterscotch candies.

The police officer, a thick, red-faced man, portly and with a club-shaped head, cut the engine, dismounted, and began to collect identity cards. Liu continued to preen, wielding Daniel's belt. Because Zhou and Liu were outside their registration area, the officer told them they must come in to the station. Zhou dutifully climbed into the sidecar. Liu scuffled, dodging and dancing around the motorcycle, sparring playfully with the officer. Finally, the officer bear-hugged Liu and shoved him into the sidecar alongside Zhou.

"We'll come find you," Fanny called out, watching to see which way the motorcycle turned when it exited the alley, thereby missing the moment when Yevgo tipped onto his side. When she turned around, Yevgo was half-lying, half-sitting, his face in shadow. She ran to him and said his name, shaking him gently, lifting his wrist, touching his clammy forehead. His eyes were closed, his mouth in a slack almost-smile; his wrist was heavy and silent, without a pulse. The crevices cutting through his cheeks on either side of his mouth were deep and sharply drawn. His hair was thick, an even mix of black and gray. She knew better than to pretend he wasn't dead, better than to imagine that she could make a phone call, summon help, summon people with expertise or technology that would restart his life. One of his fists was clenched. She pulled at his fingers and extracted the matryoshka doll, its painted-on features and clothes faded. She noticed the dense black hairs on the back of his knuckles, not a gray one among them.

Yevgo's winnings, the stack of yuan which had been on the pool table, were gone. She collected a few stray bills from the dirt underneath the table and a couple of butterscotch candies. She didn't have any idea what to do and felt unequal to the moment. She wanted to be anywhere except here beside the body of Yevgeny Velasquez. Yevgo, dead. It was impossible to accept even while she knew that she would accept it. She sat in the dirt beside him. The electric air tossed in a strengthening wind. A dark brown cloud stood in the sky at the edge of town. It shadowed Turpan like a hand and abruptly collapsed in a strong rush of wind. The air had been still one minute, and the next, a fury of black dust swept forward. Fanny shoved a hat over Yevgo's head and clapped her hands over her eyes. She bent her head against the wind.

Daniel found himself on the edge of town, to which he'd somehow walked. His teeth were full of dust. His hair, his pockets, his ears, every crease of skin, every bend of limb was caked in brown dust. Fine and gritty. He'd lost some of the yuan, which had blown away in the wind, and his mind returned to this every few minutes. The lost yuan. As if it were a great deal of money; as if it were his greatest loss. He shoved his chin into the neck of his shirt and set his back to the pummeling wind. He loathed this ugly assault of a landscape. At a tree, he crouched down, using the trunk for slight protection. He was shocked to realize that he was crying.

When Yevgo started laughing, Daniel had felt angry beyond anything he'd expected or could control. Liu was making fun of him. Yevgo was laughing at him. Everyone found him laughable. The instant attention turned to the policeman, he'd grabbed the yuan and fled. There was the matter of the belt. Pounding his thigh with a fist, he groaned. Not just a high-quality leather belt, there was a zipper on the inside which held quite a lot of cash. Unless you knew to look for the hidden zipper, you'd never know it was a money belt. That belt contained all of his money except for the small amount he carried in a wallet. He knew exactly how much money (2,785 American dollars). Without it, he was broke, dead broke. The tree he leaned against was at a crossroads in a small grove of plane trees, the two roads narrow and poorly paved. Ought he to go back, find the police station, file a complaint, pursue Liu? He'd heard that in China thieves had their hands cut off. He spat dust. In his mind were Yevgo and Fanny, Joe and Liu, at a table loaded with dishes, dining on *his* money, toasting each other. They had benefited from his intelligence, his business sense. Daniel felt the sweaty wad of yuan clenched in his fist. Play money. Useless currency. He dropped his head. *Fanny.* How had he ended up alone when he'd had a girl, friends, even a kind of work? Someone was to blame; he flipped through possibilities, his breathing shallow. Once the thought came, the feeling followed, a tolling in his chest, as if bells were clanging within the cage of his ribs. *What had happened?* Curled against the wind and dust, his head between his knees, he flicked open his eyes. Grease spot near the smooth placket of his shirt, buttons lined up. It was on him. The simplicity of it surprised him. Horrible, easy, true: *he* was the responsible party. He started to shake, adrenaline rocketing through him.

The PSB office in Turpan was a loosely run affair under the charge of a cheerful man named Inspector Fu. The beauty, Fu was unafraid to remind his staff, of being far from Beijing was that nobody cared or noticed what occurred in Turpan. This had been true since China's imperial days. Even during the reign of Emperor Li Yuan, founder of the Tang dynasty, edicts from Beijing were announced ceremoniously in Turpan, then ignored. Local authorities had always done what they pleased. Fu liked to refer to history, logic, and morality in the sermon-pep talks he delivered at staff meetings. In addition to a highly developed sense of history and a long perspective, Fu had a natural empathy. He had a kind face, a generous laugh, and an attentive gaze. He liked people and was curious about motive and desire. When questioning someone, he sat close, wrapping his hands around a crossed knee, leaning near as he listened. His eyes never left the face of the person across from him. In this way, he began to question Zhou, their two chairs facing each other in the middle of a room. Inspector Fu smiled and glanced at the identity card in his hand. Zhou Yuyi was not to fret; these questions were mere formalities. His voice was pitched to soothe. The room was plain, a table and four chairs, in a way that suggested simplicity rather than poverty. The walls were whitewashed and unadorned.

At first Zhou couldn't answer any of the questions. He coughed, began to speak, stopped. Inspector Fu called for tea and said reassuringly that the dust of Turpan scratched every man's throat. Zhou drank. He answered every question Inspector Fu put to him. He told the truth without embellishment. He said that he was Zhou Chi and not Zhou Yuyi. He told Inspector Fu about his brother's accident, about using Yuyi's license to operate Yuyi's taxi, about the offer of income from Yevgo. He said that seeing his own country had made him appreciate travel, its modulating effects on the mind and soul. He said he was not concerned with politics, that he wanted to live an interesting life, a life worthy of Charles Dickens, a great writer in another land and time. These foreigners were now his friends (except maybe for Daniel, though he didn't mention that), and the world outside of China had become real to him.

Inspector Fu listened, jotting notes now and then.

When he was finished, Zhou poured hot water into his cup from a thermos. The wind whistled through the gaps in windows. Inspector Fu was comfortable with silence. He didn't glance at Liu, who staggered up from a chair in the corner, staring and turning in confusion.

He didn't want to return to Guangzhou, Zhou said. He wished to stay in Xinjiang, maybe even right here in Turpan, find work, send his parents money. His stomach hurt but he felt tentatively happy; it was exhilarating to tell the truth, to not dissemble. The truth—speaking the truth inwardly to oneself and aloud to another—was indeed liberating. Live courageously.

This wish of Zhou's surprised Chief Inspector Fu. Everyone wanted to go to Guangzhou; nobody tried to transfer their residency permit to Turpan. He would look into it, he said.

Not me, Liu spoke up, his words slurred and loud. Send me back to Guangzhou! Please. He sobbed, hiccuped, blew his nose onto the floor. He clutched Daniel's belt like a blanket in his fist. I want to go home. I can pay. He pulled damp wadded-up bills from his pockets. Liu wiped his mouth and said he had a perfect understanding of every way in which he'd betrayed the party and his country. He vowed to live a better, more socialist lifestyle. He didn't meet Zhou's eyes.

After Fu left the room, Zhou and Liu sat quietly. Their friendship would survive, Zhou thought. Liu had fallen asleep, his head dropped back, mouth agape. Zhou turned his chair to face the window which gave onto a small courtyard. Through breaks in the swirling dust, he caught a glimpse of a bench against a wall. It looked peaceful. Nothing happened quickly in China. Probably, his request would be denied. In the meantime, he'd be sent back to Guangzhou. No doubt, he'd have to drive Liu home. Anyway, he had to return the taxi. He pulled a chair close to the window, sat, and propped his feet, as he'd learned from Yevgo, onto the sill. He tapped the glass face of his watch, which had stopped again, to see if he could get it moving. The watch stopped, started, stopped, and started so he never knew the true time. Nevertheless, the fact that he'd purchased it with money he'd earned on his own impressed him. With the watch, he was an entrepreneur. Out the window, he could see one skinny tree which was having its leaves stripped by the wind, the bench, the wall, all blurry and out of focus, as if he were looking into muddy water.

Someone fetched a donkey cart and a couple of men helped Fanny wrap Yevgo in a large piece of cloth and lay him onto the cart bed. The driver delivered them into a courtyard surrounded by high adobe walls which provided some protection from the battering wind. Sheets of brown sand blew sideways like rain. She kept her head down and her eyes shut against the blowing grit. It was twilight in the middle of the afternoon. Nothing would happen as it should: Yevgo should be cremated and Fanny should take his ashes to Tashkent. The Sad Way of the Sad Traveler. Sorrow earned, inevitable sorrow. She felt thick inside, stuffed full of feeling though she did not cry, didn't feel like crying. Ahead of her loomed bureaucratic tasks related to Yevgo's death, which would no doubt prove bewildering and complicated. Then she'd move on to another town, to other countries where the language and customs would be mysterious to her, where she'd make connections with strangers through obstacles and failures, relying on the luck of the unexpected.

She tried to think about Daniel but couldn't hold him in her mind. Were they each somehow complicit in Yevgo's death? For her part, she'd been too self-absorbed to pay sufficient attention to Yevgo's health and not insistent enough about what she had suspected, then Daniel had selfishly provoked him into that final, fatal activity— playing pool in the heat of the day, under that deadly sun. No, let go this preoccupation with accidental responsibility.

A woman, bent double against the wind, carried out a glass of tea and gesticulated vigorously, indicating that Fanny should come in out of the storm. Fanny shook her head. The woman removed Fanny's hat and swiftly, expertly, wrapped her head and face in a scarf before retreating indoors. The tea filled with grit. Snug in the scarf, only the tip of her nose and her eyes exposed, Fanny sat cross-legged and hunched over. The cart was made of weathered boards. Yevgo's body was stretched out behind her. The wind pushed at her, against her kidneys, against her thighs, as if it were trying to get her to move. Never before had she been in a sandstorm and the colossal level of discomfort impressed her: the stinging sand, the suffocating thickened air, the drifts of brown caked into every cranny. Perfect conditions in which to release the rest of Bruno's ashes; with this wind, he'd end up in Mongolia. But the ashes were back in her hotel room, sprinkled over her possessions. She tried to think about Bruno but could not hold him in her mind. The present was a balloon slowly expanding, pushing the past out of the way. It was the fall of 1989, she was in the middle of China, at the periphery of an immense desert, on an ancient traveler's route, in a sandstorm, beside the body of a friend whom she didn't know that well. The obvious was soothing: people died. Sometimes people traveled far from home. Sometimes they traveled far from home and died. The wind blew, sand and grit churned the air, scouring every surface as if to erase the visible world.